my home is far away

my
home
is
far
away

DAWN POWELL

INTRODUCTION BY TIM PAGE

STEERFORTH PRESS
SOUTH ROYALTON, VERMONT

First published in 1944 by Charles Scribner's Sons.
This edition of *My Home Is Far Away* has been published
in cooperation of the Estate of Dawn Powell.

Introduction Copyright © 1995 by Tim Page

The cover photograph of [left to right] Mabel, Phyllis, and Dawn
Powell is courtesy of the collection of the Dawn Powell Papers,
Rare Book and Manuscript Library, Columbia University.

Library of Congress Cataloging-in-Publication Data
Powell, Dawn.
My home is far away / Dawn Powell; introduction by Tim Page.
p.   cm.
ISBN 1-883642-43-4
I. Title.
PS3531.0936M9
813'.54—dc20   95-3238 CIP

Manufactured in the United States of America
Second Printing

For my cousin,
Sergeant Jack F. Sherman

foreword

UNFORTUNATELY, my fever brought back so many childhood memories with such brilliant clarity that it seems almost imperative to write a novel about the three sisters, the stepmother, Papa . . . Wrote a start from 3 to 5 A.M. with temperature."

Dawn Powell was 43 years old and in the midst of writing one of her finest satires, *A Time to Be Born*, when she entered this in her diary on January 27, 1941. In an undated section of the same volume, there are perhaps a thousand hastily scrawled words that most likely represent her feverish, aurorean "start"—an outpouring of memories: small-town Ohio at the turn of the twentieth century, surreys and steam engines, general stores with chocolate mints and jelly beans behind their counters, a loving aunt who stood up to familial tyranny, the hated stepmother with her silver whip.

Powell considered several titles for her new novel (including "Once Upon a Time," "There Were Three Children," and "There Was Another America"). Ultimately—fortunately—she opted for *My Home Is Far Away* and the book was completed in mid-1944 and published in November of that year by Scribner's.

Most of Powell's work is on some level autobiographical but with *My Home Is Far Away,* it becomes difficult to draw any sure line between fact and fiction. Like Marcia Willard, the book's heroine, Dawn Powell was the second of three sisters, all of whom would seem to have had personalities and sibling relationships much as the ones presented in the novel. Hattie Sherman Powell, Dawn's mother, died at roughly the same time and of the same illness as the fictional Daisy Willard, while Harry Willard, the well-meaning but footloose and improvident traveling salesman, was clearly modeled after Roy Powell, the author's father. Idah Hawkins Willard is a devastating but, according to surviving family members, fundamentally accurate portrait of Sabra Powell, Dawn's stepmother, while the character of Aunt Lois was based on Orpha May Sherman Steinbrueck, Hattie Powell's sister, who raised both Dawn Powell and her favorite cousin, Jack F. Sherman, from their teenage years in Shelby, Ohio.

The beloved, eternally tearful baby sister Florrie was so closely copied from Powell's own younger sister Phyllis that Powell called her character "Fuffy"—Phyllis's lifelong nickname—throughout early sketches and drafts. Of the major figures in *My Home Is Far Away*, only Bonnie Purdy seems to have had no direct counterpart in the drama of Powell's early life. And yet, even here, some aspects of Bonnie's youthful, trusting, and tender nature were apparently taken from Powell's fond memories of her own Aunt Dawn Sherman who died at a young age from a botched abortion.

Published ten years after *The Story of a Country Boy* (1934), this was the last of Powell's six Ohio novels and it must have come as something of a shock to her admirers for, in the interim, she had attained a modest but enthusiastic following as an urbane comic novelist with *Turn, Magic Wheel* (1936), *The Happy Island* (1938), and *Angels on Toast* (1940). Such rural books as *She Walks in Beauty* (1928) and *Dance Night* (1930) were long out of print. None of these early ventures had been particularly successful, critically or financially (although as late as 1957, Powell called *Dance Night* her favorite book), and it may have been assumed that she had renounced the stark solemnity and essential sadness of her Ohio narratives for the smart, boozy, bawdy, hilarious, and altogether marvellous send-ups of the Manhattan high and low life she had discovered.

Certainly her agent, Carol Brandt, and her editor, the celebrated Max Perkins, were confused by what seemed a curious mid-career detour. "Carol called to say she liked the new book very much," Powell wrote with wry sufferance in her diary after submitting the opening section, "The Man in the Balloon," for perusal. "Maybe after the second part was finished, she could tell more—'and then the first part could be cut.'"

To some degree, this befuddlement was understandable. By the early 1940s, Powell had attained a reputation for high sophistication ("Miss Powell is one of the wittiest women around and our best answer to the familiar question, 'Who really says the funny things for which Dorothy Parker gets credit?,'" Diana Trilling wrote in 1942) and nothing could be much less "sophisticated"—in the glittering, all-knowing, furiously present-tense, big-city manner that Powell had perfected—than *My Home Is Far Away.*

> This was the month of cherries and peaches, of green apples beyond the grape arbor, of little dandelion ghosts in the grass, of sour grass and four-leaf clovers, of still dry heat holding the smell of nasturiums and dying lilacs. This was the best month of all and the best day. It was not birthday, Easter, Christmas or picnic, but all these things and something else, something wonderful, something utterly unknown. The two little girls in embroidered white Sunday dresses knew no way to express their secret joy but by whirling each other dizzily over the lawn crying, "We're moving, we're moving! We're moving to London Junction!"

"At the beginning, it is written as for a child—words, images, etc., are on the table level of their eyes," Powell wrote in her diary. "Everyone is good to the three sisters, their pleasures are simple, their parents good. As they grow, the manner of writing changes—the knowledge of cruelty, divorce, disillusionment, betrayal . . ." In fact, *My Home Is Far Away* is one of the very few examples of a book written for adults, with an adult command of the English language, that maintains throughout the vantage point of a hungry, serious child. It might be likened to a memoir that has been penned not with the usual tranquility of distance but rather with the sense that everything happening to the characters is happening right now, without any promise of eventual escape, without any assurance that childhood, too, shall pass away.

It is also important to remember that *My Home Is Far Away* is a wartime book—conceived and begun in the months before Pearl Harbor, completed just after D-day, and dedicated to Powell's cousin, Jack Sherman, who was then an Army sergeant stationed in Europe. Indeed, in a 1943 diary entry, Powell called the book "propaganda—duty—to show there was another America, not just the present one of war and woe. Also, to show the things possible to learn—that in a small radius of 100 square miles in Northern Ohio, there are a half-dozen different types of civilization: a Finnish town, a Dutch town, a rubber town, steel town, and great grain farms, fruit farms, German towns, etc."

I have found that reactions to *My Home Is Far Away*—and, indeed, to most of Powell's Ohio novels—vary enormously. Well aware that I am generalizing, I should say that the strongest responses to this book usually come from woman readers; from readers, male or female, who know (and feel) the landscapes of the American Midwest; and from readers who have survived frustrating childhoods, in part by creating for themselves imaginary lives just over the horizon. (Is there another book that so vividly conveys that sense, common among gifted children, that they are human arrows, pulled back for years and years, then finally let fly to find their target?) This is not to disparage *My Home Is Far Away*, but merely to point out that it is not a "typical" Powell novel by any means and that readers who have picked this up looking for riotous wit may be disappointed.

There are many compensations, however—the lush, lyrical writing about a remembered countryside; the reaquaintance Powell provides us with our own youthful secrets and yearnings; the rare sense of a creative artist working in dangerous proximity to her raw material, to those very crises that helped determine the course of her life and artistry. The understated but excruciating way in which Powell described the death of Daisy Willard was admired by no less a critic than Van Wyck Brooks, while the portrayal of Sabra Powell/Idah Hawkins can only be called a merciless and magnificent act of vengeance. (Sabra Powell was still alive when *My Home Is Far Away* was published; her reaction to the book, if any, was not recorded.)

Powell apparently found this mixture of fiction and autobiography difficult to sustain and she was never entirely sure exactly what she had wrought. "Although I set out to do a complete job on my family, I colored it and, even worse, diluted it through a fear of embarassing my fonder relatives," she wrote in a moment of frustration in 1943. Immediately after publication, she reread the book: "My first feeling was one of queasiness over the initial establishment of a distinctly autobiographical flavor, but after a while the characters become wholly fictional, increasingly round, and with the full reality that only created characters have. Certainly few facts are here." And yet only four days later she was horrified when an unfriendly reviewer objected to her "pathetic, good-for-nothing people": "I hate to bring myself out so openly for censure, also to expose the family. It made me cringe . . ."

My Home Is Far Away sold some 4000 copies—fairly well, by Powell's sorry standards—and was respectfully, if sparsely, reviewed; in 1953, it was published in Great Britain by W. H. Allen. Powell planned a sequel—entitled, simply, "Marcia"—and worked on it intermittently for the rest of her life, finishing at least 80 double-spaced typewritten pages. What remains of "Marcia" carried the central figure on to a new life in Cleveland, and brought back the Putneys and Aunt Lois for further complications.

It is probably best that Powell let *My Home Is Far Away* stand on its own. And so Marcia Willard is forever young, alert, battered but unbowed, ready to begin her real life, at long last riding that train that will take her far away from home and to a home that is far away:

> She was still scared, but she felt light-headed and gay, the way Papa did when he was going away from home. She thought she must be like Papa, the kind of person who was always glad going away instead of coming home. She looked out the window, feeling the other self inside her, the self that had no feelings and could never be hurt, coming out stronger and stronger, looking at the fringe of London Junction and the beginnings of Milltown with calm, almost without re-membrance...

Without remembrance? On the contrary—Powell remembered everything. Eugene O'Neill called his *Long Day's Journey Into Night* a "play of old sorrow, written in tears and blood"; something similar might be said for *My Home Is Far Away*.

The critic Matthew Josephson, who was responsible for the first lengthy study of Powell's work (published in the Spring 1973 issue of *Southern Review*), wrote to Jack Sherman in August 1972 for information about Powell's early life. "I thought her novels wonderfully witty but unfinished," he said by way of introduction. "Now I like them about as they are. *My Home Is Far Away* is not for fun, and it is a masterpiece."

Tim Page
New York City
March 25, 1995

PART ONE

the

man

in

the

balloon

I

THIS WAS THE MONTH of cherries and peaches, of green
apples beyond the grape arbor, of little dandelion ghosts
in the grass, of sour grass and four-leaf clovers, of still dry
heat holding the smell of nasturtiums and dying lilacs. This was
the best month of all and the best day. It was not birthday, Easter,
Christmas, or picnic, but all these things and something else,
something wonderful, something utterly unknown. The two little
girls in embroidered white Sunday dresses knew no way to express their secret joy but by whirling each other dizzily over the
lawn crying, "We're moving, we're moving! We're moving to
London Junction!"

Down the cinder driveway between the Willard house and
Dr. Bird's box hedge rumbled the hay wagon, laden with the
Willard furniture. The sudden picture of their home, everything
that was theirs, yanked out of its familiar roots like baby teeth and
stacked up on wheels, made the children stand still, staring, uncertain. There was their little pine bed standing on end, the baby's
high-chair hanging by a rope from the corner pole, the big walnut
dresser with its front bulging out like a funny-paper policeman's;
there were the two big parlor chairs, wide rockers curved in perpetual grins, wonderful for scooting games; there was the couch
bought with coupons—bright yellow fuzzy stuff with red and

green caterpillars wiggling circles over it so that it always seemed alive and dangerous; there was the pine kitchen cupboard tied on its back to the dining-table as if it had left its little corner only when overpowered by force. Yes, there went their little yellow house itself, for without these things warming its insides, the little yellow house was nothing but empty doors and windows. They watched the wagon wheels roll relentlessly over the pansy-border and leave deep ruts in the soft new grass, but it didn't matter because they didn't live here any more. Like their furniture, now being brushed by the overhanging branches of Peach Street, they were suspended in space between the little yellow cottage, Number Twenty-Three, and the unknown towers of London Junction. This must be the reason that time, too, was suspended, for no matter how often they ran to ask their mother the time, it was always nine o'clock, a little before, a little after, but not quite starting time. So round and round they swung each other over the grass, as if this example of speed would whip up the minutes.

"We're moving, we're moving, we're moving to London Junction!" they chanted shrilly. This time they whirled through the gap in the hedge into Dr. Bird's front yard. This was a hushed space, shaded with sleek-leafed bushes, wide-spreading locust trees that dripped feathery green over fern beds below. The sun never came here or into the shuttered, vine-covered house; it was an old people's yard with a cool cemetery smell, suitable for an old man and old lady who never came out further than the plaster old man and lady in the tiny weather-house. Old Dr. Bird sat behind the porch vines, shelling peas into a tin saucepan.

"Hold on there! What's all this?" he called out in a high trembling voice.

"We're moving!" Lena answered. "We're moving to London Junction."

"Here," said the old man. "Here you are, girls. Here's a penny apiece."

They flew to his side.

"Dr. Bird," asked Marcia earnestly, "who will hold the string for you to tie up bundles when I go to London Junction?"

"Nobody," said Dr. Bird. "I'll have to do it myself."

"I'm sorry," said Marcia. "I liked putting a finger on the string. I don't see how you'll get along."

"Never mind, here's your penny," said the old man. "Run along or your folks'll drive off without you."

"Say goodbye to Dr. Bird," their mother called from the surrey now pausing in the driveway. "Well, here we go, Dr. Bird."

"Glad, eh?"

"Indeed I am," their mother answered happily. "You see, I'll be there with Ma and Lois, and besides it's a better place for Harry."

"London Junction, London Junction, London Junction!" sang the two girls and whirled each other round and round across the lawn, down the dusty path till they fell in the geranium bed laughing. Their father, a slight, jaunty figure with a little sandy moustache, in a neat brown-checked suit, came out of the little yellow house carrying the baby in one arm and the red telescope in the other. The red telescope was the very thing in which Dr. Bird had first brought the baby. The two girls had looked in it carefully every morning for over a year to see if any other babies had arrived, but so far none had followed Florrie.

"Get in, get in!" shouted their father. "Do you want to go to London Junction or do you want to stay here?"

They scrambled over the wheels into the back seat of the surrey. The horse and surrey were borrowed from the Busby Hotel where their father had clerked until today. It was a handsome outfit, the shining black surrey with tan fringe twinkling along its top, and the gleaming black horse that Papa himself had "broke" in the field behind the hotel. There were leather storm curtains rolled up to be let down in case of rain, and a silver-trimmed whip in a silver-trimmed socket. This elegance so impressed Marcia and Lena that they sat still, proudly stretching their feet in the new

Mary Jane black patent-leather slippers. Dr. Bird limped along the box hedge to the gate and watched them.

"Say hello to Lois for me," he called out. "Bring her over if you come down to Reunion."

"Of course we'll come to Reunion," their mother called back. "Ma never misses it, you know that."

She gathered her skirts carefully about her away from the wheel, and leaned over to take the baby from their father's arms.

"Let *us* hold her!" begged Lena.

Their mother stood up and lifted the baby over the back seat to them. They sat her up between them on the tufted tan cushion. In their excitement they clutched her arms so tightly that her big blue eyes welled with indignant tears.

"Don't pinch," admonished their mother, then called out, "Hurry, Harry, or we'll never get there before dark."

Their father went back to the house and to the barn again, then to the tool-shed for no reason at all, except perhaps to say goodbye, just as the sunflowers beside the old playhouse seemed to be nodding goodbye. In this moment before leaving, the clouds stood still and seemed very low, as if they might even be stroked if one stood on the treetop and reached high. Above the clouds somewhere was London Junction, beyond the far-off pine fringe that rimmed this world was London Junction, on the other side of the West Woods, sunset boundary of the world, lay London Junction. The children's eyes widened as the whip cracked and the voyage began.

"Goodbye, Dr. Bird. Goodbye, Mrs. Busby," called their mother, waving her handkerchief. A skinny brown hand waved from the lace curtains of the big gray Busby house. Their mother kept waving her handkerchief all the way down Peach Street, as certain as were the children that the whole world was watching their departure. Sure enough hands waved to them from windows, and passing the marketplace Mr. Charles, the butcher, waved his white apron, and Mr. Finney, the druggist, lifted his straw hat, and the delivery boy from the grocery-store put down his basket to salute them like a soldier.

"Where are the kittens?" Lena suddenly asked.

"In the barn, all right," said their father. "In the barn" sounded ominous to the two little girls who exchanged suspicious glances.

"Where's Towser?" demanded Marcia. "Isn't Towser going to London Junction? We've got to go back and get Towser."

"Poor Towser!" sighed their mother. "Oh, Harry!"

"What's happened to Towser?" wailed the girls, and then Florrie began to roar in the alarmingly efficient way she had, at two years old, perfected, so that the horse pricked up its ears and started to gallop, their mother reached back hastily to steady the baby, and Papa swore, pulling on the reins.

"Forget about Towser, damn it!" he shouted above the clatter of hoofs and wheels on the brick pavement. "We'll get another dog in London Junction."

"CITY LIMITS" their mother read out to them from a sign.

"Thirty miles now to London Junction," said their father.

Now they really were past the sunset woods on the edge of the world, and their mother began to sing. They all sang with her. They sang, "There was an old sailor and he had a wooden leg," and "Hark, hark the dogs do bark, the beggars are coming to town," and "A frog he would a woo-ing go." The baby stopped crying. Papa kept the whip out and the horse trotted along at a fine clip. They waved to farmhouses and shouted merry greetings to loads of hay; they waved to children perched on ladders picking cherries and to women at barnyard pumps rounding up geese, for they knew everyone. Mother had been brought up on a farm along here, her brothers' families were strewn all around, and Papa, though he came from another county, knew everyone through managing the hotel and meeting the farmers who hitched every Saturday in the hotel square. But after awhile they did not know the farms; people in fields stared back at them instead of waving. Papa and their mother fell silent.

"I wonder if we'll like London Junction," she said and her voice sounded small. "We don't know anyone but Ma and Lois and the family."

"We'll know plenty," boasted their father. "More people to know, have a better time and have more to do with. They've got asphalt streets in London Junction, and an opera house, and a baseball park."

"But it's so much bigger than Elmville," said their mother. The children, ever watchful, saw that she had taken out her handkerchief. "Of course, I want to be with my own folks, but think of all the people we're leaving. We've known them all our lives. Dr. Bird—"

"Dr. Bird won't have anybody to hold string when he wraps bundles," said Marcia. "Nobody."

Lena was holding Florrie on her lap, squeezing her so tight that now she roared again. The mighty roar that came from this Humpty-Dumpty baby made their father laugh, so they all laughed. Papa leaned over and kissed their mother and for some reason this made the girls laugh all the louder.

"Here," said their father, and handed their mother the reins. "By George, you handle a horse better than any man. Better than me, even."

"Oh no, Harry, not better than you!" their mother protested, quite shocked. "Nobody is as good with a horse as you, Harry— nobody."

Nobody could do anything as well as Harry and that was the truth. The children knew it, their mother knew it, and naturally Harry knew it.

"Well, I like horses," admitted Harry. "And they like me. That's all."

The next village was Oakville, the county seat, and here they stopped to say hello to papa's father, Grandpa Willard, at the Soldiers' Home. The old soldiers sat on benches around the grounds in wheel chairs, either talking to each other or reading, just waiting for gongs to summon them to meals, chapel, or bed. Grandpa

Willard was all dressed up in his uniform with the new cork leg his children had given him, and was sitting on a bench busily whittling a whistle out of a stick.

"I been expecting you folks to stop in the last couple weeks," he said. "I made a whistle for each of the kids."

"Getting lonesome for us?" asked Mama.

Grandpa thoughtfully shifted his tobacco to the other cheek, where it made a fascinating egg-like protuberance.

"No time to get lonesome here," he said. "Up early and reading a book or sitting out here figuring, or walking around spotting birds. Seen a couple of partridge back by the creek yesterday. Had a pest of starlings till they let us shoot some. No sirree, they's always plenty to take up your mind without getting lonesome for your folks."

Papa gave him some tobacco, and then mother gave him a new white handkerchief with his initials, R.J.W., which pleased him so much he folded it up carefully in its tissue paper, declaring that it was too fine to use and would have to be put away with his "personal belongings." He called to one of the attendants passing by, to introduce them all proudly, and asked that the event of his son's family calling be written up in an item in the *Home Weekly*.

"By cracky, other folks' families get written up when they visit. I don't see why mine can't," he said with a firm nod of the head.

Papa asked him if there was anything he'd like to have before they drove on, and Grandpa looked rather wistfully at the horse and carriage.

"I sure would like to handle them reins for about ten minutes," he said. "I haven't laid hands on the reins since I been here. Good trotter?"

Papa boasted of the horse's speed, mouth, coat, and general virtues, but then everything that was in any way connected with Papa automatically became superior to all other things of the kind. This horse, he said, was the finest horse in the county, possibly the state. He declared if he had this horse under his care for, say, four weeks he could make her the finest racing nag in the country and

Grandpa gravely agreed that this was possible. They examined the points of the animal together and Papa was a little annoyed when Grandpa found a mark on the left hind leg, so Grandpa hastily said the flaw would very likely pass away in a day or two.

"Tell you what, Harry," he said. "You might send me a picture postcard from London Junction. Some of the fellows have quite a collection."

This promise having been given, the old gentleman looked meditatively down at the children and stroked his white moustache. The children beamed back, pleased with his having only one eye and only one leg from the Civil War.

"Harry, maybe you could spare me a little change so as to give the kids something. I don't get my pension till next week."

Their father reached in his pocket and gave him some pennies and a nickel. The old man promptly presented a penny apiece to the two older girls and a nickel to the baby. Marcia and Lena watched their mother pocket the latter.

"Florrie always gets the most," said Marcia.

They regarded their baby sister speculatively.

"Babies got to have money for chewing tobacco," their grandfather said, winking his one eye.

"Thank you so much, father," said their mother earnestly. "I've started a bank account for the baby, and would you believe it, she already has nearly fourteen dollars in it?"

They climbed back in the surrey, while Grandpa made a hurried survey of the grounds to find Captain Somebody who was in charge and a very fine man it would be a pleasure for them to meet. Disappointed in this, he followed them a few yards, calling out last messages.

"Don't bother about the picture postcards if it's going to be too much trouble, Harry," he said. "It ain't a matter of life and death. And say—if they print a piece about you visiting me in the *Home Weekly* next week, I'll send it to you. There's a lot of reading matter in it, so it's worth having anyway. I always save it in my personal belongings."

They thanked him and drove away, leaving him cutting off a chew of tobacco with his penknife.

"I'd like a bank account," said Lena firmly, but her parents paid no heed.

Marcia, too, had been doing some reflecting.

"When I was the baby, I never got any nickels," she stated accusingly. "I would have remembered it if I had."

Marcia's odd and quite useless talent for remembering was a source of astonishment and amusement to her parents. Sometimes in the night her father would pick her out of bed and take her downstairs to entertain the company with her recollections. The company laughed and gasped, but the uncanniness of her memory was not an endearing trait; invariably the guests drew away respectfully from the little freak and warmed all the more to the pretty, unaffected normalcy of little Lena.

"When I was a baby," reflected Marcia gloomily in a louder voice, "Lena got all the nickels because she was the oldest. I only got the pennies."

Lena giggled. Their parents, if they heard, paid no heed but were silent till after they had left Oakville. Then their mother said hesitatingly, "Harry, I felt sorry for Father. None of his own people around. All of you boys, and yet none of you will let him make a home with you. I really think we ought to let him live with us in London Junction when we get settled."

"That's it—when," retorted their father irritably. "No, sir, he's too big a care. He'd drink up his pension and sit around the room all day chewing tobacco. That's all he'd do."

"I get along all right with Father," said their mother. "Don't be hard on him, Harry. Half-blind and only one leg, poor old soul."

The tone of their mother's voice made Marcia and Lena sorry for their grandfather. The things that made him seem wonderful before—the one eye, the cork leg, the charming companions with equally curious characteristics—all these were changed from wonders to sad misfortunes merely by the pity in their mother's voice.

Poor, poor Grandpa! And they had forgotten to sing a song for him, and to thank him for the pennies!

"Whoa, Bess!" their father called out abruptly.

They had come to a crossroads, where a grimy two-story house flaunted a sign, "Four Corners House." The sign was nailed to a dead maple tree, with a rusty pail and tin sap tube still attached to the trunk. A stone watering trough and pump were by the hitching post, and a watchdog was tied outside his kennel, growling fearfully at them. The drab exterior of the house was brightened by gay advertisements pinned to the screen door, and by a clothesline hung with red tablecloths. Their father twisted the reins around the post ring and helped their mother to the ground. Perhaps this was to be a visit, too, with even more pennies in the offing. Their father blighted these hopes by motioning them to sit still.

"You kids stay here. We'll take the baby inside with us."

Their mother jumped into their father's arms, laughing secretly. Her new brown sailor hat fell off and the curly brown bangs blew merrily over her white forehead until she had pinned on her hat once more. From the way Papa picked up Florrie and then hurried their mother into the side door of the building, the children guessed some fun was in the air that was only for grown-ups.

"I know what they're having," said Lena calmly. "They're having beer."

Marcia looked at her six-year-old sister, envious of this superior sophistication.

"Whenever they go in the side door instead of the front door of any place, it means they're having beer to drink," Lena enlarged obligingly. "Like in papa's hotel."

The little treat was plainly not a success, for Florrie's indignant bellow was heard from the moment the screen door closed on them. A few moments later she emerged triumphantly in her mother's arms, round face red with rage, fists in mouth. She was only moderately soothed by being jiggled up and down.

"Spoiled," said their father.

"No, dear, it's just that she wants to keep on riding," explained their mother. True enough, as soon as the carriage started again, Florrie fell blissfully asleep in their mother's arms. They did not stop again till they had come to Venice Corners, half-way to London Junction. Venice Corners was a pretty little village with a white frame church on one side of the main street and a fine brick church on the other. In these towns the brick churches were always the Methodist and the smaller wooden ones were Episcopal or Baptist. When they got to London Junction the children had been promised a brick Sunday school, even though they had been baptized in one of the wooden faiths.

Venice Corners had no purring flour mill like Elmville, and no little lake with rowboats like Oakville, but it countered these charms by being placed on top of a hill so that on either side the little houses marched down step by step, each with its hedge moustache, and a red chimney for a hat. It was after the noon hour now and they were all hungry.

"If we're going to see Chris and Isobel we'd better eat first," said their mother. "We mustn't be any bother to Isobel."

Chris was their mother's cousin.

They drew up under a shade tree on the Methodist Church lawn. Their mother took out the lunch basket and passed out hardboiled eggs, chicken drumsticks, and bread and jam. She wiped off their faces with paper napkins. She fed Florrie from her own lunch, and their father petted the horse, making jokes about keeping horse and carriage instead of returning them to the Busbys. Their mother put the baby in the clothes basket to nap, and began to tidy herself for the visit to Chris and Isobel. She fussed with her jabot, a ripple of white lace fastened with her garnet crescent pin over her brown-and-white checked taffeta waist. Papa tweaked her bangs as fast as she pinned them in place, until she begged, "Oh, darling, please!" She straightened the girls' hairribbons and smoothed out their mussed sashes of blue silk. Lena had a new blue bonnet with baby-blue forget-me-nots and velvet streamers. This was because she was the oldest and the prettiest and their father liked to have her look like the little girl on the Singer Sewing Machine Calendar, the one where the rosy little girl is bending over a baby's cradle. Marcia wore Lena's outgrown embroidered dress with her last year's faded straw hat, but she was not disturbed because at least she was permitted to wear her birthday locket and besides her feet were the biggest. Florrie, except for a brand-new blue bonnet with lace ruffled edge, wore the freshly starched but faded dregs of her sisters' outgrown wardrobes, and presently justified this economy by throwing up over her embroidered white bib.

"The raspberry jam," said her mother, fixing the damage.

"She always does," said Marcia critically, "even without jam."

Papa watched their mother fussing over all of them, and he frowned.

"You all look all right; what's all this fuss about?" he snapped. "Godamighty, you don't think Isobel has any more than you do, do you? Where's your watch? Why don't you pin it up a little higher? Nothing to be ashamed of. Thirty dollar watch, by God. Pin her up higher where somebody can see it."

Papa was always reminding their mother of her watch, which he and Aunt Lois and their grandmother had bought last Christmas, though in showing it off to strangers he never mentioned his co-sponsors. He had indeed forgotten about them so completely that on Aunt Lois' last visit he had boasted right to her face about the fine present he had given Daisy. Aunt Lois, pink and blond, and wonderfully perfumed, had smiled.

"Yes, it is a lovely watch, Harry," she softly agreed. "But mother and I are still waiting for your share of it to be paid."

For some reason this made their mother cry and their father swear, and the watch was seldom worn after that except when father insisted. Mother obediently pinned it up higher on her waist now, and the girls studied it with earnest admiration again, knowing that to grow up meant this dainty prize, a blue enamelled fleur-de-lys pin holding a blue enamelled locket of a watch to beat right over your own heart.

"I guess you look a damn sight better than Isobel ever did in her life," said father proudly, patting their mother.

"Well, my stars alive!" was what Isobel said when the party walked in the front gate of this relation's home. "If it isn't Harry and Daisy and the girls! Chris! Come on out and see who's here!"

Isobel was just going to pay a call on the minister's wife. She looked so pretty that Marcia secretly wished she was their mother. For instance, Isobel's skin and eyes and hair seemed all of one dusty gold color like a toasted angel's. Then she had pale tan shoes with pretty curved Cuban heels, and she had a rolled-up brown umbrella with a wolf's head handle made of ivory with little emerald eyes; her small feather toque dropped a beautiful veil over her face, so that forever after Marcia thought beauty consisted of long pale lashes on a creamy oval face delicately marked into tiny octagonal shadows by a brown veil. Even more marvellous was the fact that Isobel could talk—very fast, too—through this veil and kiss through it, too. While the parents talked with Isobel and Chris, Marcia invented a game, much to Lena's delight and admiration, called "Isobel." This was merely kissing each other through their handkerchiefs and then, on a better inspiration, through the screen door.

The Wallises lived in a house almost as small as a playhouse at the very bottom of the hill. You stepped down two stone steps from the sidewalk into the tiny yard bordered with conch-shells and red geraniums. The cottage had forgotten what color it had ever been painted and was rain-gray, with a narrow porch decorated with green Chinese shades and a green swing. Unluckily, the grown-ups at once appropriated this swing, so the girls went inside to look around. They saw at once that if Isobel were their mother and this their home there would be very little room for play, since a big brass bed took up most of the space in the parlor. It bore a snow-white spread and pillow-shams embroidered in red;

on one sham was worked "I slept and dreamed that Life was Beauty" with a lady embroidered by way of illustration watering a rosebush, and on the other "I woke and found that Life was Duty" with the same lady holding a broom. This was exactly the same as in Dr. Bird's spare bedroom and you did not need to know how to read to recognize the thought even if you did not understand it. The bay window was filled with ferns in mottled green jardinieres, two rubber plants as tall as Lena, and a tiny table of china knick-knacks: a milk-glass setting hen, a little fisher-boy in colored china holding two brown warty fish, a go-way-back-and-sit-down rug, and other souvenirs of Cedar Point, Put-in Bay, and Puritan Springs, so that nobody could possibly play train here in rocking-chairs without knocking things over. The kitchen was twice the size of the parlor-bedroom. It had measle wallpaper—or at least the colored specks looked like measles, Marcia remarked to Lena—and red-checked curtains and a red-checked tablecloth over the big dining table, and a big stove with a dishpan on it of what appeared to be salt-rising dough, from a finger's taste. One good thing about this kitchen was a large headless wire woman in the corner, with some red plaid gingham pinned around her and a tape measure hanging from her neck. Lena and Marcia were admiringly silent before this fine thing, but Lena finally claimed it by saying, "When I grow up I'm going to be a dressmaker and have a Form in my kitchen, too."

"I'm going to be a fireman like Chris," Marcia retorted coldly. "I'll be riding on a train mostly."

This crushed Lena, for Marcia always knew better things to want than she did. They found a stack of Butterick Pattern Books and sat on the floor to examine them, wishing ardently that they could cut out the figures for paper-dolls. Presently Chris came back to make some lemonade for everybody. He was a lean, tall, dark, squint-eyed young man with thick tousled black hair and white teeth. He made you laugh when he winked at you.

"Chris is my favorite relation," Lena said frankly.

"I'm going to marry him when I grow up," Marcia said, and Lena pouted again. But it was really Lena he held on his lap and when he gave them candy he gave Lena the biggest piece. Lena shot a triumphant glance from violet eyes at Marcia, but Marcia again foiled her by turning her head away proudly.

"Keep the candy, Chris," she said tensely, wanting it terribly. "I guess other people like it better than I do."

She marched out on the porch, and without her jealousy Lena found it no fun sitting on Chris's lap so she came out, too. Mama and Isobel were talking in whispers and giggles in the swing, and their father was telling them jokes while he passed the lemonade glasses.

"Come and see us when we get settled in London Junction," said their mother. "I only hope we can get as nice a place as you have. Ma says everything's awfully dear there, so we're staying with her at Lois's till we find the right place."

"We'll probably take the old Furness home on the hill," said their father. "Plenty of room for company there."

"Oh, Harry! We could never afford it!"

"Look here, now, Daisy, we couldn't make do with a little house like this here! What's the sense in moving if we don't improve ourselves. Isn't that right, Chris?"

"The Furness place is pretty big," Chris said slowly. "Biggest house in the Junction."

"We could never afford that much rent," said their mother. "Harry is fooling."

"The hell I am!" shouted their father. "You always seem to think we're not as good as anybody else in London Junction! I'll get the biggest goddam place in town before I'm through. Bigger'n Lois's place, you can take it from me!"

"Costs money, Harry," Chris said.

"I'll get money, don't you worry about me!" their father said, getting madder. "I can go on the road and make plenty any time I say the word."

"Oh, Harry, you won't go on the road!" breathed their mother, wide-eyed with fear. "You promised!"

"I'll do whatever pays me the most, by cracky!" said their father, not looking at her. "Maybe in the factory, and maybe on the road. I'm not going to sit on my patootie, though, and let the other fellas make all the money. I ain't built that way."

There was a quiet, while their mother stared at him, lips trembling, but he would not look back at her. Chris and Isobel swung back and forth in the swing, pretending not to notice how mad their guests were getting. Suddenly the children saw their father jump up from the porch-railing and point upward.

"Look at the sky!" he exclaimed. "It's coming up rain and we've got to get going. Come on, kids."

Their mother and Isobel hung behind whispering, while the girls ran ahead and Chris followed along with their father.

"Did you hear about the man in the balloon?" Chris asked. "He took off from the County Fair grounds this morning in a balloon and they tell me he claimed he'd land in London Junction this afternoon."

A man in a balloon! Lena and Marcia stared from one face to another eagerly.

"Can't tell, we may have to pick up the pieces on our way," said their father. "We had a fellow in a balloon at Elmville last summer. Went up two hundred feet from the courthouse, then came down in Morton's cow-pasture."

"I do hope we see him this time!" said Marcia. "Maybe he'll fall."

"This one never wants to miss anything," laughed their mother, tweaking Marcia's ear.

As soon as they were back in the surrey, Florrie still sleeping, Papa picked up the whip and they started off very fast. No one said anything, for their father's anger had spread around them like a frost. Something had happened that they did not understand and it was somehow Mama's fault. Presently they were in the country again, with the sweet, dull smell of hay, then the damp mossy breeze from the deep woods and hidden frog ponds. Their father put his arm around their mother. She began to laugh, rubbing her head against his cheek.

"Oh, Harry, you kill me!" she chuckled. "The Furness house! Why not Buckingham Palace?"

"All right, Buckingham Palace," agreed their father, laughing reluctantly. "You don't think I mean what I say, Daisy. It makes me mad when you won't believe me. You never think I can do the things I say, but you wait."

"But you won't go on the road, darling," pleaded their mother. "You said you'd take any other job rather than leave me."

"I said I wouldn't go on the road," their father shouted. "All right, if I said I wouldn't, then I won't. That's all there is to that."

Above, the skies darkened suddenly as if a lantern had blown out. A wind blew up, rattling the storm curtains warningly. Clouds as black as midnight rode over the horizon and the baby began to cry loudly. They stopped to put up the storm curtains, but the wind whipped them into their father's face as fast as he buttoned them. Lightning flashed and the horse whinnied in terror. Both the girls were scared but their mother told them to hush. She held the baby tight but it still wept lustily; the horse threw up its head and galloped wildly down the road into the gathering storm. It was barely three o'clock but the earth was drenched in darkness. As they dashed by the farms, horses whinnied, dogs barked, cocks crowed, bells rang in the wind, voices cried out in the fields.

"We can make the edge of town, I think," shouted their father.

"Look!" cried their mother.

When they looked they saw a dark object drifting across the sky like a bat across the ceiling.

"The balloon! The man in the balloon!" exclaimed their mother.

Marcia and Lena, arms tight around each other, looked upward, frightened and fascinated while the balloon drifted slowly downward, barely missing a barn cupola. They could see a dark figure outlined in the ship, a fairy-tale monster, omen of thunder and darkness and nightmares to come. The lightning sprang behind it like hell-fire from the Bible pictures, and the horse reared. It was like that picture in their old dining room of three horses and night lightning. The children stared helplessly, filled with sick loneliness and fear, as if the creature flying up there had brought the clouds and lightning and the blight to their perfect day, and no one, not even a father and mother, could stop his wicked vengeance.

"I wouldn't want to be up there in his shoes, by God!" yelled their father. Fearfully, they twisted their necks to look back at the balloon which was being driven back by the wind in a circle, though when the lightning flashed again they could see the balloon-man's upraised arms as if he were calling on dark spirits for more terror. Looking back as the galloping horse bore them to the city pavements, they saw the man in the balloon lost in black clouds, sailing higher and higher, roaring prophecies in thunder until he was lost in black sky.

"We'll make it!" their mother called out, for the London Junction signs could be seen as the first big drops began to fall. A railroad ran down the middle of the main street like a streetcar track, and they had to pass a switching yard filled with snorting engines and freight-cars which frightened their horse even more. They drove down a wide pavement and dashed in a driveway just as the torrent came. They drove straight into the barn and their father lifted them out on the straw-covered floor.

"Run right in the back door—quick!"

They had no time to look at Aunt Lois's house beyond their fleeting pride in its bigness, but scurried under the grape arbor, through the woodshed and in the kitchen door, which welcomed them with the smell of frying chicken and cake-baking and lights as bright as a church. Aunt Lois came running from the front of the house in a white muslin dress, looking so much like a good angel that they ran to her desperately. She hugged them and they began to cry simultaneously into her lap.

"Why, you poor babies! The storm scared you, didn't it?" Aunt Lois soothed them, drying their tears with her apron.

"No, it wasn't the storm, it was the man in the balloon," whimpered Marcia, still shivering. She buried her moist face in her aunt's soft neck. "Don't let the man in the balloon get us! Please! Please!"

2

EVERY NIGHT IN LONDON JUNCTION Lena cried and sometimes their mother rocked her in her arms, big girl that she was, and sang to her. Sometimes she cried, too, leaning over to hide her tears on Lena's yellow curls, and sometimes this sniffling woke up the sensitive Florrie who would set up a great sympathetic bellow and have to be taken up, too. Marcia stood in front of this emotional spectacle, puzzled and unmoved.

"What's Lena bawling about?" she asked repeatedly, and her mother always answered, "She's homesick for the old house on Peach Street."

Marcia tried in vain to understand. Lena had been as excited as she herself had been to come to London Junction. All right, now they were here. They had their wish, didn't they? Just as they'd made it so often on loads of hay and falling stars. But instead of being happy Lena had to bawl. It didn't make sense. Mama cried, too. Florrie always cried, so that didn't count.

"Well, I do miss Towser," Marcia thoughtfully acknowledged, but she could go no further in comprehending her sister's delicate and doubtless more mature emotions. In less triste moments, Marcia studied her for other signs of the strange difference between them, a difference she longed to rectify, if she could only understand it. Sometimes she begged for a demonstration for the benefit of her playmates.

"Show Georgie how you cry when you're homesick," Marcia would urge, but Lena would only be snappish and run away, blushing.

Marcia was five years old now, fifteen months younger than Lena, but she was half an inch taller because she took after the Willards instead of the Reeds. It was an understood thing that Lena was the pretty one, with her yellow curls and rosy cheeks, but Marcia was proud of having bigger feet so she got new shoes first, and the fact that she could hold her breath longer. She did admire Lena's social poise, her not being afraid of boys but stalking past them, nose calmly in air, and she desperately envied Lena's birthmark, a strawberry basket on her neck, caused, it was said, by her mother's passion for strawberries. Lena, for her part, was envious of grown-up solicitude over Marcia's health, remarks that she looked "peaked" and sickly. Marcia had a memory, too, though this was a matter of wonder and pride to Lena more than envy. Marcia could remember everything that ever happened, almost from her first tooth. She could remember knowing what people were saying before she could talk and she could remember bitterly the humiliation of being helpless. She remembered being carried in her mother's arms to a family reunion and given ice cream for the first time. She had cried over its being too cold and her mother said, "Here, Baby, I'll put it on a stove to warm it." Any fool of even less than two could see it was a table and not a stove, but for some philosophic reason Baby Marcia decided to let the thing pass without protest. If her mother wanted to think a table was a stove, she would just have to wait for a bigger vocabulary to argue the matter. This was the beginning of a series of disillusioning experiences with adult intelligence, and the recurrent question of whether adults were playing a constant game of insulting trickery, or whether they just didn't know much. Lena was gravely shocked by Marcia's spoken doubts, so Marcia kept her thoughts to herself.

Lena went to Primary School in London Junction now and no longer considered Marcia a fit companion in public, but walked home with a girlfriend her own age named Mary Evelyn Stewart.

The double name was very fascinating so Marcia changed her own name to Marcia Lily and Lena took the name of Lena Gladys. They tried to make Florrie use her full elegant name of Florence Adeline, but with her customary obstinacy she yelled defiantly, "Me Florrie! Me Florrie!"

"All right, then, be Florrie," Lena Gladys said contemptuously. "But Mary Evelyn and I won't ride you around any more in your go-cart after school."

Lena and Mary Evelyn had a glamorous life in Primary that set them far above Marcia. They had to learn pieces to speak on Exercise Day once a month. Since Mary Evelyn's mother worked in the Fair Store, both children learned in the Willard sitting room, while Marcia, burning with jealousy, played by herself in a corner, cutting out lady paper-dolls all with two names. Marcia couldn't go to school till next term, although she had read and written almost as soon as she walked and talked. This, like her memory, was a dubious talent, for it was not healthy to be different from other children. It wasn't healthy to learn Lena's and Mary Evelyn's pieces the second time she heard them laboriously spelled out, and it was certainly not tactful. Her mother, with a little schoolgirl on each knee, looked down at Marcia helplessly.

"Marcia, you're supposed to be playing paper-dolls!" she protested. "If the girls haven't begun to know their pieces by this time, there's no reason why *you* should."

"She isn't even six," Lena Gladys said coldly to her personal friend, Mary Evelyn. "Now, I'll begin mine again. 'The gingerbread dog and the calico cat—' "

" 'Side by side on the table sat,' " Marcia shrieked, and ran out into the yard yelling the rest of the piece until her mother caught her and boxed her ears.

This correction, not being understood, was forgotten on Exercise Day the next month, when Lena (and of course Marcia) had learned "Little Orphan Annie" with gestures. Mama left Florrie at Grandma's and took Marcia to visit the First Grade. It was an exciting day with the rustle of mothers' best silks, the smell of chalk-dust and newly scrubbed halls, and the squirming of the children sitting two at a desk to make room for the Second Graders. Marcia and her mother sat with the visiting mothers and smaller children in folding chairs on one side of the room. The teacher had drawn a flag in colors on the blackboard, and there were pussy-willows and autumn leaves on her desk. She tapped a little silver gong on her desk when everyone was seated, and she said, "Before we begin the Exercises, perhaps some of our little visitors have a piece they would like to recite for us." Without further urging, Marcia slid off her mother's lap and marched over to the platform, where she recited at terrific speed with glib gestures "Little Orphan Annie." The performance was marked by her mother's horrified face and the sound of Lena sobbing softly into her Reader, "That's my piece! Now I haven't got any piece!"

Even after a punishment for this breach of etiquette and her stout defense, "But Lena didn't know it anyway!" Marcia continued to steal Lena's arithmetic or reader and run easily through the homework while Lena was patiently working over one word in her Speller. Marcia could not understand why it took her sister or Mary Evelyn so long to learn things when they were like candy— you saw them, ate them, and that was the end. Nor could she understand why it was bad for her to find the books so simple, just because she wasn't in school yet. It was confusing to be scolded for doing Lena's lessons, and then overhear her father chuckling about it to Mr. Friend. These were all matters that would clear up certainly when she started going to school so there was no use puzzling about them.

They lived in one side of a two-family house next to Friend's Grocery Store, after the summer at Grandma's and Aunt Lois's house. Often the children walked past the Furness mansion on Main Boulevard and pretended they lived there just as their father had promised. The big house was empty and they could stroll around the orchard, and even peek through windows of the buildings, unless the old caretaker happened to be around. Through the bars of the cellar windows they could see the basement bowling alley, and back of that the greenhouse with broken panes and cracked flower-pots with dead ferns, for no one had lived in the place since old Mrs. Furness had died. They took their shoes off and went wading on the porch, for the rain leaked through the roof to make delicious puddles and a wading-pool of the garden fountain. The great overgrown lawn was a treasure of four-leaf clovers, mole cellars, garter snakes and hoary dandelions to be blown away in a wish. This was their real home, because their father had said so, and any other place was only marking time.

"It's a good thing I decided not to take the Furness place," their father said to their mother. "I understand the heater used to eat up ten tons of coals a season, and with the laundry in the basement you'd be running up and down those stairs every minute. I'm mighty glad I thought it over again."

"Oh, darling, you know we couldn't—*ever!*" their mother gently protested. "I can't understand your even thinking about it."

But this lack of faith always made their father mad. He was often cross nowadays, and always tired out. Their mother was always shushing them with "Papa has a lot on his mind at his new job, so do be quiet." There were many nights when Aunt Lois and Grandma came in for what seemed to be a very grave family conference. The children were sent to bed early, but they could hear their father's voice get higher and higher, shouting down Aunt Lois's tense quick words. The nursery was over the living room and by peeking down the open register the girls could see the grown-ups and hear them without actually understanding what these meetings were all about, except that Papa seemed to be the center of them, both leader and victim. Mama sometimes cried, and Grandma's only contribution seemed as moderator, clucking out a "Now, now, there's more to it than that!" Papa usually shouted out the same answers every time. If a fellow had brains there was no sense in his working in a furniture factory for a foreman that didn't even speak English, he said. "I got brains. I got a personality. Carson's a mighty smart man. He's the boss and he knows what's what. If the boss thinks I got the personality for the road, I don't see what you women have to kick about, trying to hold me back." The arguments often had their start before Papa's arrival, with Mama complaining to her mother and sister about something Papa was threatening to do. But as soon as they offered advice and sympathy, Mama went over to Papa's side. By the end of the evening Grandma and Aunt Lois went home annoyed and baffled, and through the register the children could see Mama tenderly embracing Papa, saying, "I know they're my folks, Harry, and they mean a lot to me, but they've no right to criticize you."

"That's all right," Papa growled. "Only thing is, they get you all upset and that's what makes me sore. Carson's been mighty nice to me and you don't seem to appreciate that. He says I'd be worth a fortune to him on the road. You said you didn't want me to work nights at the factory so I told him so. He knows I'm too smart for that. Besides if I go on the road, maybe I can pick up a chance at a big job—maybe in Cleveland, Chicago, Pittsburgh. London Junction isn't the only place in the world."

"Oh, Harry! A real city?" then their mother's voice dropped. "But we've hardly lived in London Junction yet. I'm not sure I'd like Cleveland."

Scraps from these scenes were excitedly pieced together in the dark into whispered clues by Lena and Marcia; they were repeated to Mary Evelyn at recess next day, eventually resulting in Mary Evelyn's mother saying to Lena's mother at the Fair Store one day, "Well, I hear you folks are moving to Cleveland any day now. Your little girl told my little girl." Mama was surprised, then burst out laughing, though later she scolded Lena for telling lies. Lena cried, but Marcia boldly spoke up, "If Papa tells lies, then *we* can tell lies, too!" This brought Mama's wrath on Marcia, while Lena complacently ran out to play with Mary Evelyn.

The mature new life of her older sister was desperately fascinating to Marcia, now constantly left out. On Sundays she hoped to have Lena to herself for Sunday School, but even there Mary Evelyn came first. One Sunday they were dressed up in their green

nun's veiling jumper dresses with polka dot blouses and felt tri-
corn hats, ready to march off to the First Christian Church, a
penny in each little crocheted purse. But at the corner of Maple
and Fourth they met Mary Evelyn.

"Hello, Mary Evelyn," said Lena.

"Hello, Lena Gladys," said Mary Evelyn.

"Hello," Marcia said breathlessly, but Mary Evelyn paid no
attention, just staring at Lena as if they had a secret together.

"You go on to the Christian Church," Lena directed Marcia,
firmly. "I'm going to Mary Evelyn's Sunday School."

"But you can't!" gasped Marcia. "Mary Evelyn is a Presbyterian, and they sing different songs."

"Is she a tattletale?" Mary Evelyn asked Lena, as if Marcia
was a doll and couldn't talk for herself. Mary Evelyn was tall for
her age. She had a velvet dress and a locket with an opal and
asafedita in it, a prayer book with a lock, and a nickel for collection. She had very red cheeks just as Lena had, and a fat black
braid down her back with the ends tightly curled. She had a pink
velvet hat with a big bow under her chin, for her mother bought
all her clothes from a catalogue. She did not care to walk in public
with anybody younger than she was, so Marcia was obliged to
keep several steps behind the two older girls. As she kept shouting
remarks to them, the conspicuity was almost worse than letting
her come along with them. Lena threatened to tell Mama and this
stopped Marcia for a minute or two. Still, she would rather be lec-
tured for walking behind them than go all by herself to the First
Christian Sunday School. Presently, crushed by criticism and
threats, she stood on the corner watching unhappily while Lena
Gladys and Mary Evelyn stalked proudly down the street toward
the Presbyterian Church. She wanted to get even by going home
and tattling, but she didn't quite dare risk their scorn. Her pride
was shattered by being treated like a baby, but more than that she
was mystified by the difference between herself and Lena. What
made Lena have the courage to step into a strange church, knowing she might get spanked for doing this without permission?
What made it more fun for Lena to do things without permission,

anyway? Marcia hopscotched by herself on the corner, pretending
to have a good time in case they turned around and looked, but
they did not seem to care what she did, providing she didn't bother
them. Desolately she saw that they were actually turning in the
Presbyterian Churchyard and leaving her. She had only to turn up
East Maple and go to the Christian Church, but she couldn't bear
to go all alone. Suddenly, with a little gasp at her own daring, she
began running in the direction of the other girls, and as the last
bell chimed, she fell over the brownstone steps of the Presbyterian
Church, tearing a big hole in the knee of her stocking. A strange
big man with whiskers lifted her up and carried her into the
assembly door just as they began singing, "I washed my hands this
morning, so very clean and white—" The big man put Marcia
down on a chair where she sat rigidly, her heart pounding almost
visibly under her jumper. If it had not been for the encouraging
sight of Lena standing smugly in the front row with Mary Evelyn,
and the fact that the great door was closed, she would have rushed
wildly out again, back to her proper church. She saw that she was
in a row with boys, too, some of them giants of eight or nine years
old, and this threw her into fresh panic. She kept her eyes fixed on
Lena, standing so calmly, her yellow curls prettily ruffling out
from under her felt hat; she ached with envy of this marvellous
poise. Then she thought of what Lena and Mary Evelyn would do
to her when they found she had tagged, and this prospect was
worse than fear of her mother's scolding. She thought, too, of what
the stained-glass God of the First Christian Church would do, if
He found her in a Presbyterian Church, and it was no comfort
thinking He might do the same thing to Lena because clearly Lena
did not fear Him. She saw Georgie Hollis from across the street
making faces at her and even read his lips, "What are you doing in
my Sunday School?"

Then everybody sat down and a very big, very old woman
rustled up to the platform. She had mixed yellow and gray hair
that looked like old corn silk piled in ropes on her head and loose
downy cheeks that wobbled as she walked. Moreover, she flashed

a sparkling lot of gold teeth, a black-ribboned pince-nez and a ruffled blouse covered with brooches, and chains that clinked with authority. There was a silence as she looked over the audience. Marcia hoped her heart did not thunder out her guilty presence.

"I am going to tell you little folks about Sin," said the lady in a sweet, whining Sunday-School voice. "Look what I have here. A glass of pure water, a white rabbit's foot and a bottle of black ink. The rabbit's foot represents the purity of your souls when you are little children. The ink is black like sin and the pure water is the Spirit of Goodness. Does everyone see?"

Marcia craned her neck and saw the rabbit's foot held up.

"Now, the rabbit's foot I dip in the pure water of goodness and see? It stays as white as snow. But then I dip it into the ink of Sin and look! Sin makes the soul black."

This turned out to be absolutely true and there was a murmur as the lady dangled the black rabbit's foot before the astonished audience. Marcia gripped her seat, feeling faintly sick with the knowledge of her own rabbit's foot soul turning black with sin inside her. She heard the slow sugary voice drone on, "Now, children, what do we mean by Sin?"

No one answered. The lady looked around, frowning impatiently.

"Come, come, children, I'm sure we know what Sin is. Come, Mary Evelyn, you've been coming to Sunday School regularly, what is Sin?"

"Ice cream," said Mary Evelyn hopefully.

Someone tittered.

"No, no, ice cream isn't a sin, except when it is forbidden," said the lady sharply. Mary Evelyn pouted. Marcia felt her own hand going up almost of its own accord.

"There's a little hand. What is Sin, dear?"

"Going to the wrong Sunday School," Marcia said clearly.

This was even worse than ice cream for an answer. The lady was scowling as if she wished she had never dirtied her nice rabbit's foot for the benefit of these young stupids. Furthermore, it made Lena and Mary Evelyn turn around and look at the offender. Marcia felt her face burning hot, and her stomach felt as if she'd been riding on a streetcar. She wished urgently that she might drop dead, but then someone opened the door and called out, "Are you through, Miss Marshall? The children may go to their classes now, and we can resume the discussion at Collection time."

With a burst of desperation Marcia ran for the open door and hurtled herself into the great outdoors, falling down on the same step as before and bruising her other knee. She ran down the street toward home, certain of being chased by a pack of Presbyterians and was only reassured at the corner of Maple by the Kandy Kitchen sign. This cheery sight reminded her that she still had her penny so she went inside. At the candy counter she hesitated between a licorice shoestring and a chocolate peppermint that might have a penny prize in it. She chose the peppermint and was rewarded by biting on a coin at once, which allowed her to have a second candy. She loitered over this one, making it last till she had finished a wonderful funny paper the Kandy Kitchen man had opened up over the ice cream table. Instead of being about Buster Brown and Mary Jane, this had a magical story about some one named Little Nemo. Marcia pored over this, happily sucking on her peppermint. She felt mature and independent now, ashamed that she had ever been so childish as to tag after Lena and Mary Evelyn. Suddenly she realized that she was biting on a second penny, unheard-of good fortune, and this reward gave her an inspiration.

"Mr. Kitchen," she said to the bald top of a head on the other side of the counter, "do you sell rabbit's foots?"

Mr. Kitchen's hand scratched the bald top and he said no, but if he ever caught a jackrabbit he'd give her a foot for luck.

"I don't want it for luck," Marcia explained. "I want it to play Sin with like the Presbyterians do. I guess maybe I can make one."

She could hardly wait to run home and make herself a rabbit's foot out of cotton and string. She decided she would have to get the ink out of Papa's desk while he was mowing the back lawn.

Planning this treat, she saw Lena and Mary Evelyn marching primly around the corner, so she ran out, following them at a few paces, forgetting her vow.

"Tagtail," said Mary Evelyn loudly without turning around.

"Pooh on you," answered Marcia.

"Don't pay any attention to her," said Lena.

"She'll never go to heaven and be an angel like us," said Mary Evelyn, primly.

"I don't care, then I'll go to hell and play with all the little devils," said Marcia fiercely. "I'd rather."

This awed her elders into silence, though she could see them exchanging a look of shocked horror. Her own words had even frightened herself and she had a panicky feeling that the man in the balloon might have overheard.

"Let's not let her play house with us," said Mary Evelyn.

"I don't care, I don't care!" shrilly answered Marcia. "I don't play baby games like house. I'm going to get me a rabbit's foot and play Sin. Right now, too."

The two other girls whispered together over this, clearly intrigued. Finally Lena stopped.

"All right, you can walk with us," she said graciously. "We'll play Sin, too. How do we do it?"

"Come on and I'll show you!" Marcia jubilantly cried. If it had not been Sunday they would have run all the way home to start the game. It was too bad Mary Evelyn spilled ink on her dress, but if everybody was going to get spanked, Mary Evelyn might as well, too.

3

IN THE DOUBLE-HOUSE ON FOURTH STREET next to Friend's Grocery Store, there was a dark hallway between the two apartments and a common staircase to the second floor. The Friends' rooms were on the right side and the Willards' on the left. The Friends' baby had died but they still kept its bedroom upstairs with the Madonnas and infant Jesus pictures all over, and Mrs. Friend allowed the Willard children to look at them once in a while. But she got angry when Marcia asked if Jesus was real why the various pictures of him looked like different people. She asked, too, if they could play with the little Madonnas. After that, their mother told them to stay on their side of the hall. Sometimes Charlie Friend, a nephew who delivered groceries for Mr. Friend after high school, came over and walked down the banister in his stocking feet, waving his arms to balance himself, but when Marcia and Lena tried it, they fell downstairs. Mrs. Friend blamed Charlie for this. She said he was too big a boy to play with little girls because he always made them cry. Charlie got mad and Lena and Marcia were even madder, because Charlie swiped candy for them and penny sodas in six different flavors to dissolve in water.

The Friends gave Florrie a big white cradle, and every night Marcia and Lena took opposite sides of the cradle, rocking it and singing at the top of their voices until Florrie, for some reason, would fall asleep. Sometimes their father got out his shining yellow guitar and sang with them, teaching them to take different parts. When Mama had finished the supper dishes they had quartettes. Their father's songs had many verses and were usually sad, with old men grieving for their childhood homes across the sea, mothers lamenting their dead children, little girls lost in the snowstorm, beautiful ladies dying because they had gone to the ball with a hectic flush, poor little Joe in the cold, cold night, and above all the honest Irish lad unable to get work in the city. The last was the favorite of all and they knew all the words. It went —

> Our little farm was small
> It would not support us all,
> And one of us was forced away from home.
> So I bid them all goodbye
> With a teardrop in my eye,
> And sailed for Castle Garden all alone.
>
> When I landed in New York,
> It was hard to get work;
> I roamed about the streets from day to day.
> I went from place to place
> With starvation in my face—
> Nobody had any work, they'd say.
>
> Now I'm an honest Irish lad
> And my home is far away;
> If pleasing you I'll either sing or dance.
> I'll do anything you say
> If you'll only name the day
> You'll give an honest Irish lad a chance.

It was all Marcia could do to keep from howling in sympathy, as they sang, although Lena did not seem at all affected by these melodious tragedies. After Florrie had fallen asleep, the girls were allowed to go downstairs another hour to look at their picture books, Puss in Boots and Cinderella. But the most fun was when their mother told stories. On such evenings their father made a party of it. He would rap on the Friends' door for them to come over and listen, and he would arrange the chairs as if for a show, all of them facing Mama's chair. There was always an excitement about their father; his laughter, his rages, all of his movements were sudden; anger and pleasure exploded without warning or clear reason. When he invited the Friends, it always meant he was in a fine humor, proud of his family, tickled with everything Mama said or did.

"Come on in," he'd say, "Daisy's going to tell the kids stories."

But the stories were really for him. He would put the children into their nightgowns and red Christmas robes with rabbit slippers, then plant them in their small rockers before the big stove. Mr. and Mrs. Friend settled themselves in their appointed chairs, waiting for their host to finish his preparations for the supper to come later—sardines and cheese and beer, or maybe an oyster stew.

"Harry's a better cook than I am," their mother always said. "Harry can do anything he puts his mind to."

"By Jove, I can't tell a story the way she does and that's a fact," their father chuckled. "She can raise the hair on your head—even yours—Friend, ha ha! Go ahead, honey, begin."

Mama took the big chair and crossed her legs under her, tailor-fashion. She looked like a little girl this way, blowing her curly bangs out of her eyes, which were shining wide. The stories she told in a hushed voice were all about ghosts in churchyards, the wind going woo-oo—ooo, the dogs howling in cemeteries, the dead dancing over their graves to violins played by skeleton figures. Papa would wink at Mr. Friend, fat little Mrs. Friend would clutch her husband and gasp, "Oh, my God!" Mr. Friend smoked a pipe and whenever Mama's voice sank to a whisper as it did when the story approached its climax, he would take the pipe out of his mouth and hold it motionless, shaking his bald head in amazement. Then, as Mama sat back triumphantly, Mr. Friend would chuckle and nudge his wife, "Who believes such things? Amy, you're crazy! Nobody ever saw such things, don't be foolish."

Lena always sat rocking back and forth happily, her blue eyes fixed on her mother's flushed excited face, pleased that it was a party and that she was the oldest child. For Marcia, however, each word was agony, sowing seed for terror in darkness. She would not be surpassed by Lena, though, so she clenched the arms of her rocker and tried to shut her ears to her mother's voice. One time, unable to bear the part where the Feet dance by themselves on the treetop, she ran out of the room with her fingers in her ears. Everyone laughed at her, the way they did at Mrs. Friend, so after that she steeled herself to laugh whenever she was frightened. This fooled and pleased her father, who picked her up and held her on his knee.

"Can you beat that?" he exclaimed proudly. "She knows it's funny, already."

So Lena laughed, too, but Mrs. Friend continued to be scared, no matter how often she heard the stories, and she always cried, "Oh, my God!" with a frantic clutch at her husband's arm.

"Do you wonder why I married Daisy?" their father said, arm around his wife. "Why, I'd rather listen to Daisy than go to a show."

This Lena repeated proudly to Mary Evelyn Stewart who told it to her mother, who said there were no shows in London Junction anyway, which Mary Evelyn then told Lena who told her father, who said angrily that he did not like the idea of his daughter playing with the daughter of a woman who worked in a store. This, in reverse order, went back the same route and so for two or three weeks Mary Evelyn and Lena did not speak to each other, and Lena took "Gladys" off her name because she said two names looked silly, and she went back to her own Sunday School.

Their father was a Travelling Man, now, for the London Furniture Company. He came home Thursday nights and stayed till Sunday night. On Thursday the children would stay awake, waiting for him. They could peek down through the register and see their mother sitting at the window, waiting. Then there would be the step on the porch, the exclamations and laughter. Their father and mother would embrace joyously and, still holding each other, start waltzing around and round the room faster and faster, their father not even stopping to take off his hat and coat. When they could stand it no longer, the children tore downstairs, barefooted, and took turns climbing up their father, ending up one on each shoulder. It was fun having your father a Travelling Man because he brought home presents. He brought hats for Mama from Cleveland, funny fans and joke books, miniature decks of cards, perfume, hair-ribbons, boxes of candy, soap rabbits, pencils, calendars, and once he brought Mama a fur capelet. Another travelling man was going to sell it to him cheap if Mama liked it. Mama showed it to Aunt Lois and Grandma and Mrs. Friend, but made him take it back the next trip.

"We can't spend that much money, dear," she protested, fondly. "The kids all need winter coats and we need a new carpet."

"Better keep it, Daisy," advised Mrs. Friend. "If you don't take it, Number Two will."

This got to be a family joke. Their father would pass the meat platter to her and say, "If you don't take it Number Two will." But when he went on his long trip—the Southern territory, and was gone three weeks—Mrs. Friend said, "You should have taken the fur cape because you see you didn't get the carpet or the new coats anyway. You've got to take what your man has a mind to give you of his own accord, because he's never going to give you anything you ask for, and that's the man of it."

"The trouble with Harry being on the road," Mama said to Aunt Lois, "is that he makes more money than he would here in the shop, but he hardly ever sends me any."

"Write and ask him," urged Aunt Lois.

Mama shook her head.

"I don't want to hurt his feelings. Harry's feelings get so hurt when I have to tell him about money."

"All men's feelings are hurt there," Aunt Lois said, laughing.

Aunt Lois's visits, frequent though they were, were always exciting. She wore pretty clothes, furs, and kid gloves, beads, handsome combs in her fair hair, and her skin was soft and pink like the big dolls' in the toy store. Lena was supposed to be the spit and image of her. She had beautiful teeth and was always laughing, perhaps for that very reason. One grudge she still bore against her absent husband was that he had exploited her beautiful crinkly gold hair to advertise his own manufactured hair tonic "Blair's *Blondina*"; and since word came that he made quite a sum out of his formula Aunt Lois was all the madder. She always entered in a state of excitement about something, so it made her calls very thrilling. She brought presents, a bag of peanuts, a cake, some chewing-gum, every time she came, but usually Mama or one of the children was in tears by the time she left, just out of excess excitement.

There was nothing half-way about Aunt Lois. She was ecstatically approving or violently disapproving, never merely tolerant. She thought Mrs. Friend was an idiot, and she thought all the members of Papa's family, particularly his sister Kit, were bigheads. She said once, and she'd say it again, that Mr. Putney was the man Mama should have married. Mr. Thorburne Putney, the distinguished lecturer. Outside of his personal and financial qualifications, it was always a good thing to have a prominent man in the family, a man who'd been all over the world. Mama only laughed at mention of this past suitor, and reminded her sister of so many ridiculous stories of him that Aunt Lois ended up weeping from laughter.

If Aunt Lois seemed in a tolerant mood, Mama would confide her worries. Aunt Lois would start criticizing Harry, saying it was always a bad thing for a man to go on the road—it always meant trouble. Then Mama would be hurt and stay away from her for two or three days, making Mrs. Friend her confidante, until Mrs. Friend would say it was just exactly the way she had prophesied, as soon as a man got to travelling he forgot his responsibilities, so this criticism sent Mama back to Aunt Lois. There was a great deal of talk about money, and usually Aunt Lois or Mrs. Friend would insist on leaving some with Mama. After these visits Mama would be depressed but the moment their father's step was on the porch, everything was all right again.

"God damn it, I'm too busy to think of every little thing," the children could hear their father say after the first joyous waltz and the gossip had begun, "I wish you wouldn't talk to Lois or Mrs. Friend. They just upset you, honey."

"I don't know why I do, Harry," their mother guiltily confessed. "Maybe I'm just lonesome for you."

"Lonesome!" shouted their father. "I'm the one that's lonesome. Come home every night to a cold hotel room. No wonder, I feel half sick all the time. I'm a home man, damn it, but I got to take this job to *make* a home! I wish folks would get that in their heads!"

The next time he went away on one of his longer trips, their mother sent Marcia and Lena to Kraus's Store to see if they could use corn muffins and biscuits once a week. The Krauses said yes, so three times a week their mother baked and they took the baskets after school to Kraus's. Mr. Friend ordered some for his store and other families in the neighborhood ordered regular supplies, too.

"Only don't tell my husband," their mother would beg. "Harry is so proud, he'd kill me."

She couldn't keep the secret herself, and finally told Aunt Lois.

"I won't have to ask him for any money," she said gleefully. "That will make him wonder, I'll bet."

It was fun having a secret from their father, but they waited for him to ask questions in vain. Instead, the girls heard their mother ask him playfully after a while, "Don't you think it's funny I don't need any money?"

Their father patted her tenderly and said, "Honey, you're finally learning how to manage, that's all. That's my girl!"

There was the time he brought home the high Spanish comb and the candied ginger and the talking machine with records. They played it nights for Aunt Lois and Grandma, but Aunt Lois was bad-tempered, spoiling it all. In the middle of "Oh the moon shines tonight on pretty Red Wing as sung by Edison Records," Aunt Lois said, "Harry, how much did that thing cost you? Don't you think your family might like a few comforts before you spend your money on trash like this?"

Papa looked so bewildered and abused that Marcia felt a hot surge of anger, and she cried out in a choking voice, "We don't want any comforts, Aunt Lois! We like the talking machine best!"

"Hush, dear," said Mama, her face red.

"I'd send it back a-flying, if I was in your place, Daisy, and take the money instead," said Aunt Lois firmly.

"You're just jealous, Lois," their mother cried out hotly. "Harry loves me and brings me presents and your husband hasn't written you in ten years. I *love* the talking machine! I'd rather have it than anything in the world and Harry knows it!"

She threw her arms around his neck, sobbing, and he patted her, but his face was still dark and aggrieved.

"That's what a fellow gets when he tries to do something nice for somebody," he grumbled. "Always plenty of people to criticize."

After Aunt Lois went, Mama comforted him, and even sent him out to the saloon for a pint of beer. That night the children heard him playing the guitar long after they were asleep. He sang, "Oh, Bedelia, oh, Bedelia, I've a longing for to steal you, oh, Bedelia." When they heard the gramophone playing again, "Oh the moon shines tonight on pretty Red Wing," they rolled into each other's arms to sleep, happy because he was happy again.

4

WHEREVER GRANDMA STAYED was "Grandma's house," though the London Junction place was really Aunt Lois's, left her by her absent husband's father, and a great burden to her in size and taxes. But while Aunt Lois whisked briskly up and down stairs with mop and broom and a towel around her head, eternally busy at keeping the big house in order, Grandma rocked on the side porch with her darning bag, visiting with her friends and keeping up an air of gracious leisure. Ever since she had given up the Elmville farm she talked of having a place of her own, "being independent" as she said. But her children balked her in this by making her stay for a while first with one and then the other. She managed to sustain a feeling of independence at Aunt Lois's by making plans for a millinery store, a tea-room, or a dress-making shop. Aunt Lois was always catching her with the grass blinds of the porch drawn, in low-voiced conferences with furtive little people who had a store to let or a business to sell. Aunt Lois recently had taken in schoolteachers as roomers, but one time she found that in her absence Grandma had admitted two night workers from the Foundry.

"They can use the teachers' rooms while the teachers are away," Grandma explained. "Don't you see, Lois, they can sleep daytimes while the teachers are at school?"

When Aunt Lois expostulated that the teachers wouldn't like it, Grandma explained, "They needn't know. My goodness, Lois, I could nip upstairs and wake them before the teachers got home, couldn't I? My glory, Lois, don't you want to make a little extra money? I don't want to just work for nothing all my life. Never mind! Let it go! I'll have a place of my own one of these days."

A fine thing about Grandma was that she never seemed to admit any difference between children and grown-ups, so she was as apt to confide her career plans to Marcia and Lena as to anyone else, or if she stayed with them to let them stay up till it was her own bedtime. Marcia played here while Lena was at school, and Grandma let her stir cake batter or peel potatoes or help make beds while she talked about her plans.

"Lois has had a lot of trouble in her life, what with losing her baby and having Charlie run off on her like he did," she said. "But on the other hand there's plenty Lois don't understand. A person can work their fingers to the bone on a farm, doing chores and raising ten children, all for nothing, and that's all right. But a body with a little more ambition is supposed to take a back seat. It's not fair."

"No," Marcia gravely agreed. "It's not fair. If I was you, Grandma, I'd run away."

"I will," her grandmother said resolutely. "I'm not going to take a back seat all my life. No matter what my own flesh and blood think. Why, I got more get-up-and-git in my little finger than the lot of them. I'll show them."

She had a friend, just as Lena had, a lady named Mrs. Carmel who used to run a millinery store in town but now lived in Cleveland. Mrs. Carmel had written her to come to Cleveland and start a rooming house, as there was a perfect fortune in it. It would be a real treat, Mrs. Carmel's letter said, to have an old friend there, and she needn't mind missing her lodge work as there were plenty Lady Maccabees and D.A.R.'s and Eastern Stars in Cleveland as well as a Women's Relief Corps. Every time Aunt Lois made objection to something Grandma did, Grandma would go

up to her big front room and read over Mrs. Carmel's letter sometimes aloud to Marcia.

Grandma confided a great deal in Marcia and sometimes in
her daughter Daisy, whenever Daisy was mad at Aunt Lois. But
when her two daughters made up, Grandma knew it was no use
talking to either of them for they sided against her. Either Lois
scolded or Daisy slyly teased her. Strangers and Marcia were, however, constantly sympathetic. It was mean, they felt, for Aunt Lois
to lose her temper whenever Grandma stopped Mr. Sweeney
going by. Grandma's voice talking to Mr. Sweeney was very different than when she talked to anybody else, and Marcia finally
discovered that all grown-ups used different voices for different
classes of society. The voice Grandma used for Mr. Sweeney was a
very elegant one, and furthermore with him she never used the
words "me" or "her" in a sentence. "I and my daughter Lois get
very lonely here, Mr. Sweeney, especially at nights. It is very hard
for she, especially being a widow you might say, and a lovely-look-
ing girl as anybody can tell you. It's hard for a woman, Mr.
Sweeney, when her man is a sick man. Yes sir, my daughter's husband was taken with an old disease they call walking fever ten
years ago and we haven't seen him since. Very hard for both I and
she. You know how a mother feels, Mr. Sweeney. It would be a
privilege to me to see some lovely widower like yourself pay her
a call now and then." Mr. Sweeney had a reddish face and was
always dressed up with a big black-brimmed hat over his bald
head, a cane, and a large thick gold watch fob resting on his tight
tan vest. He even carried thick kid gloves sometimes, for his affairs
took him into fine places in distant cities. He lived in the London
Junction Hotel and rented his former home on Willow Avenue to
which he and Grandma referred in sacred tones as "the property."
He had property in Cleveland, too, and in Lesterville where his
wife's parents had been very well fixed.

"A real gentleman," Grandma told Marcia, "and your Aunt
Lois don't even appreciate what I'm trying to do for her. It's
enough to break a body's heart."

"My daughter Lois wondered what your opinion was of the present situation," Grandma would say, just to keep Mr. Sweeney another few minutes. "She was saying to a party the other day that Mr. Sweeney is about the only person you can talk to in this place, I mean the only person who gets around and knows."

Mr. Sweeney would stand a little closer to the porch, careful not to disturb the spot where grass was planted but never grew, raise his big hat and mop his head thoughtfully, replace handkerchief in back pocket and cough. "It's likely we're in for some more hard times, Mrs. Reed—*but,* we got some good men in the country, J. P. Morgan, John D. Rockefeller, Andrew Carnegie—I guess we can trust them to look out for the common people in a pinch."

What made Grandma mad was that Aunt Lois would peek out and see who was there and go right back in the house, which hurt Mr. Sweeney's feelings so that he would lift his hat and go on his way with dignity. It made Grandma mad to be teased by her daughter Daisy as if Mr. Sweeney was *her* beau, when she was only trying to interest him in Lois. Even Marcia disapproved of her mother's ridicule of Mr. Sweeney, her defense being a matter of bribery largely, since Mr. Sweeney had given her a half dollar one day for bringing him a glass of water. Grandma discussed business in a low secret voice with Mr. Sweeney, and her plans to run a rooming house in Cleveland as her very clever friend, Mrs. Carmel, had advised. "It will leave my daughter very lonesome, Mr. Sweeney," Grandma confessed. "I trust you as the person she admires more than anyone else to sort of look after her. She's young and inexperienced, you know." But in spite of Aunt Lois's supposed reverence for Mr. Sweeney, she always ran away when he was there and scolded Grandma afterward, until Grandma would get red-faced and go upstairs to write other relations or— better still—Mrs. Carmel.

One day the children's mother got sick and all of them, even Florrie, were brought to Grandma's to stay, while Aunt Lois went to the Fourth Street House to nurse her sister. It was a wonderful vacation. Lena played hookey from school and Grandma let them eat cookies and milk every meal with bananas and oranges in between. They could play "Run, Sheepie, Run," in the streets after dark with the neighbor children, and Florrie stayed up till she fell asleep of her own accord and threw up unheeded after every cookie. The teachers had fun, too, for Grandma let them have beaux all over the house at all hours and cook fudge late at night.

"My daughter Daisy is a very sick girl," she said, shaking her head. "I'll have to ask you ladies to help me with the house while Lois is nursing her."

The children could empty all the drawers and trunks they liked, dress up, play opera house—anything. They got out the family album bound in green plush with an inset diamond-shaped mirror and a tasselled gold lock, and one day Grandma patiently went over the whole family gallery for them. For instance, this pretty, full-cheeked, curly-haired brunette with the lace bertha and fan was Grandma's first-born who died at the Chicago World's Fair. This plump little girl, eager, laughing, with a ball held up in her hand, was not a playmate for you at all but your own great-grandmother who was to grow up to have four babies, one of them stolen by Indians, two of the others dead. This smiling handsome young man in the high collar, checked vest and thick curly black hair was the great-uncle who ended up insane, tied to a post and chain in an asylum; he was Great-Uncle Samuel and he had been a postman leaving one family in Rhode Island to start another in Massachusetts. "Amnesia, they call it now," said Grandma. "He left your Great-Aunt Nell and all the children and was gone thirteen years, forgetting his name and home. When he remembered he came back and took a razor to his wife and children, so they locked him away."

This story hung over Marcia's mind—that laughing youth should grow up into misery and horror, that to grow up did not mean rewards but anguish; even she might go crazy, with a post and chain and a razor. It was terrifying to look at the picture of her great-grandmother, the little girl with the ball, and think of her running through dark Indian forests crying, "Baby! Baby!" and the woods crying back, "Baby! Baby!" and far off the sound of a baby crying, lost forever. She thought of her great-grandmother always as a little girl with the ball, not as the later picture, the bent old lady in cap and shawl with the tired sad face. "Did she have nice things happen to her finally?" begged Marcia. "Please, Grandma, didn't nice things happen?"

"Died in the Elm County Poorhouse," said Grandma. "People didn't have the money then they have today." It was like Papa's songs and Marcia felt that there was not enough room in her chest to bear such woe.

"Who's this one?" Lena asked, pointing to the next page, a strange foreign gentleman who seemed to have a head coming out of his stomach.

"That is an Oriental prince," Grandma's voice now swelled with pride. "He was a Siamese twin and his sister grew out of his stomach. My sister Sarah Rebecca met him on a boat trip to Italy and he very kindly gave her his picture."

"No, no!" Marcia choked. "Don't tell me any more, Grandma. No more!"

She ran out the door into the back yard, into the woodshed where they wouldn't find her slapping her own eyes to keep back tears. But tears were inside her, crying Baby! Baby! oh, Indians, give back the little girl's baby!

5

DURING THEIR FATHER'S LONGER ABSENCES, the children and their mother spent more and more time at Grandma's. Aunt Lois turned out one of the teachers and let her sister use the room for her family on the many nights they spent there, for Daisy was not so much afraid as lonesome at night. When some tiff with Aunt Lois—always about Papa—made her stay home in the house on Fourth Street for a few nights, she moved a cot into the children's room. She pushed the dresser against the door, and put Papa's revolver under her pillow. Then she wrapped her red Chinese kimono around herself and sat square-legged on the bed—her curly brown hair over her shoulders, telling stories long after bedtime. When a lightning storm came she was really happy and not at all frightened. She said burglars wouldn't be out on a night like this. In the middle of the night the thunder would begin and the rain pour. Lena and Marcia would cry out with fear and hold tight to each other. But their mother would jump out of bed and pull a chair up to the window. "Come, kids, watch the lightning!" she would cry and sometimes picked them out of bed, snuggled in blankets to sit in the chair by the window with her. It was something special to be gotten up in the night so the girls tried to be worthy of the honor but they could hardly keep back their cries of terror at each new thunderbolt or rip of lightning. They put their fingers in their ears and shut their eyes, peeking once in a while at their mother, whose eyes were shining in her rapt face, as if the storm was a story or a song to her.

"But lightning kills people," Marcia quavered.

"They would die anyway," said their mother. "If lightning didn't kill them they'd drop dead of something else. Green apples maybe."

It was fun having Papa away, a Santa Claus about to pop in with surprises any day. Besides, their mother let them do almost anything they liked. She showed them tricks she'd never showed them before: card tricks, how to twist your legs behind your neck, how to play the mouth-organ, and how to dance while she played the talking machine. She let them taste coffee and tea and told them jokes about two Irishmen and two Dutchmen. She didn't even scold them when a lady down the street reported that the children played train with her bread loaves when they delivered them. They tied a string around the loaf and dragged it very conveniently to the store or home that had ordered it from their mother. She made them a little wagon with a board and thread-spools for wheels so the lady no longer complained.

One disadvantage in Papa's longer trips was that they missed the Saturday night celebration of paying the grocery bill. Papa had made a custom of taking all three children over to Friend's Store right after Saturday night supper (always tea and toast and apple-sauce). The store was crowded with farmers in hip boots, leather jackets and stocking caps, buying their week's supplies. Marcia and Lena, with Florrie grasped between them, stood close to Papa so as not to get lost in this great crowd, and also to indicate their preferences in the "treat." The bill paid, Mr. Friend then took a brown paper bag and tin scoop over to wooden buckets on the floor filled with different candies, hard candy in one, rather gray-ish chocolates in another, horehound drops in a third. Mr. Friend made a show of letting them choose, but no matter what they said there was always a preponderance of hard candy and never enough chocolates. Marcia saved her chocolates till bedtime, but Lena ate hers at once, shrewdly enough, since later on Marcia would have to divide hers with her or be reproached as selfish by Mama. Now three Saturdays sometimes passed with no treat, and Mr. Friend's informal generosity at other times did not make up for the loss of this ceremony.

Mama was restless and moody during Papa's absences. Once Aunt Lois promised to cheer her up by taking her to Lesterville to see a show with a friend of hers. London Junction had an opera house, but it had been condemned by the Fire Department ever since the last stock company's visit. The fire hazard had been recognized only after the leading man had run off with the mayor's niece after the last act of *Dr. Jekyll and Mr. Hyde,* but after that London Junction drama lovers must travel to Lesterville for their fun. Aunt Lois's friend was an insurance man named Wilson, a business acquaintance she said, who occasionally took her to supper when she had shopping to do in Lesterville. It would be a pleasure to meet her sister. Mama was excited, and decided to take one of the children.

"I know it won't be me," Marcia said stoically. "The middle one never gets took anywhere. It's always the baby, or Lena because she's the oldest. The middle one never gets took anywhere."

Mama weighed the matter gravely, but made up her mind when Aunt Lois reminded her that Florrie would cry all the time and that Lena had just shaved off her eyebrows at Mary Evelyn's suggestion and looked peculiar. It was luck at last for the middle one. Lena was left to sulkily look after Florrie, and Marcia was fixed up in a new plaid hair-ribbon, Lena's coat since it had no patches, with white mittens strung through the sleeves for safety. Aunt Lois and Mama did each other's hair in new ways before the mirror and borrowed each other's gloves, neck-ribbons, belts and furbelows, convinced that a good time as well as *chic* depended on the wearing of borrowed trifles. Mama wore her best brown broadcloth with black velvet buttons and a short cape, and Aunt Lois wore a handsome black velveteen with narrow fur edgings at the hem and bodice. They had sachets of flower petals pinned to their underthings and Marcia was allowed a drop of perfume on her handkerchief.

Lena looked after them with a long face, pressing it against the window as they left.

"I'll probably have a bad earache when you get home," she predicted. "It hurts bad already."

They took the five o'clock streetcar to Lesterville, ten miles away. For a long time before they got there, Marcia saw the dark sky illumined with flames like a Fourth of July celebration. These were the steel mills, Mama explained. The car stopped at every other corner to pick up the workers with their dinner pails on their way to or from the mills. Riding past the gates you saw men bare to the waist outlined darkly against brilliant fire of blue or red or white, looking like the saints in stained-glass windows. The men crowded on the car smelled of dirt and sweat and pipe smoke, but more than anything else of power. Marcia withdrew into her mother's arms, afraid of these silent men, puzzled that her mother and Aunt Lois seemed unaffected by them.

"Mr. Wilson spoke of getting tickets for *Colonial Dames* at the Lyceum," said Aunt Lois. "We can take turns holding Marcia on our lap."

They got off at the White Hotel on the Square. It was Marcia's first trip to Lesterville and the biggest town she'd ever seen, but she did not want people to suspect this, so she took care not to show interest in her surroundings. They went into a palm-decorated corridor, with a marble floor and large leather chairs lining the walls with cuspidors beside them. As they entered, two gentlemen got up and removed their hats with the most gratifying reverence. One was dapper and swarthy with curling black moustaches and luxuriant black curly hair brushed back in a pompadour. He carried a rich brown topcoat over his arm, neatly folded, and wore a flower in his lapel. Marcia was so overcome with the stylishness of this Mr. Wilson that she had only a mild surprise to see that his companion was Mr. Sweeney. Mr. Sweeney bent low over Aunt Lois's hand, with the solemn dignity of one about to lead in prayer.

"I had business in Lesterville with Wilson," he said, "and when I heard you and your sister were coming over, I seized the opportunity to make it a party—my party, if you please."

Aunt Lois was very redfaced and gave Mama a deep look that was evidently meant to say volumes.

"Sweeney took charge of everything when he found you were coming," Mr. Wilson laughingly told Aunt Lois. "He says supper at the Chinatown, then out to Luna Park to see the Gaiety Revue."

Mama looked helplessly at her sister, and then at Marcia who was unable to conceal her rapture at Mr. Wilson's words and elegant manners.

"Isn't the Chinatown a little—I mean—" stammered Mama.

"I have been looking forward to such an opportunity as this for a long time," Mr. Sweeney said, fixing a look of worshipful admiration on Aunt Lois. "It is most opportune, most opportune, indeed."

It was clear that Aunt Lois's silence and rising blushes were not due to coquetry but to mounting indignation. Would the gentlemen excuse them for a moment, she asked ominously? Marcia found herself hustled out to the Ladies' Parlor where a serious conference was held.

"You stay, Lois," Mama said earnestly. "I had no idea it would be like this. Marcia and I will take the car back. If I'd realized it was to be a party of four—oh, Harry wouldn't like it at all! No, I can't stay, I just can't."

Aunt Lois said testily that she had no intention of staying either. She did not think it was any of Harry's business if his wife wanted to have a bit of innocent pleasure, but what made her so mad she could spit was that old goat Mr. Sweeney butting in.

"Ma told him I'd be here, I just know it," she declared angrily. "I'll bet a million dollars she planned the whole thing, she's so set on him. I can't stand him. He'd spoil any party. I wouldn't go with him if he was the last man on earth. I could kill him right now. It's not Walter's fault, of course, but wouldn't you think he could have done something to keep Mr. Sweeney off?"

Mama said she thought Walter Wilson looked awfully fast, and that for her part she'd trust Mr. Sweeney a great deal more than she would Mr. Wilson, but she simply couldn't stay another minute on account of Harry. Going with her sister and a friend to a show was one thing, but a foursome! Lois tartly replied, running a chamois over her crimson face, that Mama was acting like a fool, and that Walter Wilson was a perfect gentleman which was more than Harry Willard would ever be. Mama said haughtily that would be quite enough, thank you, and she would take Marcia away at once, if Lois would calm down enough to explain that Marcia had been taken sick. Aunt Lois put on her plumed black hat at a more dashing angle over her curly blond hair, but this was not for purposes of allure but a gesture of warfare. They stalked back to the gentlemen who appeared to sense some cloud on the horizon for they looked apprehensive. Mama explained that her little girl had suffered a bad stomach spell, and she'd have to take her home at once. Mr. Wilson hoped Aunt Lois could stay, but Aunt Lois said stiffly that she must help her sister. In this awkward conversation, Marcia felt the need for a tactful word from her, and as she was being pulled away she managed to smile reassuringly at Mr. Wilson and say, "Of course I'm not *really* sick."

They got on the seven o'clock streetcar going back past the mills. Marcia kept her face pressed against the window, blinking hard at the red glaring sky to hide her tears. Aunt Lois and Mama wrangled for a while as to whose fault it was the evening had been spoiled, Harry's, or Mr. Sweeney's, or Grandma's. Then both ladies stared into space with tight lips, and did not speak to each other the rest of the trip. Marcia's heart was heavy with disappointment. This would never have happened to the oldest or youngest, she bitterly reflected, just to the middle one.

6

I N THE SPRING London Junction turned into a real city, with
crowds on the street and the trains bringing in strangers every
day. This was due to visits from the carnival, Sells' Circus, a
medicine show, and later on a tabernacle with revival meetings.
There wasn't room in the London Junction Hotel for all the visitors, so the townspeople let out their spare rooms for fifty cents a
night. Aunt Lois rejected Grandma's urgent advice to make room
for Rosetta, the Rose Dancer from the carnival, but the children's
mother was finally persuaded to give up her own bedroom to her.
This was not so much Grandma's persuasive powers as the fact
that Mrs. Willard was snatching at every penny she could earn
and was lonely without her husband now that his trips lasted so
much longer.

For once Lena was jealous of Marcia who didn't have to go to
school, and could be petted by the glamorous roomer, could even
spend an afternoon in the tent dressing room, peeking at the Rose
Dance performance through a hole in the canvas. Rosetta's Rose
Dance was the high-class act of the carnival, but there were many
other wonders hidden in tents along the street and in the railroad
lot, all pointed out by her mother on an exploring expedition the
very first day. There was the white horse that could count and
spell, the fortune-teller in the gypsy clothes, the snakecharmer

with the boa constrictor pet, the sword-swallower, and the midgets. There were two midgets dressed like a king and queen who rode in a tiny royal coach drawn by midget ponies with midget footmen and coachmen in white wigs and knee-breeches. They drove through town every day at noon so that the school children might see them. Marcia was so excited over the midgets she ran away to follow them through the streets back to their tent. But she got into the wrong tent in her confusion and found herself before a long glass case wherein lay a huge snake. The snake's eyes were on a level with her own, and she stood hypnotized with terror, unable to look away. She was saved by the arrival of Charlie Friend. "I'm lost," she babbled.

"You ran away, you mean," Charlie said. "Come on home and get your whipping."

The presence in the house of Rosetta saved her from punishment, although the snake itself had punished her enough already. Rosetta gave her a popcorn ball and called her "darlin" so that Marcia at once became her slave.

Rosetta was a sharp-faced tall thin woman but she turned into a fairy princess in a golden wig, long curls falling over her shoulders, her skin coated with white powder, and dressed in the pink changeable silk skirt which she lifted up and down to simulate rose petals while a violin played "Hearts and Flowers." Mama came to see her once and sat in the front row of the tent with Marcia. They were very proud to be friends with the artist. Mama said she certainly wished Harry could be home to see this beautiful performance.

Every night at midnight Rosetta's step was heard on the porch. Their mother sat up waiting for this, reading the *Yellow Book* or sewing. The children could hear her calling up Aunt Lois earlier in the evening, begging her to come down to go with her to the carnival, but Aunt Lois wouldn't come and Mama was too shy to go alone at night. She sat on the front porch stoop with Mrs. Friend on the other side of the dividing railing, and watched the carnival lights far down the street. When the merry-go-round in the B. & O. depot lot played something familiar she and Mrs. Friend would softly sing the words to this distant accompaniment. "Just because you made those goo-goo eyes," and "Won't you come home, Bill Bailey," and "Two Little Girls in Blue." As soon as Rosetta came in, often with a man, there was excitement downstairs, enough to waken the two older girls who immediately peeked down the floor register. There was a smell of fresh coffee, the subdued rattle of dishes as if it was daylight, and sometimes the voices went on and on far into the night. They could hear their mother laughing sometimes or talking excitedly—always about Harry, Harry, Harry and then Rosetta's twanging voice with its "darlings," "honeys" and other pretty pet names she used for everybody. Rosetta was a secret, and nobody was ever to breathe to Papa that there had been a stranger in the house, that shameful thing, "a *boarder!*"

"I'll tell him myself sometime when he's in a good humor," their mother assured Aunt Lois and Grandma, "but if he hears it from anyone else he'll just kill me. You know how Harry thinks of his home."

"You'll tell him the first thing," said Aunt Lois. "You tell him everything the minute he sets foot in the house."

Their mother laughed guiltily.

"I know. I just can't keep a thing from Harry. And anyhow he sees so many things all over the country, I want him to realize that we've got things happening right here at home, too. He'll be mighty surprised when he finds I know an actress, and I didn't have to travel on the road to meet her, either."

The carnival ended Saturday night but Rosetta stayed all day Sunday, too, on Mama's invitation. Mama mended her rose-petal costume, and Rosetta showed Mama and Mrs. Friend how to shampoo their hair with the white of an egg. The three ladies in their kimonos took pails of water and basins out in the backyard Sunday afternoon and washed each other's hair, and compared lengths. Rosetta told them stories in a low voice that made Mama laugh and made Mrs. Friend exclaim admiringly, "I don't see where in the world you pick up such things." Mrs. Friend, being fair, was given a lemon rinse with the white of egg, and Mama, being brunette, was recommended vinegar. Rosetta herself put peroxide in the water and wrapped her short hair in a towel.

"I wish Harry could walk in right now," Mama kept saying. "I'll bet Harry's never met anybody like Rosetta, don't you, Mrs. Friend?"

While the ladies were drying their hair in the back yard among the elderberry bushes and sunflowers, Lena and Marcia took turns trying on the performer's rose costume and flapping their arms about to make a rose, until Marcia put her stout boot through the silk where mama had mended it, so they hastily put the whole thing back in the trunk. Florrie had whizzed around in her walker and gouged out the chocolate frosting on a newly baked cake that Mama had set on the window sill to cool, so the children, chastened by their misdemeanors and aware of imminent correction, tried to entertain themselves in more pious ways, such as washing dishes. On Marcia's inspiration they tried shampooing Florrie's scanty blond curls to shrieks of rage. When the three ladies came in, still giggling from mysterious secrets, Mama was so excited she did not notice the mischief they had created. The women sat before the dresser mirror in the downstairs bedroom trying their hair in new ways Rosetta recommended from pictures in the Sunday *Cincinnati Enquirer.* Mama read aloud "Durandel's Gossip" and "Clarabelle's Chatter of Women and Their Ways" from the paper. Rosetta ordered some soap from Mama's *Larkin Soap Catalogue* and enough geranium toilet water to win Mama the special premium of a hand-painted jardiniere. She would send the money from Mansfield where the troupe was performing next week.

"Don't forget to look up Harry," Mama said. "He'll be at the Parker House till Wednesday. Harry Willard, care of London Furniture Company."

"It'll be a real pleasure, dear," Rosetta assured her warmly. "I'll have George give him free passes to all the tents. I'll tell him you suggested it, dear."

Mama was beaming at thought of the pleasure Harry was soon to have all due to her, and perhaps at the thought of this indirect way of being in touch with him. She and Mrs. Friend sat in the bedroom talking excitedly in their kimonos long after the carnival man had come to take Rosetta and her trunk away. They cut up the cake Florrie had ruined and Mama only laughed about it because she was so excited at what a thrill Rosetta was going to have meeting Harry and how astonished Harry would be at meeting such an unusual friend of his wife's. Before dark they washed their hair again to get the white of egg out of it because, as Mrs. Friend ruefully put it, the egg dried like glue in the hair, no fault of Rosetta's of course, but their own for not doing it right.

That night Mama moved back in her own bedroom and she let Lena sleep with her because she had an earache. Marcia stayed upstairs alone for a little while and then came down purposefully.

"I have an earache, too," she stated firmly.

Her mother laughed.

"All right, climb in, rascal," she said.

But Mama didn't stay in bed. Instead she put on her kimono and went out on the front porch where Mrs. Friend was sitting rocking in the dark.

"I kinda miss the merry-go-round music," she said to Mrs. Friend. "It makes everything more lonesome now, doesn't it?"

Papa came home three days later in a new blue suit with a checkered tie and a cane and his moustache shaved off so that Florrie didn't know him and wouldn't go to him. This time he had brought a necklace of shells from Atlantic City for Mama and salt water taffy and a little box with two white mice in it and a big bath towel named Gilsey. The children played with the mice while Mama sat on his lap in the big chair. They forgot about their secret until suddenly Papa said, "A funny thing happened to me in Mansfield. An old trollop from some street show there came up to me in the Parker House and claimed she knew me. Said she was a friend of my wife's. I knew it was some kinda funny business so I walked off and next thing I see her working the same thing on Hartwell of the Eugenia Candy Company. You meet a lot of queer ones, travelling around."

"Oh, Harry!" Mama said in a low voice. Then she said, "There's something I want to tell you. You children had better go to bed now."

Marcia and Lena hung around, wanting to hear and help tell all about Rosetta's visit, but their father hoisted one of them to each shoulder and marched upstairs, whistling "Marching Through Georgia," leaving Florrie in the crib downstairs as usual.

"But we wanted to tell the secret!" Lena protested as he tumbled them on their bed.

"I can spell shampoo," Marcia said. "I can read it, too."

"You help your mother, that's all I ask," said Papa.

Later they heard their father's voice getting louder and louder downstairs, their mother's more pleading.

"But I had to get the money, somewhere, Harry," their mother was saying. "That's all I took her in for."

"So you don't trust me!" their father shouted. "If I've told you once I've told you a dozen times that I'm going to send you some money, but oh, no, you believe your mother and Lois and neighbors, take their word against mine every time! Take in a carnival trollop in my home to make some cash as if your own husband didn't look after you! Daisy, I don't understand you! Don't you love me any more, Daisy? Is that it?"

"Oh, Harry, you *know*—" their mother's voice was muffled now, very likely on Papa's forgiving shoulder. "I wouldn't hurt you for anything in the world. It's all my fault, darling. But look— here's the three dollars!"

"Keep it," Papa said gruffly. "Buy yourself a porterhouse steak with it tomorrow."

7

ONE OF THE CURIOUS THINGS about everybody else, to Marcia, was their need for a Friend. Lena had to have a Friend, Mary Evelyn; Grandma had to have a Friend, Mrs. Carmel; and even Papa had a Friend. A friend was someone who did everything differently from you and was a source of unending fascination. It was an honor to have a Friend call on you, or praise you, and you talked about your Friend proudly because a Friend was always richer, handsomer, and wiser than you—at least at first. A Friend gave you advice, sometimes presents, and his lack in any respect was well-advised, in fact a virtue.

Papa's Friend was a very important person named Hartwell of the Eugenia Candy Company and they met frequently on the road as they both had the "Eastern territory" and stayed often in the same hotels. Mr. Hartwell lived in a club in Lesterville. He was not married but went steady with the company's cashier there, a very lovely woman who had expressed the wish to meet Mrs. Willard and get acquainted.

"Why don't they get married?" Mama asked one day when Papa was speaking of his Friend.

"They've gone together so long, there wouldn't be any point in getting married," Papa explained in some exasperation.

Mr. Hartwell, who after a suitable period, was called just Hartwell and presently Ed, persuaded Papa to join the Elks, and also the Masons, as he himself was a 33rd degree Mason. It was a wonderful thing in business, Papa said, to flash your lodge pins on a customer and find that they were brothers. It paid back the dues it cost you. He'd gotten many a new customer since he'd joined these organizations, just for that very reason. Besides, there were the social advantages—smokes, stag parties, picnics, fishing trips. As these social advantages usually delayed Papa's homecomings, Mama was a little troubled about them. She was not even sure she would like Hartwell, in spite of the complimentary messages he sent through her husband to "the little woman." Hartwell bought his suits from a Pittsburgh catalogue which sent samples in return for his measurements, so Papa bought his suits there, too. People in London Junction said that Mr. Willard was a very snappy dresser. Mama and the children were very proud. When Papa came home with his new pepper-and-salt outfit and a stiff katy like Hartwell's, he was so tickled with himself that he said Mama should take herself and the children down to the Fair Dry Goods Store for new outfits.

"I guess we don't look good enough to go around with you," Mama teased him, a little ruefully, but Papa kissed her and said he had the prettiest wife and the finest family in the world. He said they would always look good to him even in rags. He said he'd seen plenty society beauties in Cleveland and Philadelphia and Buffalo that couldn't hold a candle to his Daisy in spite of their fine jewels and satins.

Mama took Lena and Marcia down to the Fair Dry Goods Store with the five-dollar bill Papa gave her. This was the store where Mary Evelyn's mother clerked and where Mary Evelyn was now proudly sorting ribbons in a box for the Saturday sale. Marcia and Lena stood on the other side of the counter watching this delicate operation in silent envy while their mother looked around. Mary Evelyn had her hair in rag curlers, and wore a ruffled black sateen pinafore over her pink-checked gingham dress. She wore curlers, as many other children did, every day except for Sunday School, parties, and Exercise Day when they were released into

half-braids with reluctantly curling ends. Marcia and Lena had
real curls but regretted not being allowed to wear rag curlers like
Mary Evelyn.

The Fair Store was a long narrow store with only one window
and a curious smell of shoe leather and wool in it, somehow identi-
fied pleasurably with new clothes. Mr. Brady owned it. He was a
bald, polite fat man who always dressed in black as his wife had
been dead many years. His manner was grave and dignified, for he
always kept in mind his duties as president of the Chamber of
Commerce, head of the School Board, and superintendent of the
Methodist Sunday School. He talked to Mama for a while and
then with a bow turned her over to Mrs. Stewart.

"I declare, Mrs. Willard, you're the only person in London
Junction that can make Mr. Brady laugh out loud," Mrs. Stewart
whispered to Mrs. Willard, unfolding a bolt of goods on the
counter. "Now here is percale, eight cents a yard, but I have some
lovely bengaline for dress at forty-five a yard. I made one myself
for Mary Evelyn, though I usually get her the store clothes."

"What color percale would you like?" Mama asked Lena.
Lena and Marcia exchanged a look of mutual understanding.

"We'd like store dresses like Mary Evelyn," Lena said.

Their mother pretended not to hear them but went on com-
paring materials.

"Four pairs of Black Cat stockings for them," said Mama. "I'd
better get that and their underwear first. Two pantywaists—gauze."

"Mary Evelyn doesn't wear Black Cat stockings," said Lena
clearly. "She wears socks. That's what we want."

"I don't wear pantywaists either," stated Mary Evelyn. "I wear
suspenders."

Mrs. Stewart laughed indulgently, but Mama firmly stuck to
her order. She ordered ten yards of percale.

"My cousin Lydia from Venice Corners is a seamstress," she
said. "She made a trousseau for Mr. Brady's niece last year. She'll
come over with her pattern books to help me make these up, because she keeps up with all the latest styles."

"I'd rather have a store dress," said Lena. "I'd rather have a store dress and a black sateen pinafore."

"I've got in some darling little dresses from Chicago," said Mrs. Stewart helpfully. "Lena Gladys would look sweet in a blue one just the color of her eyes."

"I'd rather have a pink store dress," said Marcia, feeling left out. "A pink 'cordion-pleated one so I could do a rose dance."

"I want that, too," Lena exclaimed jealously.

Mama bit her lip.

"Then I'll take twelve yards of the Val lace for trimming," she said, "and six yards of rickrack for the baby's dress."

"Anything for yourself, Mrs. Willard?" asked Mrs. Stewart, taking scissors out of her black apron pocket and snipping busily. "A pretty shirtwaist, maybe—peekaboo style?"

Mama shook her head. She said her husband had brought her some special material from the city which her cousin Isobel was going to help her with as she had a sewing-machine and a form. She thought the girls should have Sunday slippers and this surprise almost made up to them for not getting the store dresses. She looked a long time at the shirtwaists and said she might be back for the blue French tucked one with net inserts and velvet bows, but four dollars was a lot of money. When she paid for the shoes and other purchases it took all the money from her purse, her five dollars and even her bread money except a quarter with which she bought Papa a fine handkerchief. They had to hurry home to get Papa's lunch, as he was to be home for two weeks now, "taking inventory." Lena and Marcia wanted to stay and help Mary Evelyn sort ribbons, but Mary Evelyn refused their offer.

"I'm the only one that knows how to do it," she said, airily. "Mr. Brady won't let anybody but me handle these ribbons."

"My, everything is dear now at Mr. Brady's," Mama murmured, hurrying them down Fourth Street. "You need a fortune in that store."

This remark Lena told Mary Evelyn at recess the following school day, who told her mother who said that people without money shouldn't go shopping in a high-class store, which was then repeated via Lena to Papa and Mama. This resulted in Papa flying into a rage and going down to Mr. Brady's store all by himself. Mr. Brady was a brother Mason and that afternoon Papa, beaming with triumph, flung a paper package at his wife. When she opened it there was a shirtwaist, not the one she had wanted, but a black satin one with a high neck and lace bertha, besides a pair of white kid gloves and a cut-steel belt-buckle with slipper buckles to match.

"I want you to wear them to the Elks Banquet next week," Papa said, when Mama had embraced him in gratitude mixed with consternation. "By God, I'm not going to have this damn town saying anything is too dear for my wife."

"But how did you do it, Harry?" Mama cried.

"Listen, Brady gives any lodge brother all the credit he wants," boasted Papa. "I could have had the store if I asked for it. As I say to Hartwell, nothing's too good for my Daisy."

It took Mama four months of extra baking to pay the Fair Store bill, but anyhow Papa had her picture taken in the new finery just to show people. It was almost the only time she ever wore it.

8

In the summer, Papa and Mama went on a trip up the Great Lakes with Hartwell and his lady-friend. They left Florrie with Aunt Lois and Grandma, although Grandma complained she had no time for them since she was packing up any minute to move to Cleveland. Lena and Marcia were to stay on the farm near Elmville with Aunt Betts and Uncle Louie. Uncle Louie was Grandma's stepson and almost as old as she was. His wife was Grandma's first cousin, brought up with her like a sister on the old Medrow County home near Bethel.

Uncle Louie drove up to London Junction in a fine new rubber-tired buggy prepared to collect the children. He invited Grandma to come back with him, but she said indeed not, that she was branching out soon as an independent woman in Cleveland. She said her good friend Mrs. Carmel and her astute business adviser, Mr. Sweeney, were behind her in her new venture, and she did not give a snap of her finger for what Louie or Lois or Daisy or anybody else had to say. She also didn't give a snap whether she ever set foot on a farm again, because she was a body that liked to be where something was going on, where you could hear some good talk, learn something, and make a little spare cash. Uncle Louie brought in head cheese for her and a fried oyster sandwich from the London Junction Hotel and said he didn't blame her for kicking about the farm and fire away all she liked.

Uncle Louie was a thin wiry man with sandy hair, more of this in his great moustache, eyebrows, and sprouting from his nose and ears than actually on his head. He was so tall that the effort of talking to a much shorter wife and other people had made him humped so that his sharp chin seemed to rest far down on his flat chest and the back of his neck bent over almost horizontally. His face was weather-beaten and red, with his eyes as round and blue as the sky, only red-rimmed and edged with fair downy lashes that looked like chicken feathers. There was a good deal of the rooster in Uncle Louie which was only natural in a farmer and very fascinating to observe. When anybody talked he cocked his head gravely and kept his eyes fixed on them with a rooster's suspicious curiosity. Then he winked solemnly, and scratched his stomach as if he was scratching for corn. He talked little but listened to everybody intently, suddenly bursting into a rafter-shaking laugh that was half-cackle and half-whinny, and made everybody else laugh, too. He carried money in the sole of his boot and took it off to pay Papa for a brass bed he ordered from the London Furniture Store. As they rolled down the road toward Elmville he took off his thick boot again to pay for a corn-shucker in the New Amsterdam Hardware Store. When he wanted small change for drinks of "Moxie" or hard candy at corner stores, he had to unbutton his shirt where a cotton tobacco pouch was pinned containing his small change or "chicken feed." From the beginning Marcia was his favorite because she spoke up to him.

"You're my girl, Old Socks," he said, with a wink. "Pussy here can be Betts's girl."

"Will we have anybody to play with?" Lena asked. "I don't want to have to play just with Marcia all the time."

Uncle Louie cackled again, and tweaked her curls.

"Why, Pussy, you got more to play with than there is in Buckingham Palace. There's Billy, he's a goat, and Old Tom, he's a bull, and one hundred sheep and six cows and Tiddley Winks, the biggest Eskimo dog you ever saw, and a few hundred chicks, not counting the ducks and turkeys and geese and the rabbits and woodchucks and chipmunks and Almedy and the twelve Chapman kids two miles down the pike."

Lena frowned, for she hated being teased.

"How old's Almedy?" asked Lena.

Uncle Louie considered this.

"Almedy's pushing sixteen," he decided finally. "When you get them from the orphanage you can't tell, so we just let Almedy pick her own birthday."

"I'd like to pick my birthday," Lena sighed. "What did Almedy pick?"

"Almedy picked Fourth of July last year but this year she picked Decoration Day." Uncle Louie said, "Being an orphan she can pick a different birthday every year."

"Are you sure you haven't any children of your own for us to play with, Uncle Louie?" Lena persisted, still frowning, for Almedy sounded far too grown up.

"Why, Godamighty, Puss, our boys ain't been home in ten years—Carl's ten thousand miles away in Mexico and Phil's somewhere in China in the Marines, married to a Chinee, for all we know. We never hear except on Christmas. The girls both are raising families in Ioway."

Marcia's and Lena's eyes glowed with the pleasant but improbable prospect of little Chinese cousins to play with.

"Anyway, we've brought our Flinch deck if we don't have anybody to play with," said Marcia with a sigh of resignation. "We can play Muggins."

"Sure you can play Muggins, and Pit and Old Maid and croquignole," agreed Uncle Louie. "Your Aunt Betts'll teach you how to churn, too, and there's berrying and horse-riding. You won't be homesick."

"Lena will," said Marcia, a little jealously. "Lena's always homesick."

Reminded of this talent, Lena screwed up her face to cry but was as yet too interested in the ride to manage any tears. They would come later.

Uncle Louie took a different route going down to Elmville than they had coming up because he had to stop on farm business in both New Amsterdam and Willardville. New Amsterdam had windmills and a Dutch Reformed Church and when they stopped in the Ice Cream Kitchen, the waitress talked Dutch. "What nationality are we?" asked Marcia. "Dutch and Welsh and English," Uncle Louie said. "A good mixture."

The town blacksmith was a relation, so they went to the forge down a cobblestone alley between two stores. Uncle Louie let them come inside the charred, dark stable to watch the sparks fly while the smith, Uncle John, hammered out a shoe. This was a wonderful and terrifying spot, like a cave in a goblin woods with the floor half earth, half boards, black with pitch and covered with sawdust. The big furnace in the middle seemed like hellfire, spitting out brimstone, growling and roaring so that the smith was like Satan himself, dealing in fire and darkness. There was a half-loft over the back end of the place with a cot on it, a washstand and a pine corner cupboard. Little crescent windows high under the eaves let in light and permitted barn swifts to flutter in and out.

"Step up to my parlor, Louie, and have some schnapps," Uncle John roared above the din of his hammering, so Uncle Louie helped the girls up the homemade pine ladder to the loft. Uncle John, it seems, was a bachelor and though he had a room at some niece's house, he preferred to stay mostly in his own shop. The children sat on the cot, speechless with pleasure. They looked down in the pit below at Uncle John, wondering whether he was really black or whether it washed off. Certainly the black mop of oily curls and the vast black moustache would not come off. A half-grown boy ran around barefoot, fetching water and doing errands, and he too was either black or wonderfully dirty. Lena decided after scientific observation that this was dirt since he kept gaping up at her and then wiping his sleeve across his cheek, leaving small areas of almost white. Uncle John talked to him in Dutch, and called him Hans, so the girls decided that this must be

Hans Brinker himself or the little boy who saved the dyke. They smiled at him but this seemed to scare him, for he ran down the alley and didn't come back. They saw him peeking at them from behind the hitching-tree when they left and this time he grinned and thumbed his nose at them. Uncle John heaved himself up the loft. He took out a jug from his corner cupboard and before he said a word to them he threw back his head and drank with gurgling noises and an active play of Adam's apple. Then he passed the jug to Uncle Louie who drank a little, made a face, and spat it out.

"You don't need to tell me how you make your schnapps, John," gasped Uncle Louie, and both men cackled loudly. Uncle John opened the cupboard again. He took out a stone jar of oat-meal cookies which he passed to the children. Then he lifted them up to see other treasures inside the magic cupboard, little wooden windmills, boats with little sailors in them, little wooden dwarfs with nails made into anvils, all manner of toys he had carved or forged himself. Marcia hoped he would give them some but he dusted them off with a red handkerchief and tenderly put them back. Before they left he hammered crossed nails to make scissors for each of them, so it was a profitable visit after all. Lena and her friend Mary Evelyn Stewart often put crossed pins on the street-car tracks behind the London Junction school for the car wheels to crush into scissors, but the big nails in the forge made them much better. They were so pleased that they tried not to hurt Uncle John's feelings by screaming when he swung them, first one and then the other, high in the air. They carried the bruises of his iron fingers on their ribs for days afterward.

Back in the buggy they rolled swiftly down the cobblestone street on to the dusty road. Uncle Louie gave his attention to the horse which was almost running away in his eagerness to get home. Once in a while Uncle Louie would burst into a loud yodel of joy, a few bars of some song that had no words but "Hi dee hi dee hi oh de hi de hi do ho oh." Then he would wink at them and say, "How about a song, Old Socks, hey, Pussy?"

So they would sing all the songs they had learned from Papa and from Sunday School and from Lena's school. They sang, "Can you bake a cherry pie, charming Billy?" and "A frog he would a-wooing go," and "Three blind mice," while Uncle Louie chorused with a "hi dee hi dee hi dee ho" and the horse whinnied. Approaching Willardville, where Grandpa Willard's folks all settled, they began smelling something queer, which Uncle Louie explained was the Rubber Works. There was a big factory here with one big store and a row of little yellow frame houses all alike, two saloons and a public square with a bandstand pavilion in it. There was a new brick hotel by the depot with a stuffed bear in the yard, standing on its hind legs. A red automobile at the curb was a rare sight, indeed, but as all the other sights were rare to the girls they accepted it as no stranger than the stuffed bear or the smell of rubber. In spite of these wonders, the town seemed to begin and end all in one spot, huddling all its pretensions to importance in the square, the streets branching off from it being no more than country lanes.

Uncle Louie left them in the buggy while he went into the Big Store to get them each a pair of boys' overalls to play in, a pickle crock, a sack of meal, and a big tin of tobacco, all of which he put in the back of the buggy where his corn-shucker was tied. He had a bag of licorice jelly beans for Almedy, too, he said. Almedy, being an orphan and helping with the chores, liked a treat now and then. Maybe she was too big to play with them, he said, but she'd help them keep their bibs and tuckers clean.

They were nearing East Elmville Township where Uncle Louie lived and coming to Uncle Louie's neighbors. As they approached each farm, no matter how far back the house and farm buildings were from the road, Uncle Louie slowed the horse, leaned far out and yodelled "Hi-yi, Dolphie!" or "Hi-yi—Charlie!" From the distant cornfields or from the barn an echo would come back, "Hi-yi, Louie!" These echoes rode miles on the wind and were mocked by the horse's whinnying to the neighbor horses who whinnied back from fields, galloping along pasture fences beside them to the next dividing rails. On the wind, too, was the sad sweet fragrance of clover, the dusty smell of wheat, of new-cut wood lying in the green woods, of unseen fish ponds and fresh-ploughed earth. They passed the Chapmans' farm, ramshackle unpainted house and sheds all leaning against each other as if one big grunt from the sows running around in the mud would blow them all down. Uncle Louie waved the whip and yelled in greeting. Innumerable heads popped up from a row of currant bushes.

"Company!" yelled Uncle Louie, "You kids come over!"

The answering yell from a dozen throats sounded savage and derisive to the children but was probably friendly.

"Fine kids," said Uncle Louie. "Pack of hellions."

Now they came to the lane and there was no holding the horse. Lena and Marcia, gasping, hung on to their hats. Uncle Louie stood up shouting, "Hi-yi Betts, hi-yi!" A woman's voice halloed back. The horse galloped through the gates, which Aunt Betts had barely lowered in time, and ran straight into the barn. Hearts pounding, the children were lifted out; the panting horse whinnied triumph to her sisters and brothers and they whinnied welcome. Roosters crowed, hens set up an excited din. Aunt Betts— small, black-eyed, rosy, and roly-poly—came running up with her checkered apron over her head, calling greetings. The cows, now ambling up from the valley for milking, mooed, dogs leaped about them and barked, the turkey cock ran up gobbling, the whole countryside brayed and sang a welcome to the two girls.

Aunt Betts hurried them up to the big jolly house, shooed the flies off the kitchen screen with her apron, and whisked them into the big kitchen. Marcia sniffed cherry pie baking and there was a fine chocolate cake smell, too, coming from the stove. She began to jump up and down in ecstasy, but suddenly there was a bleating noise from Lena. She had her face screwed up, her underlip thrust out, and her fists in her eyes. Aunt Betts picked her up on her lap and started rocking her just as if she was Florrie.

"What's the matter, honey girl?" Aunt Betts cried out, worried. "Where does it hurt? Let me get you some peppermint."

Marcia looked on this tender scene with a cold scowl.

"She's homesick," she said flatly. "I knew she would be."

Anything to get the biggest piece of pie! Anything to get rocked and petted and called honey girl! I wish I was an only child, thought Marcia bitterly; I wish I was an orphan with a different birthday every year and no home.

9

W HAT DOES the downstairs smell like?" Lena asked, as if it was a riddle.

"Like chicken and pie in the kitchen," Marcia answered after a moment's intense pondering. "Like a churn in the parlor, and upstairs like a trunk."

"Aunt Betts smells like a churn, too," said Lena. "Uncle Louie smells like a barn, and Almedy smells like cows and strawberry patch."

They sat at the edge of the cornfield in their blue overalls and straw hats, barefooted, contemplating the universe. Marcia was very happy because Lena had no one else to play with and was forced to make a chum of her sister. They made up secrets, and played school with the cornstalks as pupils. Marcia was allowed to play principal sometimes instead of always being just a teacher. They had boys' rows and girls' rows and named as many as they could manage. They had teachers' pets, usually the smallest cornstalk in the first row, and then there were the big boys in the back who had to be scolded. They took turns being Miss Browne, the first-grade teacher, and Miss Sutton, the principal. Each stood at the head of the field four rows apart and conducted the corn in singing, numbers, spelling, and recess. The boy pet in Miss Browne's class was called Maurice and the girl pet Violet. In Miss

Sutton's class there were other pets. Pets were always addressed in honeyed tones and permitted to run errands, and were lavishly praised.

"Violet, you may take this note to the principal in Room 42," the teacher would say sweetly, and then, changing to a stern voice, add, "We will have a test in numbers while Violet is absent."

Teaching also involved tiptoeing up and down the aisles and "catching" the pupils. Except for the pets, they were a cheating, whispering, disobedient lot, inclined to throw paper-wads, chew gum, pass notes, and copy answers. Then the stern disciplinarian would come out. Whoever was Miss Browne would say in terrifying accents, "George Barnes, report at once to the principal's office!" Miss Sutton would be prepared for this with a fierce lecture and a switch. Miss Browne would simulate a snivelling, abject George Barnes, and then a recess would be declared with the two teachers eating green apples, ostensibly brought to them by their devoted "pets." This education in school technique as outlined by Lena made Marcia wild for September to come and real school to begin. On the other hand, the fun was all in being the teacher, and in the vast expanse of cornfield. Sometimes they would open up new schools in the rows further off—a third grade and a fifth, even though the courses were necessarily the same as the first grade, mixed with Sunday School. The corn stretched for miles, and it seemed a pity that only the section nearest the house could be educated. Uncle Louie said they could play in the corn but not to touch it, so when Almedy found Marcia whipping an unruly stalk for being truant, they almost had to give up the school, except Almedy finally promised not to tell if they wouldn't tell about her fellow.

Almedy's romance was almost as much fun as the corn school. Every day they walked with her down the lane to the mailbox to wait for the mailman. He came in a little white wagon and rang a dinner bell at every gate. The head of the Chapman lane was opposite the gate to Uncle Louie's lane, and Almedy's fellow was the second Chapman boy, named Elbert. He was almost a head shorter than Almedy, but he was her fellow anyway, she said. He rode on a plough-horse barefooted to wait for the mail. Almedy tried to get to her gate first, then she'd wait for Elbert, even when the mail had already been left. She would always speak first.

"Hello, Elbert," she'd say.

"Hiya, Almedy," he'd say, and that was the only thing he said to her.

He pretended not to notice them at all but he stood up on the horse like a bareback circus rider and jumped up and down. The white horse stood still as if nothing was going on at all, though it switched the flies with its long tail and sometimes this whipped Elbert's bare legs, so he said bad words. He sometimes hoisted himself off the horse to the branches of the great maple trees on either side of the gate and he swung from them by his knees, yelling, "Whoa, there, Moll! Plague on you, don't you run away or I'll whip the Jesus out of you." Moll, far from being the wild, uncontrollable colt Elbert fancied her, was so fat and old she needed no bridle, and tranquilly grazed the weeds or gnawed the leaves of the bushes. During Elbert's argument with his horse, Almedy and the two children stood attentively on the other side of the road. Marcia and Lena looked from Elbert to Almedy with grave absorption as a model for conduct in future courtships of their own. Almedy giggled every minute as if Elbert was a clown but evidently Elbert did not know anyone was watching, for he never looked at her, just yelled at the horse and did acrobatics. Finally, he would settle down on the horse, usually after a far-off admonitory shout from a distant field, reach down in the mailbox for the batch of farm papers, catalogues, samples or what not. The clank of the tin mailbox shutting again was the signal for the horse to wheel around and thump back down the Chapman lane. Almedy would stop giggling at once, and keep her thin scarred brown hand over her eyes, watching him till he was lost in the trees. She would stand for two or three minutes just looking down the Chapman lane, her sharp, plain brown face suddenly desolate and drawn up as if she too was going to be homesick. Marcia and Lena watched her, puzzled that this everyday routine should mean so much to Almedy when nothing seemed to happen at all.

"How do you know when a boy is your fellow?" Lena inquired.

"Oh, you know all right," said Almedy.

"But how?" persisted Lena.

"Oh, he walks home behind you from church or picnics," Almedy finally answered. "Elbert walks home behind me."

"What do you say to your fellow?" Lena anxiously asked, running a little to keep up with Almedy's long strides.

"Nothing," said Almedy.

"Doesn't anybody ever talk to their fellow?" asked Lena.

"No," said Almedy. "What's there to talk about?"

Almedy was so busy milking or washing or working in the fields that she was a disappointment to the children as a companion. She spoiled their games, too, just like a boy would.

"I saw a fairy in the churn today and it was turning the butter into vanilla ice cream," said Marcia.

"That's a lie," argued Lena. "*I* saw that fairy and it said it was churning chocolate fudge."

"Did your fairy have on a purple hat with a silver bell?" Marcia asked. "Mine did, and a plume too. I saw it."

"You saw your uncle's shirt-tail flying around the corner!" snapped Almedy, so the game was spoiled.

Almedy was thin and hunched like Uncle Louie, with a sharp nose and chin, and sharp, sly, brown eyes. When they went swimming in the brook she looked like a boy because her hair was short from the typhoid epidemic at the orphanage the year before. Dressed up on Sundays when the neighbors stopped to take her to church, since Uncle Louie and Aunt Betts wouldn't go, she looked more like a boy than ever, for the light blue straw hat sat up high on top of her shorn head and the made-over faded blue poplin dress hung limp on her thin scarecrow figure. The neighbors didn't bring her all the way home but let her out a mile down the road, so Almedy always took off her shoes and carried them this distance to save them. Marcia and Lena would run down the lane to meet her, but Almedy never seemed glad. She showed them her colored Sunday school cards which she saved up, but she kept gloomy silence the rest of the way.

"What happened at church?" the girls would cry.

"Nothing," said Almedy.

"Who was at church, Almedy?" Aunt Betts would ask later.

"Nobody," Almedy said.

Some people had luck with their orphans, Aunt Betts said again and again to Uncle Louie, but Almedy was no comfort at all. You could get no more out of her than you could out of Tiddley Winks, and never a word of gratitude for their giving her a home. She was as good as gold in her way, but no company. Never mind, Uncle Louie said, she was a good worker, as good as a hired man in the fields and she was about the fastest milker he'd ever seen. He'd say that much for Almedy, and that was more than he could say for other folks' orphans.

An orphan was different from people. It looked like people, ate like people, and could talk a little, but it was more like a horse or dog. Orphans were nearly always ungrateful and after you gave them a home and raised them they usually got into trouble or ran off with some fellow and you never saw them again. Marcia and Lena wondered how soon Almedy would run off with Elbert. When they saw her sitting out on the orchard fence every night after the supper dishes were done, her thin arms folded over her chest, skinny bare legs hooked through the rails for security, they wondered if she was planning to run away tonight. She kept her back to the farmhouse and faced the lane, though even in bright daylight she could never have seen beyond the thick trees to the Chapmans' gate. She just sat there till bedtime.

"Whatcha looking at, Almedy?" Marcia came up and asked.

"Turtles," said Almedy.

Marcia shrank back a little, for it was true. Two mottled turtles could be seen crawling around a mossy log under the acorn tree.

"Don't you want to come play drop-the-handkerchief?" urged Marcia.

"Naw, I like turtles," said Almedy, stonily. "I like turtles better'n anything."

10

THE FINEST FEATURE of life on the farm was the vacation from manners. Voices were never lowered; indeed, a normal tone was regarded as city affectation, and a suspicious attempt at secrecy. You could hear Uncle Louie talking far off in the barn to visitors, and even in the very same room he and Aunt Betts shouted at each other as if they were acres apart. It may have been that this constant noise kept them from being lonesome. At any rate, the shrill nasal pitch maintained indoors and out by the couple and all their neighbors managed to convey hearty good humor, open hearts and solid virtue. Marcia and Lena tried to achieve the same effect in their speech but it evidently took years of training to get your voice to come twanging through your nose that way, and when you tried it your very palate seemed to whirr like a banjo string. A good heart and honesty seemed to be so completely a matter of noise that whenever any deals with the butcher or milk company were under way you could hear the honest fellows half a mile away doing their best to out-shout each other and show how aboveboard the transactions were. Fancy table manners were also suspect, indicating a desire to seem better than ordinary folks. Such airs as "Please pass the butter" were almost insults, and likely to be reprimanded by Uncle Louie saying "What are your arms for?"

Meals were served in the big sunny kitchen on a table spread with green oilcloth, with a flypaper as a centerpiece. Jars of conserve, catsup, piccalilli, cole slaw, pickled beets and sugar were left on the table all the time, covered between meals by a red-checkered tablecloth. A person could pick up her plate and carry it outdoors to eat on the kitchen stoop if she liked. Almedy never did sit down at table, but took her plate and a chunk of bread out to the springhouse where it was always cool. Like Tiddley Winks, the dog, she did not like to have anyone watch her eat. It was Lena who discovered after judicious investigation that Almedy ate everything, even mashed potatoes, with her fingers.

Food was different here than any place the children had ever been. For breakfast there was oatmeal, mashed potatoes covered with mixed corn and tomatoes, fried ham or sausage and gravy, soda biscuits, and sometimes cornmeal pancakes and apple pie. Aunt Betts worried because the young visitors could not put away all that was placed before them. She said they both looked peaked and needed fattening up, but when they obediently tried to stuff down more they ended up with stomachaches.

Aunt Betts and Uncle Louie had such a good time eating that they kept Lena and Marcia in giggles all the time. Aunt Betts liked to sit by the stove, eating out of the pots with a big pewter spoon. Uncle Louie used a knife exclusively with fascinating dexterity. Each time he finished a plateful he'd shout "Betts, by God! More, by God!" Often for supper, which was around five o'clock, they had mugs of hard cider or homemade wine brewed from elderberries or dandelions. They would talk about things they remembered and roar with laughter till tears would stream down Aunt Betts's rosy round face. They told the same things over and over with never-failing enjoyment. There was the time the English Quaker family came all the way from England to the Quaker settlement down by the covered bridge. They had slept on the bare parlor floor on hay, with the old grandfather waking them up all hours of the night shouting, "Liverpool! Don't miss the boat!"

"Liverpool! Don't miss the boat!" gasped Aunt Betts, holding her sides, her plump bosom quivering with mirth. "Liverpool—oh, my! Oh, my sakes, Louie, stop it or I'll die laughing!"

Uncle Louie would throw back his head and cackle till the dog would run up from the barn to peer in the kitchen door, panting with sympathetic delight. The children would stand gaping, uncertain of the joke but highly pleased.

The pie races were the most fun. Aunt Betts would cut great wedges of pie for Almedy and the children. Then she would set three pies in hot pie tins down on the table, their berry juice still bubbling up through the flaky white crusts. Aunt Betts and Uncle Louie, each with a knife in hand and shaking with suppressed glee, would eye each other steadily for a moment, then cry out together, "Go!" Then their knives laid into the nearest pie, scooping it into their mouths, seeing who would get to the middle pie first. Uncle Louie always won because Aunt Betts got out of breath from laughing and had to unloose her belt, even her collar. One night they finished the cider barrel between them, drinking from the bung, and they must have had a race on the pantry too, for the fried squirrels and corn pudding were all gone by morning.

Almedy went up to her room at dark when the children did, but Uncle Louie and Aunt Betts could often be heard shouting with laughter in the kitchen till late at night.

The children's bedroom had sloping ceilings so that a grown person could stand erect only in the middle of the room. The window was very small, covered with mosquito netting which glistened like a spider web when the moonlight came through it. In the enormous black walnut bed the two girls lay awake listening to the country night noises that seemed to have smells as well somehow woven into them, a hot melting honeysuckle fragrance or the smell of rain on cedars, of wet maple leaves and dew on lilacs all mingled with the musty mothball aroma of their featherbed. A million crickets ticked out the darkness, a barn owl hooted, a loon laughed, frogs croaked down by the spring, sleeping birds gave tiny clucks, sometimes a horse let out a lonesome whinny.

It was too bad Almedy would not play with them. She would never sing with them or tell stories.

"They're all lies," Almedy stated briefly. "Songs and stories is all the same—lies."

"We could play a game," Lena would plead. "We don't have to go to sleep yet."

"Games is sinning," Almedy said, and marched up to her attic bedroom. She never read books. The only time she ever joined them was when they played ghosts once with sheets as shrouds. She entered into this game so zestfully that the children went to bed shivering with terror. After that Almedy would say grimly, "Want to play ghost?" so that they would hastily retreat, leaving her to her favorite relaxation of looking over her colored Sunday School cards.

Papa came down to take them back home in August. Marcia and Lena were so gloomy at leaving that their father was irritated. They wanted Almedy to come home with them as a souvenir of these happy days. Papa grumbled that he guessed it would be all right for Almedy to visit them, but Uncle Louie said the farm couldn't get along without Almedy.

"Don't you want to come home with us, Almedy? We've got white mice and a gramophone." They tried to coax her.

Almedy smiled, crookedly.

"When I leave this here place it won't be for no visit," she said.

Papa took them home on the train. They chattered all the way about Uncle Louie and Aunt Betts until their father sharply ordered them to hush. Aunt Lois, Grandma, Mama, and Florrie were waiting in the sitting room when they got home. For some reason, after the first rejoicing their mother acted worried.

"They've lost all their nice manners," she said ruefully. "They've turned into regular little Indians."

"Betts is nobody to handle youngsters," their father agreed. "Wait till you see how they eat."

"I can eat with a knife," boasted Marcia.

"See what I mean?" said their father. "I guess next time we take a trip we'll have to leave them some place else."

Everything that had seemed so magical about their summer was now tarnished by their parents' disapproval. After they were sent to bed, Marcia and Lena gloomily listened to the family council downstairs.

"Never mind, Betts and Louie are all right," Grandma was saying, consolingly. "They never hurt a fly."

"You said once they used to drive around together before they were married, drinking in every saloon in the country," Aunt Lois reminded her. "Everybody knows Betts used to lay around with every travelling man that came to town."

"They tell me half the kids at the Chapman farm, next to Louie's, are Louie's," said Papa, chuckling. "Look like him, too, the old devil."

"Remember when Betts was carrying on with that old bachelor at Four Corners?" said Aunt Lois. "Then when he got to wanting younger women she sent her own daughter up to him, just to keep him in the family. That was Ede, the one that went to Iowa."

"Louie still runs after a pretty girl," said Grandma. "He still sneaks off to town to see that little milliner, but then Louie's got a heart as big as all outdoors. I think he just wants to help her."

"That Almedy is going to be a handful from what the neighbors say," said Aunt Lois.

"What's Almedy got to do with this conversation?" indignantly inquired their father. "She's not even in the family."

Marcia and Lena lay in bed, puzzling over these remarks, torn between loyalty to their parents and love for Aunt Betts and Uncle Louie.

"It spoils everything," Marcia complained resentfully.

People didn't like to see other people happy, that was all. If children were happy, especially away from home, their parents insisted it was bad for them. Fathers wanted you to be disobedient so they could correct you. Mothers wanted you to be sick or sad so they could console or protect you. Marcia longed to grow up fast so she could defy them all. She would have a dress with a train, a watch with a fleur-de-lys pin, unlimited licorice beans, and she would eat with her knife faster than anybody.

I I

THE FIRST THING Marcia got from school was measles,
which she passed on to Florrie. In return for this Lena
acquired chickenpox and got the whole family quaran-
tined, a condition that lasted a long time, as one would get it just
as another was getting well. Mr. Friend put their groceries outside
the kitchen door every day with pots of soup and stew made by his
wife. Mama had not caught the germ and was determined to keep
up with her baking, in spite of the doctor's orders. She baked a
dozen loaves of bread in the middle of the night to escape his attention, then left them in the hallway for Mrs. Friend to deliver to
her customers. When Mrs. Friend, speaking through the closed
door, cautiously suggested that the bread might spread chickenpox, Mama indignantly replied that good fresh bread never hurt
anybody. If the doctor heard about it and objected, she would simply tell him she had to keep her bread customers in order to pay
his bill, and that ought to settle his hash. Mrs. Friend reluctantly
took on the secret duty of delivering what she insisted was tainted
goods. She was not amused by Mama teasing her later about her
qualms.

"Any spots on old Mr. Krug today?" Mama giggled through the
door. "I'll bet that bald head of his looks funny with chickenpox."

It was Mrs. Friend's turn to triumph when their father was
forced by the Health Officer to stay at the London Junction Hotel

when he came home from a trip. He visited the house every morning and evening, talking to them through the kitchen window,
making fun of their spots and assuring them that feathers would
sprout out next. This separation made their mother almost sicker
than chickenpox itself could have done. Papa's hearty efforts to
cheer her up did no good. In his new winter coat with the velvet
collar, his red silk muffler, derby hat and kid gloves, his nose red
with cold, he sat on the overturned washboiler outside the kitchen
window, while Mama sat in the little sewing-chair inside, wrapped
in a blue wool robe. The children had been moved, beds and all, to
the dining room to make the work easier for their mother, and to
keep them warmer.

"Don't worry about me, Daisy," Papa urged, his face pressed
to the window pane. "The Junction Hotel serves a damn nice steak
dinner for fifty-five cents. I could have the stew for thirty-five, but,
hell, the difference is worth it. I got running water in my room
and I sleep like a top. Last night a couple of B. & O. train dispatch-
ers and some drummers from an eastern concern dropped in the
room and we played poker till midnight. Went out afterward and
had as good a Welsh rarebit at the Greek's as you could get at the
Hotel Statler."

"Didn't it upset your stomach?" Mama asked, jealously.

Papa reassured her happily on this point. As further cheer he
told her that the boss, Mr. Carson, had hinted in so many words
that he was the best man he'd ever had on the road, and not to feel
that his superior talents went unobserved. This must mean a raise,
Papa deduced, for Mr. Carson was far too shrewd a businessman
to risk losing him to some bigger firm in a larger city. Say what
you would, a man with the brains to build up a business like the
London Furniture Company, known all over the world including
Canada and California, as makers of the finest merchandise, not
excepting Grand Rapids even, was not one to let a man like Harry
Willard slip through his fingers. The fact of the matter was that a
certain burled walnut dining room set, red tapestry upholstery,

eight pieces, was almost certain to be awarded to Papa at Easter time as a reward for salesmanship.

"I don't know where we'd put it," Mama said wearily. "There's no room."

"We'll throw out everything else then and make room," expostulated Papa. "Don't stand there and tell me you'd turn down a beautiful burled walnut, Empire style, eight-piece dining set—our Number 842a, the finest number in the catalogue—just to keep a lot of junk we bought once in Elmville at an auction! How do you think Carson's wife is going to feel when Carson tells her Harry Willard's wife doesn't appreciate Harry getting the salesman's grand prize for the year? Daisy, I'm surprised at you."

Either the reproach or the increasing strain of her nursing duties brought tears to Mama's eyes and this was too much.

"I come here to cheer you up. I stand outside my own home, freezing to death with a cold coming on, just to cheer you up, and you have to cry!" Papa angrily exclaimed. "That's all the thanks a man gets."

For some reason Mama did not react to his fit of temper in her usual contrite way, but permitted him to dash around the house to the street without calling him back. She quietly gave the children their supper in bed on a bread-board, rocked Florrie to sleep without singing. When they were almost asleep the doctor called, and later there was a loud banging on the door. It was Papa. He came inside and hugged Mama, in spite of her protests.

"The doctor says you might catch it," she protested.

"He don't need to know I'm here," Papa said. "What kind of a doctor is he, anyway, trying to separate married people? I've got to look after things here; you can't manage all alone. Here, I brought you something. Just won it at the Kandy Kitchen raffle."

It was a five-pound box of candy, and what the children minded most about having chickenpox was that even the thought of candy made them really sick. Marcia was even too sick to get up and peek through the portieres when Lena reported that Papa was wrapping Mama up in blankets in a chair by the stove, and was treating her as if she too was sick, and that in spite of the quarantine Mrs. Friend was there too, putting a hotwater bottle on Mama's stomach. Papa and Mrs. Friend tiptoed back and forth through the dining room, now the sickroom, from living room to kitchen all night, carrying things to Mama. It was not these odd activities that frightened the children into the conviction that their mother was sick; it was the fact that for the first time their father's voice was lowered to a whisper.

After a while they got used to Mama's sick spells, and there were compensations. Isobel would come over to look after them for a few weeks. Grandma, with wistful protests about her Cleveland plans being delayed, stayed with them for a while, and when Papa was home he did the cooking and nursing because he was the best cook and nurse Mama ever heard of. She said she was well just hearing his voice downstairs, and sure enough she stayed well quite a few months.

12

"S ING IT AGAIN," their mother begged.
So Lena and Marcia sat on the edge of her bed and sang it.
"I'm an honest Irish lad, and my home is far away,
If pleasing you I'll either sing or dance—"
Every afternoon after school they came to visit their mother,
but the rest of the time they stayed with Aunt Lois during Mama's
sickness. They enjoyed a gloomy prestige at school by their mother
having consumption, but Mary Evelyn tried to spoil it all by boast-
ing of her father dying of double pneumonia. She pointed out that
it ought to be double consumption then to equal her claim to distinction.

Grandma took care of her sick daughter most of the time, but
presently the doctor said a trained nurse must be called in. Mr.
Carson had permitted Papa to exchange routes with another salesman, which enabled him to get home every night to relieve
Grandma. Each night he brought home new medicine that some
of the fellows had recommended, and he tried them all out on
Mama from the onion plaster on the chest to the mustard pack on
her back. He was exasperated with everybody for the failure of
these remedies, and annoyed that the doctor ordered a trained
nurse, annoyed, too, that Mrs. Friend seemed to regard this as
ominous.

"It just means that she's getting better," he said. "The doctor doesn't want to trust her any more to the old lady and Lois. They make Daisy nervous. I told the doctor so myself. I came in yesterday after her mother had been looking after her and Daisy was so upset she was out of her head for a while. Didn't even know me."

"Daisy's a mighty sick girl," Mrs. Friend said, solemnly. "I only hope she pulls through."

These awesome words made Lena and Marcia look anxiously at their mother, who lay on her side with her eyes fixed on the window, paying no attention to the conversation passing over her. Her small hands looked bluish white against the covers, and the nails seemed almost gray. It was queer to see them lying so lifelessly beside her, fluttering slightly like lame birds when a sudden noise reached her.

"Maybe when she gets well she'll have a dimple like Florrie," Lena observed. "Or a scar like Marcia's got from chickenpox."

"Poor kids," said Mrs. Friend, patting their heads. "Well, I'll pray twice as hard to the Blessed Virgin and maybe the trained nurse can pull her through."

"We're not Catholics," said Lena coldly. "It wouldn't do any good for you to pray to the Virgin on our account."

When their mother roused herself again she had them sing some more, and even tried to sing herself. Their father was so exuberant over her good spirits that he dashed out to get her a present and came back with several parcels which he dumped proudly on the bed.

"Open 'em up," he commanded, rubbing his hands. "I bought out the whole damn Fair Store, honey. Wait till you see."

Mama shook her head, smiling, so Mrs. Friend had to open up the packages.

"Why, Harry Willard! Silk stockings!" she gasped. "And a real silk nightgown and a pink chemise with hand embroidery. And a gold mesh pocketbook. Why, it must have cost a million dollars!"

"Brady's a brother Mason, that's all," Papa explained, proudly beaming. "Try 'em on, Daisy. It'll make you feel better."

The children jumped up and down on the bed, pleased with the celebration, but their mother, in spite of Mrs. Friend's assistance, could not seem to keep her head above the pillow. She did put one leg out from the covers and they got one silk stocking on, but then she turned her face listlessly to the wall, whimpering, "Where's Harry? Tell Harry I want to go back to Peach Street."

"The children had better go back to their aunt's now," said Mrs. Friend. "She's sinking."

"She'll feel better when she gets a good look at that gold mesh bag," their father declared positively. "I may be no doctor but I do know my Daisy. You're coming around all right, aren't you, honey? Daisy, listen to me. Hartwell's lady friend was asking about you. Isn't that nice of her? She says her brother had the same thing and now he weighs two hundred pounds. Are you listening, Daisy?"

"I want to go home," repeated their mother, staring dully out the window. "I want to go back to Peach Street. I want Harry."

"Here I am, honey," their father said, leaning over her, but she looked past him as if the Harry she wanted was nowhere near. The children were half-persuaded that this was a new kind of game their mother had invented, but this time it was a game their father did not like at all, for he scowled, then picked up the presents from the bed and dumped them into a dresser drawer.

"She's too sick to appreciate things," Mrs. Friend consoled him. "She'll enjoy them when she gets well."

"I'll bet if I could get her downstairs, sitting up, she'd be all right in a jiffy," Papa said. "I could pull her out of this if I was in charge, doctor or no doctor, but every time I do anything Lois comes in and starts raising Cain with me. Says the doctor knows best."

"You'd better let the doctor handle it," Mrs. Friend said. "You keep on cheering her up, that's the main thing."

Papa nodded a thoughtful agreement to this.

"I guess she'd snap out of it if I got that dining room set I promised her," he said. "She'd be so tickled to see that eight-piece set moving in here she'd like as not jump right out of bed."

Mrs. Friend said not to worry about new furniture. The thing now was to get the new trained nurse.

Papa met the Columbus train the next day that brought the trained nurse, and since the depot was near Aunt Lois's house he escorted her there at once to meet the family. The nurse was a small, thin woman in her late twenties, with a thin pointed dead-white face, colorless lashes and brows that made her eyes gleam like dark gray marbles. She had a trim figure in her white uniform when her blue cape was thrown aside, with a tiny waist accented by a tightly drawn belt. In spite of her small stature, her hands were large, knobby and red. Conscious of this, evidently, she kept putting them under her apron, or twisting them nervously around the long chain on which she carried her pince-nez. Her hair was faded blond and obviously prized, for she had gone to great pains with an elaborate frizzed coiffeur of pompadour, nests of curls, and many combs. Papa was very proud of her and appeared to be working hard to impress the city person favorably. His efforts won him the only smiles she was willing to spare.

"Meet the second Mrs. Willard," was the way he had jovially introduced her, much to Aunt Lois's glowering disapproval.

Her name was really Hawkins, first name Idah, spelled with an h, if you please. She had a low, cautious voice, and she murmured that she hoped to be of service, although the Lord gave and the Lord took away. In any case she would not tarry over supper but would hasten at once to her case and do what was in her power, though she admitted she was merely human and could do no more than she could.

"I feel better just having her around," Papa confided in a surge of new spirits, but Grandma and Aunt Lois looked with hostile eyes at the intruder who knew more than they did about Daisy.

That very night Florrie, who had been weeping steadily and with almost mature understanding for her mother, was allowed to go see her, in the care of Mrs. Friend. Marcia and Lena had gone to bed, when the telephone ringing awoke them. Presently their aunt came upstairs and instructed them to get dressed. Their mother had had a spell of loneliness and wanted to see them at once. This rare suggestion, coming after ten o'clock, was most exciting and seemed proof that their mother, as always, was arranging a special treat for them. They struggled into their clothes, with leather leggings and rubbers, for a heavy snow was falling. They wanted to take along their Christmas skates, even though they hadn't learned to skate, but Aunt Lois brusquely refused this. She would take them on the sled, she said, unless the snow was already too deep.

Outside was a magic night of crisp twinkly stars, snowmuffled cottages and white trees. Aunt Lois drew the sled down the middle of the icy pavement, for the sidewalks were filled with drifts. This was indeed growing up, Marcia felt, to be out after bedtime in the dead of night and in the middle of the street. She sat in front on the sled with Lena's legs around her and a blanket tucked around them both, their breath curling out in the frosty air like smoke. Sounds were grown-up sounds, too, at this hour; the constant jangle of engine bells, a warm jolly sound that cut through blizzards and darkness like a dog's welcome bark. Aunt Lois's arctics crunched swiftly over the snow, and the snowflakes whirled like tiny stars around the street lamps. Down the street they could see their house with all the lights on, downstairs and up, as if it was Christmas Eve. Night was the best time of all to be outdoors, they thought, especially in winter and in London Junction where the smell of train smoke mingled with the tangy snowflecked air and tickled the nose. Darkness, snow, smoke, and stars made a special London Junction smell, just as mittens and their wool mufflers drawn tightly up to their noses and moist from chewing had a fuzzy snowball taste.

At the door of the house they were met and shushed into silence by Mrs. Friend. Miss Hawkins stood primly by their mother's bed, and Doctor Andrews was gravely holding their mother's wrist. Grandma sat in the sewing-chair in the corner, tears sliding down her cheeks, silently rocking Florrie.

"Mama doesn't like Florrie rocked any more," Lena stated. "Florrie's too big to be rocked to sleep every night, Mama says. It will spoil her, won't it, Papa?"

No one paid any attention to this. Papa sat on the other side of Mama, staring at her with an expression of bewilderment and pain. It was clear that something dreadful was happening but it seemed to be happening to Papa instead of to their mother.

"Do you want us to sing, Mama?" Lena asked. Marcia was proud of Lena's efficiency. She knew what to do more than the grown-ups did. When their mother did not hear, Lena repeated the question louder, and this time the sick woman turned her haggard face toward them.

"Little pickaninnies," she murmured. "Come on, hop on the wagon, pickaninnies, we're going back to Peach Street."

Delighted with the game, they climbed on the bed beside her.

"Give her the whip, Harry, we've got to get there before dark," urged their mother. "Hang on, pickaninnies, here we go. Hurry, hurry, hurry."

They could almost feel the bed rising in the air like a fairy-tale carpet, and they hung on to it tightly, their nervous giggles dying in their throats into whimpers at the sudden strangeness in their father's face. He knelt by the bed and put his head in his hands.

"Don't do it, Daisy, don't do it," he whispered. "I'll give up the road. I'll get you the Furness place—I swear I will. I'll have the dining room set put in there right away. I'll do anything you say, Daisy."

"Don't fall off," cried their mother harshly. "Harry, where are you? Look!" She raised herself up on her elbows, her eyes staring fixedly ahead. "Look, it's the man in the balloon! Look out!"

Their father caught her in his arms and laid her back on the pillow. Miss Hawkins pulled the children abruptly off the bed and pushed them into the hall, closing the door on them. They could hear Florrie burst into a panic of sobs.

"This is it," they heard the doctor say, but they could tell no more, for Mr. Friend took them back to Aunt Lois's at once. They did not know what "it" was until late the next day.

13

THE FUNERAL PEOPLE suddenly filled the Fourth Street house, their dim unknown faces haunted the dark hallways upstairs and down, the murmur of their funeral voices rose and fell like the sighing of the wind, their catfeet slipped back and forth on whispering errands. The minute a heart stopped beating, these shapes assembled as if this was the cue that brought them to life, and the final clang of the iron cemetery gates would shoo them back into designs in the wallpaper and shadows behind doors. The first of the funeral people to materialize was a large shapeless whispering woman in black serge, with woolly black hair and eyebrows and fat moist hands, scaly red cheeks, swollen legs (she wore rubber stockings under her black cotton hose), and a mighty black cotton umbrella which might well have been her means of transportation from funeral to funeral. She was wonderful with funerals, everybody said, and she didn't need to be told to come, but had a sense that informed her of death and even of its direction. Like a hawk circling over the dying sheep, Aunt Lizzie circled over sick relatives, ready to pounce at the right moment. She said she had been packed for a week for Daisy's funeral and Something told her, the way Something always did, that this was the day. She went to the deathbed at once, and after a sibilant conference with Mr. Fanzer, the undertaker, she took charge of Daisy, bathing her, combing her, permitting no one else in the room, not even Papa or Grandma. Marcia heard her talking, and peeked in, wide-eyed, to see if Mama had come to life.

"I always talk to 'em," Aunt Lizzie said comfortably. "They's always a chance they can hear."

The children were ordered to stay at Aunt Lois's, but Marcia hung back and hid under the living room couch to watch the funeral catfeet shuffle to and fro. She could tell Aunt Lizzie by the soft, heelless kid shoes with holes cut out for bunions, but even without opening her eyes she could recognize Aunt Lizzie by the moldy smell scattering from her black skirts.

"Like cellar rats," Marcia thought, sniffing again to make sure there wasn't a faint whiff of sheep barn in it, too. She could hear the insistent questions, "What's to become of the children? Who's to take the children?"

Isobel and Chris came, Grandpa Willard came, Aunt Betts and Uncle Louie came, and all of them changed into funeral faces, so it was as if you had never known these favorites any more than you'd known the other innumerable aunts and uncles.

"We wanted to be with you in your sorrow," they all chanted to Papa, Grandma, and Aunt Lois.

So this was Sorrow. Sorrow smelt of carnations and cellar rats and potato salad. People sat in the kitchen eating potato salad at all hours of day and night, as fast as Aunt Lizzie made it in the wash-boiler. Sorrow separated you from everyone else and Sorrow was a puzzle with no answer. Sorrow wasn't bad or good; it was just there making each person strange and lonely. Sorrow made Lena keep her face screwed up, sniffling, as if something hurt her.

"Where does it hurt?" Marcia asked, mystified. "Is it like being spanked?"

"It doesn't hurt exactly," Lena replied. "It's more like being homesick. You ought to cry, too. I heard people say it was funny you didn't cry."

"I didn't cry because I was glad to see Aunt Betts and Uncle Louie," said Marcia. "A person can't cry when they just can't."

Florrie was noisier than ever in her grief. She cried steadily until Mrs. Friend was afraid she'd have a convulsion. Her little body stiffened, a look of wild terror was on her face, and she refused to be fed or let anyone touch her without screaming. This manifestation was looked upon by all the funeral people as highly satisfactory, and Marcia heard many say, "The baby is the only one who realizes. The middle one hasn't any feelings at all."

It was a commendable thing to have feelings, for feelings were to feel bad with, and feeling bad was what everybody liked to see. Marcia watched Florrie and then Lena to find the secret of feelings, but her only sensation was one of limitless wonder at why people were different from herself. She thought maybe she was bewitched, for she was sure her secret self, the one with no feelings but intense sensations, was utterly separate from a little girl in a blue hair-ribbon named Marcia Willard. The little girl named Marcia could be pinched or bruised without feeling pain, because she was filled with the numbing fragrance of death, an immense thing by itself, like a train whistle blowing far off, or an echo in the woods. There were no people in it, not even Mama, here or gone. But nobody knew this. Nobody knew it but Marcia's secret self, and it filled her to the brim with such a tangle of desperate wonder there was room for nothing else.

Miss Hawkins stayed on for the funeral "at no extra charge," Papa told everyone with deep appreciation. She even wore a black dress like a member of the family, having brought the garment along with this occasion in mind. What moved Papa the most was that Mr. Carson, the president of the London Furniture Company, sent a pillow of pink carnations, a token of the esteem in which he held Papa even more than a tribute to the dead. Papa showed the pillow to the girls with tears in his eyes.

"I want you girls to realize the kind of man your Papa works for. I want you to remember this when you grow up, and if Mr. Carson ever needs a friend and I'm not here I want you to take my place."

The worst thing for Marcia about the funeral was having to sit on Aunt Lizzie's slippery lap (it had no shelf at all) and seeing grown-up people cry. Now she had feelings, Marcia thought, when the quartette of Papa's brother Masons sang "Rocked in the Cradle of the Deep," but it made her angry to have feelings and lose the strange sense of sorrow. She didn't like to see her father crying on Aunt Lois's shoulder, either, because feelings seemed to have made him forget that he didn't like Aunt Lois one bit.

Their father held them up, one at a time, to look at their mother, lying on the pillow of carnations in the clothes Papa had gotten for her at the Fair Store that time.

"Doesn't your Mama look beautiful?" Aunt Lizzie crooned, standing behind them.

"I don't like her looking that way," said Marcia stiffly. "I don't like her hair fixed that way."

They weren't allowed to ride to the cemetery because Florrie was still screaming, and the two others had to wheel her around the house in her go-cart. The undertaker's men came then to take away the rented chairs. Aunt Lizzie made a final boilerful of potato salad and then vanished with her massive umbrella, never to be seen again in London Junction. Florrie was whisked back to Aunt Lois's, and the two girls were put to bed in Mama's own bed. It smelled of disinfectant and carnations, and Marcia couldn't sleep. In the night she suddenly knew what she wished. She wished Mama had taken her with her and let her lie on the carnation pillow, but of course it would never have happened that way. It would have been Florrie or Lena, because the middle one never got taken any place.

PART TWO

the
shepherdess
in
the
snowstorm
ball

14

HODGE STREET was the greatest adventure since the day they moved to London Junction. Hodge Street was in Cleveland and was the particular location that Mrs. Carmel, in her infinite wisdom, had chosen as the ideal spot for Grandma to "branch out." The old lady was a little chagrined to find her young kin moving in on her new-won independence, but Harry, as she confided with a sigh to Mrs. Carmel, could always get around her. Somebody had to look after the poor kids. After their mother's funeral the children grew accustomed to being addressed as "you poor kids" with sad head-shakings. They grew accustomed to hearing their problems discussed candidly wherever they went, and were surprised to discover their future was not a matter of their own choosing but dependent on who was "willing" to look after them.

It was embarrassing to find that their favorite relatives were not responsive to suggestions of living with them. There were arguments as to whether it wouldn't be wiser to separate them instead of trying to farm them out in a lump. Lena favored this, because there was a chance she might be allowed to live with their darling Isobel and Chris, but thoughts of separation left Marcia stricken. Papa said no, their mama would never want them separated. During these conferences, they huddled together, even

Florrie numbed into silence by their new importance, the sense of which overwhelmed them to the exclusion of grief.

Aunt Lois finally volunteered to keep them, reluctant as she was to make things any easier for Harry, until Harry made permanent plans. She said poor Daisy would turn over in her grave if they had to go to an orphange, which was where they would end up if it was left to Harry, because he was certain to neglect them just as he had neglected Daisy.

Lena, with her new authority as female head of her family, suggested Uncle Louie's. Uncle Louie himself said regretfully that he thought he and Betts were getting too old to manage a new family. Aunt Lois said that nothing would upset their mama up in heaven more than the thought of them turning into heathens at Uncle Louie's. Busy as she was with her School Board work and her two teacher boarders, she would look after Daisy's family, providing Harry could be made to "do the right thing." If Harry had "done the right thing" in the past, poor Daisy would be alive at this minute. This phrase nettled their father mightily. He said nothing would upset poor Daisy up in heaven more than the idea of her children being bossed by Lois. If Lois had looked after her sister better when Papa, through force of circumstance, had left her in her own kin's care, poor Daisy would be alive now. He haughtily announced he would leave his brood in the care of Mrs. Friend until he found a suitable housekeeper. He had arranged for Isobel to make them each a purple dress and coat from a bolt of serge he had thoughtfully purchased on the Big Four out of Columbus, from another commercial traveller. He mentioned that he proposed to give Lena music lessons, a wish of poor Daisy's. He sternly advised Mrs. Friend to try and break Florrie of nail-biting, and to teach Marcia to answer when she was called, instead of acting deaf and dumb.

Mrs. Friend, much moved by this trust, took over her duties with tears in her eyes. They stayed in their old rooms with the two apartments thrown into one. She petted Florrie, deferred to Lena's authority as the Oldest, and taught them all to be good Catholics.

Papa came home only once a month usually bringing Mr. Hartwell to cheer him up. After a few months Papa got righteously indignant at Mrs. Friend's suggestion that he buy shoes for the children and contribute a little to their board. Papa's feelings were so deeply hurt by this lack of confidence that he ordered the children packed up at once.

"Blood is thicker than water, Mrs. Friend," he declared sternly, and forthwith carted Florrie to Isobel's in Venice Corners, and escorted the older two up to Cleveland as a surprise to their grandmother.

He did not fully explain his reasons for breaking with the Friends, but hinted that it was a religious matter.

"She was bringing them up Catholics," he said, and Mrs. Carmel, present at the time, was even more horrified than Grandma, and promised a safe refuge here from popery, every opportunity on the other hand to attend the beautiful new churches for Christian Science and Spiritualism. Harry, with grave injunctions for them to go to whatever Sunday School Grandma suggested—but, please, no rosaries for Mama's sake—then departed on a business engagement with his friend Hartwell, whose main factory was fortunately right on Hodge Street.

Hodge Street was barely half a dozen blocks from the Public Square and not far from the lake docks. While some carping souls would not have regarded Hodge (including Hodge Lane, Hodge Court, and Hodge Alley) as a proper location for the rearing of children, Marcia and Lena found it ideal, with the constant noise of trains reminiscent of London Junction, the froggy boat whistles, and the fragrant presence of the Eugenia Candy Factory, which perfumed the very air they breathed with fumes of sweet chocolate. Up and down side streets off Hodge were rooming houses whose tenants varied from genteel widows with pensions to shrill females who sat on the narrow porches in Japanese kimonos and kid curlers till dusk. "Light housekeepers," Grandma called them. These females kept the porch blinds discreetly low, and were prone to hastily pull their kimonos together at a man's approach, but this pious symptom of modesty never carried itself to the point of going indoors and dressing. Such a step would have meant losing a few neighbors' remarks, missing a street accident, or being the butt of gossip oneself. These ladies preserved their social standing by referring to each other as Mrs. M., Mrs. B., Mrs. R., and so on, as if the full use of the last name was too great a liberty. They were mostly of middle age, and although they maintained a well-bred reserve about their earlier life and never "gave away" anything, there must have been a basic similarity in all their experiences to have brought them to the same tastes and same habits. Whenever anyone passed, these females hushed up, but barely had the somewhat self-conscious passerby got out of hearing before every detail of costume and bearing was laid open to discussion. The high standards of fashion and figure verbally expressed by these ladies was particularly surprising, since they themselves so rarely put on a corset or dress, though to hear their morning critical consideration of the May Company advertisements you would have imagined they were about to make some impressive purchases that very day.

It was Grandma's habit to go down one of these side streets and back the other on her marketing in order to exchange a little gossip with as many of these ladies as possible. She was sorry that the purifying presence of her grandchildren limited the scope of her own roomers' conversation. Mrs. Myers and Mrs. Benton (better known as Mrs. M. and Mrs. B.) lapsed into morose silence when Marcia and Lena took over the porch as playground. With their bare feet usually adorned with Blue Jay corn-plasters, thrust in lopsided worn mules, they clattered in to Grandma often to complain that the doll clothes, banana peels, and orange rinds scattered over the porch made the place "not look nice," particularly since this was Hodge Street proper and not one of its cheaper tributaries.

Aunt Lois visited the children to make sure "Harry was doing something about them." She demanded of her mother what these women did for a living, a query much resented by Grandma who coldly explained that they were women bereaved by law or death of their husbands, too-high class to take employment or to let themselves go to seed in some hick town like London Junction. Aunt Lois wanted to know if and how Mrs. B. or Mrs. M. paid their board, to which Grandma indignantly replied that both ladies received registered letters every few weeks, indicating to any idiot that they had property somewhere, or an income coming in somehow.

"Do they pay you?" Aunt Lois relentlessly insisted. "Do you see any of this big income?"

Grandma said that in Cleveland you did not do business that way. In Cleveland you didn't ding and ding at high-class people (like Mrs. M. and Mrs. B.) whose status was established; you gave credit. Otherwise, as Mrs. Carmel herself would tell you, you lost your customers. Grandma suggested that her daughter go to Mr. Sweeney for corroboration of this statement, since Mr. Sweeney was the only man in London Junction with a grain of sense. Growing heated, Grandma added that she was on her own now, an independent woman at last, thank God, and she wouldn't take any criticism from any child of hers, because if such a child was so darned smart, why hadn't she known how to hang on to a husband? Aunt Lois flushed and changed the subject to her late sister's husband. Did Harry tell her what he planned for the children and did he send her any money for their keep? Did he get them the shoes they needed? Did he stay with them when he was in Cleveland or did he hang around the Eugenia Candy Company as usual all day with Ed Hartwell? Grandma said that Harry was more like a son to her than any of her own blood. It was a pleasure to have him in the house and Mr. Hartwell, too, a true gentleman who did her the honor of taking a room when Harry was in town, as they were devoted friends, and a finer man never breathed, except possibly Mr. Sweeney.

"Mrs. Reed," Mr. Hartwell had said, gravely shaking her hands only a few evenings ago on coming in rather late, "I apologize from the bottom of my heart for my condition. I can promise you

as a gentleman to a lady and a mother, God bless her, that you will
never see me in this shape again."

"So he was drunk," said Aunt Lois, with satisfaction. "Harry
too, of course. No respect for poor Daisy, not dead a year. I wish
they'd both walk in right now. I'd give them a piece of my mind."

Not ten minutes later her brother-in-law actually did walk in,
bearing white silk scarfs for his daughters, and accompanied by his
friend Hartwell, both in a praiseworthy state of grave sobriety. This
put Aunt Lois out of countenance. Grandma went on knitting a
green hug-me-tight for Mrs. M., hiding a demure smile as Mr.
Hartwell turned his masculine charm on Aunt Lois. There was no
use denying that Papa's friend made a good appearance, with his
broad shoulders, square jaw and big white teeth, carefully oiled
brown wavy hair and large Masonic diamond ring. He wore his red
pin-dot tie knotted in the latest style, bulging the exact degree out
above his vest and secured with a conservative onyx pin rimmed
with chip diamonds. His collar and cuffs were stiff and snowy,
though no whiter than Papa's, Marcia jealously noted, and from the
way his watch chain, hung with an elk's tooth, lay across his vest,
Mr. Hartwell was on his way to acquiring a bread-basket as distinguished as Mr. Sweeney's. Papa was proud of his friend's elegant
appearance but particularly proud of his rich fruity baritone. He
watched admiringly the effect of this magic sound on Aunt Lois,
for she could not disguise her pleasure in its resonant flattery.

"Willard, you never told me your wife's sister was the spit and
image of Lillian Russell," exclaimed Hartwell in a reverent tone.
"The very same complexion, the flaxen hair, the same figure! I'll
bet you have a lot of strangers staring at you in the street, Mrs.
Blair, taking you for Lillian Russell. A younger Lillian, of course!"

Aunt Lois blushed, giggled, and tossed her head. Grandma
winked slyly at her son-in-law, who was luckily escaping a "good
talking to."

"That reminds me. Eddie Foy is playing here at the Hippo-
drome," said Hartwell. "Willard, I'm going to ask a favor of you.

Will you give me permission to escort your sister-in-law there tonight? We might have a little supper afterward at the Hofbrau."

Under the spell of Mr. Hartwell, Aunt Lois forgot her plan to give Papa a "piece of her mind." In her effort to do her hair more like Lillian Russell's, she forgot even to continue her probe into Grandma's business.

Lena and Marcia were relieved that Aunt Lois was not going to take them away this time or to scold Papa. They were unhappy and bewildered that anyone should accuse him of being an indifferent parent, for he brought them, in addition to the scarfs, a bag of oranges and a box of Eugenia Chocolates, discarded from Hartwell's sample case as being a little stale.

Papa took them in the kitchen, leaving Hartwell to Aunt Lois and Grandma. As soon as he was away from the radiance of his friend, he grew silent and moody. Marcia and Lena tried to cheer him up. They liked Cleveland, they said. They would like Florrie to come up there and all of them live there together. They didn't need anything, in spite of what Aunt Lois might tell him. To further reassure him of their loyalty Marcia put out her scuffed shoe.

"These shoes are still good, Papa," she said earnestly. "So are Lena's. We put paper over the holes. We don't need new shoes anyway because we don't go to Sunday School here."

"I like your brown suit," Lena said, trying to add to his pleasure. "Now you've got a blue suit and a gray suit and a brown suit just like Mr. Hartwell."

Papa gloomily patted her on the head.

"You'll both have new outfits, from head to foot, next time I come in," he declared. "I told your grandmother last time I was here to take you down to May Company and get you outfitted right, regardless of expense. I'm too busy to do it. She could have done it, and charged it."

"Maybe they don't charge in Cleveland," Lena suggested.

Papa noticed Lena's hair now and said disapprovingly that it looked dirty and had lost its curl.

"Nobody brushes it," Lena explained readily. "It got into such a big tangle that Marcia had to cut it out in two places. Marcia got fleas in hers."

Marcia beamed.

"Not fleas, nits," she corrected. "We got nits in our mattress. It was from the Hunkies that stayed here."

"The Hunkies wouldn't pay their bill because they said they was bedbugs," Lena amplified. "Grandma got the policemen after them but they got away. Then we found the nits, so we have to shake the sheets hard when we make the bed."

"Grandma and Mrs. M. put gasoline on the mattress," Marcia added happily. "Now it smells like gasoline all night."

This brought a look of deep annoyance to their father's face. He got up and paced up and down the kitchen, stroking his chin.

"How long are we going to stay here? Are we going to go back to London Junction? When are we going back to school? Are you going to live with us?"

Their father threw his hands up impatiently at this flood of questions.

"Never mind, I'll get a housekeeper myself, if your own flesh and blood can't look after you any better," he vowed. "You kids need looking after. I'm surprised at your grandmother. You ought to be in school. By George, it's a goddam shame you can't trust anybody to do the right thing! Mind you, keep on saying your prayers every night, even if you don't go to Sunday School, and don't forget God bless Mama."

They asked him where his guitar was and if he wouldn't sing something. The guitar was at the Friends', he said, and he didn't have time to sing right now, for he was up to his ears in work. He had to do the work of ten, he said, because Mr. Carson depended utterly on him to keep the business going. They were cudgelling their brains to think of other intimate details of life at Grandma's when he patted their heads abruptly and sauntered out to the porch. They heard him out there in a quick change of mood joshing Mrs. M. and Mrs. B. He wanted to know what a couple of good-looking women like them were doing without half a dozen fellows hanging around, and had they heard the new one about the drummer and the chorus girl? Mrs. M. and Mrs. B. could be heard chuckling with the special secret kind of laughter that follows a special kind of joke, until Mrs. M. cried out coyly for him to stop before they died laughing.

"Did you hear what Mrs. M. just said to Papa?" Lena whispered later to Marcia in amazement. "She said he had two of the darlingest little girls she'd ever seen and anybody'd be mighty proud to be a second mother to them!"

"Maybe she won't chase us off the porch after this," Marcia said hopefully. "Maybe she'll stop picking on us."

Listening at every keyhole during their father's brief talks with Aunt Lois and Grandma, they could not gather what the plans for their future were to be. They did deduce that their grandmother had no intention of keeping them there for good, and that Aunt Lois would let them live with her only on condition that "Harry straightened out and did the right thing." It seemed they were a big responsibility—not a desirable one, either. They sat on the back-stair steps meditating glumly till bed time, Marcia getting her cue for gloom from Lena, who scowled and wouldn't talk.

"I'm good and mad," Lena finally said mysteriously.

"So am I," said Marcia, not knowing what there was to be mad about but anxious to share her sister's mood, and not to betray such ignorance as to suggest a game of jacks when this was the moment for gloom.

"They all pick on Papa," said Lena. "What do they mean, he don't treat us right? He brought us oranges, didn't he, and candy?"

"My piece had a worm in it," said Marcia.

"That's what you get for taking the biggest," said Lena. "Let's go to bed without being told, just to spite them."

They rather hoped their father would come in to their room to see them before they really got to bed. Their dark mood did not prevent their jumping up and down on the bed for the customary interval, followed by the conventional pillow fight. Later they were wakened by thunder and with one accord they rushed to the window to watch the lightning, hugging each other fearfully at each roll of thunder. It was thus their father found them when he came up to say goodnight to them.

"Your mother used always to love lightning and thunder," he said.

"That's why we always do, too," said Lena. "We always watch it ever since."

He took them on his lap and they sat in the dark, quietly watching the storm the way Mama used to do.

15

THE CHILDREN didn't have to go to school while they stayed with Grandma. Marcia was worried that this meant she wouldn't "pass" and moreover they had to hide when the school inspector came around. When he saw them, Grandma explained that "my daughter's children are visiting me for a few days before they go back to their school in London Junction. The poor kids have lost their mother." Other inspectors called regularly, too. When the gas inspector came the children had to rush through the house warning tenants to detach the rubber hose connecting the pipe with a one-burner gas plate, since this was against fire laws. The police inspector called, too, after a Mr. Barmby had skipped his bill one dark daybreak, leaving a suitcase containing a revolver and several bolts of brocade stolen from a nearby merchant. The police called again to confer with Grandma on the two young ladies with red cheeks in the light housekeeping front bedroom, who were not young matrons as they claimed but fourteen-year-old runaways from Chicago. Things were always happening at Grandma's, and the old lady was happy as a lark, whispering in the halls with Mrs. B. and Mrs. M., listening at doorways to strange sounds, pattering and puttering about, visiting with her friend, Mrs. Carmel. She lived in fear that Aunt Lois would pop in some day when she was having trouble with a roomer, or explaining some little difficulty to a policeman, or taking off Mr. Hartwell's or Papa's shoes when they came in late so exhausted that they fell asleep on the floor or bed with all their clothes on. Aunt Lois might call all the family together to get Grandma back to the propriety of private life in London Junction, a flavorless prospect for a woman now hell-bent on an independent career. If Daisy had only lived, she sometimes sighed, Daisy would have approved of her new life. Daisy never would have nagged her mother; Daisy would have pitched right in and helped out; Daisy would have sung and told stories such as Mrs. B. and Mrs. M. had never heard. Go ahead and tell them, Marcia; tell one of your mother's ghost stories now to Mrs. B.!

The children were permitted real grown-up duties such as making beds, except for changing sheets which wasn't necessary often anyway, for a little wrinkle or bits of grime in bedclothing never killed anybody. An Irish girl named Mary did the hard work, to a constant flow of instructions from Grandma.

A fascinating feature of Grandma's residence was that it was one of fourteen three-story frame houses, all exactly alike, and joined together at their foundations. The cellars had connecting doors, allowing the exploratory young visitors to wander almost a full block in an underground labyrinth of coal bins, jam closets, gray furnaces with swarming pipes, wood piles, broken furniture, trunks, and rat traps.

The backyards of these houses were separated by high weather-beaten picket fences. Here were garbage pails, ash heaps, clothes-line props, the lines sagging constantly with grayish washings. Lean tomcats scurried about, city cats with business on their minds, so they tolerated no petting. A tramp from the Union Station train yards would rest occasionally on a sloping cellar door, eating his handout. Grandma declared that Cleveland tramps were not as high-class or as educated as the London Junction tramps, who usually paid their way either in wood chopping or instructive conversation about the government.

In the basement of Grandma's house lived Uncle Wally, Grandma's oldest brother, who had suddenly come home from several years' wandering in the Far West. His daughters and sons in Elmville refused to take him in because, they claimed, he had turned Unitarian in his travels, so he took up quarters at Grandma's. He indicated his intention of staying, by thoughtfully taking charge of the furnace the very hour he arrived, then mending the washing machine, almost the last lick of work he did, once he was established on a cot in the furnace room. He was sixty-five years old now, and didn't care much about anything but a warm bed and plenty of coffee. He kept his own coffee pot piping hot always on the furnace. He had a big armchair beside the cot and kept his treasures on the broad sill of the barred cellar window. These treasures consisted of a deck of soiled cards for solitaire, a Holy Bible rusty with age, and a stiff collar which he was saving for his funeral. Under the cot was a slop jar with a pink crocheted lid, a cuspidor, and a tobacco box. When the children prowled through the basement, they found him usually sitting on the bed, hands on his knees, staring at nothing. If they made too much noise he snarled at them, but otherwise paid little attention to the busy life going on around him. Papa's visits cheered him up, and he usually would say something that would keep Papa chuckling for a long time.

"Martha used to say a man was too dirty for a house. Keep him in the barn or the cellar, she said, and by golly maybe she was right," he once volunteered philosophically. "Course every man's bound to have some woman at him, wife or daughter; he might as well get used to it or clear out like I did. The thing is to hold on to your temper, keep out of the way, and keep your hat on."

Next to Uncle Wally's furnace room was the laundry with the washtubs, an ironing board and a mangle in it. It was always filled with the smell of steaming Fels Naphtha soap and of wet woolens. The children were frightened of being caught in the mangle, as Mrs. Myers was always warning them, but could not be kept out when the tubs were emptied to drain off the cement floor and the opportunity for wading barefoot was at hand. Grandma padded in and out in the bedroom slippers her aching feet demanded, telling Mary to hurry, hurry, there was plenty work upstairs waiting. Roomers sometimes came down with a shirt or nightdress, calling out, "Put this in, Mary, will you? It won't cost any extra, now that you've got the suds there." The children had learned that in any spot where women were at work they were bound to scold about everything. Another point was that any time women were at work meant a clear field for mischief or adventure in other quarters. It was the time to idle away with ball and jacks on the front stoop until the ice cream sandwich man could be seen wheeling his cart far down the street. Then Lena delegated Marcia to creep into Grandma's room and get two pennies from the saucer of change on the walnut highboy. Lena wouldn't get it herself, because she said it was stealing. Money secured, they raced down the street with a pack of other screaming children who burst out of alleys, gutter drains, and thin air, holding high their pennies in tight fists. The fresh smell of the lake was in the wind, and steamer smoke, train smoke, a smell of wheat dust and coffee warehouses, threaded with the dim far-off clamor of the docks.

"I wish we could stay here for good," Marcia said sincerely. "It's fun doing as we please."

"I don't like Mrs. M. and Mrs. B. always bossing us," objected Lena. "Besides I want to stay with Papa and Florrie. I want to live in London Junction again and see Mary Evelyn."

Whenever they asked Papa if he had found the housekeeper he told them to hush up and stop bothering a busy man, all tired out from trying to make a living for them. On his rare visits he sat on the porch with Mrs. M. and Mrs. B., chuckling and teasing them. When a new roomer brought out a guitar they heard Papa singing to them, "Our little farm was small; it would not support us all." Mrs. M. and Mrs. B. both commented many times on what a card Mr. Willard was, and he certainly would have no trouble getting a mother for his little ones. Mrs. M. said three was, to her mind, the ideal number of children, as they sort of looked after themselves, leaving the parents, who might be still full of life, to go on good times together. Or for that matter the children could be left a good deal with their relations. Mrs. B. said that from Mr. Willard's dressiness she judged he made a nice little salary and could afford help to look after the children, leaving the new mother free to shop or go to her card clubs and keep up appearances. Both agreed that those little girls certainly needed a mother's care. But when Ed Hartwell was with Papa the two men made a bee-line for downtown and spent very little time with the roomers.

Mr. Hartwell made some side remarks to Papa about Mrs. B. and Mrs. M. being Battle-Axes. Soon afterward Marcia asked Mrs. M. what a battle-ax was, and received a sound box on the ears. The girls tried to keep awake till their father got in, but sleep usually overtook them. In the morning he was cross if they waked him, and often he left without a goodbye. "He's just like a chicken with his head cut off without Daisy," said Grandma to Mrs. Carmel. "He don't know what to do with the kids because he's just a kid himself."

16

GRANDMA'S FIRST YEAR ON HODGE STREET was a great success, she often stated, and she could never thank her friend Mrs. Carmel enough for her excellent advice. No one who applied for lodging was ever turned away, though this resulted sometimes in older tenants being forced out of their beds or else to sharing them. Living room and dining room were divided by screens or calico curtains strung across into dormitories for three or four people, and in especially busy times Grandma slept in the dining room in the folding bed with the children, since a private room for them was now out of the question. In spite of the number of lodgers and light housekeepers, there seemed a lot of financial difficulties. Grandma had mixed fears, one that Aunt Lois would come up and see her serious difficulties, and the other that she would *not* come up and help her out. Aunt Lois came up scolding once a month, forcing Grandma to admit that very few people found it convenient to pay their bills. Aunt Lois said it was an outrage that Harry never paid any board either for himself or the girls, and she would give him a good talking to. Lena and Marcia heard these accusations with gloomy forebodings, not lessened by Aunt Lois buying them underwear and shoes with the remark, "Your father will have to pay me back for these." Sensing trouble ahead for their father, Marcia insisted they needed nothing; if they did, then Papa would get it at the right time. When their father was told of Aunt Lois's action, he was angry at the implied criticism.

"Besides, the shoes hurt us," Marcia willingly declared. "Anyway the underwear isn't the kind Mama used to get us at the Fair Store."

Papa at once took them out and bought them new hats and hair-ribbons, the kind their mother would have liked, he said. They overheard him having a long talk with Grandma about what was to be done with them, but while the plans seemed exciting they also seemed confused. He was going to take a house in London Junction with a housekeeper, he was going to board them at the London Junction Hotel, he was going to send them to boarding school, he was going to move to California and take them there, also he was going to take an apartment with Ed Hartwell in Lesterville and have Ed's girl look out for them. These contradictory plans satisfied Grandma, and the five dollars he gave her as token of good will completely won her.

"Harry and I could always get on," she told Mrs. Carmel. "Harry and I never had a word."

She was gratified to hear that Mrs. Carmel respected Harry, and that she agreed with Grandma that Lois was too hard on everybody. Mrs. Carmel reminded Grandma that Lois had always tried to stand in her way, and hoped Grandma kept in mind that the Cleveland venture was all Mrs. Carmel's idea.

"I'm a business woman myself," said Mrs. Carmel. "I recognize a talent for business and you've got it. Your daughter doesn't see it."

Grandma was so flattered that she saw no need to mention Lois's required contribution to her business success.

Mrs. Carmel ran a millinery store in East Cleveland. She was a gaunt, dark woman always draped in innumerable black shawls, capes, veils, rustling skirts all blowing out like bat wings when she scuttled down the streets. She held her elbows stiffly out as if tacking to the wind for speed, but actually this posture was to secure many bags, large black ones, crocheted or velvet, all stuffed to capacity with old letters, ancient cancelled bankbooks, receipts and recipes, gumdrops, sewing kit, samples of brocade, bone hairpins, tangerines, Butterick patterns, keys to long-forgotten rooms in long-lost houses, photographs of owlish children naked on bear rugs or heavily muffled up on bamboo chairs, but in either case long since grown up, addresses, stamps, obsolete coins, streetcar tickets, ribbon remnants, pincushions, and many other useful objects which could not be left in bureau drawers for thievish servants. Mrs. Carmel veered and zoomed around street corners as if wound up by the toymaker and liable to be stopped only by direct collision with an immovable object, and the curious motor noise she made as she zoomed was her mutterings to herself with parched lips smacking and false teeth clacking. These mutters were as documentary as the contents of her bag, "May Company, Baileys, Taylor Arcade, Woodland car, half a cup of sugar, picture postcard," passersby would catch as she poised on a curb before flight to another corner, and often they took a second look at the eagle's beak under the black veiled bonnet, the sturdy wart with curling tendrils on her chin, the beetling black brows and restless beady eyes. Some superstitious strangers even crossed themselves or made a wish as she brushed by, but for all this strange appearance and behavior Grandma stated that Mrs. Carmel was as bright as a dollar, with a heart as big as all outdoors. Her girls worked their fingers to the bone for her and were rewarded in their "bad times" by a nice nip of gin which Mrs. Carmel herself was obliged to take medicinally to keep up her strength. It was amazing that Mrs. Carmel made a living, amazing that any customer could be found in any walk of life for the bonnets which she gorged as generously with odds and ends as she did her pockets.

The shop was so tiny, it was squeezed out of existence by two larger stores. Inside there was only one counter, and that as well as the shelves was stacked with hats of all ages for all seasons. A large bin in the corner held untrimmed felts, and in spite of the overpowering smell of camphor, fat dingy moths waddled comfortably in and out of this perpetual banquet. The darkness of the showroom and the smallness and dullness of the mirror aided sales undoubtedly, and since Mrs. Carmel never bought new stock but churned her old frames and ribbons about seasonally, the overhead could not have been great. Some people, including Grandma, were certain there was a secret treasure hidden in one of the black bags, indeed were so convinced of this hidden security that they gladly handed over the fifty cents or so Mrs. Carmel requested, usually after a busy clawing through her purse and the preface, "I seem to be a little short of cash."

Mrs. Carmel, called Em by Grandma, seldom talked above a coarse, rasping whisper or at best a croak, because all of her conversation was strictly confidential. She did not like large groups and even in a small company she would wring her hands restlessly, protruding upper teeth gnawing at under lip till chance permitted her the exclusive attention of one person, usually Grandma. These teeth were incidentally purchased for the long-deceased Mr. Carmel the very day of his death, and as an economical measure his widow instantly had her own fangs removed and wore these new teeth which might not fit perfectly but stayed in fairly well and worked a little better than her bare gums. They provided, too, an interesting sibilance to her speech, and heightened the air of secrecy to her remarks. She usually looked around the room in the middle of a sentence, to whisper, *"She* wouldn't be at the door, would she?" After the first greeting the secrets began, with some such opener as, "Well, I saw the Party finally and I passed on that remark I heard about our Friend. Well, I wish you could have seen his face!" This was a game dear to Grandma's heart and part of Mrs. Carmel's fascination for her. "No!" Grandma would cry, edging up her chair. "I wish I could have been there! How did the Party take it?" Mrs. Carmel would click her teeth and permit herself a windy chuckle. "They gave me a kinda funny look and then this other Party spoke up and mentioned such and such a price for the property—wait till She hears that!" Grandma was as delighted with this mystery as a child and all but clapped her hands at each fresh clue from her guest.

"You mean She didn't know the Property was for sale?"

Mrs. Carmel nodded twice very slowly. "She still goes to that Place I told you about."

"No!" cried Grandma, flushing with excitement. "How in the world did you know?"

"I saw the letter," whispered Mrs. Carmel, with a cautious glance at the door. "I ran into the other Party's lawyer at the Lecture, and he showed it to me."

It was Grandma's turn to throw a bombshell and she drew back in her chair as if to give it more power.

"Well, don't repeat this for the world, but this Party I told you about from Akron told me yesterday she knows for a fact the will's been changed in *his* favor."

"That's a lie," Mrs. Carmel said stoutly. "I can't tell you who told me but I can assure you the will is not changed one iota in any way, shape or form."

"You don't mean—!" gasped Grandma, eyes sparkling, and now beginning to rock her chair happily to and fro. Such code information was exchanged between Mrs. Carmel and her friend at every visit, leaving both participants glowing with secrets only half-revealed. The children, sometimes discovered too late in the closets or under a sofa, could make neither head nor tail of what they heard, nor for that matter could any adult intruder, so that Mrs. Carmel's intense fear of eavesdroppers was quite unnecessary.

Mrs. Carmel carried grudges among her other impedimenta. She was in a constant state of war with the landlord of her tiny place, and he was forever doing something that "made her hot French blood boil," for she was French by marriage and proud of it. When the children came to live with Grandma they stood in a row, jaws agape, staring at Mrs. Carmel, watching her chin waggling in perpetual croaks and sibilants, half anesthetized by the camphorous lavender sachet exuding from her drapes; finally Mrs. Carmel would tweak their cheeks with bony claws and cluck, "I always get on with little folks. No, sir, I never have any trouble with children, never, not an iota."

A gumdrop apiece, flavored faintly with mothballs, and then off she zoomed into the night. They would press noses to the front window, watching her nebulous black wings fluttering under the street lamp, then plunging suddenly homeward into darkness. No one else was ever able to bring such glamor to Grandma's busy life or to leave such a gratifying afterglow intrigue, subrosa, entre-nous-innuendo.

It was a pity Mrs. Carmel finally sided with Aunt Lois in saying the children were too big a handful for Grandma. There was a noisy conference one weekend with everybody crying about poor Daisy, Aunt Lois sternly accusing, Grandma vacillating, Mrs. Carmel stating that Grandma could put a little shop in the space occupied by the children and make a mint of money. The word "imposition" occurred several times.

That very night Papa, red-eyed and desperate, packed them up and took them to the station. It was a shock to find nobody at Grandma's was desolate at their sudden departure.

"Run along with your dad," said Uncle Wally. "Maybe there'll be some peace around the place now. Keep your noses clean."

Mrs. M. and Mrs. B. were equally stoical about their loss.

"I hope somebody teaches them some manners," said Mrs. M. "The younger one is as impudent as they come. Battle-Ax!"

"Will we see Florrie?" Marcia begged to know as their father hurried them through the Union Depot. "Are we going to London Junction?"

Papa didn't get their tickets at once but stood chewing a cigar thoughtfully for several minutes. They didn't know where they were going till they got on the train, but they were glad to be with Papa again.

17

"WHEN I SET OUT TO DO A THING, I do it," stated Papa several times and with increasing complacency. No one, least of all his three doting daughters, could deny this. There they were, almost by magic, so swiftly had Papa acted, back in the London Junction Hotel for the season, under the eye of the manager's wife, Mrs. Purdy. They had been escorted by Papa to the school superintendent's office and examined for their proper places in school, Florrie admitted to the kindergarten. They had been regally outfitted on credit at the Fair Store; they had been assigned a small, unpainted table in the hotel kitchen for their private use; and Papa and Mr. Purdy had sat up late, vowing friendship over a bottle of whiskey. Friendship was what men had as protection from the cruelties of women and fate. Mr. Purdy declared that in all his twenty years of hotel business he had never come across as decent a fellow as Harry Willard, and he didn't care who heard him say it. He said it was a rotten shame that life had treated him so badly, leaving him helpless with his family, but then life was, as that piece said, like a game of cards. The figure was so apt that he and Papa soon vanished into a distant chamber with a pair of Chicago shoe salesmen to check on the simile. The girls still dazzled by their swift re-establishment, didn't see Papa again for a week; but the Purdys, in fact the whole hotel, took good care of them.

The hotel was in the middle of town, with the train tracks running directly in front of it and the ticket office opening off the hotel lobby. The freight office and yards were further down, connecting with the ticket office by a long covered shed. An all-night cafeteria was on the other side of the ticket office, and here those railroad men who were not dressed for the privileges of the regular hotel dining room might feel at ease. Train talk was the thing in both places, however, with the daily schedules of Number Nine, Number Forty-six, Number Six, etc., all discussed as if they were race horses instead of engines. Indeed, these engines panted and snorted as joyfully into the very doors of the London Junction Hotel as if they were pet stallions showing off for their proud masters, anxious for a pat of approval. Their records hung conspicuously in both cafeteria and hotel lobby, and were studied intently by everyone, regardless of any plans for travel. "Did you hear about Twenty-six? Broke down twenty-two minutes out of Columbus, had to back up for repairs, got in an hour and forty minutes late. Shorty was firing. Old Hank in the cab." The commercial travellers liked to know all these things—something to season their conversation while they were selling.

The hotel was four stories high, of red brick, with glass-walled lobby, behind which the residents lolled in Morris chairs and viewed the passing trains, or, as they shifted from view, the marketplace on the other side of the tracks. Mr. Purdy, owner and manager, was a man of forty, thin, beak-nosed, bald, with a nasal eastern voice and general air of cosmopolitan distinction, due to a neatly cropped brown moustache, rimless glasses on a black ribbon, and a fur-collared greatcoat. He kept his wife and other family details tucked away somewhere in the back of the house, and was known to freeze Mrs. Purdy with a look when she ventured into the doorway of the lobby. The rule was that she was to use the back entrance, and though Mr. Purdy dined with his guests in the dining room, and so did Mrs. Hazy, his housekeeper, Mrs. Purdy was protected from this commercial scene by being screened off with her offspring into a corner of the kitchen. Far from being displeased, Mrs. Purdy basked in the special protection provided for her, not at all resentful that it was her money which had bought the hotel so that she might have deserved some say in its management. The isolation had further point in that the Purdy offspring, at two years old, showed signs to all but his mother of being imbecilic, though in a silent, unobtrusive way.

Papa had engaged a large corner bedroom for his family, with two big brass beds in it so that when he was at home he could sleep there too. In the mornings the chambermaid helped them get ready for school. The older girls brought Florrie home from kindergarten at noon and she was permitted to tag at the chambermaid's skirts the rest of the day. Mrs. Purdy's niece, Bonnie, the cashier, also took a personal interest in Florrie, and allowed her to play in the lobby under her fond but casual eye. Florrie took turns sitting on the laps of the various residents, ate limitless bonbons and cookies, and showed off.

"Where is your Mama, Baby?" the gentlemen would ask, and Florrie would point heavenward. This always resulted in someone pressing a coin upon her, and a display of handkerchiefs with several sentimental bachelors blowing their noses ostentatiously. As Mr. Sweeney, who was frequently present, said, "There are times when a man isn't ashamed to shed an honest tear."

Bonnie Purdy was a trim, complacent little figure, very stylish, since she had a pass on all the railroads and could make trips all over the country on the spur of the moment to see shows, buy hats, or go to parties. She was considered full of life, admired for her jauntily swaying hips and high-stepping when she was fixed up, and the intimations of plumply curved legs revealed by her skirts. She was no chippy, the men respectfully declared, but a fine little girl, high school and business college graduate, a little lady even if she did work around men. She was up on all the latest songs and taught them to Marcia and Lena, accompanying them on the dining room piano. She even took them with her to Eastern Star Entertainments, where she had them sing. She was an earnest performer herself, specializing in musical recitations. For these she looked particularly fine, wearing a white Greek-style wool dress with a red collar that set off her smooth black hair, parted in the middle and drawn smoothly back like pictures of the Madonna. Her cheeks were full, her eyes large and expressive, her mouth childishly pretty but solemn. She sat on the platform in a large armchair, and recited "Sandolphin, the Angel of Mercy, Sandophin, the Angel of Prayer," while a lodge sister played the Flower Song on the piano. It was considered a very refined performance. She always came up to say good night to the children, bringing them glasses of milk, and anxiously assuring them there was nothing to be afraid of. But no one could be afraid with the genial trains romping in and out of the room all night—or so it seemed—and the friendly male voices in the halls or outside on the train platform.

Florrie still sobbed in the night for her mother. Marcia, too, had one recurrent dream of her mother. She saw her crossing a street, in her dream, bent over with a bushel bag of potatoes on her back, and her face so tired it did not even smile. Another time she saw her mother carrying her bed on her back, again all bent over like an old woman. In her dreams her mother never smiled, but was always bent with a heavy burden, so Marcia dreaded these dreams and was glad if Florrie woke her up with her crying. Then she would manage to keep her quiet by telling her stories, neverending stories, in the course of which they both fell asleep. The stories were about a boy named Niky who was a million years old and lived in a tree, with a Whistle Fairy who could transform him anywhere in any shape when Niky whistled. If Florrie was fretful, Marcia made extravagant promises of producing Niky in person, though at the crucial moment she announced he had been disguised as the tangerine Florrie had just eaten. As Lena considered this sort of thing childish, Marcia tried to save it for the nights Lena spent at her friend Mary Evelyn's.

It was to be expected that Aunt Lois was perturbed over Harry's solution to his domestic problem but, as the other relatives felt too, she realized that interference meant taking on the responsibility oneself, and she had worry enough with Grandma. She insisted that they spend Saturdays and Sundays with her, scrubbing them from top to toe, mending and darning them, and looking over their report cards. She wanted to keep Florrie, indeed everyone wanted to keep Florrie, even Isobel and Chris, poor as they were, for Florrie was a "little doll," they all said. But Papa vowed poor Daisy would never want the girls separated. Besides, it was Florrie who looked after him, trying to do all the things she had seen her mother do, bringing him his matches and ashtray, admiring his neckties, worrying over his frowns, lisping consolation.

"She's a second Daisy," declared Papa fondly. "I wouldn't take a million for her."

The kitchen help at the hotel provided spontaneous entertainment and occasional discipline for the children. Their love affairs, the town and hotel scandals were freely aired, and later conducted to school by Marcia and Lena for the recess secrets with their classmates. Mrs. McGuire, the cook; Pete, the pastry cook; Kitty and Fanny, the two helpers, knew everything that was going on in town, and were not afraid to make suitable comments. Sometimes on the Friday night Knights of Columbus dances in Eagle Hall, they took Lena to sit by the orchestra and watch the dancing. In good-humored idle hours they taught the children to waltz and two-step and schottische, and twice they took all three girls to the dances to show off Marcia and Lena dancing together and all three singing "Absence Makes the Heart Grow Fonder." After school they rode in the engines in the switchyard with the engineers, and played in the telegraph tower with Oley, the Swedish operator. He let them hang on to wires and get electric shocks unless the inspector or dispatcher was around to chase them.

"I hear you're going to get a new mama," the trainmen and the kitchen girls were always saying. "Is it that chippy in Newark your dad's running with?"

"Your papa's sweet on Bonnie, isn't he?" the kitchen girls demanded, curiously, and receiving an astonished negative from Marcia they pursued the point with, "What was he doing with her at the Luna Park picnic last Sunday, then? What does she look after you kids for then? Believe me, it ain't for money."

It was true that every few weeks their father drew them on his knee for a grave conference.

"How do you like keeping house for your papa?" he would ask earnestly.

They would chorus their pleasure. Then he would whip out a cabinet photograph of a lady from his pocket and ask, "How would you like this lady for your new mama?" Ever pleased at any dramatic change they always expressed approval, though the ladies varied from the one in a long white robe with her hair down, seated at a harp, to a pop-eyed plump brunette in a black picture hat, leaning on a parasol. Whenever they confided excitedly in Bonnie about these ladies, Bonnie got cross and, one time, burst into tears. They couldn't imagine what was the matter.

"It just goes to show," Bonnie, weeping, explained. "A person does the best she knows how but all the good it does! A person could eat her heart out for a kind word for all some people care!"

"My papa likes you, Bonnie," Florrie volunteered one day.

"Your papa hates the ground I walk on," she stated darkly. "You can tell him I said so."

Mr. Hartwell came over often, sometimes with his lady-friend Mabel. On these occasions Papa borrowed a screen from Mr. Purdy to place around the children's bed, while he acted host to his two guests and Bonnie when she got off duty. Mabel was definitely stout, "a fine figure," as Papa declared, with tightly curled bangs and yellow hair, a pink and white face, and two gold teeth. She had been Mr. Hartwell's lady-friend for ten years, and was still half-dazzled and half-resentful of his hold on her, so that she divided her time between rumpling his glossy hair in her two plump little fists and cooing, "Whose honey sugar are you?" and next minute snapping, "Oh, shut your big mouth, you big fourflusher. I said Shut Up." Mr. Hartwell usually remained polite toward her during both these treatments, since, as he often said, he had too big a respect for a real lady like Miss Purdy and his friend Willard to kick her rump right through her shoulder blades as many less cultivated men might do on similar provocation.

A card table was set up during these gay evenings and Five Hundred enjoyed with a pitcher of beer, pretzels, and cheese. Papa kidded Bonnie about all her beaux and treated Mabel with the cagey respect due a pal's lady-friend. Sometimes he played the guitar for Bonnie to recite or sing, but often in the very middle he would stop abruptly and put the guitar away. "I guess it reminds him of Mama," deduced Marcia and Lena, in bed listening but pretending for their own purposes to be asleep.

Mabel slept in Bonnie's room on these occasions, and Mr. Hartwell tucked in the other brass bed with Papa. They snored and filled the room with fumes of cigar smoke and beer. In the night Florrie always stumbled into her father's bed. Mr. Hartwell and Papa were usually waked up by Florrie putting her feet in their faces or butting them in the stomachs in her restless tossing. These were good times, the children thought, being part of Papa's life, but after his parties he was silent and moody. Bonnie was always finding some reason to call when he was home, but he never seemed glad to see her when no one else was around.

"How's Mr. Willard today?" Bonnie asked gayly. "I don't suppose any power on earth would make him take a poor girl to the Elks' dance in Lesterville tonight."

"An old family man like me's got no business at a dance," Papa answered. "All I can do to get around on crutches as it is."

"You wouldn't have to dance," Bonnie said. "I don't give a snap about dancing, myself, but I enjoy good music. Maybe you'd like to walk down to the Band Concert later, when I get off. It always cheers me up."

"I don't want to cheer up," Papa said. "I got a lot on my mind. You get one of those young fellows from the Yard. You don't want an old boy like me to tag along."

"Mr. Willard, you're not much past thirty," Bonnie tremulously protested. "I suppose you think I'm too old, too, being twenty! You don't need to always act as if you were my father."

"You're a nice girl, Bonnie," Papa said. "You go have a good time."

"I pressed your suit, Mr. Willard," Bonnie said, standing in the door, unwilling to leave without a friendlier contact. "No, don't bother to pay me. I was pressing my own things anyway, so it was no trouble. Well, so long."

Still she didn't go. Papa started dealing himself a round of Solitaire on the bed, pretending not to notice Bonnie's uncertainty. The children, laboring over their school books, glanced up curiously at this scene, not understanding Papa's gayety in crowds and his moodiness when alone with their gay, beloved Bonnie.

"I suppose you'll be gone three weeks this trip," pursued Bonnie, swinging her keys nervously. "Maybe I might be running down to Columbus next Saturday, myself."

"That so?" Papa listlessly said.

"Oh, something else," Bonnie pursued, watching his face anxiously. "The lodge is putting on a show next Thursday night in the hall, and I thought the girls could sing 'Go to Sleep, My Little Pickaninny,' then 'Hello, Central,' for an encore. They'll get paid fifty cents."

Papa beamed now, and looked over with pride at his offspring.

"Their mama would be tickled to hear that," he exclaimed. "By George, they're getting to be real professionals."

"I taught them," Bonnie reminded him. "I thought it would be cute if they had Florrie in a cradle, rocking her for the first song."

"Blacked up like a pickaninny?" Marcia asked, excitedly.

"She's too big for a cradle," said Lena.

"I am not," wailed Florrie, clinging to Bonnie's skirts. "I want to do what Bonnie says."

Bonnie consoled her, finding a solution to her own vague embarrassment by picking her up to take downstairs with her.

"No objection to my sitting at your table for lunch, Mr. Willard, I hope?" she asked jauntily, and when Papa only shook his head she went away humming, with Florrie on her shoulder.

"Bonnie's awful good to us, Papa," said Lena. "Sometimes she reminds me of Mama."

"Hush! Nobody's like your Mama," Papa said harshly. He got up and put on his hat. "Get to work on your lessons now, no more fooling!"

No matter how gloomy he was, alone in the room with them, he changed as soon as he entered a group. They tiptoed down the back stairs to listen outside the lobby or dining room door while he told stories and joked with the other men and the waitresses. No matter how quiet the place would be, Papa's entrance made it immediately merry. His daughters huddled in the back hall, listening to the roars of laughter and their father's contagious chuckle, not knowing what was so funny but proud as Punch when somebody cried out, "By George, you can't beat Harry Willard! No, sir, he can't be topped!"

The hotel and the intimacy with Papa was exciting for a while, but then it grew lonely, for the longer his absences were the more brusquely people treated the children. Mrs. McGuire and the kitchen help found them underfoot too much, and scolded, till their only refuge was in swiping cookies and oranges from the icebox and having some really good reason for a scolding. Lena stood up haughtily to the constant, though not really bad-tempered, nagging and regarded herself as an adult, not to be confused with her two younger sisters. She had a dignified private life with her friend Mary Evelyn, and made personal visits to the Friends', and to her Aunt Lois to discuss family affairs and receive rewards due her advanced years in trinkets, small change, new bonnets, and ribbons. When Mrs. Purdy commissioned her to look after the idiot baby, Lena proudly announced that she was no nursemaid and

stayed at Mary Evelyn's for two days. The job therefore fell to
Marcia. Even though Mrs. Purdy gave her twenty-five cents a
week, it was humiliating to be caught by her classmates, wheeling
the Purdy baby up and down back alleys. Florrie was a comfort, in
that she liked to wheel anything, and ran along beside, begging to
push the go-cart. Eventually Marcia perfected a scheme whereby
she let Florrie wheel the empty go-cart around and as soon as Mrs.
Purdy got out of her apartment for her missionary committee
work, Marcia plumped the baby on the living room floor, barri-
caded it with chairs, and then sat on a stool outside the pen,
reading all of Mrs. Purdy's books. School work was easy to the
point of boredom, but here in Mrs. Purdy's overfurnished parlor
was the culture of the ages. *Last Days of Pompeii,* the works
of Mrs. E. D. E. N. Southworth, *Lucille,* Miss Mulock's works, *The
Old Mamzelle's Secret, Three Musketeers, If I Were King, Wormwood,*
Henty stories, Horatio Alger books—all these Marcia devoured in
a state of ecstasy unmarred by her inadequacy to digest many hard
lumps of language or meaning, for the thrill was in the reading.
Florrie loyally warned her of Mrs. Purdy's approach, so the books
and chairs could be replaced and the ever-ready explanation given
that the baby cried so she brought it inside. When they weren't
counting the days till Papa returned, Florrie and Marcia were
wandering up and down past Mary Evelyn's house, hoping for
Lena to come out.

But whenever they were fortunate enough to catch her, Lena
was quite likely to strut past them with Mary Evelyn (dressed as
nearly alike as their totally dissimilar charms would allow), and
if she did speak, it was in no friendly spirit. "Go home and wash
your face," she was likely to admonish Marcia curtly. "You ought
to be ashamed going around with your petticoat showing. For
heaven's sake, take Florrie home and blow her nose, and don't you
two come tagging around Mary Evelyn and me, or I'll tell Papa."

Dashed but not discouraged, Marcia and Florrie swiped sleeves
across their faces, jerked at their offending skirts, yanked their
garters and, after gawking at their fashionable sister's progress

down the street with her proud friend, they followed doggedly, utterly fascinated by the busy life Lena was able to make for herself. Lena and Mary Evelyn took walks to gather violets or mushrooms, they went to Epworth League meetings, they joined the Loyal Temperance Legion, a mysterious secret society that met after dark and sang songs and took pledges never to touch rum. Lena and Mary Evelyn did their studies together and made fudge, and they sewed things on the sewing machine. Marcia and Florrie were a little unhappy at Lena's individuality, but proud and astonished too at her initiative. They tried to think of games to rival Mary Evelyn's inducements, but the only thing that would hold Lena was Marcia's final desperate offer to spend her quarter on ice cream, instead of saving it for the *St. Nicholas Magazine.* During Papa's visits Lena gave up her friend, in case Papa would offer some treat which she might miss. She felt her responsibility, too, and usually devoted the first evening with Papa to a grave report on the bad behavior of her two sisters. Marcia was kept after school twice for not answering when spoken to, she was sent home by the teacher to wash her hands, she was slapped for impudence when she called the teacher a chippy. Florrie had bawled all during Sunday School, so they said she couldn't come again, and she had jumped on the bed till it broke the slats. Lena then produced her report card with an A in deportment, which she felt offset the C's in her studies, and partially convinced Papa, so that he saw only the D in Marcia's deportment and not the A's and B's in studies.

"I don't like deportment, that's why," Marcia belligerently explained. For her part she was able to tell Papa that Lena visited Aunt Lois all the time and told her everything that Papa was doing, so that Aunt Lois was madder than ever at him. She added that Lena now swore, and said "Lord" and "For heaven's sake," just like Mary Evelyn. This retaliation impressed Lena with her sister's strategic abilities, so she treated her like an equal for fully three days.

Papa didn't go on a trip for over a month. When Mr. Hartwell came over they didn't celebrate, but talked in low voices far into the night. Bonnie Purdy came in at midnight, bringing coffee and sandwiches which she declared were just going to waste in the icebox. The children sensed something queer was going on from Papa's silent spells and letter writing. One morning Bonnie came in at daybreak in her dressing gown to wake Papa for the Chicago train. He was gone two days. When he came back he had his hat once again cocked on the side of his head and chuckled at everything. Bonnie ran in the room after him, and they saw her reach up and kiss him warmly.

"I knew you'd get it," she cried. "You can get anything you ever go for, Harry Willard, if you'd just listen to me!"

Since there was no other audience available, Papa was obliged to do his talking to his small family. He paced up and down the room, with his thumbs in his vest, and said, thank God, he didn't have to slave for a flathead like Carson any more, a man who wouldn't trust an old employe, criticizing expense accounts, pinching pennies like no first-class company ever did. He was glad he could lift his head up again on his trips, hold his own with other men representing high-class firms such as the London Furniture Company could never be with a dumbbell like Bert Carson at the head, a spying, suspicious old cheapskate who didn't appreciate what a hell of a lot of guts it took to build up a business on the road. He should have listened to Hartwell two years ago and quit then instead of waiting for this kick in the pants. But you couldn't keep Harry Willard down, no, sir! He was signed up now with the Emperor Mausoleum Company, travelling out of Chicago, working for one of the biggest men in the business, Colgate Custer.

"You can tell that to your Aunt Lois next time she tries to pump you," Papa instructed Lena. "Just say your father's making twice the money and working for Colgate Custer. I'll drop in on your grandma next week and tell her. She's the only friend I've got in the whole damn family."

He went off next day in high spirits, without saying when he would be back. Mr. Purdy came in to see him and was surprised to find him gone.

"Did he leave anything with you?" he asked Lena.

Lena said no, and Mr. Purdy, after a thoughtful look around the room, went out, stroking his chin.

"I suppose Papa never paid this bill, either," said Lena, scowling. "I get sick and tired of it!"

Florrie and Marcia stared in horror at this evidence of rising disloyalty to Papa.

"Aunt Lois says we owe everybody in town," Lena stated.

"Mary Evelyn's mother said Papa's never paid a bill in his life, and the only reason the Purdys let us stay here, never paying, is that Bonnie Purdy is stuck on Papa. Aunt Lois said Papa borrowed fifty dollars from Mr. Sweeney for the first month we were here and never paid anything since."

Florrie began to cry. Every word Lena said hurt Marcia. Even if it was true, you couldn't come right out and say such things, not, oh never, about Papa. Lena's pretty, rosy face was drawn into an angry frown, her lips pulled tightly together. She looked almost grown-up and very much like Aunt Lois, with her hair frizzed and pulled back into a bun.

"I don't believe what Mary Evelyn's mother says," Marcia said. "She's just a store clerk."

This high-handed attack again impressed and surprised Lena so that she looked at Marcia with grudging respect. Carried away with her success Marcia made so bold as to ask Bonnie outright, before Lena, if Papa owed a lot of money.

"He'll pay it back, don't you worry about that," Bonnie said firmly. "You children ought to be ashamed criticizing your father. Why, your father is one of the finest, loveliest men that ever breathed."

"What will Mr. Purdy do with us if Papa doesn't pay the bill?" Marcia asked.

Bonnie merely tousled both girls' heads, and looked fondly down at them.

"You poor kids worrying that way!" she exclaimed. "But don't you go worrying your papa about things! He's got enough on his mind, three motherless children, nobody but strangers willing to look after them, poor man!"

As usual Lena's pride was roused.

"We have plenty of relations, we don't have to have strangers," she said with a toss of her head. "We've got Chris and Isobel and Uncle Louie and Grandpa Willard, and plenty other relations."

"They never come to see us," said Marcia candidly. "When Papa wrote we were coming to visit them they never answered."

"They were just afraid they'd have you on their hands for good," Bonnie suggested. "It costs money to bring up three children, and they maybe weren't sure they could afford you."

"But we only wanted to visit them," Marcia said. "Papa told them."

"I guess they didn't believe him," Lena said.

Bonnie shook her finger at them.

"Not another word about your father, now! Lena, don't you listen to that bad Mary Evelyn. Your father's doing the best he can; he's a wonderful man and don't you forget it."

Lena was as pleased as the others to have this reassurance. She punished Mary Evelyn by staying home and allowing Marcia to spend her ten cents on nougats which they ate playing Casino on the floor.

18

It astonished Marcia to discover that other children lived in an almost incomprehensibly different way than they did. It took a long time for this fact to penetrate, since she spent very little time with her schoolmates. They played silly games at recess, like Water, Water Wildflower, and Crack the Whip, all involving a lot of running and whooping around, when the time could be spent in the school library, reading books not recommended, or studying words in the big dictionary. Lena always walked home with Mary Evelyn and an older new friend, Myrtle Chase, who had just moved to town from Detroit and was an object of worship to Lena and Mary Evelyn. Marcia walked home alone, carrying on imaginary conversations with characters in the books she was reading. The other children had birthday parties, which filled Marcia with vague dread, for everybody else knew what to do and, besides, she never had any presents to give. They had peanut races, and the mothers told them what games to play, and to save their favors for "memory books," whatever they might be. These children had pretty little bedrooms, doll houses, little pianos, all kinds of story books, and sometimes they had bicycles or ponies or rabbits in the backyard. They lived on Park Square, far from the railroad center of town, or on Main Boulevard; they took dancing lessons every Saturday from a Miss Brumby, and music lessons, violin or piano, from a Miss Cory from Oberlin. Their fathers were at home all the time and owned a grocery store, a real estate business, a hardware store, or were executives in the furniture factory, the banks, or the telephone company. At the parties something awful usually happened. The mother would ask Marcia where was her "hankie," and, finding she had none, would take her upstairs to lend her one. Or she would exclaim, gently, "Little girl, is that a nice way to eat? Just look at your frock—or was that stain on it before?" Dishes broke as soon as they reached Marcia's hands. Some adult would usually draw her out of the group to say, "That's not nice language for a little girl," with Marcia sulkily uncertain of what word had been wrong, only knowing that the kitchen help and the lobby gentlemen at the hotel always chuckled when she said it.

In school she was looked upon with suspicion, and her quick answers usually brought out whispers of "Cheat! Cheat!" until she learned not to answer. Lena was frankly ashamed of her, though she rose valiantly to her defense when the teacher punished her for copying in a test, unable to believe Marcia remembered whole pages word for word almost in one glance. Lena assumed her authority as Oldest, and called on Marcia's teacher for redress, saying with dignity that her young sister was the smartest girl in class and the teacher ought to know better, and if she didn't stop picking on Marcia she, Lena, would take it up with the principal. On this happy occasion Lena elected to march home holding on to Marcia's arm protectively, and she showed her how to crochet as a special favor.

Papa, at their urgent request, packed up all three of them to go to Uncle Louie's that summer, and he said maybe he'd have a house when they came back. This time everything was different. Uncle Louie had had bad luck with his crops, Aunt Betts's rose cold turned into a siege of asthma, and Almedy worked so hard she had no time for company. The girls missed the careless freedom of the hotel, and country games seemed silly after the grown-up pleasures of London Junction. Florrie got a rash from sliding down the haystack on her bottom and all three got poison ivy. Uncle Louie and Aunt Betts weren't as jolly this time, and didn't seem to want them.

"How long did your father say you were going to stay here?" asked Uncle Louie at the end of a week.

"As long as we like, he said," Lena reassured him.

"I guess that's the size of it," said Uncle Louie moodily. "By George, he sent along all your winter clothes, too, mittens and skates even. Does he think we have to be responsible now for you?"

"Now, Lou," Aunt Betts wheezed, "it isn't the children's fault. Like as not they didn't know a thing about it. Don't make Florrie cry." For Florrie always wept at criticisms of Papa.

"That's so," granted Uncle Louie. "Harry's got a hell of a nerve, though, not even asking by your leave. If he can't raise his own family, why don't he put 'em in a home? I like the kids all right, but I'm not going to let Harry impose on me on that account."

As usual, Lena's pride rose up again, though Marcia was only mildly uncomfortable at these discussions. Lena laboriously wrote a letter to Papa and another to Aunt Lois, stating "we don't want to stay anywheres we're not wanted so pleas send us tickets." Aunt Lois was frantically adjusting Grandma's affairs in Cleveland, and Papa was in the West, so after waiting impatiently two or three days Lena announced they were leaving that very day for London Junction. Uncle Louie was abashed, and tried to coax them to wait till Papa wrote, but Lena was firm. She packed up the trunk again, herself, and saw that Marcia and Florrie got into their train clothes.

"You'll have to buy our tickets, Uncle Louie," she said stiffly, as he drove them to the train. "Papa will send you the money later."

Uncle Louie was disturbed by their sudden departure, but afraid to tempt Fate by forbidding it. They didn't need tickets after all, for a freight train ambled along with an engineer and brakeman from the London Junction yards, so they rode free in the caboose, singing all the way for the edification of the other occupants, the county sheriff and a swarthy gentleman handcuffed to him, en route to the state penitentiary. The swarthy gentleman was stimulated to sing "Santa Lucia" and "Funicula," in Italian, and readily taught them to the girls, so they felt the trip was highly worthwhile.

"What'll we do when we get there?" Marcia asked as the train came into the switchyards. "Mr. Purdy said he had to have our room for the stock company this month."

"You wait and see," Lena said mysteriously.

Florrie and Marcia watched their competent leader with satisfaction. At London Junction she held up a hand for the cab.

"Drive us to Mrs. Lois Blair's," she commanded, and after they got in she said, "You're to charge this to Mr. Harry Willard, please."

"Oughtn't we to run in and see Bonnie?" Marcia asked.

Lena shook her head.

"No, sir, we're not going any place we're not wanted," she declared. "I'm sick and tired of it. Aunt Lois will have to keep us because she's our aunt, isn't she?"

They were all excited at the idea of moving into Aunt Lois's big house, and all pleased with Lena's masterly management. Aunt Lois, just back from Cleveland, was caught in the right mood, much impressed with their Italian songs. She laughed appreciatively over Lena's account of their difficulties. They did exactly the right thing, she said. Whenever they were in trouble they must come straight to her. She'd manage somehow.

19

A T THIS TIME Aunt Lois was thirty-four years old, buxom and handsome and, according to Papa's grumbling admission, worth nearly ten thousand dollars! Apart from her house, she had done well with her stock in the Lesterville Steel Mills, even though she was always being tapped by all of her relations for loans (never to be repaid). She enjoyed her position as leader of the family, feeling that her generosity entitled her to dictate the lives of all her dependents. She kept in touch with all the northern Ohio relations, passing on their marriages, schools, diets, jobs, pleasures, and clothes. Each year she had one hobby which she obliged the rest of the family to share. One year she insisted that the cure for all diseases was to wear Ground Gripper shoes, the next year it was a front-lace corset which she would have gladly foisted on the men, too. Then came the fireless cooker year, the cooking-in-paper-bags year, the linoleum-over-the-whole-house year, the cement porch year, the shower bath year, and each one of these obsessions received the passionate devotion of a new religion, working its way into her conversation on any subject, and invested with powers little less than magical of renewing health, wealth and happiness. The relations, bound by debt to Aunt Lois, had to admit the common sense of her advice, and permitted themselves to be badgered into following her commands, particularly since her zeal led her to advance further loans for carrying out her wishes.

The only rebellious members of her family were her mother and her brother-in-law. "Mother is slippery as an eel," she said. "She won't argue, always seems to agree, then she goes right ahead doing what she pleases." She itched to regulate her brother-in-law's life, and was irked that the children's hotel life carried them out of her control. But now they were under her roof, and their dependence on her gave her a gratifying hold on their father. She wrote him immediately that she was taking the children, "straightening out the absolutely shocking effect on their manners and language of their life at the hotel," and she would expect regular sums for their support. For answer Papa sent them a large box of salt water taffy from Atlantic City and a series of pictures of himself and Mr. Hartwell wearing false noses and opera hats on the sides of their heads. Aunt Lois did not share the children's delight over the communication.

They missed their old liberty, but their new life seemed to be a step upward in respectability, besides being luxurious beyond their wildest imaginations. They were convinced that nowhere in the world existed advantages superior to Aunt Lois's home. There were no teachers rooming there now, though Aunt Lois did make extra money by selling insurance policies in her spare time. One of her recent whims had been to sell all of her old furniture and do the entire downstairs over in stylish Fumed Oak. The big parlor had gas coals in the fireplace, a Story and Clark player-piano, an elegant rainbow-tinted glass chandelier with a red bead fringe, a bust of somebody (possibly Ulysses S. Grant), a bowl of goldfish with a wondrous castle inside, leather cushions with pictures of Indian maids burnt on them, a rack containing the piano rolls, sheet music out of the Sunday supplements, *Etudes,* and magazines old and new—*Burr MacIntosh's, Ainslee's, Munsey's, Delineator, Young's, Smart Set,* and the *Blue Book.* Most of these had been marked by Aunt Lois, and the favored poems or epigrams were carefully memorized by Marcia and pondered upon in the night. "Love is a flower, passion's a weed"; "Men love women, women love love"; "Gods weep, the half-gods can only laugh." These fruity thoughts gave a pleasingly theatrical background to Marcia's impression of Aunt Lois's house. Lena and Florrie were more impressed with the fireless cooker and the piano, where Lena, with Aunt Lois's help, learned "Shepherd Dance," the "Weasel Waltz," and "Dorothy, A Country Dance."

Much to their surprise, the children discovered that not only did Aunt Lois find Mr. Sweeney tolerable now, she even welcomed him as a regular caller. She instructed them not to mention this to their father, who would be sure to put an evil meaning to it, and as further safeguard she sent them upstairs during his calls. If they escaped banishment by reading quietly in the corner, they found the conversation fully as baffling as Mrs. Carmel's. Mr. Sweeney always stood for a moment in the doorway, head bared and bowed as if scarcely daring to enter the sacred presence of Pure Womanhood. Receiving Aunt Lois's hand, he bowed low over it and entered with grave dignity. He placed his hat, cane, and gloves on the hall table; then, with another bow, presented Aunt Lois with a large, beribboned box of De Klyn's Bon Bons, or for variety Chandler & Rudd Salted Almonds. These rites observed and properly applauded by Aunt Lois, he then drew up a straight chair to Aunt Lois, who implored him to take the big chair. Her entreaties, based as much on the demands of his bulk as on politeness, finally prevailed over his humble wishes, and with a "May I smoke?" he relaxed comfortably. Aunt Lois, who could never be idle, crocheted or mended, and in low tones vibrant with conspiracy the two murmured such phrases as "six per cent," "common," "two hundred shares preferred," "stockholders' meeting," "dividends." The quality of their voices was so charged with excitement and secret pleasure that it was hard to believe money, and not romance, was its cause. Aunt Lois's fair head bent breathlessly toward Mr. Sweeney's flushed heavy-jowled face, and when he left she sat smiling abstractedly at her work as if words of love instead of mere financial profit still lingered on the air. Whenever Marcia reminded her of the old jokes between Mama and her about Mr. Sweeney's pompous airs, Aunt Lois reddened and said sharply, it took a long time to appreciate some people.

"Don't you tell your father I said so," she added.

Every Saturday Aunt Lois went to Lesterville on business, and these were the days Papa elected to call on his children if he was in town. He stayed at the Elks' instead of the hotel because, he said, things were getting too thick at the hotel.

One time Lena boldly asked him if he was intending to pay board at Aunt Lois's as she had insisted. A look of hurt surprise came over his face as he regarded his daughter reproachfully. Then he took out his checkbook and wrote out a check for twenty dollars. Later, Aunt Lois said the check was no good, which wounded Papa even more.

"Looks like a man can never suit some parties no matter how hard he tries," he said, wistfully, so that even Lena felt ashamed for her forwardness. He brought them red tam-o'-shanters, and fur-topped boots for Florrie, and a sample picture book of famous mausoleums erected by his company in all parts of the earth. He talked of buying a mausoleum for Daisy, too, when Lena said Aunt Lois thought Mama should have a gravestone. He brought them a song book from Bonnie, advising them not to tell their aunt from where it came, and taught them "Take Me Out to the Ball Game." They were confused and sorry when he left, for he criticized Aunt Lois, and they were already mixed up in their feelings by Aunt Lois's steady attacks on him. Florrie remained steadfast, vowing complete adoration of Papa, unmarred by her devotion to Aunt Lois, but Lena swayed from one to the other.

There were more secrets to be kept, later on, when who should be found lolling on the parlor sofa one day but Mr. Hartwell, Papa's friend. Mr. Hartwell gave them each a quarter and told them that under no circumstances were they to tell Papa of this visit, while Aunt Lois sternly admonished them never to speak of it to Mr. Sweeney. Mr. Hartwell's visits, which became regular, and took place usually while they were at school, were quite different from Mr. Sweeney's. Aunt Lois laughed a lot at everything Mr. Hartwell said, and he followed her around when she cooked, patting her shoulder and tweaking her curly yellow hair. He, too, brought candy. He saved pictures of Lillian Russell to show how much she looked like her, and made her blush by calling her his "Evening Star." He was very much at home around the place, taking naps in the downstairs bedroom when he came in from the train, and helping himself in the icebox. Aunt Lois was always cross after his visits, scolding the children for eating the cake she was saving for him, and complaining of how tied down she was, just at the age when she could have a good time. There was something very secret about Mr. Hartwell's visits, and he frequently used the back door because it was handier, he said. Once some woman telephoned there for him, and Aunt Lois answered that she knew no such person as Hartwell. None of the children liked Aunt Lois's change of manner under Mr. Hartwell's influence. Usually arrogant and dignified, she giggled and flirted and blushed in a silly way, not becoming an elderly woman. Lena said she had a good notion to tell Papa on her, but when she did she was taken aback by Papa's roar of delight.

"The old son-of-a-gun!" he kept chuckling. "Wait till I get hold of him! By George, I'll tell him I heard it from Mabel. That'll serve him right for being so foxy!"

His opportunity did not take this form, but gave him even more satisfaction. Aunt Lois was home when he called one day, "full as a tick," as she described him later to Mr. Sweeney. She promptly attacked him for his snappy new topcoat when the girls needed clothes; she wanted to know if he seriously intended to pay for Lena's piano lessons as Daisy had always wished; she also wanted to know what about all this talk about Bonnie Purdy chasing all over the country to meet him, making herself the talk of the town, staying in the same hotels in Cleveland and Toledo with him; what kind of father was he, after a wonderful wife like Daisy, chasing a chippy like Bonnie Purdy, so that his little girls would grow up with a bad name?

Papa got white at this, unable to speak for a moment. When he did his voice trembled.

"I can't help where Bonnie Purdy goes," he said. "At least I'm not taking her away from somebody. You can't talk, Lois, while you're fooling around with Ed Hartwell. You know he's got Mabel. You mind your own reputation. I'll look after mine. People are talking about you more than they are about me."

Aunt Lois must have been stunned into silence by this; certainly she acted strangely and secretively after that, and was snappish at the children. Mr. Hartwell did not come any more, but on her weekly trips to Cleveland she always brought back a box of Eugenia Candies, and a *Cosmopolitan,* his favorite magazine. Though she said these trips were to visit her mother, she was vague in her news of Hodge Street, and was preoccupied a great deal of the time. She did not like Lena bringing Mary Evelyn home after school, finally forbidding it outright because Mary Evelyn's mother was a gossip and troublemaker, she said. Lena was not to be denied her social life, and visited Mary Evelyn's home instead, because her papa said she could. When Papa said she was not to wear her Sunday shoes to school, Lena answered that Aunt Lois said she could, so she was able to manage an agreeable state of independence.

It was Lena's fault that Mary Evelyn was present and able to inform the town the day Mr. Hartwell's Mabel called on Aunt Lois. Lena had defied Aunt Lois by bringing Mary Evelyn in for cookies, inasmuch as Aunt Lois wasn't expected home from Lesterville till six. Marcia and Florrie were playing jacks on the front stoop when a large blond woman, dressed elaborately in velvet and feather trimmings, came up the walk. Marcia was pleased to see this was Mabel, part of the old hotel parties. But Mabel was in no state for friendliness.

"Where's your aunt?" she asked.

Marcia and Florrie reported in unison that she was away. Mabel set her jaw and said she could wait. And wait she did, sitting upright in the parlor without taking off her kid gloves or hat for nearly an hour. Lena and Mary Evelyn peeked at her from time to time, curiously. A few minutes after six o'clock a cab drew up and out stepped Aunt Lois, laden with bundles, accompanied by Mr. Sweeney. As soon as they entered the house the lady visitor began to shout. There was a scream from Aunt Lois, a sound of bundles dropping and panting voices, with Mr. Sweeney softly exclaiming, "Ladies! Ladies!" Presently Mabel came running out, red-faced and dishevelled, many tears streaming down her cheeks, muttering, "Oh, oh, oh, oh my God!"

Mr. Sweeney consoled Aunt Lois, who lay back on the sofa white as a sheet, trembling.

"I really believe she had a gun," said Mr. Sweeney. "What on earth was she after you for? What was she shouting about her man and who is she? I'd better call the police."

"No," said Aunt Lois briefly. She drew her hand restlessly away from Mr. Sweeney's soothing touch. "She's some crazy woman that mixed me up with somebody."

"I'd better stay here to see she doesn't come back," said Mr. Sweeney gravely, patting her hand again.

"Oh, for God's sake, leave me be!" cried Aunt Lois desperately, pushing him aside. "Can't you see I'm upset?"

Mr. Sweeney was so offended at this ungrateful suggestion that he got up, buttoning his coat with great dignity across his broad vest and walking majestically out of the house.

"It's not my business, of course," he stated at the door. "But I must say I do not understand this incident, not in the least, Mrs. Blair."

Other people in London Junction were more astute, easily making interesting deductions from Mary Evelyn's fortunately detailed report. At school the new girl, Myrtle Chase, told Lena she was not allowed to play with her any more, and the mother of

Marcia's seat-mate requested that her daughter's seat be changed. Papa unexpectedly took Aunt Lois's part in public discussions and went so far as to tell Ed Hartwell that Mabel was not a lady in any sense of the word. Ed replied sorrowfully that sometimes a fellow found that out too late. He said that when a woman like Mabel came right out and refused to be a lady, she ought to have her bucket kicked right up between her shoulder blades. He said if she ever laid a finger on Lois again he'd do that very thing, in spite of being the best-natured fellow in the world.

20

M<small>RS. J<small>ANE</small>'S ROOMING HOUSE</small> in Lesterville was on West Park Street, convenient to the markets and to the steel mills, which was perhaps the best that could be said for it. On one side were warehouses, old houses made into bakeshops, and stores with rooms to let upstairs, and on the other side the offices and outlying buildings of the steel works began, ending far off in the glaring sky above the mills themselves. Mrs. Jane's had been mentioned to Papa by a stranger in the station, so it was here the Willard family found itself, bag and baggage, as suddenly as it had found itself once before, on Hodge Street. The reasons for this move were similar too—vague reprisals on Aunt Lois, Fate, and all the other elements that forever challenged Papa. The children were puffed up with pride at being claimed by Papa and almost keeping house for him, you might say. Papa was working now for the High Class Novelty Company of Lesterville and was to be home nights—at least, he wasn't to travel on this job for a time.

"I want a rest from the road, get my health back," he said confidentially to Mrs. Jane when they moved in to the parlor floor. "The fact is, those cold hotel rooms and drafty trains can get a man's constitution down in time. Many's the night I've sat in some damn hotel room, shaking from head to foot with a chill, first hot, then cold, hands shaking so I could hardly hold a glass. Only thing for it is to carry a little brandy on you, take a swallow every five minutes or so till the spell is over."

Mrs. Jane said she had spells of terrible dizziness, much the same, and found brandy the only cure. As Papa appeared on the verge of a chill and Mrs. Jane seemed to sense a dizzy spell coming on, they had a glass of brandy then and there, as they settled the fees and privileges of the new living quarters. The chief advantage of the new arrangement was that Mrs. Jane had lost three children herself—stillborn, accidents, and "cholery morbus," so she was particularly well equipped to keep an eye on three motherless little girls. (Both Papa and Mrs. Jane wiped their eyes here and looked mournfully at the three girls who were comfortably playing Robber Casino on the bed.) Mrs. Jane had plenty to do, with her millhand roomers, night and day workers, but she would make these three little dolls her special care, provide from her own table for them, at least once a day, see that they washed their ears and didn't run the streets like hoodlums. So the deal was set and Papa said with satisfaction that he could stand just so much criticism from certain people, then he liked to step in and show them up.

"You write your grandma and your Aunt Lois to keep their hands off; your father is looking after you now," he instructed the children, and with a promise to install them in the proper school the next day he put his hat on the side of his head and was off to the Lesterville Hotel, where Mr. Hartwell was stopping, because he didn't have much chance to see his old friend any more.

The children examined the rooms curiously, wanting to be pleased but a little bewildered. The room which was to be their bedroom, living room and kitchen still bore traces of its original purpose, which was an old-fashioned family kitchen, but parlor and bedroom perquisites had been added for lodgers' needs. There was a bird's-eye maple folding bed with a bulging front for the children, a worn Morris chair, a richly carved, black walnut armchair (some of this carving proved later to be examples of pet- rified Spearmint), a clothes rack in a niche formerly used for the stove. The floor was camouflaged with a mottled, scuffed, brownish linoleum, which stopped at the middle door to join a scuffed, greenish linoleum. A card table with dangerously inclined legs was disguised by a tasselled plum velvet drape, the stain in the middle almost hidden by the pewter dish of colored clay fruit from Mexico. This room opened by lofty arched sliding doors into the dark alcove, formerly dining room, in which Papa's brass bed and an enormous black walnut wardrobe were wedged. Another sliding door leading to Mrs. Jane's own rooms was boarded up with odd pieces of water-soaked beaverboard. In here a small, high window was hung with ruffled dimity curtains, dusty and flyblown, but as coy as if they gave on some sunny daisy field instead of an airshaft. A black stovepipe came mysteriously in one aperture near the ceiling, crooked an elbow and went out another for no purpose but decoration, since whatever stove was ever connected with it had long since been junked, but Mrs. Jane said the pipes looked better than holes in the plaster.

Mrs. Jane was a thin, flabby woman of forty-five, with a putty-colored face, liverish lips permanently curled up in what was meant to be a heartening smile, ready to widen into a merry cackle the more honest because it revealed palate, bridgework and tonsils without affectation. A tendency to jaundice gave a yellow cast to her eyeballs and patches of brown spots on her lean neck. She had a high, little girl voice and a way of fondly cocking her head to one side, but this coquettish effect was only to reassure the suspicious, and not to lure the opposite sex, because, goodness knows, as she made haste to explain to Papa, none of her men lodgers needed to worry about her setting after them. She'd had her chances, still had; but just because she felt sorry for a nice looking young man with three motherless children didn't mean she was looking for a man. Papa said a woman with her figure didn't need to look far and she agreed that he had certainly said it. Mrs. Jane spoke often with pleasure of her figure, though it was seldom revealed to proper advantage. She wore a bungalow apron and lace boudoir cap for marketing, since her head was always armored in steel curlers. For household chores she wrapped her head in whatever dustcap, towel, or napkin was handy, and shuffled around in bedroom slippers, bare legs, and a ragged crepe kimono, flowery sleeves pinned back on her shoulder. This working costume gave an impression of slavish domesticity, but like many a dustcloth around the head often indicated merely that there was a lot of work to be done but not right now. A scrubbing pail of suds was usually abandoned on the hall steps; a mop, broom, or carpet sweeper leaned against a door to clout the unsuspecting as they entered; a dustpan of debris sometimes sat all day on a stair step; a washing half done in the backyard, a stew burning dry on her stove—these were ambitious projects started at breakfast by Mrs. Jane and deserted for others that occurred to her: an attic cleaning, a bargaining tour of the markets. Lodgers commented on Mrs. Jane's industry when they saw her implements about, and Mrs. Jane, possibly abandoning all for the daily paper in the porch rocker, would reply in a cheery whine, "Woman's work is never done." This uproarious *mot* sent her into peals of laughter.

A great deal of Mrs. Jane's time was spent in locating her pet, a large tiger cat appropriately named Tommy. Her voice could be heard wailing, "Tommy! Tommy! Where are you, Tommy dear? Come, Tommy!" from morning to midnight, and scarcely a day passed that she did not have a few hours' anguished conviction that Tommy had been stolen or run over. The cat's chief pleasure seemed to be in providing this daily drama for his fond mistress. During her distracted calls and search for him, often accompanied by sobs, Tommy lay blinking under the porch or on the roof, observing her frenzy with what might be a sardonic masculine smile, and after pleasuring himself with the sight of his dear madam making a fool of herself over him he stretched himself and ambled leisurely to his cushion on the back stairs where, in due time, she would find him manicuring his nails and tidying his whiskers as if nothing had happened.

"They know!" Mrs. Jane declared proudly, indicating the intelligent animal. "You'd be surprised how they know!"

Mrs. Jane felt that the Willard children were almost like her own, she said, which meant they had to run errands and help her with the chores. "Get your beds done now, girls! Have you done your baseboards, Marcia? Have you dusted your dressers?"

Marcia hated this use of "your" not wanting any connection with household unpleasantness. "They're not *my* baseboards," she would mutter. "They're *hers!*"

After the first genial conference, Papa and Mrs. Jane did not further the intimacy, though Mrs. Jane did her best. She asked questions of the girls. "I guess your father's got a sweetheart some place," she said. "Some young girl, I suppose, young enough to be his daughter. Your father's got a lot of snap to him, the way he steps, the way he wears that hat of his. I guess he shows the girls a good time all right. One of these days I'm going to fix myself up, branch out in a new navy blue suit. I'll bet he takes notice then, by golly! I still got my figure and I got all my teeth, that's the mainest thing."

Mrs. Jane talked of a day to come when she would retire to sunny California and lie around one of those bungalows in a bungalow apron, in a hammock all day. If she found the right man, maybe some widower with a little snap to him, she would hand over her savings and off they'd go. If the widower had any children she'd be a second mother to them. These implications depressed the children and made Papa wary, even though deceptively genial. When Mrs. Jane suggested opening the sliding doors between their suites, he generously declared he wouldn't permit it because lots of people would get something in their heads. Some people had that kind of mind. Mrs. Jane said she was old enough not to care what people said, especially if she liked a person, but Papa told her she wasn't fair to herself. He said a person in her position in the community couldn't be too careful and he intended to help her keep up this respected position.

After that he spent some time pushing the wardrobe against the sliding door to Mrs. Jane's room, in case the beaverboard strips might not hold against the hurricanes of circumstance.

21

Papa sat in the carved chair, knees crossed, eyes gazing dreamily upward, and plucked at his guitar.

"Picture tonight, the fields are-a snowy-a-white," he sang tenderly. "Come on, Florrie, sing it after me. The other kids know it."

Florrie sat on the foot stool directly in front of her father, her small hands clasped, and her large earnest blue eyes fixed worshipfully on him.

"Pitcha taneye, a feelsa sowee why," she dutifully sang.

"After this let's sing 'Honest Irish Lad,'" urged Marcia, and Lena said, "Then 'Poor Little Joe.'"

"How the old folks would enjoy it," went on Papa, ignoring them.

He scarcely ever would sing the old favorites. When the girls sang them he would interrupt with a command to go on an errand, or he would himself go out, frowning. It was as if these songs were buried in the Mapleview Cemetery with Mama, all covered with myrtle and graveyard flowers. Marcia shut her eyes sometimes and saw Mama behind those final iron gates, wandering forlorn, eyes blind with death, the heavy pack on her back, the homeless Irish lad beside her, and poor little Joe shivering in rags. About these three the snow danced and swirled as it did in the glass Snowstorm Ball on Mrs. Jane's mantelpiece, the storm finally engulfing them just as it did the little shepherdess in the glass ball. Maybe, thought Marcia, this was the way Papa, too, thought of the old songs, and wanted to forget.

"How about a new song?" asked Mr. Taylor, Papa's new friend.

"That's the trouble with giving up the road," Papa complained. "You get behind the times. By the time a song hits this town, it's a hundred years old."

"I heard a pip in Columbus last week," boasted Mr. Taylor. "Name of it was 'If I Had a Thousand Lives.' Fellow came out and sang it in a full dress suit, then in a kinda frame-like behind him some girl would light up like a picture. Made you all choked up. End up with her coming out of the frame and walking over to him, so they walked up and down together, her in front of him, ahanging on to his arm. They musta sung it five, six times."

"How'd it go?" Papa asked, interested.

Mr. Taylor scratched his nose.

"If I—no, it was lower than that. If I—dum de dum. Well, hell, a song's just a song. Those fellas are always singing something or other. I pay no attention."

"I'll take Detroit any day in preference to Columbus," stated Papa, resuming his guitar. "I've seen some of the finest shows in the world in Detroit, Michigan. I'll say that much."

"I guess you've never been to Detroit, have you, Mr. Taylor?" asked Marcia brightly.

Mr. Taylor looked moodily at her.

"How about the kids going out to play?" he suggested, whereupon all three girls favored him with a reproachful frown.

Mr. Taylor was Papa's new friend for Lesterville. He was a dried, sandy little man with a long, pointed nose like a rat's, a feature that seemed to fascinate him as much as it did other people, for he was always tugging at it, then squinting down to see if any change had come over it. Between these diversions he wrinkled it into a perpetual sniff, accompanied by rapid blinking of his small, raisin eyes. He sniffed at words and people as if his nostrils did the work of all other senses, and he could sniff out a thought or even a person's financial status quicker than a beagle could smell a fox. He lived in a men's hotel down the street, and was proud of it because it was called The Hermits' Club, just like the one in Cleveland, though the Lesterville Hermits were bound by no convivial ties, only by their common need for a hall bedroom cheap. Mr. Taylor had several calling cards printed up with his name and club on them, which he passed around to strangers unfamiliar with the "club." Its privileges, apart from a bed and the use of the elevator, were so limited that he came over to the Willards' rooms frequently, especially on Sunday, where he could have room to spread out the funnies. His favorite was "Hee Haw! And Her Name was Maud," and he often used that expression to clinch an argument.

He never took off his cap, a baggish, greenish plaid number with a big visor sliding down over his nose, and he kept a match behind his ear as a precaution against any delay in getting a smoke the instant the desire struck him. He wore a bow tie and a brick-colored Norfolk suit. He had one silk shirt which Papa said he never took off, but his vanity entitled him to snap his fingers at Papa's other friend, Ed Hartwell, the finest dresser Papa ever saw.

When Papa first brought Mr. Taylor to the Lesterville rooms the children burst out laughing, for he was small and droll like a monkey. But like many a droll, twinkling-eyed little man with a funny, nasal, cracked voice and clownish ways, he was not funny at all. He had a way of eating the best candies Mr. Hartwell brought to them, of pinching their cheeks, pulling their curls, and ordering them about as if he was a teacher or a relation instead of just a fellow worker at the High Class Novelty Company.

"Mark my words, the novelty business is here to stay," he said, nodding wisely. "You wouldn't catch Charlie Taylor traipsing around the country selling tombs like you did, Willard. Stay in an up-and-coming boom town like Lesterville and get in the novelty business; that's my advice to anybody."

Papa agreed heartily, in fact too heartily, that there was a lot in this clever statement. He didn't intend to stay in Lesterville all his life, but it was a relief not to be kicked around by a cheap outfit like the Mausoleum Company, run by a big crook like Colgate Custer who, it was said, had Negro blood the way all the Southerners did; you could tell by the fingernails. Naturally, a high-spirited fellow who'd been all over, as Papa had, knew what it was all about, missed the cosmopolitan advantages of the road. The latest songs, for instance, oyster cocktails—try and get one in Lesterville!—lobster Newburgh, peach melba. Still, they weren't everything. At the High Class Novelty Company a man was treated like a gentleman, even though he didn't get the jack you got on the road. But you got a chance to know everyday folks and there wasn't a finer man in the business than Troyan, a foreigner, yes, a Bohemian, but the Bohemians were the finest class of people when you got to know them. They didn't try to catch you up on expense accounts; they knew how to appreciate a first-class salesman. Mr. Taylor silently twigged his nose during Papa's praise of the boss, venturing no answer but, "A fellow's got to work for somebody, what the hell? It's either that or starve, what the hell?"

Marcia and Lena resented Mr. Taylor, for either he interfered with their games by his presence or made their evenings lonely by keeping Papa out, usually, it would appear, at Stein's Saloon over by the steel mills.

Papa defended his new friend by saying he was a man who had a lot of trouble—wife ran away with another man, leaving him with a little boy, of whom Mr. Taylor didn't see much. He had efficiently deposited him on his erring wife's mother who had been made to feel it her duty to do penance for the scandal in the family. Now he sat on the arm of the battered Morris chair, whirling his watch chain around, whistling out of tune, spoiling Papa's song. Marcia sat on the floor, legs crossed, writing in her composition book, and Lena played Solitaire, waiting for their turn to sing with Papa.

The remains of Sunday dinner, canned beans, buns, and weenies, were in the sink in the corner, and steaming on the gas plate was a teakettle for dishwater. The kettle was a rusty, misshapen affair, wearing another larger kettle's lid which slid down over the snout, giving a startling resemblance to Mr. Taylor.

"What the hell, Willard, you going to hang around here all day?" Mr. Taylor restlessly demanded.

Florrie's lip began to tremble.

"I want to learn the song!" she began to sob, so Papa hastily resumed the lesson, for Florrie was his pet.

Mr. Taylor picked up his coffee cup with the spoon in it and rattled the spoon around, scraping the last bit of sugar from the cracks, and watching the children meditatively as if, Marcia bitterly whispered to Lena, he was planning to eat them if no other plan for their disposition presented itself.

"Make yourself at home for a spell, Charlie," urged Papa. "I got to quiet the kids for a while."

Mr. Taylor put down his coffee cup on the floor and rattled his keys. If he couldn't rattle or scrape something he tapped on whatever was handy, or snorted, coughed, whistled, anything to cheer himself up and make his presence felt. Now he got up and helped himself to the one piece of candied fruit Lena and Marcia had been quarreling over. He glanced down at Marcia's composition book.

"Copying something?" he asked.

Marcia gave him an icy look.

"I don't copy," she said. "I make up."

Whistling jauntily at the rebuff, Mr. Taylor made a leisurely tour of the rooms now, peering in the wardrobe, tapping the pipe, and looking through the kitchen curtains at the high black wood fence barely two feet away. A trickle of noonday sun lit up this pleasant prospect, accenting tenderly a tin ash pail now being investigated by Mrs. Jane's cat, Tommy.

"What do you pay for this hole?" Mr. Taylor inquired, wrinkling his nose.

Papa put the guitar back in its case and the girls cast reproachful eyes at the intruder.

"Seven-fifty a week," said Papa. "It's an outrage, but then the old lady keeps an eye on the kids. Why, we had one of the prettiest little homes in London Junction for only ten dollars a month, when my wife was alive. The best furnishings. Fact was I had a brand new dining room set ordered the very day Daisy died. She always wanted the best. Wait a minute. I got a picture of an actress here, looks just like her. Found it in last week's *Leader*."

He produced from his vest pocket a newspaper clipping and the children ran to look over Mr. Taylor's arms. It did look a little like Mama. The name here was Mabel Taliaferro, but Papa had clippings of other actresses who reminded him of Mama, either in the bangs or the tilt of the head, or a little expression around the eyes. The children fell in with this habit, saving pictures of every beauty in the news, disappointed if Papa silently shook his head after a study of them, justifying their mistake by pointing out that the watch or the ribbon or the earring was like Mama's. Mr. Taylor scrutinized or rather sniffed the clipping indifferently, then handed it back to Papa.

"Don't look like nobody to me but this Mabel Whatsername here, what the hell," was his comment, but Papa looked again at the picture, holding it up to the light with a stern, searching expression as if he was commanding it to be Daisy herself. Then he put it carefully back in his pocket.

"Why didn't you leave the kids with their aunt back in London Junction?" asked Mr. Taylor. "None of my business, but this is no place to raise kids, what the hell."

"Their grandmother got in some trouble in Cleveland and Lois had to stay up there for a while," said Papa, but the children knew there had been another quarrel between Aunt Lois and Papa, mutual accusations resulting in Papa's hotly packing them off to Lesterville.

"Roomer at their grandmother's left a cigar burning and burned down half the street—fourteen houses," said Papa, referring to the catastrophe which had ended Grandma's Hodge Street adventure. "Law got after the old lady, besides her losing all of her furniture, and most of the roomers beat their bill in the middle of the excitement. I guess Lois has her hands full, but the old lady's bound to start in again. Going in the millinery business now with a friend of hers."

"We'll get free hats," prophesied Lena.

Mr. Taylor shrugged impatiently at these family details.

"Let's go over to the hotel and get Hartwell," said Mr. Taylor. "Cook up a game there. Let the kids go play, what the hell, no good their sticking in here all the time. They're big enough to amuse themselves, ain't they?"

Marcia and Lena again looked resentfully at him and Marcia made bold to pull her nose in angry mockery, so Florrie had a fit of giggles, very irritating to Mr. Taylor, suspicious of its cause.

The truth was that they didn't know how to go about playing in Lesterville. In Cleveland the Hodge Street district had been a little village in itself, but Lesterville, in bursting from village into busy, industrial town, was too big for one center and too small for several centers. At the big West Park Street School everybody belonged to "the bunch" except the foreigners, who kept to themselves. There was no welcome in either group for strangers. Lena and Marcia dreaded recess, when their isolation was most conspicuous. Fifth graders didn't mix with fourth graders, so Lena would not dream of easing her own misery by sharing Marcia's. In Marcia's class a big, athletic girl named Burnadetta dictated the games, the fashions, the catchwords ("Oh, that'll be peachy!" "Oh, you kiddo!" "If you don't like it, lump it!"). The stone-paved schoolyard rang with the cries of her devoted followers: "Come here, Burnadetta! Look at me, Burnadetta! Where's Burnadetta? Oh, Burnadetta, Burnadetta, Burnadetta!" A name like Burnadetta is as good as a pony or a big play yard for prestige, or even a roguish nickname like Jerry, that of the tomboy leader of Lena's class. Whatever qualities besides appealing names these girls had for leadership the outsiders could not guess; they could only be fascinated audience to the inner circle's fun, tagging behind while the eager slaves jostled each other for the privilege of walking next to the idol. "I'll carry your books, Burnadetta! . . . I'll draw your map for you, Jerry! . . . You can copy my composition, Burnadetta! . . . Oh, you kiddo! Oh, oh, what'll we play next, Burnadetta, Jerry!"

Lena and Marcia dreamed of strange, incredible adventures in which Burnadetta or Jerry said, "Hello," and even walked through the school gates with them, to the envy of all. This, they felt, could be accomplished if Aunt Lois in all her beauty and efficiency would suddenly come to school for them, showing these children of plain mothers that a beautiful aunt was much more desirable. But these were dreams and not to be counted upon.

School clothes were different here, too, being Peter Thompsons or middy suits, purchased in the Juvenile Department, and not at all like the grown-up hand-me-downs made over by Isobel and sent over twice a year. Lesterville school children had allowances, ate lunch in the school cafeteria, and travelled back and forth to school in "bunches" on the streetcar, or went to The Sugar Bowl for banana splits at recess. Uninvited to do this, even if they had the money, Lena and Marcia hid in the basement toilet at recess or pretended to have nosebleed, and at noon walked all the way home for bread and milk and ginger snaps. Florrie, being in the first grade, and completely trusting, was fortunate enough to be Teacher's pet, so she was launched in games by her patron and often invited to share Teacher's lunch. Saturdays and Sundays were days when other children had mysterious club meetings, picnics, picture shows, visits to the park or menagerie; Papa had to work Saturdays, so there was nothing to do but skip the rope in front of Mrs. Jane's house or just sit on the stoop in silence. They were afraid of the busy street clanging with streetcars, factory bells and ear-splitting whistles, and crowded with the steel workers jostling each other along with grim, intent faces, sometimes shouting bad words that made the very air shiver.

So they sat on the narrow front porch which jutted past Mrs. Jane's fern-filled bay window, two steps above street level. They made up guessing games and thought of what they wanted most in the world, like high heels, a croquignole board, a lavalliere like Burnadetta's, a visit from a relation or Bonnie Purdy. On Sundays they had Papa for a little while unless he'd been out all night with Mr. Taylor, after which he lay in bed all day, shouting to them for God's sake to shut up. They were afraid to go to the big stone churches because here you had to wear gloves and carry a Bible or prayerbook and have patent leather slippers. Lena noticed these religious rules and decreed that they must not try to break them, even though there was a Membership Campaign on at the East Park Presbyterian Church, and Burnadetta herself had asked them to sign up on her team ("the Blues") so that she could win a star.

"You have to give a dime there," Lena disclosed gloomily to Marcia. "Even the juveniles can't give pennies."

At least Papa was home on Sundays, so they could sing; that was a comfort. But here was Mr. Taylor ruining their one day by suggesting that Papa leave, and that they "go play."

"Why don't they go down to that new Athletic Club just opened on the Square?" persisted Mr. Taylor. "Swimming pool, sand piles, games. I seen kids running in and out. Free, too."

Papa hadn't heard of this and listened with interest. To the girls, the idea sounded so entrancing that they looked at Mr. Taylor more favorably, and were glad when Papa urged them to get into street clothes. In Papa's impressive company, they were positive no snubs could occur. Papa led them straight to the big new building with the football field beyond it and tennis courts in front. At the "Children's Entrance" he bade them have a good time and he'd come after them at five to take them home on the streetcar. Lena, with a great show of assurance, led them to some stairs marked "Swimming Pool" but a buxom young woman in a bathing suit said they must bring bathing suits for the Pool. Having none to command, Lena then led them to the Gymnasium, where children were riding stationary bicycles, tumbling on mattresses, climbing monkey cages, chinning themselves, and playing ball. They did not need to be told that here also a costume was necessary, since all the girls wore bloomers and middies, absent from the Willards' wardrobe. Florrie, unconscious of this, flung herself joyously into a double somersault, exposing her underpants to the jeers of some small boys until Lena hastily dragged her away. Another room yielded a group listening to a Story Teller, but a glance indicated that these drab, bespectacled, morose little folks were the doomed ones, left out of everything else and unpopular, so to join them would certainly be admission of defeat.

"That old story!" Marcia scornfully exclaimed as they withdrew. "Everybody knows 'Peter Pan'!"

"I don't," said Florrie, hanging back.

"Come on, then, I'll tell you," Marcia said, and inasmuch as she had heard of Peter Pan only dimly she made up a hasty story about a magic boy who lived in a skillet and granted wishes to a kitchen slavey when anything beginning with a "b" was cooked in the pan, but caused an earthquake if by some horrible chance cornmeal mush was ever cooked in it.

Wandering through the bare whitewashed corridors, they peeked in several rooms where gym classes were in progress, but there seemed no possible way of joining any group. These other boys and girls seemed to have been born in bunches, happily complete, looking with indifferent, even hostile, gaze at the three strangers. In one room an empty ping-pong table inspired them to experiment with the game, but two young ladies appeared and calmly announced they had "signed" for that hour. They finally found a Reading Room with a checkerboard in it but no checkers or any reading matter as yet, equipped merely with empty shelves and a long table and a *Silence, Please,* sign.

"I'll bet Mr. Taylor knew all the time it would be this way," said Marcia, as they sat down on the chairs. They played "I Love My Love With an A" for a while, then strolled out to the hall where a lady sat at a desk, with a green reading shade over her eyes.

"Did you sign up for what hours you want to use the pool?" she asked in a brisk, metallic voice. "Tuesday afternoons and Sundays for children."

Lena, with an important cough, immediately took the pencil and put down, "Sundays, 2–4," to the immense admiration of her sisters; then wrote all their names in the proper column in the new backward-slanting handwriting the girls in her class used.

"Willard," repeated the lady, running her finger down a big list. "Is your father George Willard?"

"No, Harry Willard," said Lena. The lady frowned.

"We have only one Willard here. How long has your father been a member?"

Lena looked blank, so Marcia stepped up.

"About six months," she said.

The lady then shuffled some index cards, shaking her head.

"Perhaps he's been dropped for non-payment of dues," she said. "I don't see you children down as Junior Members, either. Have you paid your fee?"

"I don't remember," stammered Lena, getting very red. "How much was it?"

"The regular membership fee is ten dollars, and two dollars a month dues," said the lady. "If your father had paid that up, your union fee would only be five dollars a year. Otherwise—"

"Does everybody have to be a member?" asked Lena.

The lady now removed the reading shade and passed a hand over her harassed brow, regarding them with some thought.

"Monday is Free Day," she said. "Get your schoolteachers to write a statement that your parents cannot afford regular membership. That entitles you to all the Privileges on Free Day."

"We'll come Sundays, if we come, because our father is a member," said Lena loudly. "Somebody here made a mistake, I guess, and he'll have to see about it. We don't want to come on any Free Day."

She pushed Marcia and Florrie ahead of her out the front door, her lips drawn tight to keep from screaming her fury. They stood outside the front door, waiting for five o'clock to come, but Papa didn't come back, and finally at half-past they straggled home, asking the way from a dozen people. It was Mr. Taylor's fault. They restored a little of their spirits by imitating him with such success that when their father came home in an extraordinarily hilarious mood himself he found them in shrieks of laughter, pulling their noses and blinking their eyes and shouting "what-the-hell" in unison.

"I guess you kids had a good time," he said, and they laughed some more.

22

I HATE LESTERVILLE! I hate Lesterville!" Lena was the first to come out and say it, though it was in a low mutter that only her sisters could hear. If only they could have stayed in dear London Junction, they mourned, and Lena went as far as to write firm letters to Aunt Lois and Mrs. Friend, suggesting that a long visit to the Junction would be appreciated.

"There is no use our going to school any more because the bunch just talks about the new Athletic Club and we can't go there because we're not members. Marcia's teacher won't pay attention when she holds up her hand to answer, then she gives her F on her grade card. Florrie hasn't any party dress, so she can't go to parties when she's asked. Nobody asks Marcia and me, ha ha. There is a rat in the kitchen. I wish Mama was alive. Mrs. Jane is mean to us. If somebody doesn't take us away from here we will run away, anyhow me."

Marcia was disturbed over this candid letter, since she had just sent a long letter of her own of a far more romantic nature, describing her beautiful new wardrobe (seen in the Smith Store catalogue), and telling of gay parties in the fashionable homes of Jerry (Lena's chum) and Burnadetta (my chum), Papa's eminence at the Athletic Club ("he is president of it") and her own and her sisters' triumphs in the Epworth League, Dancing School, and

Gym Club. She dared not admit her guilt to Lena, and trusted to the usual delay in Lena's acquiring a stamp.

It was true that life in Lesterville seemed a series of misfortunes. Marcia's teacher suggested calling at her home to talk over grades, and inquired who looked after their homework. Marcia said, "Our housekeeper." When the teacher did call she reported to the Community Charity Service that the children were neglected and, to their mortification, a box of groceries was delivered in the Charity Service truck.

At sight of this, Mrs. Jane assumed that Papa had lost his job and harried him every night for back rent and advance as well. The cashier of the Bakery Lunch, who roomed on the third floor, lost a cameo ring and said one of those fresh little girls had stolen it. Lena talked back to her and was slapped in the face. Later Florrie found the ring in the hall, but Lena wouldn't let her give it back because the woman would be all the more certain of theft. At school Marcia got first prize in Composition but was ignominiously retired to third prize because the principal, who was judge, said the theme showed she had had outside help. And Florrie had broken Mrs. Jane's glass Snowstorm Ball because the shepherdess looked like Mama and she wanted to save her.

It was no good telling Papa these woes, because they made him so mad he banged out of the house and stayed out all night playing poker with Mr. Taylor. He was gloomy whenever he was home, and always gloomier after a visit from his old friend Hartwell, now back on probation with Mabel. Mr. Hartwell said Papa was too big a man to be stuck in a cheap outfit like the High Class Novelty Company. A first-class salesman was going to waste, he declared, and it was a damn shame. He brought messages from the waitress at the Toledo lunch room, from Kitty over in Detroit, from the Clark crowd in Akron, and he described gay parties in fashionable roof gardens ("don't mention this to Mabel") where Papa's fund of anecdotes would have been highly prized.

"No, sir, I'm through with that," Papa declared a little more emphatically than was necessary. "I've got a good thing, here, a raise promised. Had a hint from Troyan the other day I might be asked into the firm. I've had plenty of offers to go back on the road but not me. Got a letter just today from my old firm wanting me back. No siree."

Later on Lena found the letter and showed it to Marcia in alarm. The Mausoleum Company wanted to know when Mr. Willard was going to make good the funds he had collected and been unable to account for at his dismissal. The sum was one hundred and four dollars, and they were wasting no more time on letters, but would bring action at once. Meantime they would refuse references in the event he sought work elsewhere.

"I wish we'd stayed in London Junction!" Lena said, as if that was the only thing to be said in this fresh catastrophe. They worried about the hour when police would close in and cart them all off to prison. Papa's worry took the form of scolding them, until Lena talked back again and Florrie cried. The night steelworkers sleeping in the room upstairs banged on the floor. "Shut that brat up!"

How wonderful in the middle of these adversities to see Bonnie Purdy suddenly appear one Saturday afternoon at their door, a little plumper but as jaunty as ever. They rushed to her as if here was salvation, and Bonnie did not hesitate to promise anything they asked. Would she stay with them, would she take them to the picture show, would she ask Mrs. Jane to let them have the cellar for their playroom, would she take them back to the London Junction Hotel? Poor Papa's face lit up when he came in from work and saw Bonnie. "I happened to be passing," said Bonnie, "and just happened to see the number and I thought I'd drop in. Now that I'm here I might as well fix the place up a little."

"We don't need anybody to fix us up," Papa said. "If you just dropped in to criticize you might as well leave."

Bonnie reddened.

"I wasn't criticizing, Mr. Willard, only the children—the place—well, those stories going around in the Junction made me so cross. I thought I'd come over and help."

"So you happened to pass by," said Papa disagreeably. "You can tell anybody in London Junction to mind their own goddam business, and I'll do the same."

Bonnie bit her lip and then decided to ignore Papa's mood. She gave a gay laugh.

"I'd be sore if I didn't know you were always kidding, Harry Willard!" she said. "You wouldn't be cross to an old friend like me. I know you like me too much for that. Just for spite, I'm going to give you a big kiss."

This was done, with some embarrassed remonstrances from Papa, and then suddenly capitulating he waltzed Bonnie around the room in a tight embrace, to the delight of the girls.

"Just like when Mama was alive!" they exclaimed in chorus.

Papa stopped abruptly, leaving Bonnie dizzily hanging on to a chair, laughing breathlessly.

"Bonnie looks like Mama, doesn't she, Papa?" said Marcia.

"Not a bit," Papa said. "Your Mama never painted her face."

Bonnie rubbed her cheeks.

"I guess the first Mrs. Willard was a mighty pretty woman," she said.

"First and *only* Mrs. Willard," Papa corrected. Having succeeded in making Bonnie dab at her eyes with a handkerchief, he seemed cheered.

"I hear you're going steady with every fellow on the Big Four," he said, smiling. "Got to have your good time, I guess, haven't you, Bonnie?"

"I don't like to sit around being lonesome for anybody," Bonnie said, chin now going in air. "Speaking of paint, I don't lay it on the way certain Lesterville women do, folks you seem to think are all right or you wouldn't be chasing them, from stories I hear."

Papa laughed amiably.

"I'm not chasing anybody," Papa said. "If I was chasing anybody it wouldn't be somebody that got herself talked about in every saloon from here to Cincinnati."

"I don't know who you have reference to, Mr. Willard," Bonnie said, voice trembling.

"Getting engaged to three fellows at once, dating up a dozen others on the side," Papa said. "Not that it's anything to me. I just hate to see a nice girl make herself look cheap."

"I can't help who says they're engaged to who," Bonnie said. "Personally, I don't intend to get married, ever. Not on a bet."

"That's fine," Papa said. "Anybody that gets herself talked about can't expect a decent man to marry them."

"A decent man doesn't hang around those girls in Stein's Cafe," Bonnie said. She was trying not to cry. "A decent man doesn't get a girl started caring for him, then act huffy when she shows a little affection. If he acted a little nicer, maybe she wouldn't go round trying to have what little pleasure she can."

"Staying all night at Cedar Point," Papa said, musingly. "A fine thing."

Bonnie burst into tears.

"If you knew so much you could have stopped me, Harry Willard," she sobbed. "What have you got against me, anyway? What have I done except be a friend?"

Papa was at a loss over this, and looked scowlingly at the floor.

"It's your coming over here to criticize," he said. "All I get everywhere I go since Daisy died is criticism. By God, it's more than a man can stand, working night and day, doing his best, taking care of his family all alone, friendless—"

"Ed Hartwell is over at Mabel's," Bonnie said. "They're your friends, aren't they? To tell the truth, I was on my way there this minute."

She began pinning on her hat, her lips still quivering.

Papa said nothing and at the door she turned.

"Any message for Ed?" Bonnie asked. "Maybe you might drop around. Far be it from me to suggest."

"Couldn't do it," Papa said.

The girls watched Bonnie leave, resignedly. No picture show, no streetcar ride, nobody ever kept promises, not even Bonnie.

And Papa had been cross with her, so perhaps she'd never come again. He didn't even say goodbye to Bonnie when she went, but after a little while he picked up his hat and left. He didn't come back that night, nor was he back the next morning when Aunt Lois marvellously appeared, just as Lena had begged.

"You mean your father hasn't been home since yesterday afternoon?" she exclaimed, after the first joys of reunion. "What did you have for lunch this noon?"

"We made hot water soup," said Lena. "You boil the water and put in salt and pepper and buttered crackers for oysters, so it tastes like oyster soup."

Aunt Lois looked thoughtfully around the rooms, made no comment while they admiringly described the details of Bonnie Purdy's costume, and the news that she was visiting Mabel and Mr. Hartwell. Presently she accosted Mrs. Jane in the hallway and there was a low-voiced conference, clicking of tongues, shaking of heads on both sides, sighs, shrugs, sorrowful glances at the girls, all ending up in Mrs. Jane helping Aunt Lois find a suitcase into which to put their clothes. Lena nudged Marcia. "We're going back to London Junction," her lips formed the words.

"But we can't," Marcia lamented in a whisper. "The truant officer will come after us tomorrow if we don't go to school."

"We'll be in school there," said Lena rapturously. "With Mary Evelyn."

"Put on your coats, you're coming home with me," said Aunt Lois, buckling the straps of the wicker suitcase. She shook her head significantly at Mrs. Jane. "It's beyond me. I honestly wouldn't have believed it, well as I know Harry Willard. I advise you to get your money from him, Mrs. Jane, before he skips. That's the way Harry is. Oh, you poor kids!"

There was delay in leaving, eager as the older two were to go anywhere and have something happen, anything at all. Florrie sat on the floor and sobbed that she would not leave Papa, that she wouldn't leave Mrs. Jane's tomcat, Tommy, and that she had to look after her dear Papa because he had said so. Marcia suddenly remembered she had two library books out, *The Green Fairy Book* and *The Blue Fairy* Book, and unless she took them back tomorrow she would have to pay four cents or else the police would come to London Junction and get her. Mrs. Jane promised not only to deliver the books but not to give her address to the police in case of delay. Florrie stuck to her guns till the threat of leaving without her brought her, weeping, after them. The faint twinges about Papa's reaction were lost completely in the unexpected treat of being driven all the way back to London Junction in Mr. Sweeney's new Winton car. The three sat in the back and sang the songs they knew, very loud when they passed Burnadetta's house on East Park. Aunt Lois sat in front with Mr. Sweeney, talking earnestly in the low emphatic tone which always meant "something was going to be done about the girls."

PART THREE

home

is

far

away

23

THERE WERE DIFFERENT KINDS OF HAPPINESS, Marcia decided. What most people wanted was the happiness of having what other people wanted. Then they had brief moments of an inferior happiness when they only got what they themselves but nobody else wanted. This rather spoiled things. Some people made mistakes in their opinion of what other people wanted, but if they didn't find out they managed to be happy, maybe wondering a little once in a while what everybody wanted this for. Others wasted so much time trying to have what other people wanted that sometimes they never knew they were perfectly happy without it. The biggest jolt in growing up was to discover that you didn't like what others liked and they thought you were crazy to like what you liked.

Marcia thought the greatest happiness was to be left alone. If anybody was around they kept you from thinking or reading or else made fun of your diary or whipped you or scolded you about something. Lena wanted everything other girls wanted, whether she really liked it or not, and since these were all tangible objects costing money, Lena was unhappy a good deal of the time. Florrie's happiness consisted in having people love her and fondle her and refrain from unkind words about anybody. There were definite barometers for people's happiness, too. You could tell Aunt Lois's by the sudden richness of her laugh, and the way her blond curls kinked up of their own accord. You could tell Grandma's by the way she smiled secretly to herself over her mending, moving her lips and nodding complacently as if at her age she knew better than to have her pleasure spoiled by telling it to some jealous confidante. You could tell Papa's by the cocky set of his hat and by his walk.

It was evident that Papa was pretty happy about something that summer of 1911 because his stiff straw hat sat snappily on the side of his wavy brown hair or else tilted itself merrily over one eyebrow. His hat was as sensitive to the master's temper as Aunt Lois's hair was to hers; it seemed to rejoice all of itself in a happy secret, rearing itself up at the slightest touch of the hand, never sedately straight as in his somber moods. Papa's shoes, too, seemed to dance along by themselves, and in these happy moments his footsteps coming down the sidewalk sounded like a tap dance. He had a travelling job again for the Cleveland Excelsior Cement Company, working for a Mr. Balzer who, he declared, was just about the biggest man in the cement business, as well as a hell of a fine man. Give him a German any day, he said, in preference to these Bohemian novelty men; he'd said it before, and he'd say it again: the cement business, when managed by a superior fellow like Oscar Balzer, was about the most exclusive and up-and-coming business a man could get into. He visited his daughters every three or four weeks on his London Junction trip, and usually brought them a box of Chandler & Rudd salted almonds, or peppermint candy hearts, or joke books. He almost pacified Aunt Lois's prejudices by presenting her with a box of Mama's jewelry, including the fleur-de-lys watch and pin, and the garnet pin and her garnet earrings. They both cried over this, and said how pleased Daisy would be at his disposal of her jewels. Aunt Lois said it was about the sweetest thing Harry had ever done.

"You'll find out the kind of man I am one of these days, Lois," Papa said, wiping his eyes. "I'll betcha anything Daisy knows how I try just as well as if she was alive. You've always criticized but you'll find out I'm always looking for some way to do what Daisy

would want of me, and that's all I ask. Well, by George, I think
I've got a chance right now to please Daisy and when I do it you
can bet your sweet life Daisy up there is going to be tickled to
death."

Aunt Lois said cautiously that she didn't know what he was
up to but she sincerely hoped it would be for the best. She said so
far as she was concerned she'd never had anything against him, except the way he ran up bills and neglected his children, but she'd
always said he'd come through in the long run. At least she hoped
so. She said Daisy had always thought the sun rose and set on him,
and that was why it seemed a shame, seeing him run around with
girls like Bonnie Purdy, who couldn't be mentioned in the same
breath with dear Daisy.

"You're absolutely right and I'll shake on it," Papa agreed
solemnly. "You know what's what, Lois, in spite of being so bull-
headed about everything. Yes, sir, I may have had too good a time
now and then, but something always held me back from getting
in too deep. It was like Daisy was whispering to me, 'Now, wait a
minute, Harry. Think of the kids. Is this the right thing for them?'
And I'd back right down. That's the way it's been from the day she
died and that's a fact."

Aunt Lois pinned the fleur-de-lys pin on her fresh pink poplin
dress, and Papa looked at it with moist, sentimental eyes. Suddenly
he said, "Tell you what, Lois, I'd better get that watch cleaned and
repaired before I give it to you."

"I can have it done right here, Harry," Aunt Lois said.

"No, I know a fellow in Cleveland who'll do it for nothing as a
favor to me," Papa said. "I happen to have done a few favors for
him and he'll be glad to fix it up good as new. The clasp is a little
loose, and I wouldn't want you to lose it."

"We—ell—"

Aunt Lois reluctantly handed over the watch, which Papa
quickly wrapped in the chamois bag and pocketed with a suspicious air of finality. This put a little dampener on the reconcili-
ation, especially since Papa immediately left the house, whistling

"The Whistler and His Dog" as he jauntily stepped down the walk. Aunt Lois looked moodily after him.

"I don't know what's got into him to be so darn tickled with himself," she observed, and repeated the incident to Mr. Sweeney, later on, over a plate of oysters he had brought from Lesterville.

"Some woman, take my word for it," said Mr. Sweeney.

This turned out to be the truth. Papa was about to get married. As he frequently boasted later on, the news of the wedding was written up all over the country, in three newspapers to be exact. He had the clippings to prove it. Aunt Lois thought the children should have been invited to the wedding, especially since the bride's own child by a former marriage would be present; however, it meant railroad tickets and new dresses, so Papa vetoed the suggestion. Besides, the bride said that one child underfoot at a wedding was enough; time enough to take the others on after they were settled. Aunt Lois held out that Florrie at least should go, being Papa's favorite and a decoration to any gathering, but Papa was too impressed with his new wife's family to agree. In his preliminary discussions of the marriage he had proudly boasted not of his fiancée's beauty or virtues but of her folks.

"Finest people in Daleport," he stated. "Genuine old Western Reserve stock, not like London Junction folks at all. Originally from Vermont, fine old New England folks."

Aunt Lois, ruffled by the turn affairs had taken, retorted that most everybody came from New England at one time or another, because there was no place else to come from unless they were immigrants, and the reason they came was they were such mean skinflints they wanted to get whatever property they could for nothing, and if they were so fine they wouldn't have needed to leave Vermont in the first place. Papa was dashed by this for a moment, but he would not have his triumph spoiled. He reminded Aunt Lois that the new Mrs. Willard was second cousin to J. B. Hawkins of Ashtabula, one-time Congressman. Aunt Lois replied that this didn't make Mrs. Willard a Congressman, and she didn't see what was so wonderful about being cousins, especially *second*

cousins of anybody, because second cousins never left you anything, and besides she'd read in the *Literary Digest* that the entire
white race was thirty-second cousins of each other. The onion being
the cousin of the lily didn't make it any posy, she said, or smell any
the better.

Papa had brought his news to her in a genial, all-forgiving
mood, certain that at last he was doing the right thing, so that
Aunt Lois's testy reaction gave him more sorrow than anger. His
proud, beaming smile changed to an expression of grieved bewilderment.

"I don't understand you, Lois," he said, shaking his head.
"You've been raising Cain for years about my running with the
wrong women, so I go out of my way to get a real lady, someone
Daisy would be sure to say would make a good, refined mother for
the girls. And already you're giving me hell for it. If they aren't too
tough for you, they're too refined; that's about the size of it. God
damn, what's a man to do, trying to do the right thing and always
getting kicked in the pants for it?"

He stalked out of the house, glowering, leaving Aunt Lois
to pursue her unfavorable reflections aloud to the children. They
were puzzled as much as their father had been by her indignation,
since she had often darkly hinted at the day he would some day
disgrace them all by marrying Bonnie Purdy. Marcia and Florrie
had hoped this disgrace would happen, but Lena, who was more
socially advanced now, had primly informed Papa one day that
she would run away if he married Bonnie, because Mary Evelyn's
mother said Bonnie wasn't nice. Papa was a little afraid of his oldest daughter, but he said he guessed Bonnie Purdy was about as
nice as Mary Evelyn's mother, but he had no intention of marrying
either one. When news came of the new marriage, Lena gravely
thanked her father for following her advice. Marcia was glad of
any change, but Florrie wept that she did not want any new mama;
she had only one mama, and nobody could make her have another
one. Eventually they received souvenir postcards of Niagara Falls
and the three clippings of the wedding.

"Friends of Harry Willard in London Junction," said the *London Junction Register,* "will be interested to learn of his recent marriage to Mrs. Idah Hawkins Turner of Daleport. Mr. Willard has recently taken a position as manager of the London Junction Furniture Company's Retail Store and Funeral Parlor on Main Street. He is the brother-in-law of Mrs. Lois Blair, long a resident here, with whom his three children have made their home."

The *Daleport Sentinel* said, "Mrs. Idah Hawkins Turner, age 36, became the bride yesterday of Mr. Harry Willard, 37, of London Junction, in a small but tasteful ceremony at the home of Mrs. Turner's mother, Mrs. Minnie Hawkins. The bride was formerly a trained nurse in Columbus, but retired three years ago to marry the well-known Daleport dentist, Dr. Ephraim Turner, who died last year at the age of 61, leaving one infant, little Minelda May. The couple was attended by Mr. Ed Hartwell of Lesterville, as best man, and the bride's sister, Mrs. Burns, as matron of honor. Reverend Timothy Thompson was the officiating clergyman, and delicious refreshments were enjoyed by all."

The *Elmville Republican* said, "News has reached friends here of the second marriage of Henry Willard, formerly of Peach Street, and the Busby Hotel. The first Mrs. Willard, affectionately remembered here as Daisy Reed, passed away six years ago leaving three little daughters. Mr. Willard's new bride attended his first wife's last illness in the capacity of nurse, and after her first marriage resided in Daleport, where the present wedding took place. She is the second cousin of former Congressman J. B. Hawkins."

The big news, such as to stun Aunt Lois into silence, appeared in the London Junction paper two weeks later. "The Main Street Realty Company announces the sale of the Furness house, long vacant, to Mrs. Idah Hawkins Willard, recently married to Harry Willard. Mrs. Willard has been negotiating for the property for some time, and on a recent flying trip to the Junction arranged for its repair. It is expected the property will be in readiness for the couple on their return next month from a month's honeymoon."

"The Furness house!" gasped all who heard. "So Harry married money! Well, what do you know!"

Aunt Lois eventually found the right answer to this.

"Money, of course she has money. Why else do you think she put her hooks into that dentist, an old man twice her age? Everybody in that part of the state says he was dying when she nailed him and had him sign over everything to her on the wedding day. Left her close to fifteen thousand dollars! At that, she got a bargain on the Furness house. Trust Harry Willard to land on his feet!"

This made Aunt Lois madder than anything else. Now Papa was reaping rewards for extravagance and mismanagement, while she, who had made up to his family for his delinquencies, could barely keep her head above water. As she said to Mr. Sweeney, Daisy would turn over in her grave if she but knew.

24

EVERYBODY IN LONDON JUNCTION talked about the second
Mrs. Willard's trousseau, and several ladies had even paid
formal calls for the express purpose of examining it. There
was her off-white satin wedding dress with the short, pearl-se-
quined veil, her fawn-colored broadcloth traveling suit trimmed in
brown soutache, with a peg-top skirt, brown horsehair toque and
gloves to match, her purple taffeta petticoat and umbrella, her
peach-colored *crepe de chine* party dress with beaded panel down
the front and baby blue velvet forget-me-nots appliqued around
the flounce, and her big horsehair picture hat weighted with huge
roses. For every day she had the clothes left over from her mourn-
ing period for the late Dr. Turner. Her early weeks in London Junction were marked by magic transformations from mousy little
grub by morning into radiant butterfly by dusk, radiance graded
to suit whatever occasion was on hand. Papa strutted when he
escorted this fashionable figure down Main Street on Saturday
nights to the picture show or on Sundays to the First Methodist
Church, wheeling little Minelda May in the very latest go-cart
from the Store. Marcia, Lena, and Florrie followed at an admiring
distance, proud of the stares at their new mother's city dresses, and
shocked to hear later that their own shabbiness was as much a subject of comment as their stepmother's elegance.

It was like a dream to walk home from school straight up the Furness front walk. After a while Mrs. Willard ruled that they were to use the back alley and back door, because they tracked up the new broadloom carpet. Their first rapture over the change in their fortunes was not easily quenched. It was true that the Furness place, after years of neglect, was no longer the show place of London Junction, but it was still to them the fairytale castle it had been when Papa first promised it to Mama, and they had played there, pretending to own it. It was far too big to refurnish, so several rooms were shut up. The three girls used one big bedroom, with a cot in the alcove for Florrie. Their new mother said that girls' rooms shouldn't be cluttered up with a lot of junk, so, to tell the truth, it looked more bleak than the house's exterior grandeur would indicate. Downstairs, the big parlor was decorated with the very latest in furniture, rugs and drapes from the Store (payment deducted from Papa's salary for the next thirty months), with a grand piano in the middle of the room. A purple plush scarf, with gold roses painted upon it, added a royal richness to the piano, crowned in addition by a funereal-looking amphora of gilded wheat. The piano was queen of the parlor, with two bright blue plush chairs, overstuffed and tasselled, as its duchesses. These were placed before the fireplace (made up-to-date with artificial gas logs) and their dignity enhanced by a stiff hand-embroidered sofa cushion laid against each right foreleg. A vast blue davenport between the chairs was so rigidly overstuffed that its cushions popped up waist high. The parlor seemed made not for living inhabitants but for these regal pieces of furniture which frowned at any violation of their lofty privacy and brooked no touch but the reverent dusting ministrations of their priestess, Mrs. Willard.

Behind the davenport was a mahogany refectory table bearing a top-heavy gold pagoda of a lamp. On one side was placed a limp leather volume of Whittier's *Snowbound,* and on the other a silver framed photograph of the wedding party, with Minelda's diaper showing. The "changeable" wallpaper of purple into rose permitted but two works of art to "mark up" its distinction, one of these a small violently colored view of a rose-covered cottage doorway, the other a large gold-framed copy of a shallow brown brook with a deer peeping through brown willow branches beside it. Culture was modestly represented by an old golden oak bookcase reclaimed from the Friends' attic and properly hidden behind two potted palms. The old books were there as they had been in Mama's day, but to save wear and tear they were locked up. Florrie's big doll was locked in here so she wouldn't break it, and also her sisters' gilt-edged diaries, because Mrs. Willard was a careful woman and felt that all possessions were better locked up, since it was regrettably impossible to lock up their owners.

"I want to teach the girls to take care of things," she told Papa. "They've lived such a helter-skelter life, they've got to learn how nice people act. Supposing some of my relations, like Cousin Jay from Ashtabula, would come to visit us. Why, he'd think they were little hoodlums."

"That's the ticket," Papa agreed, with satisfaction. "I want you to make ladies of 'em. God knows, I can't do it, because it takes a lady to make 'em act right. That's what their own mother would want."

The girls were in a daze over their sudden ascent in the world. Imagine living in the big Furness house, with a piano and pictures and balconies and thick rugs. Every day there was some new luxury added to the household. Mrs. Willard considered it stylish to subscribe to a magazine of some sort, and, after discussing the matter for several evenings with her husband and callers, settled on *The Delineator*. A magazine rack was immediately purchased for this, and to keep it company the *Lesterville Weekly Courier* and the London Junction Furniture Company catalogue. The girls were not allowed to touch this collection, however, because they would muss up everything. At first they were too awed by their new splendor to resent the rules for its protection. At school they boasted of their new mother and their new house, the dumb-waiter, the big empty stables, the fountain that didn't work, the iron dog. Lena, always more courageous than her sisters, even planned and issued invitations to her classmates and teachers to a big party (with favors and games and prizes like Myrtle Chase's parties), date to be determined later. It was just as well that she had a fight with Mary Evelyn over the invitation list, because it gave an excuse for calling the whole thing off with no loss of dignity. Their new mother, they announced, was richer than anybody in London Junction; she had a whole cedar chest full of Philippine embroidered underwear; she owned a cottage at Silver Lake where undoubtedly they would henceforth spend their summers lolling in rowboats and collecting shells; she had a fabulous brother Vance who spent a year or two in military school, and had been to New York City, and she had relatives of great consequence in the East, in addition to her cousin, the Ashtabula Congressman. Papa overheard these vulgar boasts and reprimanded the girls severely, though he himself was making important references to these advantages at his lodge and around the Store.

Papa was actually walking on air, between his residence in the Furness house and his magnificent new title as manager of the Store. He had cards printed with his name and a new middle initial he had added for style—"Mr. Harry J. Willard, General Manager, London Furniture Store, London Junction. Your Home is Your Castle, Let Us Furnish It. *Undertaking Parlors.*" The Store was the newest business building in the Junction, with plate-glass windows on one entire side, and the wholesale offices and catalogue department located on the two floors above. A great billboard advertising the Store rose above the roof, giving a respectable impression of a five-story building to fascinated passengers whizzing by on trains. Papa took his daughters down to look over his new headquarters very soon after he settled there, but on the advice of his wife finally forbade them to come in the Store except on the most vital errand. It was too bad, for all three had spotted wonderful corners for play in the great showroom. There was a smell of varnish and new wood as soon as you stepped inside, and an impressive vista of glossy dining tables, buffets, Windsor chairs, settees, crowds of fat overstuffed chairs adorned with tassels, fringes, tapestry insets, and so pompous in their new-ness and overstuffedness that it must have taken great courage to invite one to take its place in a simple parlor with lesser pieces. Floor lamps and table lamps of all shapes and sizes were lit all day to demonstrate their charms; some were ingeniously attached to the arm of a chair, a smoking stand, or built into a center table. A mezzanine floor with elegant gold-trimmed balustrade held the many styles of beds from veneered bronze maple to burled walnut. The place really got its elegant tone, aside from its artistic furni-ture, from a Chinese incense burner hanging in the living-room suite department, blending its Sen-Sen and strawberry shrub fragrance with that of furniture polish and glue, also from the huge Victor Talking Machine with megaphone which boomed out richly over the Store and on to the street a perpetual chorus of "Come, Come, I Want You Only." It was worth the price of ad-mission just working in a place like that, Papa said happily, and with a treat like that on the premises he didn't see how he could keep the customers out. His old Lesterville friend from the High Class Novelty Works dropped in one day (Mr. Taylor), and after a tour of the place shook his head and said it was too rich for his blood. He was so awed by the sight of Papa in white collar, black suit, and shiny black shoes, moving gracefully among all this lux-ury, changing the Victrola needle, relighting the incense burner, conferring with the mortician glibly on choice of coffin linings, that he skulked out of the place while Papa was still showing off, and was never seen in the Store again.

All in all the Willard girls felt that they had come into a fairy-tale world, and the town itself was impressed. Papa adopted a brisk but somber manner suited to his new position, kept away from the Elks' Club and the London Junction Hotel, spoke to his former cronies from his travelling salesman and railroad life with the proper mingling of friendliness and aloofness. It seemed to him that every person he met in his day's work was looking at him with awe and inwardly exclaiming, "Harry Willard, of all people! A self-made man, by George, a living success story. Said he'd make good and darned if he hasn't. Leading citizen, topnotch business-man, well, well, well!" His daughters looked at him with rever-ence for this magic he had wrought. They bragged about it to their schoolmates and by night they gloated over it to each other.

But the adjustment to good fortune is sometimes as hard to make as the adjustment to bad fortune. Anxious as they were to live up to the new standard, there seemed to be not one single thing they could do to suit their new mother. They didn't even know why it was wrong, because she just stood shaking her head in despair and sometimes throwing up her hands as if there was no coping with such stupidity. They didn't open or shut doors right, they walked on their heels instead of their toes, they wiped their hands on their napkins or else they didn't, they sat on the bed, they sat on the chairs, they sang till the place sounded like bedlam, they went around in old clothes, looking like perfect little tramps and shaming their elders, or else they wanted to wear their best clothes and ruin them. Efforts to do right in the face of these confused complaints seemed hopeless, and even Papa was unsympathetic. Coming home at night beaming with his new triumphs, he was righteously annoyed to be brought down to earth by his wife's complaints about his children.

"I'm surprised at you girls," he scolded. "I got a fine new home for you, just like your own mother always wanted for you, and you don't know how to act right. You don't say 'thank you' and you don't mind. If you don't try to behave yourselves, I'll send you off some place, I swear. You got to learn to appreciate what people are trying to do for you. Lena, you're the oldest. I'm going to count on you to keep the others toeing the mark. You're grow-ing up and it's time you learned how to be ladies."

But it was Lena who made the first big mistake. She was anxious to be the new mama's pet, so she earnestly tried to ingratiate herself by relating the defects of her younger sisters with gloomy prophecies of what would become of them if they didn't follow her own example. She said that Marcia did not wear her galoshes or mittens and hid them in a tree trunk on her way to school, and that in the school cloakroom she rouged her face with red crepe paper. She said that Florrie was always dragging around a dirty kitten named Snowball and hiding it in the bedroom until she, Lena, was afraid they'd all catch the mange from it. She was afraid they'd catch roup from the sick chicken Florrie had carried around for a day or two, too. The new Mrs. Willard approved of Lena's helpful information and instructed her to punish these misdemeanors if they came up again. Heady with power, Lena brought Mary Evelyn home one day to show off the house, taking care to do so when she thought no one was around, so she could take her in the front door.

"This is the parlor," she said with a wave of her hand. "Twenty-two by thirty."

Mary Evelyn could not disguise her admiration and envy for a moment, then inquired with a mean smirk why the piano was locked, and was it because nobody was allowed to play it. Taunted by this, Lena was driven to look for the key in the kitchen cabinet, where unfortunately she did find it in the broken sugar bowl. She haughtily invited Mary Evelyn to join her in a duet and they were seated playing "Chopsticks" when suddenly a figure loomed in the doorway. It was the new Mrs. Willard in her fawn-colored suit. Her face was white and stony, her marble eyes sparked with fury. Not quite sure what was wrong, both girls froze at this image of wrath. The lady stalked over to the piano and shut down the keyboard almost on their very fingers.

"Give me that key," she commanded in a low hoarse voice, and as Lena weakly obeyed she said through her teeth, "You are not to touch this piano, never, do you hear?"

"I was only—"

"None of your impudence!" Mrs. Willard snarled. "Who told you you could come in this room? I won't have you little demons trooping in and out, pawing my good furniture with your filthy hands. Your father will hear of this."

Mary Evelyn was out of the door and halfway down the block in a flash. But Lena, after her first shock, stubbornly stood her ground.

"I guess I'm supposed to have my music lessons, like my father promised," she said haughtily. "Where am I supposed to practice?"

"I don't know and I don't care," muttered Mrs. Willard. "Just stay out of this room with your dirty boots."

On the front porch Minelda, still in her carriage, wailed loudly to be brought inside.

"Let her yell," Lena said in a loud voice, and ran to join Mary Evelyn.

The former Miss Hawkins stood for a moment darting her eyes about the room, studying what must be done to repair the desolate ruin that twenty minutes of invasion had wrought. Without taking off her hat—it was the big one with the flowers— she ran for a dust cloth and began frantically to polish away imaginary stains from the piano. She tested a few notes to see how much out of key the abuse had left the sensitive instrument, then for a final test sat down to play her one and only selection, "Work for the Night is Coming," with one hand. The notes seemed unimpaired, but she shook her head convinced that some interior damage had been done, then she locked the keyboard lovingly. She got down on her knees to wipe from a very red rose in the car- pet the mud tracks she fancied must be there. It took her several minutes to arrange *Snowbound* at its proper angle on the refectory table, and even then her earnest inspection could not inform her whether its contents had been violated by the intruder's eyes. In the midst of these repairs she suddenly realized that Lena had ac- tually drawn up one of the white shades, and this atrocity brought from her a moan of genuine anguish. Her eyes were red rimmed when Papa came home, and when he asked what was wrong, she put her head on his shoulder and sobbed, "Oh Harry, Harry, what am I going to do? I can't stand seeing our home wrecked by these children. You've got to speak to them, dear, before they pull the whole place down around our ears!"

25

AFTER HER FIRST DIFFICULTY with her stepmother, Lena refused to take any orders except from Papa. She said she was too big to be looking after other people's babies, and if anyone had to wheel Minelda after school it would have to be Marcia. Marcia did not mind this chore very much, since it let her out of playing games with the schoolchildren, and besides she felt there was no use arguing about it. She got a book out of the library every day and read as she wheeled. If Minelda yelled too loudly, she was sometimes exasperated to the point of giving her a good pinch. Minelda was two and a half, sickly and inclined to whimpering, brought on by the thorough manner she was bundled up by her devoted mother, even in summer. Minelda tossed and squirmed under her usually wet woolens, suffering from prickly heat, and her pinched little face was white to the point of blueness. Her steady squirming and tugging at her little harness did not penetrate Marcia's consciousness, absorbed as she was in her book. Even when Minelda managed to wriggle half out of her go-cart, her little caretaker paid no attention, since the sobs presently subsided into chokes and gurgles as she hung herself by her strap. Sometimes a book would be so entrancing that Marcia, resting the open book on the buggy's handle bar, would be wheeling for several minutes peacefully before noticing that the go-cart was empty.

Emerging from her daydream, Marcia would presently recognize distant shrieks and there would be Minelda, far back in the ditch where an unexpected jolt had thrown her. As soon as they were near home Minelda set up a defiant howl proclaiming all these indignities until her mother rushed out of the kitchen to snatch her up into protective arms.

"You poor, poor baby, what has that bad girl done to you?" she cried out, which set Minelda off into new sobs and indignant glares at Marcia. "Where did this bruise come from? And just look at the way she's dirtied up your nice clean pillow! Get a rag and wipe off these wheels this very minute, Marcia Willard! I never saw such a disgraceful sight. No wonder the poor child cries!"

Attention being directed to the damage done the go-cart and Minelda, Marcia registered mild astonishment on seeing that there were dents in the carriage where she had absentmindedly banged it into a tree or wall. Remnants of twigs and gravel on Minelda's bib indicated a misguided feast on definitely inedible items.

"She'll be sick!" moaned her mother. "Why did you let her?"

"I can't help it if a person wants to eat caterpillars," Marcia argued in self-defense. "If that's what she likes, I can't stop her."

"Wheel her down the paved streets after this," Minelda's mother commanded. "Why must you always take these back alleys?"

"Because my dress is torn, that's why," Marcia said.

"I'd be ashamed to be so vain," said her stepmother. "Nobody is looking at an ugly little girl like you, anyway. Wait a minute, now, what are you hiding under your jacket? Is that a book?"

The crime was out, try as Marcia did to conceal her book. Mrs. Willard snatched at it.

"That's why you're so careless. Head so full of nonsense and silly stories you don't even know you're alive. No wonder! Well, I'll see to it you get your library card stopped."

The glamor of their new life slowly sifted down to its disagreeable reality. Here they were in a fine big house with a new mother who had pretty clothes and a piano, and with their father a dignified public figure "out of the woods" at last, as he himself proudly put it. Mr. and Mrs. Harry Willard were mentioned at least once a week in the *Register* as being present at the Masonic Banquet, guests at Mr. Carson's Memorial Dinner, patrons of the London Junction Boosters Annual Minstrel Show, with invitations to be members of the Bridge Club, and Mrs. Willard elected second vice-president of the Women's Century Reading Club. Such social prominence was more than the family had ever dreamed of, and was commented upon enviously by all the relations. But try as they would, there seemed no place in this charmed life for anybody but Papa, Idah Hawkins Willard, and possibly Minelda. The night the Willards took their turn at entertaining the Bridge Club (refreshments of beer, pretzels, ice cream and cake; prizes, a handembroidered muffin towel and a burnt leather wallet) the children were instructed not to show themselves downstairs under any circumstances. Marcia and Lena exchanged a look of consternation, having boasted for several days to their schoolmates of this great event.

"When it meets at Mrs. Carson's, Barbara passes things," Lena said.

"Maybe they could come down and sing something," Papa suggested.

"What would they wear?" his bride inquired. "They'd look like little tramps and nobody wants children running around at a nice party."

The Bridge Club was a really devastating blow. Lena and Florrie had invited their intimate friends to come play with them during the party and they were desperately wondering how to ward them off. Lena sneaked down the back stairs during the party and brought back cruel reports of the party's progress. Two of Florrie's classmates had been brought by their parents to play with Florrie, and were seen enjoying ice cream and cake. Furthermore, Lena had heard her stepmother explaining that the reason Florrie couldn't come down was that she was sick. Worse yet, one child was permitted—even urged—to render her piece, "Angel's

Serenade," on the piano, when Lena could play it much faster if anybody would ever give her the chance. This shocking event brought gloom to the bedroom when Lena reported it.

"Didn't Papa do anything about it?" Marcia asked.

"Papa clapped," Lena said. "Then he and Mr. Chase said they would go downtown and get some more beer, and they haven't come back yet and She is mad as hops. She keeps getting up from the card table and emptying the ash trays even when there's nothing in them."

"I'm not a bit sick," Florrie brooded, sitting up in bed. "She oughtn't to tell lies about me. I won't even try to call her 'mama' like she said we should."

It was the beginning of calling the new mother "She."

26

THE BRIDAL CHAMBER was on the second floor, and was so beautiful that the door was kept locked. No matter how often the bride went in and out She carefully took her keys from her pocket and shut off this paradise from prying little eyes. As the bookcase, parlor, piano, icebox, clothes chests, and closets were also kept locked, the girls were resigned to the bedroom's beauties being denied them. They had viewed it once on a tour of the house with Aunt Lois, and once Florrie had taken a little colored girl of her acquaintance up over the porch roof to peer in the window, for the secrecy had persuaded her there must be fairy queens and magic carpets there. But there was only the canopy bed left from the Furness estate, draped in pink silkalene, and the new bride's gold dresser set and knicknacks. At night they could hear the door being locked and what seemed sounds of quarrelling—"Now, Harry! Harry, now stop! Harry, if you don't stop, now, I'll never forgive you. Now, now, now, Harry, stop!"

The second Mrs. Willard had changed very little since her first appearance in London Junction as Idah Hawkins, nurse to the first Mrs. Willard's last illness. Motherhood had added no curves to her slight figure, so She resorted to modest padding here and there for style, and Lena on a snooping trip reported that the lady's suit with weights and paddings actually weighed more than

She did. For dressy purposes there was a jar of Hygienic Vegetable Rouge, which She rubbed carefully into a small circle in each cheek. Her faded scanty hair was decorated with switch, curls, and other devices of a richer golden hue, and when other ladies admired the coiffure She modestly boasted that it took three-quarters of an hour to get it that way. She said most women didn't have the patience, but She had always taken pains with her appearance and saw no reason for a real lady to let herself slide. She liked her little girl to look nice, too, and it was funny to hear the poor child cry just because the other girls had dirtied her up. When someone referred to her first encounter with Harry Willard, a twinkle came into her pale marble eyes and She tittered, "I had my eye on him right off, even then." It seems that when her first husband, Dr. Turner, passed on, the very first thing She had done was to buy some stock in the London Furniture Company. Then She asked Mr. Carson, the company president, what had happened to Harry Willard and Mr. Carson said, by George, he needed a man like Willard again, so he sent for him. That was how it started, what with her business trips to the Junction, and Mr. Carson trying to locate Harry again, old differences forgotten.

"Well, it takes a lot of courage to marry a widower with three little girls," Mary Evelyn's mother said, the day of her call, for which she had had fifty new calling cards specially engraved, in addition to purchasing a new Alice blue suit with red buttons and trimming to show that other ladies in London Junction besides the new Mrs. Willard knew the styles. The new bride gravely acknowledged her guest's compliment.

"The thing is not to let them take advantage," She explained. "They've been spoiled so, it's going to take a lot of managing, but it's just like I told Dr. Turner when I found out how spoiled *he* was. 'Your mother may have let you spill your ashes all over the floor, but she's dead now, and if you are set on smoking you take it right out to the garage where it belongs.' You have to let 'em know where you stand right at the start."

In spite of this statement, Mrs. Idah Willard's "stand" was so elaborate, and involved so many contingencies, that her new family despaired of ever getting it straight. First, they were to stay out of the house except for sleeping and eating. Second, they were not to sit out on the lawn mooning where everybody could see them, nor were they to go visiting relatives or school friends or have them call. They were not to use their school paper for games, because it cost money, nor were they to keep reading in their school readers for fun after their lesson was learned. They were to make themselves useful, instead of ornamental, but on the other hand She'd rather do all the housework herself than have them singing songs while they made beds or washed dishes. Their duties were to pick up scraps on the front lawn, tend to Minelda, and run errands. They were not to go places where townspeople would talk about their ragged clothes, but they were not allowed to use their sewing boxes either, because needles and thread cost money. They might sit in the old carriage barn, but they were to just sit there, not pretend they were riding or indeed pretend any other kind of nonsense, and if they tracked in mud when they came in to supper She would straighten them out. The "straightening out" was unpleasant, since She was so small She had to resort to tricks for her force, such as pinching them or cracking their heads with her diamond ring. Marcia found a handsome silver-tasselled little whip in the street after the circus parade, and this She at once appropriated, saying grimly as She locked it in the closet, "You'll get your whip when you ask for it." When Marcia stiffly refused to react to her whippings, She complained to Papa that he would have to punish the girls, since they were so wayward they wouldn't even cry. Florrie had croup and She tied a coal-oil bandage around her neck which burned her fearfully all night. Marcia and Lena sat up all night thinking maybe Florrie would die of pain but they were afraid to call out or tell Papa because they were sure this was part of Her plan. In the morning, She took off the bandage and when the skin came off with it She tittered, "My goodness, I forgot to put vaseline on first." There was no use telling these things to Papa, because She always told him something else first, and as he often said, it looked like his sister-in-law, Lois, was putting the kids up to mischief just to spoil the first break he'd ever had. She was afraid to whip Lena, however, since Lena threatened to tell Mr. Carson's daughter, Barbara. Lena was pretty independent, and all She could do was grind her teeth when Lena did as she pleased. Lena wouldn't come straight home from school, because she was organizing an exclusive after-school group of three into the "Buckeye Girls Sewing and Secret Society." The organization didn't have anything to sew so they changed the name to "B. L. G." (Buckeye Lark Girls), a purely pleasure club. Some boys found out the secret meaning of B. L. G., so the club met again to change its name to U. K. U. K. (U-Know-Us-Kids).

After this last monumental step forward, the club sagged into inactivity, till Myrtle Chase's mother took a kindly interest. She suggested they make it a nice little reading club like her own Century Club. To make it more fun and grown-up they should observe "parliamentary rule," which they could learn out of her own *Roberts' Rules of Order*. After a gloomy session with Mr. Roberts and Mrs. Chase's copy of *Tales of a Wayside Inn*, Lena said that if people's mothers were going to butt in they'd give up the whole project. Just then She got wind of Lena's secret society and told Papa Lena belonged to a club whose purpose was to read dirty books. Papa's nerves were ragged from the friction in his family, so he lost his temper and ordered Lena to come right home after school instead of getting herself talked about with her dirty books. Lena indignantly confided this to Mary Evelyn, who eagerly asked where you got those "dirty books" and that was a fine idea for a club, much better than Mrs. Chase's. They decided, after pondering the matter, that if Lena's stepmother knew so much about them she must have some. This incited Lena to further daring. She stole the house keys again and after earnest prowling discovered a book in her stepmother's bureau drawer called *Sex Talks*.

She sneaked this out with palpitating heart, and soon had a much larger reading club than Mrs. Chase had anticipated. Since any type of reading was a chore for Lena's group, and this book was full of big words, they were only kept going by the conviction that anything hidden must be worth while. Besides, at last they had a secret. Finally, She discovered the secret, and this time Lena was whipped reluctantly by Papa at Her insistence. He was mad at Her, though, afterwards, and went out alone that night, slamming the door. When he came home, the girls heard him coming upstairs on his hands and knees, and they heard Her crying out, "Oh, Harry, you've been drinking! You can't even walk upstairs."

"I can walk upstairs if I want to, God damn it," shouted Papa. "Anybody can walk upstairs, but *this* is the way I like to go upstairs, and this is the way I'm *going* to do it."

All of these domestic upsets grieved Papa.

"No matter how hard you try, something's always going wrong," he said, but he couldn't be down long. He was too dazzled by his new importance as a solid citizen, actually on the Chamber of Commerce, on the Church Entertainment Committee, and manager of the remodelled Retail Furniture Store and Undertaking Parlor. Whoever managed the furniture salesmen automatically became assistant undertaker, since the duties had always gone together like those of jeweller and optician. The simple facts of embalming, selecting a coffin, and directing the funeral procedure were passed on by his predecessor, and Papa was ecstatically pleased over his emergence as a professional man, respected by all, particularly on those sorrowful occasions when he tiptoed about in his new funeral black, wearing white gloves and whispering consolation to the bereaved. "A more cheerful personality than Fanzer has," Mr. Carson himself said, referring to the undertaker in charge. These personal advantages in his career so intoxicated Papa that he was enraged to hear doubts expressed on the wisdom of his marriage. Mrs. Friend told him old friends of Daisy thought his new wife favored her own child at the expense of her acquired three. Papa vowed he would never forgive such an impudent comment. He swore that Lois had put the children up to mischief because she was jealous he had the Furness place. He forbade the girls to visit their aunt. But there seemed no way of keeping his children up to his own social level. On Sundays, when he and his stylish bride wheeled Minelda in her Sunday best down Main Boulevard, he was sure to meet his three daughters wandering glumly and shabbily down the street. Could they have money to go to the picture show or to the Kandy Kitchen? By George, he indignantly replied, he was not made of money. Let them go home and catch up on their homework, instead of running the streets.

"Can we have the key?" Lena impertinently asked. "How can we go home if we're locked out?"

Mrs. Willard murmured to Papa that they wanted the key just to scratch up the piano and muss up the Sunday paper. She said they took such poor care of their clothes She personally was ashamed to have passersby see them on the front porch, so they had better keep in the back of the house. Papa almost hated them for their silent, gloomy faces, for their interfering with his just rewards, and for their unconscious reminder that his new affluence was not sound. There wasn't any more money than there ever was, for the upkeep of his wife's house took three times more than he had ever dreamed. And, as She herself said, you couldn't expect her to spend the late Dr. Turner's bequest and her own little savings on those three spoiled kids. There was an end to even her patience, She declared.

27

GRANDMA WAS BACK IN LONDON JUNCTION "on her own, too," as she jubilantly boasted, definitely not living with kin. After her Cleveland disasters which she blamed mysteriously on politics, she had been obliged to make a visiting tour of her children, a very disagreeable experience for a lady who had once branched out into a career.

"Not one of my children ever minded me," she complained. "I don't see why they think I should mind them now."

They expected her to live with them and look after their children.

"A grandmother doesn't like children any more than a mother does," she declared. "Sometimes she's just too old to get out of tending them, that's all, but I'm not. Never felt better in my life."

It was that fine man, Mr. Sweeney, who came to her rescue with a loan, just as before. Since Aunt Lois had paid him back the last time he had come to the rescue, she was mad enough at this new negotiation to take a train for California, where Aunt Betts had gone for her asthma. She said if Grandma wanted to get in hot water again she would have to get herself out this time. She said she would not forgive Mr. Sweeney for aiding Grandma's wildcat scheme.

The present wildcat scheme was a collaboration of Mrs. Carmel and Grandma. Rheumatism had hampered Mrs. Carmel's gift for hat trimming and idleness made her restless. They would go in partnership in a notion shop in London Junction. With Mrs. Carmel's savings and Grandma's loan from Mr. Sweeney, they would make a fortune. They took an apartment over the Fair Store, with the living room as their shop. The notions consisted of knicknacks from Mrs. Carmel's bags, ancient handkerchiefs slightly yellowed, silk remnants also somewhat sun-faded, postcards, dusty marchpane fruit with a pungent flavor of mothballs, patterns, magazine subscriptions, hairpins, fans, souvenir spoons shined up to look like new except for a dent or two where some baby had teethed on them, bibs, and sheet music. The sheet music was far from being the latest thing, and had been sampled by mice and moths so that a page crumpled away at a touch. However, for a genuine musician there were many treats here, vocally and instrumentally, "The Little Romp Quick-step," "Father is Dead, and Mother's So Poor," "Velocipede Gallop," "Stay Home With Me Tonight, Tom," and "Mama, Why Don't Baby Cry?" As Grandma said, at least it made a nice showing. By way of a specialty, they sold homemade candy, butterscotch, peanut brittle, and sea-foam. The candy was inspired by finding among Mrs. Carmel's treasures an old paper-backed volume called *Young Folk's Candy and Good Times Book*. Recipes were adapted to the unscientific cook, reading "add some water, a little more sugar if it seems too thin, stir only if necessary but not too much, dash of flavoring to taste, set aside to cool and cut up into squares." If the results were good, Grandma dipped into them until there was scarcely enough for three customers at twenty-five cents a box but a careful packing job could spread it out to five, what with each piece wrapped in waxed paper and an extra cardboard at the bottom.

The Fair Store was right in the busiest section of town, around the corner from the railroad and directly opposite the bandstand. From their front bay window they could watch the crowd at the band concerts, and from their side windows they could watch the passing trains. With proper lighting conditions they could even see some life going on in the back of the London Junction Hotel. Across the corridor from them was the Odd Fellows Hall, the scene of dances and banquets. Sometimes a dance orchestra competed with the band concerts, so that Grandma, relaxing happily under the spell of all this music, could produce a humming arrangement of the "William Tell Overture" all mixed up with "Give My Regards to Broadway." She liked a good tune to hum and felt aggrieved that she could never get beyond the first bar of "Oh, You Beautiful Doll," because the 8:41 Cincinnati Express always roared through the rest of it.

The apartment had a big square front room with pine woodwork and a light wallpaper mottled with an intricate design of bilious morning glories. Shelves had been built along one side for their wares, and a counter placed beneath them. A wax head decorated the counter, wearing a blond transformation made apparently of rope rather than hair. A Perfecto Cigar Box served as cash register. A dark closet opening from the front room turned out to be the kitchen, from which issued the smell of escaping gas and burnt sugar. Another door led to two small cubicles which were called bedrooms, and were also used for fitting of corsets. Mr. Brady, owner of the Fair Store, allowed the ladies his Irregulars. Grandma felt that most women's figures were irregular anyway, so they might as well save money by buying irregular corsets. It only took a jiffy to cut off the garters from the bust section and sew them on the right end.

The arrival of Grandma in London Junction had a devastating effect on the Willard girls. A person goes through life accepting his lot with equanimity, till a moment of complete happiness reveals to him that he has up to now had a perfectly wretched existence. Marcia and Lena and Florrie had reluctantly adjusted themselves to their stepmother's rule, working out their own routine for dodging her displeasure. Suddenly Grandma was in town, and the flash of hope this brought made them see their life in the Furness home as unendurable torture. The possibility of escape to

Grandma's and a revival of the easygoing days on Hodge Street made them look with mutinous indignation on their lot. Why must they be made to feel guilty of some crime? Why must they wake each morning with leaden hearts, tiptoe glumly downstairs to breakfast, waiting for the almost certain morning greeting from Her, "Don't dig your heels into my new waxed floors! Don't put your filthy hands on my clean tablecloth! Stop coughing; your cold's all gone!" If Minelda had a rash or stomachache or sore throat, it was ascribed to Marcia who had in her wickedness let Minelda eat a banana, walk on the grass, or throw her bonnet on the sidewalk.

"I'll tell Grandma," Lena and Marcia whispered to each other in the dark. But how could they when She wouldn't let them visit her? And how could they when it might bring criticism on Papa? They sat upstairs in the dark, forbidden to read because lights cost money, forbidden to sing, forbidden to play games because it might shake the floor, forbidden to go out because they'd track mud back indoors. If Lena boldly ventured downstairs to ask Papa's permission to sit in the kitchen or to unlock Florrie's big doll from the closet, Papa flew into a temper.

"What's the matter bothering me with fool questions like that?" So She always won out, smiling crookedly down at her mending as Lena had to retreat back upstairs.

"Our own Grandma in town and She won't let us see her," Marcia and Lena muttered angrily. Grandma in town gave Marcia confidence to creep downstairs and sneak *Parlor Recitations for Young People* out of the bookcase without asking permission. Caught red-handed just as she was learning "My Mother Calls Me William," she was jerked by her arm into the kitchen, and her own silver-tasselled whip was administered smartly. Stonily impassive during this punishment, Marcia looked contemptuously at the former Miss Hawkins, who sank back flushed and trembling into a chair.

"Next time you'll cry," she gasped. "I'll get a bigger whip."

"I don't care how big a whip you get," Marcia said coldly. "Just don't touch me with your hands, if you please."

She stalked upstairs triumphantly in spite of the red whip marks across her cheek and arms. This she did mind, for now everyone at school would know that she, a big girl of nearly twelve, was still getting whippings. Everyone would make fun of her.

When could they visit Grandma, they begged their father, trying not to seem too eager or She would find a way to stop them completely. Papa gruffly told them whenever their mother gave permission.

His wife tightened her lips and cast her pale cold eyes around the three with a look of satisfaction.

"No sense in their picking up bad manners again," She said. "I've had a time breaking them of all the bad habits their grandmother taught them, and their Aunt Lois and, goodness knows, who all. They only want to carry tales. If their grandma wanted them around she'd have sent for them before. Nobody wants three young ones around; oh, no, they leave that kind of dirty work to me."

Papa was fidgety between his wife's complaint and the steadfast accusing gaze of his daughters.

"It's her place to call on me first," She went on in a thin fretful tone. "Harry, I'm surprised you aren't offended by her not calling."

"That's right," acknowledged Papa, glad of a reasonable stand. "She ought to call on us first."

"Why?" asked Marcia.

Her stepmother threw up her hands.

"There! That's the back talk I get all day from these girls!"

Papa was glad to get out of the house on pretext of mowing the lawn. But Grandma's presence in town had its effect on him, too. Every night he told trivial anecdotes about things that happened long ago on Hodge Street, cautiously sifted recollections of episodes in Grandma's life, expressions she used, samples of her generosity and good nature, with head-shakings over her business innocence and how often his advice had saved her. His wife listened silently and clamped her jaw grimly when finally, to no one's surprise but his own, Papa announced that, disagreeable as the task was, he supposed he owed it to the old lady to give her the benefit of his advice in her present undertaking.

"I might as well go down after supper and get it over with," he said, lowering his eyes to hide the sparkle of eagerness. "The old lady will think it funny if I don't drop in for a talk, and nobody else can handle her the way I can. Besides," he was inspired to add, "when she goes I'll probably come into quite a lot of property because she always claimed she'd leave it to me."

"How much has she got?" his wife asked with interest. "We could get a machine, maybe. We could go on a tour. Why don't you find out?"

"I'll feel around," promised Papa, glad to have the matter closed amiably. "I'll take the girls over right after supper if they can behave themselves!"

It turned out there was another reason for Papa's eagerness to leave the house that night. He grasped Florrie by one hand and sped down the street, beaming, Marcia and Lena breathlessly skipping along behind. At Jake's Saloon near the hotel he stopped and peered in the door.

"By George, there's Ed Hartwell in there!" he exclaimed in profound surprise. "You kids wait while I go and say hello. He must be making the Junction on his new route. Well, well."

He hastily ducked inside and the immediate burst of laughter from inside was like old times. Marcia and Lena exchanged a comprehending look.

"He knew Ed was here," stated Lena. "He knew he didn't dare ask him to the house so he made up this excuse."

Hello took some time so the three girls walked back and forth impatiently in front of the saloon.

A fog of stale beer fumes surrounded the place, and from inside they heard "Too Much Mustard" jangling on the mechanical piano. Some boys from Lena's class came along and yelled "Hello, sweetheart," at Lena, who tossed her head indignantly. Marcia wished they would yell at her, too, but boys never looked at anyone but Lena. If they had a home like other girls they could have parties at night and make fudge and play Post Office. Marcia mentioned this to Lena as a prospect for their possible future at Grandma's, but Lena suddenly drew away and said with a faraway look, "Maybe only one of us can stay at Grandma's, and I'm the one because I'm the oldest."

It was half an hour before Papa emerged from Jake's, arm in arm with Ed Hartwell, and chuckling away in the highest spirits. Mr. Hartwell was even more elegant looking than before, for his sideburns and moustache were now lightly tinged with gray, and his figure had increased impressively. It seemed that Mr. Hartwell felt that he, too, should call on Grandma.

"Harry, your mother-in-law is one of the finest," he declared warmly. He shook hands with the girls, picked up Florrie to carry but found his wind not up to it, so put her down. He gave each of them a quarter on the spot, and pinched Lena's rosy cheek with an exclamation that, by George, she was getting to be a little beauty. He patted Marcia's head and observed that she looked bright as a little button.

Both men repeated complimentary remarks about the old lady, and what guts she had, and how anxious they were to see her. However, they delayed the visit a little longer by recollecting some private matter that needed attending in the Elks Club. In spite of their impatience at the second delay, the girls were cheered to hear Papa laugh again all the louder, and to hear him saying things that made Mr. Hartwell roar with deepest appreciation.

"By George, there's nobody like you, Willard!" Mr. Hartwell declared, slapping him on the back. "I don't know whether your wife realizes how lucky she is, and you can tell her I said so."

"How's Mabel, Mr. Hartwell?" Marcia asked, politely. "Are you married yet?"

This set Mr. Hartwell and Papa into another fit of laughter right in the middle of the street. Mr. Hartwell shook his head admiringly.

"That one always hits the nail on the head, don't she, Harry?"

Marcia was pleased but mystified at the merry reaction to her question, and seeing her puzzled frown Mr. Hartwell hastened to say that Mabel was in the best of health and gaining steadily, at last report weighing two hundred pounds and fit as a fiddle.

"A bull fiddle," said Papa, which convulsed his friend.

It was nearly eight o'clock when they reached the Fair Store building. A dark doorway led to the upstairs apartments and ballroom. A small blue light at the landing gave a grisly glow to the hall, dimly indicating a rotten board in the floor and a broken banister. Bad plumbing and the circumstance of street cats using the vestibule for a comfort station lent an intimate aroma to the place, not particularly mellowed by the Corylopsis incense burning in the ballroom's Ladies' Parlor. On the first door of the second floor was a placard bearing the news, "Odd Fellows Dance. Admission Fifty Cents, Ladies Free," and issuing from this spot could be heard sounds of an orchestra tuning up. Other doors led to the Fair Store stockrooms, a Christian Science Reading Room, a dentist's office, and at the end of the hall the Novelty Shop. This was Grandma's new headquarters. Marcia clutched Lena's arm as they heard the well-remembered slippered footsteps coming to answer their knock. Lena jerked her arm free.

"Remember what I told you," Lena whispered sharply. "I'm the one that's going to stay here."

It was always discouraging to have others calm in moments your own heart was thundering with wild rapture, and Grandma was as calm as ever at sight of her callers.

"Grandma. Oh, Grandma," cried Marcia, flinging herself at the old lady the instant the door opened and trembling with delight. But Grandma's pleasure in seeing her family was in no way proportionate to the visitors' estimation of the joy they were bestowing. She accepted their embraces with moderate warmth and welcomed them into her parlor with more pride in a parlor of her own than in the callers.

"They can't take away my independence," she said, patting Mr. Hartwell fondly on the arm. "So long as I've got friends like Mr. Sweeney and Mrs. Carmel here I don't need to take anything from my family."

Mrs. Carmel, it seemed, was busy in the kitchen over a large iron pot of fondant, muttering like a witch as she stirred it. She hoped they would excuse her for continuing this chore, because the truth was their chocolate fondant had caught on like a house afire, and they had to be on their toes every minute, meeting the demand. London Junction might be behind the times in some ways but not in its candy tastes.

"You folks have a good talk," she benignly advised, and then with a wheezy chuckle, "you gentlemen take a good look at my partner there and see if you notice anything."

At this Grandma blushingly stroked her hair, and all exclaimed at once on this startling change. Yes, she said, it was true she was wearing a transformation. For years it had been recommended to her by friends who found it astonishing for a woman of her youthful appearance to have gray hair. A purchase of a box of oddments from a fire sale had yielded this wig, and since no one wanted to buy it Grandma had appropriated it for her own use. Moreover, in this business, closely connected with fashions as it was, a woman had to look her best. The wig was nut brown and reared up in luxuriant tiers to a crown of tight curls falling neatly over a high amber comb.

"By Jove, you don't look a day over thirty-five!" exclaimed Papa.

Grandma explained that she dared not wear the device all the time, for fear her daughter Lois would see her in it and go into a jealous rage. She might be obliged to give it up altogether if a customer should take a fancy to it. She said she had happened to learn from a high-priced authority in Cleveland that this very transformation represented the finest workmanship of its kind outside

New York City. Little experiences while wearing it had borne out this theory. For instance, on streetcars in Cleveland perfect strangers would stare and then accost her.

"Excuse me, madam," they had said more than once, "that is one of the most beautiful wigs I ever saw." Parties would cross the street, staring, and say, "You don't know me from Adam but I just have to ask you where you got that wonderful transformation. I've never seen anything like it and I've travelled all over the country."

"I feel younger in it, too," confessed Grandma. "Mrs. Carmel's been after me to get my teeth pulled out too and get a set but that means money."

"I tell her if she wants to beautify herself, might as well go the whole hog," whistled Mrs. Carmel, chuckling so that the velvet bow she wore in her own hair fell in the pot of boiling candy and had to be fished out with a dipper.

The strains of the orchestra came through the walls and a drum roll shook the floor.

"Dance," Grandma explained complacently. "There's something going on here every minute. Sometimes two things."

She produced a bakery cake and a pot of coffee from the stove, and passed these around.

"You can't beat bakery cake," she said. "Nothing tastes better than good bakery bread, too. I like being up to the minute. I don't listen to all that talk about old-fashioned home baking. I've tasted plenty of soggy home baking, I can tell you."

Mr. Hartwell and Papa examined the wares with professional interest, recommending a touch here and there. Mr. Hartwell recalled that by chance he had a bottle of whiskey on his hip he had happened absentmindedly to pick up in his room and begged permission to serve himself and friend Willard. Permission was granted at once.

"A drinking man don't feel right when he's not drinking," Grandma stated. "That's why Wally never felt good."

"Where is Uncle Wally?" asked Marcia.

"Went back to his daughter in Elmville after the fire," Grandma said. "Slept in the barn there, and when he didn't show up for meals for a couple of days they went out and found him lying there in the hay, dead as you please. Martha said the horses wouldn't touch the hay for days."

Marcia thought of poor old Uncle Wally all still and cold in the haymow, nobody missing him for days. That was what people did to old men, maybe old ladies too, only women were stronger.

"Well, we all got to go some time," Grandma added comfortably.

Lena was singing "Wrap Me in a Bundle, Dear, and Take Me Home with You," with the orchestra next door. She and Marcia danced to it, counting carefully. Florrie sat on a stool in the kitchen, greasing pans for Mrs. Carmel. Florrie loved helping, but her stepmother wouldn't let her. She wanted to pick up some hairpins scattered over the floor, but Grandma said no, that if she needed a hairpin she knew right where they were, one under the counter, one under the big rocker, and one under the sink. Once you started putting things where they belonged you never knew where anything was.

Mr. Hartwell said Grandma had more common sense in her little finger than most women had in their whole body. He applauded the two girls' dancing and nudged Papa.

"I'll take your daughter in for this dance," he said. "How about it, Lena?"

"But it's not free," Lena protested.

"Nothing's free," Mr. Hartwell merrily answered. Marcia watched, in an anguish of jealousy while Mr. Hartwell took Lena across the hall to the Odd Fellows' Dance. It was some consolation to think of how mad it would make Her when She found it out. Marcia went out to stand in the hall, watching. She saw Bonnie Purdy dancing with a tall man from out of town. You could always tell people from out of town because they looked better and had a mysterious swagger. Maybe everybody looked better out of town. Mr. Hartwell was holding Lena off proudly as if she was a little doll, and Lena was tossing her head and pointing her toes carefully, pretending not to notice Marcia watching.

When the dance was over Mr. Hartwell didn't bring Lena back but stood in the middle of the floor tapping his foot and clapping his hands for an encore. Marcia went back to Grandma's. Papa was sitting on a stool by Grandma, holding her hand. They both looked very weepy.

"No, sir, Harry, there'll never be anybody like Daisy," Grandma said. "I remember when I sat up with her over the third baby. When she came to I said, 'Well, Daisy, that makes three.' And she said—she was always teasing me—'All right, mom, isn't it about time you told me the facts of life?'"

"We were always laughing, having a good time over something," Papa said, wiping his eyes. "Sometimes I think we shouldn't ever have left Peach Street."

"No, sir, I don't think you should have," Grandma said, solemnly shaking her monument of curls. "Things wouldn't have turned out this way if you'd stayed there. Well, you've got a new wife now. I hear she's got a nice appearance."

"And we've got the Furness house," Papa said. "I always told Daisy we would but she wouldn't believe me. Maybe I tried to do too much for Daisy."

"Maybe you did, Harry," Grandma admitted. "All Daisy ever wanted was you. I guess you wanted to spoil her."

"I did," Papa said, wiping his nose. "I wanted Daisy to have everything, but Daisy didn't need fine clothes to look good. She looked good in any old rag."

Mr. Hartwell brought Lena back, with a deep bow of thanks. She looked, he said, more and more like her Aunt Lois. It was time to go, and Mrs. Carmel gave the girls each a bag of candy mixed with salted peanuts. Mr. Hartwell and Papa had a final drink out of the bottle before leaving, and they both informed Grandma that she was just about the finest woman they'd ever had the pleasure of knowing. Mr. Hartwell said he would give a thousand dollars if his own mother, also a wonderful woman, could meet her. He hadn't seen his mother for five years, he said, and a man felt pretty bad when he hadn't seen his mother for five years. Grandma said it was too bad his mother didn't live nearer to him, but he said it wasn't that, but every time he was in his home town, Chicago, he was so head over heels in work he didn't have a chance to run out to see her.

Marcia and Lena waited with falling spirits for a chance to tell Grandma their own problem but there wasn't any way of getting her attention without Papa hearing. Glumly, Marcia wondered if Grandma would save them anyway. Nobody was interested in anybody much but themselves. Maybe Grandma would take sides with their stepmother.

"I'll call on your wife one of these days," Grandma said to Papa. "Soon as business lets up I'll drop in. I've never been through the Furness house."

They left Mr. Hartwell at the Elks House, and almost at once their gaiety vanished. Marcia walked behind, thinking her heart would break. Mr. Hartwell had danced only with Lena, and if anybody was to stay with Grandma it would be Lena. There was never any hope, anywhere. Even Papa's steps lagged as they approached their house, their good time forgotten in the apprehension of what was awaiting them. It was after ten and the house was dark. The girls started for the back door but Papa harshly ordered them to follow him up the front walk to the front door. He took out a key and unlocked it as his wife, in a night hair net and blue flannel kimono, turned on the stair lights. "You're not bringing them all in the front way, Harry!" She cried out. "Wait, I'll open the back door."

"I'll come in any damn door I please," shouted Papa. "I'll come down the chimney if I damn well like."

He tramped upstairs, roughly brushing her aside. The girls tiptoed up behind him, careful not to scar up the stairs or the banister, but their stepmother followed them on her knees, wiping each step. Papa went in the bedroom and banged the door.

"Did your father stop anywhere on the way to your grandmother's?" She asked Lena sharply.

"No," said Lena.

"No," said Marcia.

"No, Ma'am," said Florrie, lips trembling. "Oh, don't whip Papa, please!"

28

I FEEL SORRY for Her," Florrie said one day, in troubled tones. Her older sisters regarded her with a baleful look. They had been forbidden to leave the house or to play cards, because it was Sunday, and they could not go to Epworth League meeting because word had gotten round that these services ended up in kissing games in the choir loft. (Lena had taken a prominent part in these activities, though Marcia had unfortunately not been invited.) They could sit on the porch if they liked, but they didn't like because they had been forced to change from their Sunday dresses to patched blue calico, and someone might see them, especially since it was their gloomy conviction that She made the patches big on purpose. So they sat in their room, sulking in the twilight.

"What are you sorry for Her about?" demanded Marcia. "She slapped your hands for crocheting, didn't she?"

Florrie acknowledged this.

"She cries all the time, though," she said.

"Let Her cry," said Lena, scowling at the tenderhearted little sister. Then curiosity overcame her and she added, "What does She cry about?"

"It's about money, and Papa cries too, I think," Florrie said. "Her eyes are red all the time, and She never puts her rats in her hair any more. She even scolded Minelda, too."

"She's getting meaner every minute, ever since Grandma's been in town," Marcia said. "She shook you for coughing tonight, and said you just did it to make Papa worry. I don't see why you feel sorry for Her."

"I feel sorry for Her because She can't help being mean," Florrie said guiltily, knowing this confession of weakness would not please her sisters. "Marcia can't help spilling things and breaking things, and Papa can't help his temper, and She can't help being mean. I guess that's why Papa doesn't get mad at Her; it's because he knows She can't help it."

Lena and Marcia frowned into space, speculating on what mighty catastrophe could cause tears in Her eyes. The muffled voices of their father and Her in their own room down the hall encouraged Lena to creep down the hall to listen. She came back, nodding with satisfaction.

"It's about money, all right," she said. "She keeps saying, 'Oh, Harry, why didn't you tell me before? You know I trusted you.' Papa's getting sort of mad. He keeps saying, 'Can't I get it through your head that I wouldn't have touched a penny of your damned money if I hadn't thought I could put it back? How many times have I got to explain it to you?' She says She can't get over his lying about his salary, and now that She's used up all her money She can't run the house on what little he makes, and pay taxes and pay his old bills. He says nobody would be after him about the old bills if he didn't live in this big house, and that's Her fault."

"Maybe we'll get sent to an orphanage," Marcia said hopefully.

"Florrie, maybe, but we're too old, I think," Lena said.

Marcia took a turn at eavesdropping next and was able to report that there was mention of Grandpa Willard coming, and something about his pension coming in handy. This was cheerful news, because there was the fond belief that a visitor in the house would keep Her from nagging at them. The third floor rooms might be unlocked then, too, and She wouldn't dare refuse them books or magazines if some relative was around. Things would certainly be different.

The next day Papa dragged out one of the attic mattresses to be aired, indicating that a visitor was expected. Marcia disobeyed the order not to go to Grandma's except with special permission, and played hookey after morning recess in order to inform her grandma of the happy prospect. It was disconcerting to have Grandma shrug off the news with a patronizing comment that the old man was better off in the Soldiers' Home. Later, when Grandpa Willard appeared in brand new civilian clothes Marcia heard him inquire benignly of Papa after the "old lady."

"Is she still alive? Well, well!" he exclaimed, shaking his head in amazement. "Got all her faculties still? Well, I'll be doggoned. When I saw the old lady ten, twenty years ago, it seemed to me her memory was beginning to fail a little. Well, well, thank goodness I got my memory."

Old men didn't like old ladies any more than old ladies liked old men; far from common experiences making them sympathetic, it made them even gleeful over a contemporary's infirmities, as if life was a see-saw, the other going down made you automatically go up. Marcia resented this contempt her grandparents had for each other's antiquity, and caught her grandfather in a memory lapse, after his slighting reference to Grandma Reed's failing. Grandpa gravely considered her accusation.

"No, my memory ain't going one bit," he declared. "It's just that there's a lot of things I never knew right in the first place, that's all."

Grandpa and Papa had a talk on the back steps after supper. Papa said the way he figured was that it was lonesome spending your last days in a Home when you had children ready and willing to board you. Daisy had always wanted him to live with them, but it never worked out that way. But now that they had this big house Papa figured it would tickle Daisy to know Pa was at last staying with them. He could mow the lawn and help around the garden, and take it easy the little time remaining to him. Staying with his folks he got his full pension instead of the Home taking most of it, and he could pay board. Grandpa said money never meant anything to him and he'd just as soon turn the whole pension over to Harry and just keep out enough for tobacco and reading matter, maybe a beer now and then. He didn't want to be any trouble to anybody, and She might as well know that right away. He'd make his own bed and keep his own room tidy, and get his own meals. Papa said he'd send word to the rest of the family around the state to come see him there, but Grandpa said that would make trouble for Her and not to bother.

It took Grandpa very little time to gather the situation, especially after his new daughter-in-law had hidden his pipe tobacco, thrown out his pile of the *Home Weekly,* and put newspapers over the floor of his room so he wouldn't step on the parquet. Without saying a word to anyone he took his cot down to the cellar and fixed up a corner by the bowling alley for his room. Papa didn't say a word when he came home at night and found this change made, but he rummaged around the attic for a washstand and couple of chairs to add to the cellar room. Neither did his wife mention the move, but silently set to work scrubbing and fumigating the little bedroom which Grandpa had just vacated. She did think of little things each day to remind Grandpa that a room in the cellar was no excuse for slovenliness. He must keep the windows locked so that burglars wouldn't get in that way, and he must not go prowling in the potato bins or the preserve closet, for sometimes things would turn, just having sick old folks breathing on them. He wasn't to smoke in there either, because what with his pipe chugging away and his pile of old dirty papers, like as not he'd set the house on fire and they'd all be burned in their sleep. Grandpa promised to step outside when he wanted to smoke, and keep his part of the cellar clean as a whistle. He got up early in the morning and went out, nobody knew where, and came home at supper time to smoke out in the yard. Marcia and Lena sat beside him, Florrie on his lap, asking for stories about when he was a drummer boy. If the occasion was opportune, they told their own stories about Her. Grandpa listened discreetly to these confidences, offering neither advice nor consolation. He wasn't any help at all, the girls decided, any more than Grandma Reed was. Old folks were just as afraid as children were; you couldn't count on them for anything. Marcia, reflecting on this, felt a sudden wave of fear. Supposing when she grew old—that is, providing there would ever be an end to this awful eternity of childhood—she would have a daughter just like her stepmother, and the daughter would make her sleep in the cellar like Uncle Wally and Grandpa had had to do.

"I won't have any daughters then," she decided. "No family at all; that's the only safe thing."

She spoke of this to Lena and Grandpa when they were raking the grass. It was fun raking, but they had to pretend it wasn't or She wouldn't ask them to do it. She already suspected that this chore was not sufficiently in the nature of punishment, for She peered out the kitchen window and called out, "For goodness sake, don't ruin that rake, and there's no need chopping into the turf that way! Looks like a herd of buffalo had been let loose on it."

"We've got to walk *some place*. We can't fly over it," Marcia said in a loud enough tone to be considered audacious by Lena, but not loud enough to reach the kitchen.

Grandpa had a crick in his back and took time out for a chew of tobacco.

"If you don't have any family you'll just be an old maid," Lena said crushingly. "How do you think you'll like that, smarty?"

"I'd like it fine," Marcia boldly replied, hoping God wouldn't hear this and take her seriously. "I don't see any sense in getting married and having a lot of family to be mean to me."

"You get used to it," Grandpa said comfortably. "If it ain't your own family it's other people's. Might as well be picked on by your own flesh and blood."

"Marcia's going to be an old maid whether she wants to or not," Lena said complacently. "The boys don't like her because she's so crazy."

This had such a ring of authority that Marcia kept a moody silence. It was a fact that boys sent Lena notes all the time and followed her home from school as far as they dared. The only boy who sent Marcia notes was little David Gross, who was only eleven, small for his age, and called sissy by the class. Even the high school boys and railroad men in the Elks Pool Room whistled at Lena as she passed, but Marcia walked past much slower and oftener with never a whistle. If she had heard one she would have shrieked out her delight, "Oh, thank you, thank you, thank you!" It was Lena's yellow curls that did the trick, and then her rosy cheeks. Nobody ever liked hair-colored hair, straight at that, like Marcia's. The future looked very gloomy so far as romance was concerned. Probably there'd be nothing left for her but to be rich and famous. But even famous people, married or no, often ended up with cruel landlords and mean uncles throwing them into institutions, locking them in attics, or putting them on the street. Marcia thought very likely Lena would be the one to turn on her in her hour of need and order her off to a cot in the cellar. Lena was sometimes almost as bad as her stepmother. Lena walked on the other side of the street rather than walk to school with Marcia, and whenever Marcia told her anything Lena exclaimed coldly, "Oh, you're crazy." If it was something Marcia had read in a book, Lena said it was just poppycock, because the only persons Lena trusted were Mary Evelyn and Myrtle Chase.

Grandpa was a great reader and discussed books with Marcia. His son's wife was fit to be tied when She found out he had brought a box of paper-backed novels from the Soldiers' Home. There was no way She could forbid his lending them to Marcia, however, because She did not dare say all the things she'd like to Grandpa—not yet, anyway. Marcia read countless novels by E. P. Roe, Charlotte Braeme, Bulwer Lytton, Mary J. Holmes, and others, but they left her baffled and angry.

"The lord always marries the governess," she complained earnestly to Grandpa, "but it turns out in the end she is really a princess anyway, so it doesn't prove anything. I'll bet he wouldn't have married her if he didn't know she was going to turn out to be rich and noble. No, sir, there isn't one story where the governess stays just a governess, because if she did nobody would ever marry her."

"Now, don't be so critical," rebuked Grandpa. "Read all the books you like but don't go round criticizing."

"Well, I just don't see any sense in the way these people in these books act," grumbled Marcia. "I should think if anybody could marry whoever he pleased it would be a lord, so what do they make so much fuss about it for?"

"You don't know what you're talking about," Grandpa stated flatly. "The party that writes up all these stories ought to know whereof he speaks. If that's the way he likes to have people act, he's got a right to make them act that way."

"Marcia's always crazy," said Lena.

There was no use talking to anybody because nobody understood anything, except maybe Florrie, who was so anxious to be obliging that she agreed with everybody. Whenever you said outright what you were thinking people stared at you curiously, as if thoughts were something you should keep to yourself.

Still, there was David Gross, even if he was a sissy. Marcia hoped her stepmother wouldn't find out about her secret intimacy with the Gross family. Lena might tell. Florrie knew about it because she went there with Marcia often. The Grosses lived in the brick house behind the schoolhouse, so that Marcia and Florrie could run in and out (the front door too, and without knocking, at Mrs. Gross's own insistence) during recess or any time they had a chance. David and Marcia acted out stories they had read or made up together. David's mother taught Florrie to crochet and to play the piano, but Florrie had to keep her new accomplishment secret from her stepmother for fear She would scold, fearing some future violation of Her own piano which was for looks. David's mother read out loud to them and let them sit in the living room or play games anywhere in the house, make fudge in the kitchen, race up and down stairs or take any books they liked out of the bookcase. Nothing was locked in the Gross home. They had a gramophone and Mrs. Gross explained the stories of operas to them when she played the records. She was a soft-voiced, plain, gentle woman with curly gray hair and ruffled dresses. Florrie worshipped her because she let her hug and kiss her, a privilege Florrie was denied by her self-conscious sisters and even by Papa, since it irritated Her so much to see. She did not look like other mothers in London Junction, but seemed more like somebody's sister, or like their Cousin Isobel. It was certain that Mrs. Gross was not beautiful the way Aunt Lois was, or like Isobel, but her way of talking and smiling with her eyes, which had unusually heavy lashes, presented a new definition of beauty. It must be Eastern graces, Marcia decided, and determined that she too would go to Philadelphia or Washington when she grew up and learn little ways like Mrs. Gross.

The Grosses had moved to London Junction from Washington, but after the first excitement over a new family in town, with the local ladies leaving cards, the different ministers' wives calling, and invitations to town functions issued, they were left to themselves. Mrs. Gross had not responded to the welcome and, without being rude, had quietly established her family as being self-sufficient. David did not join in the school games, and was too clever in his studies to be regarded with anything but contempt and suspicion. Moreover, he was almost two years younger than the others in his class and a head shorter than Marcia. He wore thick glasses, braces on his teeth, in addition to pronouncing grass "grahs" and water "wottah" instead of "worter." His doom so far as popularity was concerned was sealed the day he came running into class late, apologizing to the teacher, "Pardon my dishevelled appearance, but I've been in the woods collecting some botanical specimens." A low hiss went around the room, in which Marcia joined, though she was secretly impressed with this bold speech. A few days later she settled her own hash by using "feminine prerogative" in a composition and was met with the same hiss when the work was read aloud. Compositions were exchanged for students to grade each other and David wrote on Marcia's, "100% plus." So they were obliged to be friends, quietly, and helped each other with their compositions. David explained to Marcia that "Helas" was not a girl's name, and Marcia explained to David that the seven sisters in his story could not be just three or four months apart in their ages. It was a stimulating and helpful friendship, even though Lena jeered at it.

There was in the Gross family an older sister named Fannie who was hump-backed and painted copies of famous masters in a room she called her "studio." (She gave Marcia her copy of the Rosa Bonheur picture that used to hang in the Elmville house.) Then there was a little old lady in a wheelchair, called Aunt Rachel, who muttered in a foreign language and had a mat of fuzzy white curls. Hump-back, foreign language speaker, and sissy in the family were social hurdles that even a fictional noble-woman could not take without some embarrassment, so Marcia and Florrie endeavored to disguise their intimacy with the new family. Mr. Gross never appeared because, David explained, his family, with the exception of Aunt Rachel, who was a little crazy, had never forgiven him for marrying a Gentile. So, to conciliate his aging parents, he had gone back to stay with them in the East.

"But Fannie and I aren't Gentiles," David proudly explained. "Mother has Aunt Rachel teach us our Bible and once a month she takes us to Cleveland to the synagogue, because she knows it pleases Father. When he comes back he'll be proud of us."

Florrie wanted to know what a Gentile was, and Marcia im-patiently explained it was some kind of people in the Bible.

Mrs. Gross, in spite of being a Gentile, seemed like anybody else, so that except for the soft speech, different from the nasal shrill voices of other London Junction women, she had no strange Biblical characteristics. Marcia was puzzled when David declared she too was Gentile, and hastily assured him that she was no such thing, being First Church of Christ and part Welsh and English and Dutch. Later she asked Grandpa about this, and after some reflection he said they might be Gentiles when you got right down to it. He gave her a little dictionary for her birthday so she could look up things. She kept this in the carriage seat in the barn so nobody could take it away, and also her composition books where she wrote down things that nobody, not even Grandpa, would discuss. Mrs. Gross loaned her new novels to let Grandpa read, such as *The Calling of Dan Matthews, The Beloved Vagabond,* and *The Girl from the Limberlost.* Sometimes she was so deep in these worlds that she hardly noticed she was still being whipped for not answering when spoken to. Florrie did her crying for her. They didn't tell the Grosses about their stepmother, because they were ashamed. It would be terrible if people got to feeling sorry for them the way they were for the barefoot poor children who lived in shacks along the railroad. It would be terrible, too, if people wondered why Papa didn't notice what was going on, but Lena's theory was that he did but he didn't know what to do about it, especially since She was good to him at least. After they went to bed, She tiptoed in their room, and while they pretended to be asleep She noiselessly went through all their dresser drawers and took away anything she thought was nonsense, such as Lena's La Blanche Face Powder and the samples she was always sending away for. She finally found Florrie's crocheting and took that away, and even after Marcia hid her novels under the mattress She reached under and took them out, so the only way she could get them back was to say they belonged to the Church Library.

"As if I would still be reading the church library books," Marcia later exclaimed to her grandfather. "In those books the moral is always that the poor boy can go to heaven quicker than the rich boy, but then the story has the poor boy get a lot richer than the rich boy, so finally there isn't any moral, except you'd better get rich to be on the safe side."

"Well, that's the way books are and you gotta take 'em that way," Grandpa advised her. "If books was anything like real life nobody'd want to waste time reading 'em."

Florrie had nightmares from being waked up by creeping hands under her pillow, so she was punished for this. She sometimes walked in her sleep and it made it all the worse for her when she yelled, "Don't let the witch get me, don't let her." She didn't dare tell Mrs. Gross the crocheting had been taken away, so she said she got tired of it. But secretly she got a piece of twine and a bent hairpin and hid it with Marcia's notebooks in the carriage seat. She couldn't resist bringing it in the house one night and hiding it under her pillow. It was going to be a penwiper for Marcia, she promised, when she finished crocheting it. But in the morning it was gone. The next night Florrie cried herself to sleep and then walked, in her sleep, straight into Papa's bedroom and shouted in an awful voice, "Give me my string and hairpin; I want to crochet. You give it to me or I'll tell the devil on you."

Papa woke up, frightened out of his wits, and picked up Florrie. Minelda, in the crib, started to bawl, too. Florrie woke up at Papa's voice and burst into hysterics, telling the whole story about her crochet hook and the string. Papa was very quiet and asked his wife what this was all about.

"Of course, I put it away," She said stoutly. "Florrie's fidgety enough as it is without giving her more things to fidget with. Next she'll have St. Vitus' dance."

Papa carried Florrie back to her bed, where she sobbed, trembling for hours. Lena and Marcia were afraid they would catch it on Florrie's account but they heard Papa arguing in the next room for a long time, and in the morning their stepmother's eyes were as red-rimmed as Florrie's, and she was more subdued than they had ever seen her. The next day, however, Marcia could not find her notebooks or dictionary and her stepmother found her looking for them all over the barn.

"If you're looking for that trash of yours, I just burned it," She said shrilly. "I'm not going to look after a loony child in this family."

Marcia's chest filled with murderous fury. She felt faint with the desire to kill Her. She looked around to see if Grandpa and

Lena had heard her precious things called "trash" and burned, but they pretended not to hear. That was the trouble with everybody in the same boat; they wouldn't lift a finger to help you because they were afraid of catching it themselves.

"That was a twenty-five-cent notebook," Marcia said icily. "My father gave it to me."

"It'll be a long time before your father gives you another twenty-five cents to waste on such junk, when you're needing schoolbooks," She said, her eyes glittering. She started to go indoors, but decided to round off the discipline.

"Mr. Willard, you don't need to sit out front gabbing with those girls so everybody can hear you a block away. Anybody eating us out of house and home ought to make themselves useful."

"You can't talk that way to Grandpa," Marcia shouted, shaking her fist.

"Hush," said Grandpa quietly. He didn't look at Her as She locked the screen door to prevent them coming indoors without permission, but scratched his head thoughtfully. Then he stumped down the front walk, holding himself very straight, the way a drummer boy should. Marcia and Lena did not look at each other. Marcia shut her lips tightly together. Make yourself numb, she said to herself, draw deep breaths. Pretend you're dead. If you're dead it doesn't matter about notebooks or dictionaries or crochet hooks or Grandpa. Nobody can hurt a dead person.

It was some satisfaction to have Papa worried about Grandpa not showing up for supper, and Her sullen uneasiness. She chewed her fingernails every time Papa went down the cellar to look for Grandpa, and gave a gasp of relief when the familiar step was heard on the front walk, finally.

"Your father's been drinking, that's what," She said loudly. "Listen to the way he's walking. Well! Just one thing more on my shoulders!"

29

THE MIRACLE that had failed to take place with Grandma in town and with the arrival of Grandpa Willard actually occurred when Vance Hawkins moved in with them. Next to Minelda, She prized her younger brother Vance, and talked about him so much that Papa often got jealous. Vance had been everywhere. ("A lot of other folks have travelled around, too," Papa said to this.) He had spent a year in military school, so that he had many rich friends contacted there. ("Why doesn't he go stay with them then, if those rich people are so crazy about him?" Papa inquired.) Brother Vance was an expert telegrapher and was going to work in the London Junction Western Union office for sixty-five dollars a month, temporarily, of course, since his opportunities with his rich friends were unlimited. He had dropped telegraphy to work for the National Cash Register people in Dayton, but some girl named Mildred started chasing him and blaming things on him that were none of his doing, so he had to clear out. In Detroit he had worked for Ford Motors at thirty-five dollars a week, if you please, but had been lucky enough to catch his toe in some machine and received $3,000 damages. "It's not a fortune," he had modestly written concerning this triumph, "but it's a start. You don't need a big toe to walk with anyway." The reason he said he was taking the London Junction job was that he had invested his little sum so shrewdly and in such a tight way that he could not get at it somehow. He wrote quite frankly that he wanted to make sort of a visit with his favorite sister instead of boarding at some stranger's, because he wanted to save his salary with the purpose of settling in California.

Papa said the family was big enough as it was.

"It's all YOUR family," his wife plaintively answered. "It's not mine. If you see fit to have your father live with us in the house my money paid for, I certainly have a right to ask my only brother. Goodness knows, it's time I had some of my own kin around for protection. As near as I can make out, Harry, you want not only all your own family but your first wife's family living off of us. If I didn't put my foot down I'll bet you'd have old lady Reed move in on us."

She liked to talk that way about Grandma because it annoyed Papa as much as it pained the children.

"Will Vance stay in the cellar with Grandpa?" Florrie innocently asked.

"There's an old mattress in the potato bin. He could fix himself up pretty comfortable there," Grandpa chuckled, fondly patting Florrie's head.

But Vance was to have not only the biggest bedroom on the third floor but the freedom of the house as well. The girls first recognized the miracle when they came home from school one day and found a young man reclining easily on the parlor davenport, with his feet thrown over the arm. They peeked in, mindful of their place, and were shocked when he genially urged them to come on in and get acquainted. Their stepmother impatiently nodded permission. She was flushed and smiling with pride in her visitor, so excited she forgot to scowl warningly at the girls as they walked gingerly over the broadloom carpet. Even the piano was unlocked and had three pieces of sheet music arranged on it as if anybody that wanted could sit down and run through these gems, "Till the Sands of the Desert Grow Cold," "Put On Your Old Gray Bonnet," and "Come, Josephine, in My Flying Machine."

One good thing was that Vance did not look like his sister Idah. That was something. He was long and lean, with a way of leaping around as if he was made of rubber. He had a hook nose and fishy gray eyes set astonishingly close together for the simple reason that his narrow face left no room for them to spread out. His long head, in fact, seemed to have a dimension missing, being all profile, rising from lively Adam's apple over the nasal hump and up to the peak of his scalp, from which a fountain of greasy yellow hair sprawled in all directions. It was a pity he did not have his sister's cosmetic privileges, for his skin was decorated with a pink rash which, She explained to Papa, had been faithfully his since infancy.

"His blood is too rich," She explained proudly. "All the Hawkins have rich blood."

As if these charms were not enough, he had a habit of holding his mouth agape in a half smile, revealing an extraordinary set of pale salmon gums studded with cigarette-stained stumps of teeth. The reason for keeping his mouth open appeared to be no vanity over his remarkable expanse of gums, but a convenience for jumping into the conversation with no loss of time. It was plain that listening to anybody was a hardship; he could scarcely wait for his chance to hop in, usually with an anecdote prefaced by the phrase, "like the fellow in the show." His words were lost in uncontrollable chortles in which Papa, coming home early to welcome his in-law, only feebly joined. Vance had a baffling way of darting his eyes around and behind you, so that you found yourself following his gaze uneasily, half expecting some strange tropical bird to be wafting about your head, or possibly some psychic phenomena to be manifesting itself. His sister could not restrain her pride in him, and nodded triumphantly around the room at every remark he made. There, that's the way to talk, she seemed to say; here's a party that knows what it's all about.

Papa made a polite effort to be amused by the newcomer, but it had never been his nature to be impressed by anybody but himself, so in due course his basic irritation betrayed itself.

"I guess there's not many towns of any size in this country that Vance hasn't seen," his sister declared. "It's an education just listening to him tell it."

"I covered a good deal of territory myself," Papa reminded her. "I guess I've been around as much as Vance here."

Vance said, all joking aside, his mind was pretty set on making California his permanent home. With his damages he could live pretty well, working when he felt like it, laying off when he pleased. There was a chance of getting more damages too, he said, if anything should complicate the condition of his foot. He'd seen to that, all right, and didn't need a lawyer to tell him. Papa said personally he didn't give a snap of his little finger about California, or Dayton, or Detroit either for that matter. Give him a real town like Cleveland or, say, Atlantic City, or Buffalo. Or if you wanted good climate and plenty of sun take a little place like Elmville, where the sun shone all the time and a man could raise a family on the fat of the land for fifteen dollars a week, eggs twelve cents a dozen, all the berries you could put up free.

During the evening Grandpa listened for a while silently then disappeared. The girls were pleased with this new life in the house and the change in their stepmother. Vance was taken with Lena, ogling her with open admiration. He called her "Blondie" and pinched her cheeks. He held Minelda on his lap until she dampened it, a crisis that brought an angry oath to his lips and resulted in Minelda being dumped wailing on the floor.

"My best gray suit," he said reproachfully, shaking his head. "I got two others but this is my best. Always wear gray 'cause it don't show the dander like blue."

The episode brought an end to the gala evening and reminded Her that the girls had been neglected in discipline, so they were sent off to bed with instructions not to horse around up there and bring the house down.

"How about me and Lena taking a little walk first?" Vance asked, but his sister said, a little sharply, that Lena was no age to be going walking with boys, especially a grown man of twenty-six.

After the first excitement of the new arrival, the family settled down to normal; that is, She made it clear that Vance's freedom with the house was no reason for the others to follow suit. He had a front door key and sometimes when he came in late at night he even brought company with him. They could be heard rattling around the kitchen, eating snacks. When Papa heard this he would go to the head of the stairs in his nightshirt and roar down, "What's going on down there? That you, Vance? Can't you let people sleep, damn it?" This would wake up the rest of the house. Minelda would start bawling and asking for a drink of water, or her teddy bear, or the washcloth she chewed herself to sleep on. Her mother would protest that Harry mustn't be too hard on Vance; he was just a kid. Papa would say kid, nothing; at twenty-six he himself was raising a family. The girls would sit up in bed, whispering conjectures about what Vance was up to, and morning would find everybody sullen or irascible.

Vance brought presents to Lena, and could not, as he himself cheerfully confessed, keep his hands off her. He went to dances in Lesterville and brought her souvenirs from there, and heart-shaped candy boxes tied with big blue satin bows. He even asked her to go with him to dances, but Papa wouldn't allow it, much as Lena wanted to go. But he got them in trouble by inviting them to come in the parlor. His sister came in one day and found Florrie playing "Glow Worm," taught her by Mrs. Gross, while Vance taught Lena the schottische, with the carpet rolled up. As might have been expected, Vance did not take any blame for this outrage, but watched with a shrug while his sister hustled the girls out of the room, Florrie by the ear.

"You take things too serious, Idah," he said, dropping on to the sofa again with his copy of *Argosy*. "You're way behind the times."

Papa did not talk much when Vance was at supper, because Vance did all the talking, with his sister's approving interpolations. Grandpa did not even come to meals. Papa said he thought he was living on the free lunch at Jake's Saloon, and bags of gumdrops he kept in his dresser drawer. It was just as well he didn't come, because meals were skimpier and skimpier. Suppers were half-cooked potatoes fried in lard, a few gray little sausages, some stringbeans or peas, also mysteriously gray and greasy, and burnt cookies or maple syrup and soda biscuits, so consistently overdosed with cream of tartar that the girls thought it was deliberate. Papa did not eat much, and his daughters found out that it was because he dropped off at Grandma Reed's before coming home every day, and had a bite. They knew he did not like Vance being the king-pin in the house, but he did not quarrel with him. Having Papa gloomy made him seem closer to them now, and his irritation at Minelda's whining seemed something in their favor.

Marcia stopped in the Western Union office whenever Vance was on duty, and he let her read all the telegrams, and showed her how to type on the Oliver Invisible Typewriter. Next door to the telegraph office was Chase's Music Store, and in no time at all Vance had made an intimate friend of Gertrude Chase, the young lady who demonstrated sheet music. He let Marcia run the telegraph office while he went next door and sang, "Give Me Once More the Sunshine of Your Smile," through his nose, with Gertrude earnestly banging out the accompaniment. Marcia was to tell any impatient customers that the operator was checking on some mix-up at the tower, the railroad telegraph office, but anybody could tell this was a lie, hearing Vance's adenoidal warble echoing through the piano showroom next door. Nobody else in London Junction had time to hang around a music store singing the new songs. As many of the telegrams were concerned with Papa's business, saying "Aunt Sade low, come at once," or "Funeral Tuesday at four," or "Order coffin for Father at Carson's," Papa had even further reason for annoyance at his house guest.

"He's costing me a fortune," Papa declared, "just by never being on the job. Why, God Almighty, he spends hours at a time in the music store. You can even see him leaning over the piano there any time of day, through the plate-glass window."

"I guess if any harm was done the inspector would let him know," said Mrs. Willard. "He's quicker than most boys, so he can do his job a lot quicker."

But She confessed frankly that she was worried about all the town girls chasing after Vance. They just wouldn't let him be and one of these days he might give in to one of them, he was so good-natured. Papa said he guessed Vance could take care of himself if they started taking his clothes off. Vance himself declared the London Junction girls were pretty slow. The girls in Toledo knew how to show a fellow a good time, and when you got in the right crowd in Erie, Pennsylvania, you could have the time of your life. As a matter of fact, Vance said wherever he went he tried to get in with the right crowd right away, because it made all the difference in the world. The trouble with London Junction was that there wasn't any right crowd. You met the same bunch at the Odd Fellows' dances that you met at Sunday School picnics or Cosmopolitan Club balls. It made it hard for a fellow just come to town to pick out his bunch. Papa sarcastically replied that he guessed Vance had picked his bunch all right when he took Sadie Murphy behind the freight house and paid her off with two poker chips, so Sadie had indignantly told the town.

The more Vance burgeoned out as the town beau, the more depressed Papa became. Grandma Reed told the girls she hadn't heard Harry laugh since the night he and Ed Hartwell came to see her. Papa said it wasn't up to the manager of a funiture and funeral parlor to go round laughing at every little thing. The fact was that laughing took your mind off business and a fellow pushing forty didn't feel much like laughing anyway. At his age a man with Papa's responsible position had to watch his step. He got disgusted with these flybrains that ran around town with out-of-town girls, or went on excursions to Cedar Point with ladies who were far from wives. It was a shame, honest to God, to see some of these men his own age get into a room at the London Junction Hotel and drink and play poker all night. You could tell they didn't have the right kind of wife and home. Papa said the young women were getting worse all the time, too. He could see them passing the Store on Saturday nights, letting some fellow hold on to their round, bare arm, knowing damn well what he'd be after next, but these modern girls didn't seem to care. He said when he walked home late Saturday nights from the Store he could hear the couples spooning and giggling on the dark porches, sometimes lying down together in the hammocks. No yelling of "Now, now, stop! Now, I warn you. Stop, I say!" with which any decent woman repelled a man's vulgar approaches. It made Papa shocked to find that there were so many girls in town who let these young fellows get away with murder. Take the family that lived in the double house on Fourth where he and Daisy used to live. The daughter there wasn't much older than Lena, but she had some fellow kissing her on the porch and playing the banjo every night. If Papa had been the girl's father he'd kick the chap out before he got her in trouble.

This was Papa's new moral attitude brought about by Vance's presence in the house, and Vance's doing all the things Papa used to like to do. But the really staggering blow came when Papa and wife and four daughters came home from Minelda's baptism at church one evening and found Vance sitting on the front porch with Bonnie Purdy and another couple. Papa turned pale and could not even speak for a minute in answer to Bonnie's teasing "Hello, stranger." The girls flung themselves on Bonnie rapturously till Papa harshly ordered them to go indoors.

"Can we sit in the parlor while Bonnie is here?" Florrie asked eagerly. This innocent betrayal of her stepmother's rules annoyed both Her and Papa, especially since Bonnie laughingly said, "Isn't she darling? As if it wasn't her own home!"

After this remark there was nothing to be done but invite the whole group into the parlor, where Bonnie gayly played the piano for Vance to sing, and the girls sat, carefully motionless so as not to spoil anything, on the sofa. Papa wouldn't look at Bonnie, because Vance sat on the piano bench with his arm around her.

"Come on, Harry, get out your guitar," Bonnie urged. "Girls, do make your father play like old times. I don't get to London Junction much any more, and I'd like to hear him for old time's sake."

Papa said brusquely that he had no time to tinker around like that any more. His wife sat stiffly on a straight chair, biting her fingernails and glaring at Bonnie's taking liberties with the piano. She could not resist getting a cloth finally and wiping off the keys the minute Bonnie took her hands off of them. The other girl who had come with Bonnie sat on the lap of her escort quite as if it was a matter of form rather than pleasure. She and Bonnie had come over from Lesterville, where Bonnie now worked, in the young man's automobile and they were driving back late that night. Bonnie was still pretty, but had new city ways such as crossing her plump legs rather high, showing her clocked black silk stockings and a pleated ruffle of purple taffeta petticoat. She had a purple silk scarf wound round her head for motoring, with strands of black hair looped out over her pink cheeks, and she had a rose silk jersey suit.

"Going with the boys yet, Lena?" she asked, which caused Lena to look in hasty apprehension at her stepmother.

"Yes, she does," Marcia jealously answered for her.

"I do not!" Lena flared up, glancing from her father to stepmother.

"Lena's my girl," Vance said. "Prettiest girl in the Junction, if you ask me."

"Florrie's my favorite," Bonnie said, picking up Florrie affectionately. "Remember when I used to look after you, Florrie? Remember what fun we used to have at the hotel—you girls and your father and—"

"Florrie was too little to remember," Papa said in a harsh voice.

"No, no, I do so remember," Florrie cried out. "I remember Bonnie because she was always good to us, always, always."

"I'm glad somebody remembers me," Bonnie said. Vance pinched her cheek and Papa abruptly got up and left the room.

"Hey, Harry, how about fixing us a little treat?" Vance called out. "I bring in some company; you might treat 'em right."

Minelda, who had enjoyed being the center of attention at her baptism, began to whimper at Florrie being petted, so her mother took her off to bed. At the door She paused, trying to catch Marcia's or Lena's eyes and thus convey a disciplinary silent warning, but both girls carefully avoided this opportunity, because they wanted to stay up with Bonnie.

"I don't think we're very welcome here," said Bonnie's girlfriend. "Your sister glared at me as if she could eat me alive, Vance."

"She does that to everybody," Marcia reassured her.

"Oh, she does?" Bonnie asked, with lifted eyebrows.

"Come on now, let's have 'On Mobile Bay,'" Vance said, pulling Bonnie down to the piano bench again, this time on his lap.

Papa came back in the room with a plate of gingersnaps, and stopped dead in front of the piano just as Vance was nuzzling Bonnie's neck.

"God damn you, don't you know how to treat a lady?" he said in a trembling voice.

Bonnie giggled.

"Don't worry about Bonnie; she's been kissed before, plenty," Vance said easily, and this time turned Bonnie's face around for a real kiss. The next minute Papa had yanked him off the piano bench by the coat collar and knocked him down. The children screamed, Bonnie and her girlfriend clapped their hands in terror, and She came running downstairs into the room to find her pet brother sitting on the floor holding on to his jaw with a foolish look of utter amazement. Papa stood panting beside him.

"Not in my house you can't do that sort of thing," he choked. "Not by a damn sight!"

"Your house?" his wife shrilly cried. "Your house? You ought to be ashamed of yourself, Harry Willard. Oh, poor Vancie, did he hurt you?"

"He couldn't hurt me, not him," Vance said sullenly, getting to his feet and stroking down his hair. "He's just going crazy, that's all. I won't stand for it either."

"Then get out. Get out and stay out!" shouted Papa, eyes blazing.

"Oh, Harry, please!" Bonnie murmured, pulling at his arm. "He didn't mean any harm. You know it didn't mean anything."

"I'd be a fool if I thought that," Papa said.

"What business is it of yours if Vance wants to make love to his girl?" demanded Vance's sister.

"That's what I'd like to know," Vance added.

"I just don't like it, that's all, and that's enough," Papa shouted. "Now get out before I throw you out."

"I don't need to be told that more than once," Vance said. "Come on, folks, I'm getting out right now."

He pulled Bonnie and her friend toward the door, Bonnie with averted face and the other girl pop-eyed. Florrie began to cry, but Lena and Marcia were highly pleased at the privilege of being present at this show, even if they were frightened at seeing their father in such a fit of temper. He stood there shaking visibly while Vance and his friends left, and did not move when his wife came back in.

"All right, throw my little brother out. Two can play at that game," She said in a cold fury. "I told your father next time he came in late I'd lock him out and this is the time I'm going to do it. You'll be sorry for what you did to Vance, Harry Willard!"

She ran out and they heard her feet clattering down the cellar steps. Papa did not pay any attention, but wiped his forehead finally and muttered, "Get to bed, all of you."

This was the night, then, that Grandpa came home in the pouring rain and found the doors locked. He must have been drinking, it was said later, or he wouldn't have wandered all over the Junction switchyards the way he had. Mr. Purdy called them up before breakfast the next morning and told them the old man had been killed by a third rail.

"She killed him," Lena and Marcia whispered to each other. "She'd like to kill all of us."

Vance's moving to the hotel was lost in the shock of Grandpa's death. It served a purpose, in a way, for She dared not nag Papa for putting out Vance, since she had admitted in front of everybody that she was going to lock out Grandpa. She didn't dare talk as much as she wanted about the four hundred and sixteen dollars Grandpa had left to his children, though she made it clear the money would repair the roof and get a new furnace and washing machine. Papa merely said that he had written to the rest of the brothers and sisters scattered around the state, and said he was using Grandpa's fortune to get him the best goddam coffin the Carson Furniture and Funeral Parlor could supply. It was the least they could do for the old man, he told them, and though there were some whimpers from some of the relations it was too late. Papa himself got a new suit for the funeral and made a down payment on a Ford. He urged them not to deliver the car yet, as it wouldn't look right for him to go riding around so soon after his old man died. Even so, his brothers and sisters continued to write him nasty letters for years.

"There's no pleasing your own relations," Papa said, shaking his head. "You can do and do for them but still it ain't enough."

30

MARCIA WAS PLANNING to run away. Florrie knew about it, but they didn't tell Lena because she was sure to tattle to Mary Evelyn and it would get back to Papa. Marcia had made this decision after the Speaking Prize trouble. Every year at commencement time, a prize consisting of a brass medal on a red satin ribbon was awarded to the best recitation at the Grammar School Holiday Exercises. This had been awarded to Marcia for "The Raven" (expression and gestures coached by Fannie Gross). The winner of this medal was then invited to represent her town in the Mid-Summer Educational Conference in Lesterville, where the county winner would win an even larger medal and ten dollars. The participants would receive a handsome certificate merely for competing. They were to be judged by the *Courier* editor, the Methodist minister, and the high school principal. The requirement that loomed most important to Marcia was that the girls were to wear white dresses and white shoes and stockings.

Since she had no white dress or white shoes, Marcia asked Papa to buy them, a request that enraged him. He had just paid his taxes, he said, and if he bought for one he would have to buy for all three. Business was poor, now that these young men left town as soon as they got a girl in trouble instead of marrying her and buying furniture. As for the undertaking end, folks were all going to some new quack doctor in town and getting cured, instead of patronizing old Doc Franks, who knew his business. Besides, it would take two or three dollars for carfare and to spend the day in Lesterville, so he didn't see that ten dollars would be any profit supposing she did get it, which wasn't likely. It was a terrible blow to Marcia. Even Lena was generously indignant, but in making her complaint to Papa she did not improve matters by stating that they all needed white shoes and stockings anyway, and she thought she'd better accompany Marcia on this important mission. She explained that she would be in the contest herself, since she spoke every bit as well as Marcia, but for the fact that her teacher was so dumb she couldn't make the students remember anything, so that Lena had broken down in the middle of her piece. Papa scowled over these supplications, and was definitely set against it when his wife called out that if he was going to buy white things for the girls he would have to pay the laundry bill, and the laundryman had just been around for his last bill. So here was her great opportunity nipped in the bud by Papa himself, and Marcia made up her mind to run away. She would somehow find a way to enter the competition and get the cash prize, so that she could live comfortably in some distant city until she got work. Other girls her age worked, and it must be a fine thing to have dollar bills in your pocket and no one to tell you how to spend them. It seemed to her, on a judicious study of herself in the mirror, that she would look about sixteen with her braids wound around her head and high heels; wearing glasses might help too. She was certain she knew enough to teach school, knowing more than any grown person she had ever met so far, if people would only give her a chance to tell it. David Gross recommended that she go straight to his father in Washington, who would employ her at once, but Marcia said she didn't want to go to anybody's parents, as parents were bound to cause trouble, no matter what you did. She could address envelopes anyway, the way they advertised in the papers, or she could sell magazine subscriptions and make all kinds of money.

She hinted to Mrs. Friend that she was contemplating taking a position. Mrs. Friend wanted to know what sort of position. Marcia said she had thought of being an amanuensis to a famous author or else a companion to a wealthy old lady, travelling abroad and bringing her wraps on deck when the evenings were too cool. Mrs. Friend gave her a quarter to copy some letters, and Marcia put this in a special sachet bag toward her carfare to Lesterville. To leave no stone unturned in the way of future career in case she didn't get the ten dollars, Marcia also copied drawings in magazines which said, "Copy this cartoon and win a free scholarship to the International Cartoonists' Institute in St. Louis, jobs to graduates guaranteed." This took a lot of paper, in fact almost the whole quarter's worth, since so much erasing wore holes in the drawing, and Florrie, usually slavishly optimistic about Marcia's genius thought so many smudges might count against her.

"Will you come back to London Junction ever?" Florrie asked tremulously.

Marcia shook her head firmly in the negative, and Florrie sobbed over this imminent parting until Marcia promised to come and get her some day. If she won the Lesterville County Elocution Prize, she would take up acting instead of art, and she promised that Florrie could see all her shows free.

While Marcia was desperately plotting ways to run away, and an immediate means of getting to Lesterville for the big day that would open all the gates, the Chautauqua came to town. Mrs. Gross took David and Marcia to a Dramatic Reading. One lady took all the parts in "The Lion and the Mouse," changing her voice, jumping up and sitting down all over the stage, conjuring up invisible scenery, until Marcia was in an excited daze, resolved that this would be her chosen work. She managed to find a copy of the play at the library and read it softly in the toilet (changing her voice marvellously and stopping dead when anyone came in), and she hoped to hear more of the lady's talents, but the next performance was on the "Poetry of Rabindranath Tagore," and Marcia decided it couldn't be much or the Woman's Century Reading Club wouldn't be going in a body. The high school boys did odd jobs around the Chautauqua tent, and there were college boys who travelled with the management. This was all that interested Lena and Mary Evelyn, who managed to hang around the grounds making acquaintance of many strange boys by the simple process of cutting across the road to walk in front of them in dignified conversation, sometimes pausing to frown at the boys "following" them, until a sparkling interchange of repartee ensued. Lena walked with one boy and Mary Evelyn with the other. Lena stayed all night with Mary Evelyn on these occasions, and Papa did not dare forbid this for some reason, in spite of his wife's protests that Lena was having dates. She reported that her brother Vance, now staying at the hotel, said he and a tony friend from Lesterville had dated up Lena and Myrtle Chase one night and gone riding all over the country. Papa said he didn't believe a word Vance Hawkins ever said, so no action came of this. To make up for this leniency he forbade Marcia and Florrie to go out nights to watch people coming and going from the Chautauqua.

Marcia eagerly followed the billboards announcing the daily offerings of cosmopolitan entertainment: The Trouville Opera Company, in scenes from "Cavalleria Rusticana"; Mr. Abner Snively, World-Renowned Humorist, in Monologues, Assisted by Consuela Chapman, Concert Violinist; The Occult Sciences and Philosophy of the Orient, by Dr. Cass Bittner of the University of Virginia; Italy and the Dalmatian Coast, with Slides, by Sir Wade Frisbee, Explorer, Naturalist, and World-Traveller. Mrs. Gross took David and Fannie every night, and Marcia listened enviously to their accounts. Lena said the whole thing was too much like church, and she wouldn't be caught dead inside the tent. Papa said it wouldn't look right if he, as a leading citizen, stayed away from this community treat, so he selected Abner Snively, the World-Renowned Humorist, and the next day Mary Evelyn's mother told Lena she never heard anybody laugh so much in her life as Papa did. Papa told the jokes over and over again at supper, tears rolling down his cheek as he told about Pat and Mike, Rastus and the Colonel, Hans and Fritz, the Native and the Missionary Lady. He declared that in all of his experience he had frankly never heard such a genius as Snively, and he guessed he had heard the best of them, of course before he settled down. His wife said she thought, if you were to ask her opinion, that Mr. Snively got pretty close to being off-color sometimes, but maybe that was the type of thing Harry liked. Marcia said that if she were to take the County Elocution Prize she would very likely go around the country with a Chautauqua, telling jokes and giving dramatic readings. This made Papa sober up, and he said he wouldn't have any daughter of his charging around the country performing like some actress, and so far as the County Prize was concerned she might as well get it out of her head because he had talked the thing over with Idah and there was no point getting any white clothes for Marcia anyway, because she'd have them dirty and torn before she got there.

Marcia wanted to write Aunt Lois out in California for the white dress, without which no talent could be heard, but it would take too long. Mrs. Gross finally heard of the trouble and said she could fix over a dress of Fanny's for her, though she wasn't much good at fixing, and Marcia could stuff some cotton in her own white shoes. She stole a visit to Grandma and explained the situation. Grandma said if she had the money for the fare she'd give it to her in a minute, but the fact was it took every penny she and Mrs. Carmel had to get their business on its feet. They were doing fine, understand, and stood in the way of making hundreds, maybe thousands, but it just took a little time, and until then she couldn't do what she'd like for her grandchildren. She couldn't even spare the change for a Chautauqua ticket, since she'd had to borrow from Mr. Sweeney again for the Women's Relief Corps picnic last week, a pretty dressy affair held in conjunction with the G. A. R. Reunion in Elmville. (A pity Grandpa Willard wasn't alive for it, Grandma said, since the other old gentlemen, many of

them over seventy, seemed to enjoy it so much.) After this unsuc-
cessful interview Marcia wandered wistfully over to the Chautauqua tent and studied the program for the afternoon. Through a
flap in the tent she saw that half the seats were empty and there
was no reason why a person couldn't just go in and sit down, but
she didn't have the courage. The picture of the afternoon's speaker
was of a blandly beaming middle-aged man, long thin hair parted
in the middle, pince-nez dropping a black ribbon elegantly down
his face, Chesterfield overcoat buttoned up to his wing collar, and
stylish top hat in white-gloved hand over his heart. The name of
this personage was Thorburne Putney, F.R.G.S., B.A., International Authority on The Art of Living.

"Thorburne Putney," Marcia repeated, pleased with the eu-
phonious syllables. Suddenly she remembered the house on Fourth
Street, and Aunt Lois telling Mama she should have married
Thorburne Putney. "Thorburne Putney," she repeated with immense satisfaction in the coincidence, and an immediate impulse
to make good use of it. She would wait at the gate of the grounds
until he came out, and he would suddenly look at her and exclaim,
"Good heavens, who are you? You are the spit and image of my
long lost and only love, Daisy Reed. Can it be possible?" Then,
skipping all details, Marcia saw herself immediately adopted by
the great man and whisked off in a huge automobile, going from
town to town on the Chautauqua circuit as his pampered daughter, and sometimes assisting him on the platform with a special
recitation of "The Raven." Visions of a glamorous future occupied
her agreeably as she sauntered back and forth before the gate, and
she was so deep in them that Mr. Putney and a red-haired massive
woman were almost upon her before she recognized them. Recall-
ing herself rudely from a grand ball in the White House where she
was presiding at tea as the adored daughter of President Putney,
Marcia looked up suddenly and let out a scream. The great man
stopped and bent over her in alarm.

"Are you hurt? What happened?"

"I—I twisted my ankle," Marcia gasped, forgetting her carefully planned approach. "I do it all the time. My mother used to know you."

Mr. Putney and his companion stared at each other blankly.

"My mother's name was Daisy Reed and I look like her," Marcia babbled on. "Papa got married again and we live in the biggest house in town and I'm going to go on Chautauqua tours just like you after I get the County Elocution prize."

The great Thorburne Putney shook his head in amazement, and began to laugh. It was not a jolly laugh, for he bared his teeth and shook the laugh out raspingly; it was like a rusty bucket on a rusty chain being fetched up from a dry well. Still, it was a laugh in its own way, and Marcia took it as great encouragement. She was disappointed that he gave no start of astonishment at hearing the romantic name of Daisy Reed once more, but passed a hand across his brow thoughtfully. The lady, who had the reddest hair that was ever seen on land or sea and a bosom on which she laid a variety of trinkets without even needing to fasten them, was much more friendly.

"So you get elocution prizes. Isn't that nice?" she said. "That's just how you got started, isn't it, Thorburne?"

"Maybe the way I'll end up, too," Mr. Putney said sourly. "Twelve people in the tent this afternoon. All looked like idiots. What did you say your mother's name was?"

"Daisy Reed," said Marcia. "She's dead."

She felt tears coming to her eyes and thought with surprise that she did so have feelings, no matter what Lena said.

"Poor kiddie," said the lady.

"Maybe she wouldn't have died if she'd married you," Marcia said solemnly to Mr. Putney, who stared at her.

"Daisy Reed, of course," he said. "Daisy was a dear. I took sick in a little town here once some fifteen years ago or so, and Daisy's family harbored me. Poor Daisy. Dead, you say."

"You're a nice child," the lady said, patting Marcia on the head as if she was Florrie instead of practically grown-up. "You know what you want to do with your life and that's a lot. If my little girl had lived she'd be just about your age and your coloring. How old are you?"

"Thirteen," said Marcia. "Tomorrow's my birthday but I never get any presents except underwear and shoes and stuff like that."

Mr. Putney was oiling up his laugh with pleasanter results now, and the lady's laugh shook all of her trinkets.

"That's too good to pass up, Burnie," she said, and with a giddy sensation that she feared might be fatal Marcia saw her reach in her chain handbag and extend a tiny coin, too little even for a dime.

"Here's a birthday present," she said.

Marcia looked at the coin with a sinking feeling. It was just a medal or something.

"What is it?" she asked, trying not to show her disappointment.

"A five-dollar goldpiece," said Mr. Putney. "Haven't you ever seen any before?"

"Oh, sure, but I get them mixed up with ten-dollar goldpieces," Marcia stammered, joy leaping once more through her body. "Oh, thank you, thank you."

"Write to me what you do with it," the lady said, and handed her a card. "Here's our regular address."

They walked with Marcia to the railroad tracks before the hotel, Mr. Putney half-amused, half-sarcastic at the lady's senti-mental insistence that her own Dorothea would have been exactly like Marcia had she lived.

"I never expected Dorothea to turn out a beauty," she said seriously. "She was too much like her father for that. But she was bright as a button from the time she could talk, just like this one."

Marcia was getting good and tired of being bright as a button, to tell the truth, but if that was the only compliment she was ever going to get from people she might as well resign herself to it.

"There are buttons and buttons," Mr. Putney said, pronounc-ing his words in a carefully clipped way, like an actor would. You could tell when he was meaning to be funny, because he put his finger to the side of his nose. "For instance, there is the wool-covered button. Not that Daisy's daughter is that type of button; I merely suggest that you watch your figures of speech. Watch them like a hawk, my dear Beverly."

"There are hawks and hawks too, Burnie," the lady said, a little roguishly. Marcia decided they must be married. She was so dizzy from this marvellous adventure that she did not know what she was telling them, and afterward she thought it was certainly not the sort of cosmopolitan talk of which she fancied herself capable, because Beverly laughed too much. Beverly talked too, and afterwards fragments floated back to Marcia's mind, but at the time one phrase boomed away in her head, drowning out every other impression—Five-dollar goldpiece, five-dollar goldpiece, five-dollar goldpiece. She wanted to bolt down the middle of the street shouting this miracle to the whole town, though she could not very well break away from the flattering attention of Mr. and Mrs. Putney. She was glad Lena was not around, for if they ever saw how much prettier Lena was than she they would probably take back the five-dollar goldpiece and give it to her. No one had ever made so much fuss over her, and these were great and famous personages too. They had a home in Cleveland and almost in a dream Marcia heard herself being invited to visit them, because they were very lonely when they weren't on the road. Mr. Putney inquired after Grandma Reed and declared he would like to call on her if he had the time, but they were leaving the next day. He presented Marcia with his pamphlet, *The Art of Living Richly,* with his autograph, "To a very bright little button," which rather spoiled it for Marcia.

She ran all the way home and seeing Lena and Mary Evelyn across the street shouted her news at them.

"You'd better not tell Her you have the money or She'll take it away from you," Lena cautioned, and added thoughtfully, "Maybe you'd better let me keep it for you."

"Why don't you go visit the people and get one yourself?" suggested Mary Evelyn, and this seemed such a practical idea that

Lena at once accepted it. Marcia watched them go off in the direction of the hotel with some uneasiness. Lena was always spoiling everything. She would probably tell Mrs. Putney that Marcia's birthday wasn't tomorrow at all, but six months off. Lena was tricky that way, always telling on everybody. It turned out that on the steps of the hotel Lena and Mary Evelyn ran into Vance Hawkins, who took them to an ice-cream parlor, so they didn't have a chance at the Putneys.

It was Florrie who really made trouble. She had been whimpering every night at the idea of Marcia running away forever, and when she heard about the five dollars she was certain that this would speed up the parting. She went to Papa and begged him to let Marcia go to the Lesterville Prize Contest, because Marcia was sure to win, and maybe if she wasn't allowed to go she might run away and get killed like Grandpa Willard. Papa flew off the handle at once, and said he wasn't going to take any criticism on the way he was raising his family, no, sir, not even from the family itself. He said he and the children's mother had gotten along without traipsing around the country speaking pieces, spending a fortune on white dresses, and so on, and carfare, and he guessed his children could do the same. He said that if he caught Marcia out of the house on the afternoon of the exercises he would give her the hiding of her life. Marcia went upstairs and sulked over this, but Florrie tried to appease her by saying Papa wasn't really mean, he was just mad that he didn't have money for the white outfits and carfare, and it made him madder that he didn't dare ask his wife to buy them, so he had to take it out on somebody. Marcia told this to David Gross, who said if she wanted to run away right away he would help her. He said Destiny had sent Thorburne Putney to London Junction at this crucial moment in Marcia's career, almost as if her dead mother had willed this to happen, and to allow anything to stand in her way was sacrilege. Marcia scarcely slept that night, planning and planning ways of escape, and when she did doze off she dreamed of Mama crossing the road with the burden tied to her back, and no matter how hard Marcia willed her to turn around and smile she could not make it happen until the last instant. Then her mother's face blended into Bonnie Purdy's face and Cousin Isobel's and Mrs. Gross's, until Marcia thought with consternation she had forgotten her mother's face, and now it would never come back to her.

The day before the Lesterville Exercises, Marcia's great inspiration came, approved by David Gross and Florrie, but a deadly secret from everyone else. The most important thing in the competition was, after all, reciting the piece and wearing the white dress before the three judges. There was no use hoping to get to the exercises after her father's warning, but she would take the car to Lesterville early in the morning while Papa and his wife were at the Carson's making preparations for Mr. Carson's mother's funeral. She was supposed to be in charge of Minelda during their absence, but Florrie thought she could manage her. Once in Lesterville she would make straight for one of the three judges' addresses, wearing her white dress which was now hanging in Mrs. Gross's bedroom; she would recite her piece, get the prize, and take the next car home before her absence would be noticed. Then with her prize money she would run away. Florrie's awed doubt that she would ever dare do this strengthened Marcia's courage. Next morning she wanted to confide in Lena, but fortunately they had a fight over a box of cactus candy Aunt Lois had sent from California, so they stopped speaking to each other. Marcia got into Fannie Gross's made-over white dress, which still dipped quite a lot on one side in spite of all Mrs. Gross could do; the shoes stuffed with cotton didn't wobble too much, and anyway they were white, which was the main thing. David kept a lookout for anyone who might tell on her until Marcia had gotten aboard the eight o'clock streetcar, five-dollar goldpiece in her hand.

The conductor could not change the five-dollar goldpiece and said she didn't need to pay. It was a wonderful thing having money and going into the world by yourself. Everybody smiled at her; a man gave her a chocolate bar, another man told her where the *Courier* office could be found; in fact, the world was filled with marvellous strangers all devoted to you, who would take your part against your relations on any occasion. Marcia looked out the window, passing the steel mills and Mrs. Jane's house, and fancied she saw Mrs. Jane herself sweeping off the front stoop, with a handkerchief tied around her curlers. She waved her hand and it really was Mrs. Jane but she looked up blankly at the streetcar, not recognizing Marcia in the white dress. Marcia got off at the Square, as the man had directed, and there was the little *Courier* office. It was not open yet, and Mr. Andrews was not likely to be in for some time, the janitor said, because the paper came out the day before and the rest of the week Mr. Andrews took it easy. Marcia stood in the hallway waiting, however, and murmuring "The Raven" to herself over and over, to insure herself against stage fright. It was nearly ten o'clock when a Ford drew up and Mr. Andrews arrived. He was a gloomy-looking, gray-complexioned little man with an unexpected little potbelly which he patted constantly as if he feared it might slip away. His suit seemed wrinkled and a size too large, wrinkling around his ankles till he hitched up his belt. He seemed uneasily conscious of his appearance, for he looked around pugnaciously the minute he got out of the car, ready to face down any criticism. Seeing only Marcia, he got out his keys and swung them around uncertainly.

"I can't come to the exercises, but I've got my piece and I came to speak it for the judges before the exercises," Marcia said. "It says you get a certificate and the prizewinner gets ten dollars. Here's my Lesterville medal."

Mr. Andrews was baffled by this, to the extent of taking off his shapeless gray hat and running his hand over his bald head. He took his swivel chair at his desk and frowned at Marcia.

"I guess since you made the trip specially I could give you a certificate," he said. "No need to speak the piece though. Not for me."

"Oh, yes, I have to," Marcia hastened to correct him. "It says here in the rules that you have to be heard by the judges and wear a white dress and white shoes before you can get the certificate. I'll begin."

Mr. Andrews shook his head uneasily and opened his mouth about to protest once more, but Marcia had firmly planted herself before him. The janitor came in and began sweeping around the musty shadows behind the file-case, and Mr. Andrews looked hopefully at Marcia to see if this interruption would distract her, but she was sailing into "The Raven" in her best platform manner, waving her right hand over this word, pointing upward at that, and lowering her voice to a croak on the "Quoth the raven, nevermore." Mr. Andrews fixed his eyes steadily on the back of his hand, which he had placed over his knee so that he missed the best part of the expressions and gestures. At the end of every stanza he made a motion to get up, then relaxed despondently as Marcia sailed briskly on. She didn't forget a word or a gesture, humping her shoulders and ducking her head like a raven on the last phrase. The janitor stopped sweeping and applauded briefly at the end of the piece, while Marcia stood before Mr. Andrews with her hand outstretched for the certificate.

"I suppose I have to go to the principal's office now and recite it before I can get the certificate," she said after a pause, during which Mr. Andrews drummed moodily on the table without looking at her.

"No, no, you can't do that," he hastened to say, reaching out to hold her back in case she tore out the door on this ambitious errand. "This isn't regular at all, and I don't know who gave you the idea that it was. But you speak real well, and you went to the trouble of this trip, so maybe I can get the principal and Dr. Bosley on the phone about it. If they say it's okay I'll give you your certificate right now."

Marcia wanted to ask what about the ten dollars, but she didn't dare. She listened with pounding heart while Mr. Andrews made his phone calls, explaining that there was a kid in the office reciting pieces like a house afire, because her folks wouldn't let her come to the regular exercises, and was it all right to give her the certificate. Apparently this was all right, for he started shaking his fountain pen over an impressive document.

"What put it in your head to want this certificate anyway?" he asked, stealing a curious look at her.

"Because I want to get a job, and it shows what I can do," Marcia explained, "especially if you aren't in high school yet."

Mr. Andrews allowed that that was right, and after thoughtfully drumming on the table some more said there wasn't anything he could do about the prize without his two fellow-judges, but he was pretty sure they'd be glad to chip in with him on a private award for ambition, and here was five dollars.

He advised her to put it aside in a savings bank as a start towards college, maybe a great career—look at Edison who came from a little town not a hundred miles off. Mr. Andrews began warming to his subject, which was evidently a familiar one, possibly the very speech he had delivered at the public school commencement exercises. It was Marcia's turn to look embarrassed as the sole recipient of this inspirational talk. In the middle Mr. Andrews even got up and pounded his desk when he mentioned the government, which he said would never be the same until we got Teddy Roosevelt back in office. Marcia wiggled from one foot to the other, wondering how much more she would have to listen before she got the five dollars. Mr. Andrews stopped abruptly in the middle of a sentence and sat down, mopping his forehead. Not knowing exactly what to do Marcia clapped her hands, which embarrassed the editor to the point of hastily handing her the five dollars and muttering something about work to be done.

On the streetcar going back to London Junction, Marcia thought she might have won even more money by going to the other two judges, but it was too late, and besides she would be getting home before noon. It was a great day. It was too bad she couldn't show off her white dress to Lena, but the best thing was to leave the outfit at Mrs. Gross's and go home in her checked gingham in case She was home. She was so full of excitement that it was a blow to come into the kitchen and find that Minelda and Florrie had not only tipped over a pan of biscuit dough on the kitchen floor, but had tracked it into the forbidden rooms. Marcia angrily set to cleaning up the mess, knowing she would get scolded for letting it happen, then for not cleaning it up right. It was awful the way your home and your family could take all the joy out of life.

31

HOW OLD MUST YOU BE before you learn to hide yourself completely and thus protect yourself? When Mrs. Gross stated that she was going to ask Mr. Willard personally if Marcia couldn't share David's French lessons next fall, Marcia was bursting to say, "But I won't be here this fall. I'll be working some place far off, because the first chance I get I'm going to run away." But she dared not even trust Mrs. Gross. Mrs. Gross might say that nice children didn't run away, and think how it would hurt her parents' feelings; then Marcia might blurt out something about Her and being whipped and all the things that no one should know or they would feel sorry for her, and the worst thing that could happen to anybody was public pity. Mrs. Gross was likely to report her plan to Papa "for the best," and Grandma might tell "for the best," too. Either people spoiled your plans because they were downright mean or because they meant it "for the best." When Marcia felt her secret unbearably near her lips, she started talking giddily about a riddle, a book she had read, or something that happened a long time ago. Her stepmother declared she never heard so much nonsense in all her life, and there wasn't a truthful bone in Marcia's whole body. Marcia did not shake inside with rage at this the way she used to do, because she had ten dollars pinned in a sachet bag to her undershirt, and ten dollars was better than the Holy Bible to make you feel calm and safe from wounds. She woke up often in the night with a shock of fear, remembering that she was going to do something tremendous, something was going to happen to her, to her alone, not to Florrie and Lena. This wasn't pretend either. It was as if she was bewitched by that other person inside her making her do something instead of pretending. She didn't know how or when she was going to do this, but every day seemed the last. Every moment sharpened her sensations. This is the last time I will pass the burned Holy Roller Church, she would think every day; this is the last time I'll wait by the Gross barn for the wind to shake down crab apples; this is the last time I'll start numbing myself coming in the back door in case She's laying for me with a switch or scolding; this is the last time I'll walk past Mary Evelyn's front porch hoping she and Lena will wave and ask me to come and play with them. It was funny knowing you were gone, but not knowing where, and having other people treat you as if you were still present. It was funny having that other person inside you, strong and invincible like Lena, when outside you were resigned to whatever came up. The very wind, heady with dying lilacs and the constant smell of train smoke, apples rotting in roadside ditches, the heavy sweetness of preserve kettles boiling over in hot kitchens bore a solemn warning to Marcia that this is the last summer, this is the last time, the very last. She saw each familiar face and spot with the desperate clarity of farewell and this time she knew it was not pretending. She tried to remember when she found out pretending was no good. Was it when she gave up waiting for Aunt Lois or Grandma or Cousin Isobel to come rescue them, or was it the day she met the Putneys and discovered that reality could be as good or better than pretending?

She knew the day had almost come when the newspaper told the details of the new school and set Papa to raging. It seemed that the town fathers had decided to charge tuition in the new high school. Papa stormed about this at supper time, declaring that between Lena's and Marcia's fees he'd go bankrupt. He said the best people in the Junction had gotten along without any new expensive schools (gymnasiums, domestic science and manual training departments, business courses, and all those newfangled ideas), and he guessed his daughters could do the same.

"You mean we have to quit school?" Lena asked, eyes wide. Bad girls and poor children who had to work in the mills quit school. "If we don't go everybody will think it's because we're too poor to pay the tuition. All the other girls are ordering gym suits and domestic science aprons from the Fair Store already. Oh, Papa, we just *have* to go."

"Aprons! Gym suits! I never heard the like," gasped Mrs. Willard, eyes darting from one to the other and resting sympathetically on Papa. "Harry, I do think you ought to get up at the Chamber of Commerce meeting and give them a piece of your mind! The way youngsters now are pampered; why, I never in all my life! And what good are they at the end? A lot of good-for-nothings that expect you to do and do for them the rest of their life! The house needs painting, we have to make a payment on the car before they'll deliver it, there's our lodge dues, and our vacation expenses next month at Silver Lake, and the new washer; but, oh, no, we have to take our last penny to buy school trash for the girls!"

"But everybody in town is doing it," wailed Lena.

Marcia looked stonily into space.

"Lena's so full of boys and dates behind the schoolhouse—oh, yes, don't think I don't hear all about it!—and Marcia's so full of crazy ideas she moons around like a lunatic, don't know anybody's talking to her half the time. No siree, Harry Willard, you don't need to ask me for my money, and I won't have you taking the household money either. No siree. They're not my flesh and blood. Let them go to their Aunt Lois or their grandmother or some of those relations they're always telling about. When it comes to laying out any more money I wash my hands."

As this outburst said all and more than Papa had in his mind, there was nothing left for him but to glower at his plate.

"What's the good of us getting high honors if we can't go to the new high school?" Lena inquired. "Our own mother wouldn't want us to quit school. I'll bet we don't get allowed to ride in the automobile when we do get one. I'll bet only Minelda gets allowed in it."

Minelda's mother's bony hand flashed across Lena's cheek in a smart slap which brought Lena to her feet, scarlet with indignation.

"I won't stand it! I'll go away and never come back, never! I'll tell Aunt Lois, I'll tell everybody!" She ran out of the kitchen door, giving it a good bang. Papa got up and walked slowly toward the door, not looking at his wife. She sat gnawing her fingernails nervously. Florrie got up and went over to Papa, slipping her hand in his. Minelda screwed up her little white face into crying position and made whimpering demands to go bye-bye. Marcia could see Lena running down the street toward Mary Evelyn's or maybe Grandma's. Now Lena would be the one to run away, and that meant she'd have to stay, at least for a while. Lena always got first chance at everything.

"Goodness only knows what stories she's started telling this very minute," muttered Mrs. Willard. "I won't dare lift my head by the time she's started her lies."

Marcia thought Lena wouldn't tell though, because Lena didn't want the town feeling sorry for them any more than Marcia did. With a sudden sinking feeling she remembered that Lena had borrowed her five-dollar goldpiece that afternoon to show Myrtle Chase. Now Lena would keep it. She'd run away with it, and it was just like her, Marcia thought with rising wrath. She had even guessed that Marcia was planning to run away with it, but Marcia wouldn't confess it when she challenged her. So now Lena would run away with it. You couldn't trust anybody. Well, she would show her soon enough that two could run away as well as one.

"Never fear, she'll be back, Harry," said Mrs. Willard. "Come and finish your supper."

Papa sat down and nobody said anything. Marcia hoped he would mention the rice being burned and the bread being mildewed, but he didn't seem to notice, or if he did his wife's bad cooking was by this time no cause for comment. Suddenly Florrie began to sob softly.

"I hope Lena won't get killed like Grandpa Willard," she moaned. "Can't you do something, Papa?"

But Papa only took out a cigar and smoked morosely, never looking up to meet his wife's watchful eyes. At dark he went out. Marcia and Florrie went upstairs whispering, and watched the front window for his return.

"Maybe she ran away to California to Aunt Lois," said Florrie. "Do you think maybe she's gone to live with Mary Evelyn? Maybe Grandma will let her stay with her."

When Papa came home they heard him haranguing his wife in the bedroom, and in the midst of this they thought they heard something about Mary Evelyn's mother saying Lena was spending the night there. Mary Evelyn's mother had had the nerve to tell Papa he would have to do something about the way his children were neglected, especially Lena, before she, Mrs. Stewart, would even advise the child to go home. Papa was pretty mad at Mrs. Stewart, who he said had always had her nose in everybody's business from way back, but he was mad at his wife too. The girls could hear her protesting, "But, Harry—" and finally Papa shouted, "God damn it, why can't you cook rice without burning it? I don't ask for any Hotel Astor cooking; all I ask is a little rice that's not burned once in a while."

Florrie was desperately worried about Lena, but Marcia's concern was for her five-dollar goldpiece and the way Lena always got there first, and the way Lena never got reality and pretending mixed up, but went straight out and did things. She and Florrie could hardly sleep for the fear that Lena would never come back

and they would never see her again. Now she was out in the world
maybe, like the honest Irish lad or poor little Joe. Marcia thought
of the time their hearts had been wrung with woe over these sad
songs; maybe it wasn't the songs but the dim knowledge that the
same fate was waiting in the future for themselves.

The next day Lena did not come back and Papa said he was
not going to give Mrs. Stewart the satisfaction of asking her where
his daughter had gone. At noon he came home early to see if there
was any word from Lena, but there wasn't. Mrs. Willard buzzed
around him uneasily, telling him that Lena had been getting out of
hand lately anyway, and was up to plenty of mischief that Papa
didn't know about. She said many was the time she had spotted
Lena and a girlfriend walking down dark streets with boys on
evenings Lena was supposed to be at Epworth League meetings or
doing her homework with Mary Evelyn. She said that her brother
Vance had told her that everybody in town knew Lena left her
home looking one way, the way a girl should, but as soon as she
got to Mary Evelyn's she put paint on her face and did her hair up
and put on high-heeled slippers. She never intended to mention
this to him, since he wouldn't ever listen to any criticism of his
children, but did Papa know that Lena had been buying clothes
and charging them to him at the Fair Store? Just ask Mrs. Stewart
that, if you please, and see what she had to say. Maybe it was just as
well the young lady had cleared out when she did. Maybe she had
reasons of her own, but had aggravated people on purpose so as
to put the blame on them. If Papa wanted to find out the sort of
goings-on Lena had been up to this last year, just take a look at her
diary, the one she had stolen out of the parlor bookcase and kept
hidden—or rather thought she kept hidden—in the pocket of her
winter coat. Papa listened to this without comment, scowling into
space. Marcia and Florrie were surprised at the cleverness of their
older sister as they heard this report; Marcia felt hurt that she
hadn't been allowed to share all this intrigue and that Lena had
shut her off utterly again. She hastily went upstairs to get Lena's
diary, but Papa came up for it before she was through.

The entries in Lena's diary, written in purple ink, were not too revealing of her criminal tendencies. They went along pretty much in a monotone: "May 9—From this date on I am going to keep a record of everything that happens to me. May 10—Nothing doing. May 11—Ditto. May 12—Nothing doing. May 13—Ditto. May 14—Cora Bird's party. Not invited. May 15—Nothing doing. May 16—Circus. Not allowed to go. May 17—Nothing doing. May 18—B. G. walked home from meeting with me. May 19— B. G. and L. F. came to Myrtle's house. May 2—Had fight with B. G. May 21—Nothing doing. May 22—Ditto. May 23—Made fudge at Mary Evelyn's. We raised Cain. May 24—N. D. May 25— Ditto. May 26—Made up with B. G. May 27—Meeting of U-No-Us-Kids at Myrtle C's. We raised Cain. Pinocchio. We made a rule to keep diaries all our life, so we can show our children. May 28— Nothing doing." There was never any mention of anyone in the family, Lena's private life deliberately excluding these necessary evils. Papa stood in the bedroom doorway frowning over the little book, then tossing it on the dresser.

"Where'd she get this book?" he asked.

"We both got them from Cousin Isobel for Christmas but She—I mean Mother—locked them up and wouldn't let us write in them," Marcia said. "I guess Lena took hers out anyway."

"Where's your Aunt Lois now?" Papa asked.

"She's coming home pretty soon, I guess," Marcia said.

When night came there was still no word of Lena. Papa didn't come home for supper, but went to Grandma's and called at the Fair Store, where Mrs. Stewart gave him a suit box.

"You can give these old rags to Mrs. Willard," she said. "They're the clothes she had Lena wearing while she herself went around in all her finery. I fixed up Lena to look decent just like I would my own Mary Evelyn, and you can tell your wife I said so. You'll get the bill, never mind."

Papa was in such a rage that he vowed if Lena came home he wouldn't let her in the door, making him the laughing stock of the town. This scandal was as much as his job was worth, he said. His wife was openly pleased to find him in this frame of mind, and told Florrie that her cot was going up in the attic because from now on she would sleep with Marcia. It was as if Lena was gone forever.

32

THE LONDON JUNCTION newspaper gave the news away, and everybody in town, especially Grandma Reed and Mrs. Carmel, said it was just about the most romantic thing they'd ever heard of. "A little bird has just told us," said the newspaper, "that Mrs. Lois Blair's long sojourn in the West has not been entirely for the purpose of installing herself in the real estate business out there. On the contrary, Cupid has had a hand in delaying her homecoming. A few months ago Mr. R. L. Sweeney, noted realtor of London Junction and Lesterville, decided he too needed a western climate, and the gist of the matter is that he settled in Pasadena where Mrs. Blair was located, and the two were secretly wed over four months ago. Friends and relatives of the pair were only today notified of the union, inasmuch as the Sweeneys are expected back immediately to take up residence in Mrs. Blair's home here. The couple were met in Cleveland by Mrs. Sweeney's niece, Miss Lena Willard, who will make her home with them, according to rumors around town. Congratulations, Mr. and Mrs. Sweeney, and may you not regret your choice of London Junction as your future home in preference to the Golden State."

"I'd like to see Ed Hartwell's face when he finds that out," Papa chuckled to Grandma Reed. He had beckoned Marcia and

Florrie to come with him the minute supper was over. He told his wife this was a family matter and before he went to Lois's to bring Lena home he wanted to have a talk with Grandma, and the girls might as well come along. As usual, as soon as they got off the Furness property, he began to whistle and step quickly, almost as if a chill strong wind issued from his home, blowing him away without any effort on his part. He was plainly delighted that Lena had not taken refuge with Mary Evelyn's mother and for a moment hesitated at the corner, muttering something about dropping in to tell off Mrs. Stewart.

"At least it's all in the family," he repeated several times, after they got to Grandma's.

Grandma was sitting in her bay window in a housedress, fanning herself with a large souvenir palm leaf fan decorated with a lively picture of Teddy Roosevelt leading the Rough Riders. She was not wearing her transformation, but had her gray hair done in curl papers, with a black velvet bow thrust in the midst to brighten it up. She had the newspaper in her lap, and kept looking at it and shaking her head.

"Lena must have gone straight to Cleveland and met their train," Papa said. "Now how do you suppose that little devil knew when they were coming when nobody else did?"

"Maybe she stopped in the telegraph office and Vance Hawkins showed her the telegrams," Grandma suggested. "I can't get over their getting married without telling me. Goodness knows, I've been trying to bring them together for years, then I just gave up. Mr. Sweeney has always been mighty lovely to me though, mighty lovely indeed. I don't know where I'd be without him."

Mrs. Carmel's head popped out of the bedroom door. She was taking a "bird bath," as she expressed it, and continued to push a washcloth over her sharp old face as she talked.

"I tell Mrs. Reed she could have got Mr. Sweeney any day she held out her little finger," she declared. "What that man didn't do for her!"

"Now, now," Grandma said, blushing. "I don't say Mr. Sweeney didn't say a great many things to me that sometimes made me think. But Lois is more up-and-coming, and when she sets out to get somebody, anybody else has got to take a backseat."

"It takes a load off my mind about Lena, I can tell you," Papa confessed. "That kid is just as pigheaded as her Aunt Lois, and hell knows what she would do when she set her mind to it. I haven't slept a wink till I read this."

"Children always turn up," Grandma said comfortably. "Mine were always running away, and for that matter some of them stayed away, but there was always plenty more running around asking for cookies."

"It ain't the ones that run away you worry about," Mrs. Carmel interpolated, popping her head in again. "It's the ones that stay home. They're the ones, all right. Never get married if they're girls, never keep a job if they're boys. No, sir, the ones that run away do all right."

Papa asked Grandma if Ed Hartwell had been in to see her lately, and if he ever did show up to be sure and tell him about Lois marrying Sweeney. He said it was one on Ed, all right.

"Ed was pretty stuck on Lois," Papa said. "Lois was pretty soft on him too, but they couldn't stand up to Mabel. She'd have filled them both full of buckshot. A fella ought to think about the future when he takes up with a girl like Mabel. They ain't so bad when you marry them—I mean, take a girl like Mabel—but when you don't you're in for it. I don't think Lois ever cared for Sweeney the way she did for Ed. I guess she just gave up, being on toward thirty-six, seven, and figuring that Sweeney has plenty of dough."

"Lena'll have a good time living with Aunt Lois," Florrie said thoughtfully.

"Who said I'd let her stay there?" Papa cried wrathfully.

"Aunt Lois will let her go to high school," Marcia said.

"I'd let her stay there, Harry," Grandma advised. "The minute you start fighting over children, you lose out. If you start a rumpus and make her come back, then something'll happen to make everybody sorry."

"Folks'll talk, now that it's already printed in the papers that she's staying there," Mrs. Carmel obligingly put in. "You don't want to set folks talking."

"Maybe Aunt Lois will let us all stay there again," Florrie said hopefully.

Papa looked sorrowfully at his youngest and shook his head. "That's the way your children turn against you," he observed, but he was too relieved about Lena's return to get really angry. "Florrie is the one I thought I could always count on too. She's the most like Daisy. So you like your Aunt Lois better than you do Papa, eh, Florrie? Didn't we always have good times together, Florrie?"

Florrie's brows met in an anguish of decision.

"We used to," she answered truthfully. "Only you don't play the guitar and sing any more."

Papa laughed. He shook the ashes from the cigar on the floor and leaned back in his chair. Marcia thought it was funny about places and people; the way certain places and certain people preserved a person at his happiest and best, and other places and people distorted him into a grim stranger. With Grandma Reed, Papa was young and gay again, kidding about his troubles, relaxing in Grandma's easygoing sympathy. But with his wife he had to be on guard all the time, reminding himself that this was the right life, nice people didn't joke and whistle, nice people worried about money, appearances, tidiness, possessions, and naturally you wanted to be considered nice people. It was too bad it was impossible to be nice people and enjoy life at the same time. It was too bad, too, that if you wanted to be nice people you couldn't like the companions you naturally might prefer. So Papa felt guilty enjoying himself at Grandma's, but at the moment the guilt sensation intensified his pleasure. It would worry him later when he had time for it.

Mrs. Carmel, refreshed by her toilet, and anxious not to miss any tidbit, emerged complete from the bedroom now, wearing a rusty black poplin high-necked dress which wafted a musty, attic breeze about the room, aided by Grandma's fan. Over her finely tucked bosom she wore a variety of brooches and dangling knick-nacks, explaining to Papa that if London Junction folks didn't know enough to buy genuine up-to-date jewelry when they saw it, she herself had the good taste and common sense not to let it go to waste. If Papa saw anything on her chest that he fancied as an adornment to his wife, however, Mrs. Carmel would be glad to surrender it at the lowest possible price, since he was like a real son to her partner. She was in the middle of saying that she was sure her partner thought more of him than she did even of her new son-in-law, Mr. Sweeney, when she was taken with a sneezing attack, quelled only after some magic operations with a large blue bandana handkerchief somehow whipped out of her blouse and a bottle of lavender smelling salts which she inhaled with shut eyes and a prayerful expression.

"This climate don't agree with her like Hodge Street," Grandma explained. "I tell her any day she says the word we'll pack up and go back there. I'd just as soon now anyway if Lois is coming back. It'll be criticism from morning till night, every little thing I do, when she gets here. I wouldn't be a bit surprised if she'd put it up to Mr. Sweeney not to help me any more."

"I told you you should have nabbed him yourself," Mrs. Carmel gasped, with a flourish of her bandana before replacing it in her blouse. "Why, Mr. Willard, when this woman here was wearing that transformation she could have got any man in town. Why didn't you wear it tonight?"

"I'm not going to wear it anymore," Grandma said sorrowfully, and picked up the newspaper again with the picture of Mr. Sweeney.

Papa took out his watch and said he had a good notion to meet the seven-thirty Express in case the bride and groom came in on it. He thought he'd leave the girls for a little visit and stop back for them. Maybe he'd bring back Lena, he said. Mrs. Carmel, who had dressed up especially for her friend's son-in-law, urged him to stay and talk over the business and goings-on around town. She said she and Grandma were kind of disappointed in the Junction, things being so slow. Of course, that business about Bonnie Purdy had stirred things up a little, but being cooped up in the shop all day they didn't get a chance to hear news that a person like Papa, in an undertaking parlor, would hear. Papa had his hat on the side of his head and a hand on the doorknob, but he paused to look questioningly from Grandma to Mrs. Carmel.

"What about Bonnie Purdy? Isn't she still at the Gas Company in Lesterville?" he wanted to know.

"Not now. The party she used to run with, not to mention any names, went to her boss and got her fired after this other party stepped in. Told the whole story, so Bonnie got the sack." Mrs. Carmel happily wheezed out her information, interrupted herself to take a tremendous snort of her smelling salts, thrusting it dangerously up a nostril and placing a bony finger on the other one for maximum effect. "Don't say I said so, but Mrs. Stewart down in the Fair Store says there's other parties mixed up in it. My, what won't these girls do next! As I say to my partner here, I'm not sorry my own daughters are under the sod when I hear these stories. Why don't you ask your company to stay and have a dish of pickled pigsfeet, Mrs. Reed?"

Papa said they had just eaten supper but he might have a snack when he came back in, a suggestion which pleased both old ladies. Grandma talked a good deal about how much she hated her early farm life, but she carried its routine in a small measure into whatever quarters she found herself. The apartment always smelled of cooking, a quart of berries being preserved, a few beets being pickled, a cheesecloth bag of sour cream dripping into a pan under the sink, later to emerge as a cupful of cottage cheese, and stone crocks of various leftovers of meats being pickled, jellied or ground into sandwich paste. The room was so overwhelmed with these housekeeping demonstrations that its original commercial intent was quite obscured. The same lady in the rope wig guarded the cigarbox cash register, and the same pile of ancient sheet music was piled beside her, but Mrs. Carmel's large sewing basket sat on top, filled with patterns and half-finished garments from many years back. She selected her latest effort from the basket for her evening's work, a child's coat of a singularly unwieldy carpetlike material. It was just a remnant, she said, from a sale in a big store in Paris, France, and though she had no particular child in mind, one would turn up come cold weather.

Papa stood in the doorway, quietly brushing his coat sleeve.

"I didn't hear anything," he finally said. "What happened to Bonnie? Is she back in town?"

"The only folks she could go to were her relations at the hotel. I guess they don't know about it yet. Well, live and learn, I always say."

Grandma was rocking back and forth, fanning herself and looking moodily out the window. Florrie and Marcia were playing double solitaire on the floor but enormously interested in Mrs. Carmel's cagey conversation. Papa evidently decided not to give her the pleasure of more questions, for he abruptly bolted out the door.

"There's a mighty fine man," stated Mrs. Carmel, nodding her head rapidly at the large needle she held in her hand to be threaded. "He puts me in mind of Mr. Carmel, just as full of ginger as they come, right up to the age of fifty. I'm glad he's got a nice little wife now; she's a trim little party judging from her looks, seeing her across the street."

"I don't like a woman with little feet," Grandma said, the Rough Riders dreamily waving back and forth before her face. "I've never known it to fail, there's something mean about a woman with little feet. Not that some with big feet aren't mean too, but just the same a little-foot woman is likely to be nasty in little ways."

Florrie and Marcia kept watch out the window to see if they could catch sight of Lena and Aunt Lois when the seven-thirty came through. Florrie swore she could see Papa—she could tell him by his hat, she said—in the back room of the hotel, but Marcia didn't think he'd be there on account of the money he still owed Mr. Purdy. They wondered if Lena could be made to come home again, and if Papa and Aunt Lois might not have a fight right there at the station. Aunt Lois might want to fight, they decided, but Papa cared too much about appearances. He'd pretend it was all his idea, Lena staying with Aunt Lois, and he'd tell everybody around town that it was something he'd talked Sweeney and Aunt Lois into doing, since they weren't likely to have any children of their own, and Lena was a favorite with them. When they heard the train coming in, they begged Grandma to let them run over to the station and see.

"Go ahead," she said. "But you don't catch me going. I'm a little cross with Lois for putting this over on me. Lois has hurt my feelings just once too often."

Sure enough, there was Mr. Sweeney, resplendent in an all-white suit and a Panama hat, holding open the door of the taxicab. Aunt Lois was pointing out her bags to the baggageman, and she too was all in white linen, with a big Panama hat and white oxfords. Lena was standing demurely by Mr. Sweeney, and it was a blow to see that she too was in brand-new clothes, pink linen and pink hat to match, with a little pink crocheted handbag. Florrie ran over to her and clutched her frantically, but Lena disengaged herself.

"Don't get me all dirty, Florrie," she said.

"Hello, Lena," said Marcia jealously.

"Hello," Lena said, and looked away frowning as if here was horrid reminder of a sordid past.

"Where's my five-dollar goldpiece?" Marcia said in a louder voice.

"My goodness, are you going to harp on that all my life?" exclaimed Lena petulantly. "Can't you see Aunt Lois and Mr. Sweeney want to get home?"

There was no sign of Papa. Aunt Lois hugged them and told them she would come and bring them presents from California as soon as they got unpacked, and tell Grandma she was coming down there and straighten her out first thing in the morning. Florrie and Marcia hung back while the distinguished little party drove off, Aunt Lois blowing kisses to them, Mr. Sweeney trying not to look too swollen up with pride, and Lena pursing up her lips and folding her hands demurely in her lap.

"When I run away, I'll take you with me," Marcia said after a long silence. "How would you like that?"

"I wouldn't want to leave Papa," Florrie said doubtfully. "But if you want me to go, Marcia, I will. Can I come back when we get there?"

Marcia looked at Florrie critically for the first time and saw that as usual Lena had grounds for her snubbing. Florrie's fair silky hair was all tousled over one eye and her jumper had a portion of raspberry jam embroidered over it. In the station window she saw that her own petticoat was showing a good three inches on one side, and two buttons were off her blouse.

"Well, I don't see how a person can be expected to think of every little thing," she muttered aloud.

They started back toward Grandma's, cutting across the back way to come up the back steps. This was an error in taste, for Papa and Bonnie Purdy were engaged in deep low-voiced conversation in the shadow of the back stairs. Bonnie was doing all the talking and Papa was listening, earnestly nodding his head. The girls crept around the front way unobserved and waited a long time at Grandma's till Papa came to get them. They spent the time describing Aunt Lois's costume over and over again for the old ladies' amazement.

"Travelling in white—well, I never!" ejaculated Mrs. Carmel several times. "You wouldn't see me doing it, even in my prime."

33

MARCIA AND FLORRIE were forbidden to visit Lena at Aunt Lois's. Their stepmother said if Lena wanted to see them she could come and call on them, and, for that matter, just let that young lady show her face in the door. Setting the whole town against her own folks, causing talk, and even ruining people's confidence in her own father, so that only this very day Mr. Friend had called in an undertaker from Lesterville to attend his sister's passing. That was the sort of thing your independent young ladies could do to their own fathers. She was not saying anything, Mrs. Willard added, about the damage done to her good name by the situation; she was used to it. Stories got back to her, and she knew exactly whom to blame for not being invited to join the new Social Club. Her brother Vance had obligingly told her that the town gossip was that the Willards expected to be invited places but never returned hospitality, they were so afraid of someone dirtying up their dishes and upholstery. Well, anyone with half an eye knew who started that talk, and the somebody was right in the family, or was till she saw fit to run away to an aunt who had as good as said she was through looking after other people's children. No, declared Mrs. Willard, she would not lift a finger to bring Lena back to her proper home, and if her father tried to do so, she, Idah Hawkins Willard, would pack up and go straight back to Daleport, taking Minelda with her and the household linen which was all her personal property, proved by her initials. Lena's adventure and triumphal return under the enemy's flag seemed to have unleashed a whole horde of venomous thoughts in her stepmother, for she ranted at the table, fixing a glassy oyster-colored eye on first Florrie, then Marcia, and muttering angry monologues around her work, relieving herself of a perfect mint of bitterness, scathing memories of all the family traits—Marcia's sarcastic silences, Florrie's pouting face, and Lena's brazenness.

"I shouldn't be a bit surprised," she said, shaking a knobby red forefinger at Marcia, "if somebody right in this family didn't tell the whole town that I'm not a good housekeeper. Yes, sir, I'll bet neighbors down the street whisper behind my back, 'There goes a woman that sweeps the dirt into closets.' I'd like them to step in here and I'd show 'em every inch of the house, clean as a whistle, except when you children are around."

She took care to say nothing about Papa, for she was respectful of his temper and not a little afraid he might bolt out of her life forever. When her patience was too tried with him, she shut her jaw tightly, lips white under compression, and she was deeply hurt that this visible effort at self-control irritated rather than pleased Papa. She talked so much about Lena insulting her own father by not even coming to see him that Papa was reluctantly obliged to confess that Aunt Lois and Lena had come in the store, and they had talked over the whole matter. As might have been expected, he took the position of the whole arrangement being his idea.

"I told Lois right to her face that there was no reason she shouldn't take a little responsibility, now that she's settled down with Sweeney," Papa said. "Naturally, I wouldn't let my daughter live with strangers, and I wouldn't let her live with people that couldn't give her advantages that I couldn't give her. But, by George, Sweeney is worth plenty of money and he might as well spend it on my daughter as on some orphan from an asylum, some kid with bad blood maybe that'd turn on 'em in the end. I've got a hell of a lot of expense right now. I told Lois for the time being I don't mind somebody else in the family taking over part of the burden if it's all right with Lena. It won't be like her own home here, but it'll be a good experience for her. My dad sent me to live with my Uncle Bill when I was about Lena's age. Best thing that ever happened to me."

"She'll lose whatever manners I've drummed into her," his wife moodily said. "I can just hear them talking about me, telling lies and putting people against me. I noticed Mrs. Chase had a tea yesterday and not a word to me. Every time I go to market somebody makes some remark that shows stories are going around. I'm almost afraid to go downtown."

So their sister was gone forever, Marcia and Florrie thought with a sense of terror. They met her at Grandma's after Sunday School. Grandma was having a celebration dinner for the bridal couple, and the girls sneaked in on their way home. This time Lena was very gracious and let Marcia wear her new coral beads all the time she was there, and gave Florrie a red handkerchief with the words, "Twenty-Three Skidoo," printed on it in yellow. She confided that she had heard about Aunt Lois's train through telegrams Vance Hawkins had transmitted, and she generously suggested that both sisters run away as soon as possible—"not to Aunt Lois's though," she interpolated. She said she wouldn't stand being bossed by That Woman a second, and they were dummies to take it, and so was Papa. She said so far as she was concerned she was absolutely through with Papa, and it was just like Aunt Lois said, he was a big windbag, always blowing off about something and never really doing anything. Marcia and Florrie exchanged a stricken look over this shocking irreverence.

"Don't, Lena," Florrie begged tearfully. "Please don't talk about Papa that way. Mama wouldn't like it."

Marcia longed to confide in Lena that she too was going to run away, but she could not be sure whether Lena would be sympathetic or suddenly go to the grown-ups' side, blabbing everything so that Aunt Lois would taunt Papa with it and then she'd be locked up. It was a pity you could never trust anybody.

Mr. Sweeney, now kingpin in the Willard and Reed family, bore himself with the dignity of a man elected to a public office far above his dreams but one for which he knew himself, in all humility, to be perfectly equipped. He nodded thoughtfully over Grandma's and Aunt Lois's exchange on family matters, voiced his judgments with an impressive hemming and hawing, and all in all accepted his promotion from family adviser to head of family with suitable gravity. It was a shame that a man of such majestic manner should have to perspire like any ordinary fellow, until Aunt Lois implored him to take off his coat even if he did wear old-fashioned suspenders. The ladies asked his opinion on the seasoning of the succotash, the state of the nation, the band concert programs, and all private problems, with flattering deference to his resonant decisions. There was none of the laughter such as was occasioned by Papa's presence at a family party, though Mr. Sweeney was not without proper appreciation, observing "Very humorous, yes," to many things that were said. He addressed Aunt Lois deferentially as "Mrs. Sweeney" or "my dear," referred to the first Mrs. Sweeney as "poor Ivy," and rather annoyed Grandma by occasionally testing out the word "Mother" on her, until Grandma observed that the small difference in their ages made this form of address a little ridiculous. At sixty, she said, she could hardly have had a son of fifty-three even if she'd wanted one.

Marriage had completely altered Aunt Lois's queenly attitude toward Mr. Sweeney. She fluttered anxiously about him, patting his big red hand as it lay on the table, lighting his cigar, bringing him a glass of lemonade when he mopped his broad red forehead, filling his plate before Grandma could ask if he wanted more, putting all the white meat from her own dish onto his, and looking at the other plates with a frown as if she would like to give them all necks and gizzards just so that her master might have the daintiest bits. She buttered his buns, and slid her own coffee to him when Grandma said the second pot would take another minute. In short, she behaved as a wife should, who recognizes the

authority of her master and his superior requirements. All domi-
neering traits seemed to have been melted by marriage, and Aunt
Lois deferred completely to her husband now, explaining that
wherever they went in the West there was always someone who
mistook him for a senator or colonel or bigwig of sorts, and treated
them both accordingly. It made travelling a pleasure. Both bride
and groom had expanded in waistline and referred affectionately
to many good dishes they had found in the West. Californians
were fine people, they said, not at all stuck-up like you'd think.
True, they ate their lettuce first, that is before soup, and with
mayonnaise instead of sugar and vinegar, but then every state had
its own customs that looked funny to other states. The Sweeneys
expected to take a two months' vacation in the West every year,
and might even put Lena in a boarding school out there.

"I might visit you myself," Grandma said, "I've always had a
hankering for California."

"I understand the climate cures arthritis," Mrs. Carmel said.
Aunt Lois brushed aside these suggestions.

"Ma, now you know you'd never leave Ohio," she said. "Why,
every time she's ever been in Indiana or Kentucky, Mr. Sweeney,
she is miserable. She can tell the minute we're on the Ohio state
border, and then she perks up. Besides, that kind of a trip takes
money, Ma, and this shop doesn't look to me as if there was that
much profit in it."

Grandma was about to say in some irritation that she could
always put her fingers on cash when she needed it, but bethought
herself of her daughter's probable policing of Mr. Sweeney's
checkbook and was silent.

There was a great deal of talk about Papa, Aunt Lois declaring that if he tried to make Lena come back home she would have
the law on him for neglect. Grandma said Harry wasn't to blame,
he'd always had hard luck, and whatever had gone wrong was the
fault of his wife. Aunt Lois said he had picked his wife with his
eyes open, and she could well remember the day poor Daisy died

and Harry brought this nurse in saying, "Meet the second Mrs. Willard." That was the sort of thing you couldn't forget, with your sister lying on her deathbed and the three children scared out of their wits. She wouldn't be at all surprised but what the second Mrs. Willard had fixed up the medicine for Daisy just so she could get Harry.

"You mean this party poisoned her?" Mrs. Carmel exclaimed, beady eyes glowing with pleasure.

"Now, now, Mrs. Sweeney," Mr. Sweeney remonstrated, shaking a finger fondly at his wife. "Don't exaggerate."

Aunt Lois tossed her head sulkily, and compromised by saying Harry could have married lots of girls who would have made lovely mothers, good-hearted, hardworking girls, say, like Bonnie Purdy. Aunt Lois said, much to her nieces' astonishment, that she never could understand why Papa hadn't married Bonnie anyway, because Bonnie was fond of the children and was by no means stupid.

"But you always told him not to, Aunt Lois," Florrie said wide-eyed.

"I may have said something once in a while, but, my goodness, I never tried to run his life one way or another," Aunt Lois replied. "A real man never takes anybody's advice anyway, if he has any gumption. No, sir, Harry should have married Bonnie. If he had, the whole family would be better off and Bonnie wouldn't be in the fix she's in right now."

Marcia asked if it was true Lena would go to the new high school, and Mr. Sweeney said naturally, that was the plan. Brooding over this for a few moments, Marcia stated that she personally was going to get a job and make a lot of money maybe, she hinted, not in London Junction either. When Mr. Sweeney benignly asked her what she could do, she said she had learned the touch system at the telegraph office when Vance Hawkins let her use the typewriter. Aunt Lois wanted to know what the touch system was, and Marcia explained it was "not looking at what you're doing."

"I should think you'd make a lot of mistakes that way," Aunt Lois said.

Marcia admitted that the type did sort of jumble up, but that's the way you had to do it; you looked up at the ceiling and banged away, and that was the touch system, the first thing required of an office worker. She didn't see how anyone could be expected to have the finished product perfect when they wouldn't let you look at the keys. She also didn't see how she could be expected to be an expert when her stepmother had forbidden her to hang around the telegraph office any more, because she made trouble for Vance, telling customers that he was practicing in the music store or had stepped out to take a walk with Bonnie Purdy, until a warning came that he might be fired, all due to Miss Know-it-all.

Marcia was settling into a cozy chat when the clanging of the twelve-fifty Cincinnati Express brought her to the realization that they were already late for dinner and would have to make up some excuse for being late. She snatched Florrie's Sunday School hat and jammed it on the tousled head, yanked her out the door and flew down the street. Lena left the table to stand in the bay window and watch them as far as the turn in the street. When Aunt Lois reminded her that Marcia had forgotten to give back the coral beads, Lena said she guessed she'd let her keep them, because she liked her blue beads the best anyway. She resumed her place at the table in a rather gloomy mood, which she maintained the rest of the day. Aunt Lois did not like Mary Evelyn and disapproved of Lena going around with her. She said Mary Evelyn painted her cheeks and chased after boys, both of these occupations appealing enormously to Lena too. But if you couldn't play around with your bosom friend, you might as well play with your sisters. Only now she was an only child, Lena thought, something she had always longed to be, but it wasn't much fun really, except for the clothes and the presents, and half the fun of even these rewards was in showing them off to your sisters. Nothing ever turned out perfect.

34

I N ANOTHER WEEK SCHOOL WOULD OPEN. David Gross told Marcia of the new courses there would be in high school, the new things he was going to learn.

"General history," he said, dreamily staring into space through his thick glasses. "That's about Nebuchadnezzar and his hanging gardens. I'll take that, and so would you, Marcia. You and I would probably be the only ones that would like it."

"I know," said Marcia gloomily.

"English literature," pursued David. He got out a pencil and began writing it all down on the back of the parcel he was about to mail to his father (some fudge his sister Fannie had just made).

"I've read it all," Marcia said. "I've read more than Miss Burlington has anyway."

"Yes, but there's a new teacher taking her place, somebody from Ohio State," David said. "Everything is improved, they told Mother at the school meeting. It won't be any fun learning new things without you. And there'll be prizes and scholarships."

"Maybe Lena will get some," Marcia said.

David shook his head.

"No, she won't, because all she cares about is boys. She isn't like you."

Marcia said nothing, half-glad that her own passionate interest in the boys was not obvious, since it was not a reciprocal matter, and half disgusted with David for being so dumb as not to see this. David was like Lena said he was, a little old man. He might be very bright and all that, but Marcia felt there must be something the matter with a boy that thought she was the most beautiful girl in town. She hoped nobody ever heard him saying this or they'd make fun of both of them. It was too bad he was half a head shorter than she was, and what with always talking like a book and wearing knickerbockers when the other boys wore long pants, David was worse than no boyfriend at all, even if they did make up exciting stories together. Now that was over, and the fact that David felt so forlorn about it made Marcia more philosophical. Maybe going to the new high school would just have meant that she would have to be mean to David, because she would want to go to the dances and parties and David would never fit in there; if you felt a misfit yourself you just wouldn't dare go around with another misfit. She wouldn't be allowed to go to any of the high-school parties anyway, what was she thinking of? she reminded herself. She wouldn't have the class dues or the right dress or permission to go with a boy. Even meeting David accidentally in the post office, on an errand for her stepmother, they had to talk at the writing desk, pretending to be waiting for stamps, for fear word would get back to her home. It was lucky she was there this day, for the postal clerk stuck his head out the window after a while and called to her.

"Here's a card for one of you Willard girls," he said. It was for her, and was a picture of Edgewater Park, Cleveland, with a few lines on the back from Mrs. Putney, "We'll have a picnic supper in this park if you have a chance to visit us this summer. Bring your bathing suit."

This exciting message was shared with David and all its possibilities gone over breathlessly. She would go to Cleveland when she ran away, and it would have to be soon now, before school began. She would go to Mrs. Putney's and get a job from there. How wonderful that the postcard hadn't gone home where perhaps she would never have received it or, even worse, her stepmother would have had to find out all about the Putneys. Marcia was so excited she wanted to tell Papa, Grandma, everybody, but David reminded her that this would spoil all her plans.

In front of the London Junction Hotel bar she caught a glimpse of Papa laughing with a big man who must be Mr. Hartwell. This was the Papa they never saw any more, the gay laughing Papa with hat on the side of his head and the half-smoked cigar in his hand. Marcia looked at him a long time, feeling lonesome for him, as if he'd been away a long time. But even as she watched, the two men separated; Papa looked at his watch, straightened his hat, waved his hand, and as Mr. Hartwell took his sample case inside the hotel Papa seemed to change. His shoulders slumped, his footsteps dragged slowly and he walked with his eyes bent on the ground.

When she got home Marcia knocked on the back screen door, was let in silently by her stepmother, gave her the stamped envelopes She had requested, and tiptoed carefully up the steps, being careful not to touch the railing or put her heels on the stairs. She was supposed to wash her hands and clean up Minelda before lunch, a touchy chore, since Minelda screamed whenever anyone washed her, and her mother kept calling up frantically to stop torturing the child, sometimes dashing up to cuff Marcia and finish the job herself, unconvinced even when Minelda yelled all the louder at the change in hands. Marcia thought of the hanging gardens of Nebuchadnezzar as she combed Minelda's skimpy locks; they were all mixed up with the new high-school playground with the fountain playing in the center. In one of Grandpa's books, now locked in the parlor bookcase, there were pictures of ancient Babylon and all the places described in general history. Grandpa had given the book to her, but She had taken it away at his death and locked it up even though he'd written "Marcia's book" on the flyleaf. Marcia felt an overwhelming urge to have this book, to hide it and take it with her wherever she went, so that someday if she should meet David Gross she could say, "I know about those things too." Minelda was calm today and Marcia left her without any tumult, creeping down the front stairs into the dark parlor, reaching with trembling fingers into the vase where Florrie said the keys were now kept. She found it and with pounding heart was about to unlock the bookcase when she heard the voice of Vance in the back hallway. Marcia frantically slid behind the huge armchair, fortunately placed in the corner, and with an awful sinking sensation heard Vance and her stepmother come into the room.

"I don't want Harry to find you here, Vance; you know how he is," Mrs. Willard murmured fretfully. "Goodness knows, I've got my hands full without bringing on another fight. Now what is it? Hurry, before he gets here."

"Keep your shirt on," Vance replied in an aggrieved tone. He lit a cigarette and threw the match at the fireplace without a word of reproach from his sister. Marcia was relieved that they were sitting down with their backs to her, at least, but she was afraid she might cough and nothing short of death would be the penalty for being discovered here.

"Oh, Vancie, I can't stand it if you're in trouble again," Marcia heard her stepmother moan.

"It isn't my fault, damn it," Vance muttered.

His sister hastened to reassure him.

"I know it isn't, Vancie, but you do have the worst luck. Some woman again, I'll bet. I'd just like to lay my hands on her."

There was a moment's silence and then Vance began talking quickly and quietly, interrupted only by smothered exclamations from his sister.

"I've got to skip town and I've got to have money. A girl I've been running around with got herself in trouble and the wire just came through the office to her relations that she died in the doctor's office this morning in Lesterville. It'll be all over town by tomorrow. I've got a guy's Ford down by the office and I'm going East, only I've got to have some dough. How much you got here?"

There was another moaning sigh from his sister, and then, "You might as well tell me the rest, Vancie. Who's the girl?"

"Bonnie Purdy," Vance said, "your husband's old girlfriend. If you want to know so much he gave her the dough for the operation too. I wasn't going to get hooked when she came to me, by George."

"Harry gave her money? Harry Willard?" her voice was incredulous. "It must have been the money for the car. That's why they haven't delivered it. Of all the dirty tricks!"

"I told her to go ahead and go to him when she came after me about it," Vance went on angrily. "He was so damned careful of her he didn't want anybody else kissing her. I guess he could be careful enough of her to pay for her doctor. No girl is going to trap me that way, believe me. Only now she's conked out, everybody knew I was going with her, she told people about it, so that lets me in on a fine mess. Girls always got to blab and get a fellow in a jam just when he's getting his feet on the ground."

"But Harry—I can't get over Harry giving it to her."

"Yes, and he can pay for her funeral expenses too, he's such a gentleman," Vance snorted. "He can lay her out, if that's any satisfaction to him, and pay for the pleasure. Only that isn't going to get me out of town."

"If Harry has the money unbeknownst to me to pay for Bonnie Purdy," said Mrs. Willard tensely, "then I guess I can find some to get my brother out of trouble."

"That's the old girl," Vance exclaimed, much relieved.

There was a rustling of paper. She must keep her money in her blouse, Marcia decided, not daring to peek, and praying that they would both get out before her breathing could be heard.

"Go on, now, quick, out the front door," Mrs. Willard urged.

"I knew I could count on you," Vance's voice came back jubilantly. "I'll write Mom and she'll tell you where I land. Bye, old girl. Don't let on. You think I'm killed or something, that's the ticket."

The door closed softly, and Marcia pressed both hands over her heart to keep it from thundering too loud. She shut her eyes, waiting for the high-heeled footsteps to cross to the back hall, but after a full moment in sudden silence she opened them. For a moment she did not realize what was wrong. Then she knew eyes were upon her. Before she met them, she knew what it would be. The two marble eyes fixed on her were filled with implacable hatred. Her stepmother was bending over the chair looking down at her.

"I wasn't doing anything," Marcia choked.

"Spying. Sneaking." The voice was deadly calm, and Marcia thought this then would be the end of her, death from fright. "Trying to find out things that are none of your business so you can tell everybody lies. Well, this is one time you won't. Come out of there, and go in the kitchen."

Unable to speak and unable to move, the grim fingers gripped her wrist and yanked her briskly into the kitchen, opened the screen door and pushed her outside, locking it again.

"Wait," said her stepmother, and her steps could be heard flying upstairs. Marcia had to wait, for she did not know what to do or how she could get her legs to moving anyway. If Papa had come up the path then, she would not have dared tell him what was happening, any more than she'd dare tell anyone. In almost no time, the high-heeled slippers flew down the back stairs, and this time there was a crooked smile on her stepmother's face. She handed out the door, a big square bag, indeed the very telescope, now mouse-chewed and shabby, that the Willards had moved with to London Junction, the "telescope" in which Dr. Byrd had brought Florrie ten years ago.

"There's your things," She said. "Never come back here again. I'll tell my story of what happened, and it's not going to be the same as yours, so the best thing for you to do is clear out. Don't you dare open your mouth about anything you heard and don't you dare go to your father with any tales. You'll pay for it if you do. Get out!"

Marcia stood stupidly for a while, even after the door clicked. She didn't know what to do, because Myrtle Chase was walking past and would see her being put out of the house. When Myrtle turned the corner, Marcia picked up the telescope and ran as fast as she could across the vacant lots between home and the railroad tracks. She took the freight tracks because they didn't run through the center street but switched off a side alley till they came to the depot. She ran so fast that she fell down in the cinders once and bruised her hand. She could see the end of the street where Aunt Lois lived, and she desperately wished she dared stop to see Lena, but she might tell and then she'd be killed or might be taken back home. Coming to the station, there was a passenger train coming in and Marcia knew she would have to take it no matter which way it was going. If it was going toward Elmville she would go to Aunt Betts's, though she knew their house was full of half a dozen grandchildren now and Aunt Betts was sick. If it was going toward Cleveland—! She asked the conductor and he said it was Cleveland, and Marcia stumbled onto the coach. She dragged her bag into the women's room, so that anyone getting on from the Junction wouldn't see her and try to stop her. She stood in there trying to fix herself up and wiping away tears of fright.

Pretty soon she came out and took a seat. She felt in her waist to see that her five dollars was still pinned to her underslip, with Mrs. Putney's postcard picture of Edgewater Park. The card and Lena's coral beads were lucky, she thought, breathing a little easier as the train rolled along. She was still scared, but she felt light-headed and gay, the way Papa did when he was going away from home. She thought she must be like Papa, the kind of person who was always glad going away instead of coming home. She looked out the window, feeling the other self inside her, the self that had no feelings and could never be hurt, coming out stronger and stronger, looking at the fringe of London Junction and the beginnings of Milltown with calm, almost without remembrance. In a backyard past Milltown Village, a woman was chopping off the head of a chicken, and Marcia thought if Florrie was along this would make her cry. She thought she ought to cry just a little, out of loyalty to Florrie. She'd come back and get Florrie someday, just like she promised. But maybe Florrie would never leave Papa. It was as if Florrie would always have to protect Papa instead of the other way round.

The porter came in with the last call for lunch, and passengers began moving forward. Marcia remembered she had no lunch, but she didn't know how you acted in a diner. When a boy came through with fruit and candy she asked him how much each of his wares was. Nothing was under ten cents. As he was about Marcia's age, she did not want him to think she couldn't afford this, so she asked him how much lunch in the diner would be.

"You don't want to spend all that money," said the boy, a thin freckled boy with several teeth missing. "Look. Take this, and don't say anything."

He handed her a pear and an apple, and dodged hastily down the aisle before the conductor could catch him at this unprofessional conduct. A young lady came in looking, Marcia saw at once, as a young lady on her own should look. She was not pretty like Lena but she looked like pictures in magazines. She had black hair parted in the middle and drawn sleekly back to fine little snail-like coils on the back of her neck, from ear to ear. Marcia studied this coiffure intently, pretending to read the Want Ads in the *Leader* at the same time. "Mother's Helper—oh, no! Secretary— maybe, why not? Telephone Operator—that ought to be easy. Be a Trained Nurse—maybe. Cash Girl in Large Department Store— maybe . . ." Presently Marcia went back to the women's room and undid her long braids. In the face of some urgent pounding on the door, she finally got her hair twisted up into what seemed a similar set of coils. She looked at least sixteen, she thought with pleasure. She rubbed some red paper on her cheeks the way Lena and Mary Evelyn did, but an old lady stared at her so sternly she hastily wiped it off the minute she got back to her seat.

It was not long after noon but it was dark and raining outside, so there was not much to see. Marcia thought about what she would do when she got into Union Station. She would take a streetcar to the Putneys, and she would say she was looking for a room. She was sure they would be good to her, because strangers were always good to you. The light rattle of the rain on the coach roof made her drowsy, and she thought about telephone operating, being a salesgirl in May's, being a secretary with the touch system, and presently she was in a half dream reciting with Mr. Putney, only he changed into a very old man, so she had the platform all to herself and was taking all the parts in a play called "The Lion and the Mouse." Lena and Florrie and Papa and Aunt Lois were all there in the front row gazing worshipfully at her.

The rain came louder, beating across the window. Marcia rubbed a spot on the pane and saw they were already at Union Falls, miles and miles from London Junction. The rain covered the spot, and Marcia took her forefinger and wrote "MARCIA WILLARD" across the foggy pane.

A NOTE ON THE AUTHOR

DAWN POWELL was born in Mt. Gilead, Ohio, in 1897. In 1918 she moved to New York City where she lived and wrote until her death from cancer in 1965. She was the author of fifteen novels, numerous short stories, and a half dozen plays. Among her works presently available are *Dawn Powell At Her Best* (Steerforth Press, 1994), an anthology which includes the novels *Turn, Magic Wheel* and *Dance Night* and a selection of her short fiction, and *The Diaries of Dawn Powell: 1931–1965* (Steerforth Press, 1995).

A NOTE ON THE BOOK

The text for this book was composed by Steerforth Press using a digital version of Granjon, a typeface designed by George W. Jones and first issued by Linotype in 1928. The book was printed on acid free papers and bound by Quebecor Printing~Book Press Inc. of North Brattleboro, Vermont.